# ROYAL BOROUGH OF GREENWICH

Follow us on twitter  @greenwichlibs

**Greenwich
Centre
Library**

5/4

## Please return by the last date shown

| | | |
|---|---|---|
| | | |
| | | |
| | | |

Thank you! To renew, please contact any
Royal Greenwich library or renew online or by phone
www.better.org.uk/greenwichlibraries
24hr renewal line  01527 852385

NIALL GRIFFITHS

# Broken Ghost

VINTAGE

1 3 5 7 9 10 8 6 4 2

Vintage
20 Vauxhall Bridge Road,
London SW1V 2SA

Vintage is part of the Penguin Random House group
of companies whose addresses can be found
at global.penguinrandomhouse.com

Penguin
Random House
UK

Copyright © Niall Griffiths 2019

Niall Griffiths has asserted his right to be identified as
the author of this Work in accordance with the Copyright,
Designs and Patents Act 1988

First published by Jonathan Cape in 2019
First published by Vintage in 2020

penguin.co.uk/vintage

A CIP catalogue record for this book is available
from the British Library

ISBN 9780099583776

Printed and bound in Great Britain by Clays Ltd, Elcograf S.p.A.

Penguin Random House is committed to a sustainable future for
our business, our readers and our planet. This book is made
from Forest Stewardship Council® certified paper.

to two wild and wonderful women

Nicola Dawn

and

Rebecca Loncraine

flying forever, now, both of you

# GWELEDIGAETH/
# VISION

I remember what a fine figure she showed against the sky as she hung in the misty rain, and how the tight black silk gown set off her shape.

Thomas Hardy, in a letter to
Lady Hester Pinney, on the
public hanging of sixteen-year-old
Martha Brown, convicted of
murdering her violent husband

# EMMA

IT WAS JUST there. Saw it. And maybe I should say *her*, I saw *her*, cos it definitely had a woman's shape. Can always tell that shape – the curves an that. Floating in the air she was, just a bit below us, and I heard words.

We'd walked up the ridge to watch the sun come up. The sun was behind us cos we'd all turned to look back at the lake. They were all sleeping – them who hadn't already gone home, I mean; there was a couple of tents but mostly people were just crashed out on the shore, on the pebbles. A few fires still going, aye, but they'd nearly gone out – just smoke. Only a handful of people left, and only the three of us were awake, me and that scouse lad, what do they call him, Adlad is it? An that fuckin nutter, that Cowley, who was messing about with that iPod he'd robbed off one of the students. Didn't really want him there, me; he gives me the jitters at the best of times, he does, and I could feel the comedown starting to make itself known and I just didn't want him there but it's not like I asked him to come – he just followed us up, like, onto the ridge. It had been raining, drizzling lightly, for a bit and hadn't long stopped and all steam was coming up off the lake in these mad shapes. Like ghosts. An then there was this *glow*, like, this *glow* in the air, just below us it was but not on the ground, I mean it was in the air like, floating, and Adam was looking at me with his eyes all big like *what the FUCK?* and I looked and there was a woman in that glow. The shape of a woman. Not kidding. She was just hanging there in the air and I heard words: I heard the word 'bridge' and the words 'dig' and 'wild' and it was like she was talking to me, telling me something that I needed to know. I don't know; I can't explain. And it was like everything went away, *everything*, Adam an Cowley and the people sleeping on the shore of the lake, everything I'd done in the past, it was like none of that mattered anymore, it was like there was this great big bubble around me. There was

3

only me and what I could possibly do. My skin felt all tingly. A kind of rush went through me, it did, a million times better than the crap E I'd had which had done nothing except keep me awake, even tho it was promising to bring a crash on me. It was ... what was it? I dunno. As soon as it was over, and it didn't last very long like, the very instant it was gone I knew that I wanted it back again.

I don't remember looking at the other two. The floating thing, the shadow, the woman-shape, it just vanished into the air and I thought of Tomos and how much I wanted to see him and smell his skin and hold him so I just walked off the mountain and went home. Took fuckin ages, it did. Was knackered by the time I got home. Tom was still asleep. I paid the babysitter and got into bed with my boy, *cwtched* up and fell asleep dead quick. No dreams. Or, at least, none that I can remember.

# ADAM

I JUST FELT so fuckin happy. Can't explain it, an I don't even want to try, really. I just felt so fuckin happy. Like that shite E should've made me feel but didn't; pure fuckin caffeine or somethin, that was. All it did was keep me awake. Probably for the best, tho, really, considering.

I went up the ridge because I was following that Emma one's arse, that's all. I was about to go home and crash but I saw her, in them leggings dead tight an them little boots, heading off up the ridge so I thought I'd follow her. Get somethin in the wank bank, like. Which was me plan; home, wank, kip. Everybody was asleep on the shore or had already gone home so I was gonna borrow someone's bike and scoot off home meself. There was a row of bikes, like, mountain bikes, all lined up on the shore and I was gonna take one an leave a note – honest – with me phone number on. Didn't fancy the walk, like. Miles back into the town. I was even toying with the idea of knocking at the door of Rhoserchan, down the hill, asking if they had a spare bed for a few hours, but didn't think that'd be a wise move. An besides me plan was to get home and go to me own bed and have a big long thrap to help me nod off an then I saw that Emma going up the ridge so I followed her. We'd been talking earlier, like, getting on well, so I just went up after her. And that fuckin Cowley had followed *me*, God knows why. I felt him behind me, heard his heavy breathing as we climbed up the slope, an tinny little snatches of music coming out of that iPod he'd lifted off some student lad and was arsing about with. Wicks the dick off me, that, when people scroll through an play a couple of seconds of each song. Does me fuckin head in. Not that I'd tell *him* that. He'd been standing on the shore, in his fuckin rugby top, no coat, just standing there like Tony Soprano with a skullcrop and great big dragon tat on his neck and you could see him just *praying* for someone to say something so's he could kick off. Didn't want him around me and him farting about with that iPod was doing me head right in but what the fuck can yeh do? So anyway we gets to the top of the ridge an all this steam was coming up off the lake, looked fuckin mad it did, amazing, took the breath out me chest, no lie. It'd stopped drizzling but the air was still kind of damp and then there was this *glow* ... in the air, like, a bit below us cos we were on the top of the ridge by this time, but it was floating, this glow, in mid-air. I even thought that maybe I was asleep and I was dreaming but then that Emma one looked at me with them green eyes of hers gone big an I could see the tattooed stars behind her ear and I knew I was awake. It was like a floating glow. Can't explain it. Kind of a shadow in it, as well, a vague human shape; I mean it had a bump that could've been a head and long thin things that could've been limbs. Curves, a bit like a woman. I dunno, Christ, I'd never seen anything like it in me life. I went into a kind of trance. It was like a smack hit, that's the only thing I can compare it to. I just felt so fuckin happy. Funny how it made me feel that way, cos I mean it was just a shadow or somethin. The sun was coming up. The air was damp. Just something in the atmosphere, that's all it was. An when I started feeling, like, normal again, I looked around an the other two had gone an I was all alone on the ridge on top of the mountain so I just walked home. Took ages. Stroked me cat and went to bed and slept like a log on Mogadon. Didn't even dream.

# COWLEY

FUSS ABOUT FUCK all, mun. Jes-a fuckin blob in-a sky. Rising sun or somethin, that's all. I wazen even lookin, like, I was tryin-a find some decent sounds on that fuckin machine that I found, *not* fuckin robbed, some *stew*-dent cunt had dropped it in-a rushes like, don't even know how to work-a fuckin thing, I don't. It was all some chart shite or some arty shite I'd never even yurd of, no fuckin 'Phonics or anythin decent. Every borin twat had crashed or gone home so I jes went up-a ridge with-a others, that scouse lad and that girl. Think-a name's Emily or somethin. An it was jes-a blob in-a sky, that's all it was. Risin fuckin sun or somethin. In-a cloud or somethin. Fuss about fuck all, mun. I saw fuckin nowt.

# LOSING, AGAIN

IN THE EIGHTEENTH minute our attacker, our 35 million star signing, goes in the book for diving. Rounds the keeper and decides to do the death of Aida instead of putting the ball in the net. Fuck's sake. Despair, despair. It's all collapsing. This season's gonna end on a low.

Sion shakes his head at me from over at the bar. Didn't even notice him come in.

—Did yeh see that? Pony-tailed pillock.

—Is right.

—Orange juice aye?

—Ta.

—Drop-a vodka in it aye?

Just smile, Adam lad. Just smile back at him. Gallons of fuckin orange juice ... sure I'm developing a tangerine tinge to me skin. Watch a game in the pub and I leave lookin like an Oompa Loompa. Or a worker at a perfume counter back home, WAG-mandarin. And needing a piss five times a night as me body tries to get rid of the glut of vitamin C.

Ah well. Better than the alternative, I suppose. Nothing's ever easy.

Sionie puts a Britvic on the table and sits opposite with his Guinness.

—And once again our star man royally tits it up. Fuckin holy show, this.

—Holy show? What's that mean? Scouse-ism is it, aye?

—No. Everyone says it. Means making a twat of yourself. One of me ma's favourite expressions and she's from round this way originally. Never heard it, no?

He sips his pint. I know how it'll taste, that Guinness; I've heard it's a decent pint in here and I can feel it on me tongue, cold and a bit thick and steely and malty. I start to salivate. God I'm like a fuckin dog. I drink some of me Britvic an crunch hard on ice.

—It's a good description anyway. Entire team's a holy fuckin show.

I can barely watch, truth be told. It's a thing you never get used to. And of course there's always some fuckin prick who thinks that yer not quite suffering enough for their liking, isn't there? An there he is, knobhead at the bar, fin haircut and Home Counties accent, bound to be a student, wearing a shirt with '20' on the back of it which he turns to show his mates, jerking both his thumbs backwards over his shoulder. Listen to the bellend:

—See the curves on the 2? Like a woman. Oh that number. I caress her, I stroke her. Such a lovely digit, innit? I worship it. Her.

Give me fuckin strength, man. I've got a nicer number for you, dickhead: 15,000. That's the amount of 'fans' who leave before the final whistle whenever your bunch of pampered and indulged boy-men are losing at home. Buncha wankers. Not happy unless someone else is *un*happy. There was a time I would've been *right* in the face of someone like that. And what's him and his blert mates doing in *this* ale house anyway? Should be back in town in the Varsity or somewhere. Some student pub. Fuckin prick, I'll—

The glow, lad. Remember that glow.

—Yew okay to be in a pub, Adam?

—Why shouldn't I be, Sion?

—Temptation, like. All the smells n that.

There's a moustache of Guinness froth on his top lip. —I can handle it, lad. I put on a deep, African voice: – Strong like lye-on. An besides, where else is there to watch the game? Only boozers show it, don't they?

—Aye. Altho why we're wanting to watch this cack is beyond me.

The inevitable goal goes in. On the screen I see red shirts pointing accusingly at each other in the penalty box and the goalie bending to pick the ball out of the net and at the bar I see Tit-head 20 slapping his knees, I mean he's actually slapping his fuckin knees as he roars with laughter. *Roars* with laughter. His mates are watching this performance and sniggering and some of the people at the bar, the *proper* people like, are glaring daggers at him.

I must avoid all temptation. I must be absolutely honest with myself at all times.

I stand up. —Come 'ed.

—Where we going?

—Back room. This is doing me head in. *He's* doing me head in.

I nod in the direction of 20 who's now hanging onto the bar as if his laughter might bring him to his knees. Theatrical cunt. Christ there was a time when ...

The glow.

—Can't watch this shite. Neither the game or *that* prick.

—Agreed.

We take the drinks into the back room where there's no telly or knobhead; this is the serious drinker's room. Blokes at the bar not talking, each with a pint and a chaser in front of him. Scraggly beards and baseball caps. Bad teeth and yellowy eyes. The only food on offer a sweaty roll in cling film or whatever comes out of vending machines – peanuts or M&Ms. M&Ms! Sugary chocolate with booze? Yick. Never saw the attraction in that combination meself. And I can't see M&Ms these days without thinking of that advert where the big red M&M has a voice like Willem Dafoe: *you get in the bowl*. The feller puts him in a bowl and gives it to his girl-friend and the sweetie's legs and arms are dangling over the sides. *Couldn't find a bigger bowl, huh?*, he says. A living M&M. You'd have to take big bites out of him, eat him alive like, and he'd either be screaming in pain and thrashing his little legs and arms or he'd be making sarcastic judgments and comments as you ate him: *Whoops, don't crack your dentures, there, honey* ... Either way it'd be a fuckin nightmare. Adverts these days, God. They're incomprehensible on the one hand and fever dreams on the other.

Voices in the other bar are raised. Sion asks me if I need a smoke and I tell him I do. There's a bit of a charge off him, a little bit of shaky energy. He's a feller of a bit of a nervous dispo-sish, is our Sionie. Harmless feller, not a bad bone in his body.

We go out into the beer garden and roll cigs. Well, I say 'beer garden' ... a placcy chair and four flagstones. But it's outside. It's a nice day an I can hear seagulls an smell a briny whiff from the nearby sea.

—Benny'll be here soon. He's coming straight from work.

—Is he? On a Sunday?

—Got to unload a wagon or something. Be a load of mad stuff from Germany. Pickled herrings n stuff. Sour Krauts.

—Hope he's getting double time.

—From Lidl? Nah, not a chance. It's not even ovies, this, just a normal shift, like. No one pays moren normal time anymore, do ey? He works over forty hours a week an he's in debt up to his eyeballs, him. Living wage is a thing of the past, mun. He spits a shred of baccy off his lip. —Got an interview meself next week. Warehouse work out at Glan-yr-Afon.

I have to laugh; he sounds so woebegone.

—What are yew laughing at?

I use the word, speak it like, cos it's a good one: —You, lad. You sound so fuckin woebegone.

—Well, wouldn't you be? Twelve-hour days for buttons, slogging me bollax off? Not looking forwards to it at *all*, mun.

—You haven't even got the friggin job yet. Haven't even had the interview.

—Kind of hoping I don't, either. Not fuckin looking forwards to it at all. But I'm skinto. An if I get it an don't take it they'll stop me dole. Mad for their fuckin sanctions, they are.

The phone trills in me pocket. It's Benj.

—Where are you? I'm in the pub but *you're* not.

—Having a smoke outside, Benj.

—I'll join. Orange juice is it?

—Nah. Sick of the stuff. I'm alright.

—Sionie with you?

—Aye.

—He on the Guinness?

—Aye.

—There we are, then. See you in two.

I put the phone back in me pocket.

—Benny?

—He's at the bar. Be out in a minute.

I'm thirsty. So thirsty. The familiar thought creeps in; just one. Just one drink, one pint. Guinness, all black and cool and creamy with condensation on the glass, drips running across the gold harp, a shamrock in the foam. Just the one won't hurt. It'll be a test, a test I'll pass, I'll have just the one and savour it and then go back on the juice, just for the taste like it would be, not the buzz at the back of the neck, just the taste cos it's utterly unique, that taste, nothing comes close, just that cool and slightly burnt taste. One won't hurt.

Except it fuckin will. It'll hurt me and everyone around me. It'll hurt everything. Just the one and it'll end in only one way and that'll be chaos and fuckin ruin.

The *glow*.

—You alright butt?

I nod.

—Yewer lookin a bit sweaty there, mun.

—I'm alright. Don't worry about it.

The door thwacks open against the wall cos Benny, hands occupied with drinks, has hoofed it open. There's a great big grin on his face and his hair's all sweat-matted with dust in it. Two stripes of muck on his cheek like war paint.

—*Boys bach! Shwd y chi?*

—Sound Benj.

He passes a pint to Sion then necks half of his own in one go. The thirst coming off him in waves but it's a good thirst, somehow, different to the thirst that hangs heavy over the heads of the drinkers in the back bar of the pub. It's like a force or something; a kind of pulse in the air around his head and body.

—*DuwDuw*. Some right arseholes in yur tonight, inner?

—'Swhy we're out here, mate. Wanted to gob him.

—Mister 20 we talkin about, aye?

—Yeah.

—Think someone's about to do it for yew. Second goal's just gone in as well.

—Oh for fuck's sake.

—Aye but yur's me just paid an I bear presents. Football be fucked.

He puts his pint on the wall an digs in his pocket. The froth on his glass has the shape of an elephant's head, the trunk craning upwards in mid-trumpet.

—Hold yewer hand out, Sionie boy.

He drops a wee white pill onto Sion's palm.

—Jes a very mild ecko, that's all. Very mild. Jester nice little buzz, like.

—Sure it's mild? Only I've …

—Oh God aye. Had one with me cornflakes this morning, jester get me through-a shift, like. *Very* pleasant, very mellow. And for me favourite scwelsh ex-junkie …

He hands me an ounce of American Spirit.

—Don't smoke it all at once, now.

Ah. God bless the boy. —Starman, Benny.

—Anyway. I could've gotten yew a pill too cos yewer back yewsin, now, aren't yew?

—What?

—Urd yew prolapsed, I did.

—The word's *re*lapsed, Benny. But no I haven't. Who's told you this?

—Up at Pendam last week. Bit of a rave up yur, wasn't there? And some pills going around in which yew indulged? Or so I was told. So I've yurd, like.

—Oh Jesus Christ. Which gobshite told you this?

—Word gets round, mun. Small town.

The seriousness on his face. A great big concern in his eyes which I find touching and funny.

—What's so worth grinning about, then? If this is yew *re*lapsed then I don't see what's so funny.

—This true? Sion says.

I shake me head. —It wasn't even MDMA. We were ripped off. Caffeine pill or something, swear down. No hit from it at all, it just kept me awake. Don't worry yerselves, boys. I'm grand. An nor was it even a rave – equinox party or some shite. Few dopeheads and a crappy sound system, that was it.

—Takin a bit of a risk, tho, weren't yew? Cos I mean ...

—Nah, not really. I mean even if it hadder been proper MDMA ... I give a shrug. —Crack n smack, now, aye, but no more, man. Never again. And the bevvy of course. But I was never bad on the E. Wasn't my thing. Never got its claws into me like.

—Yeah but still n all. I'm finding it difficult to approve, feller-me-lad.

Ben's right, really, I should've done a Grange Hill and Just Said No. But. Just sometimes I get so fucking bored. —I appreciate the concern lads and everything and God knows it's nice to know that yis care. I put my right hand over me heart, national anthem. —But why the worry? Youse didn't know me when I was running wild anyway.

—No but I've urd stories, I yav. Tales from when yew were up at Rhos. In that right Sion?

Sionie nods. Dead solemn.

—What kind of stories? And from who?

—Never yew mind. Benny taps the side of his nose with his index finger. A fly circles the curls on his head, them tight curls all matted and knotty with sweat and dust. —Jest urd some things.

—Cack. I was a model fuckin pupil up at Rhos, lar. Poster boy for rehab, that's me. Was more or less clean before I even checked into the place.

—Was yew?

—Aye. Hadter be, didn't I? Wouldn't've let me in otherwise.

—So why bother with it then? If yew were clean, like, why'd yew need Rhos?

—I've told you before. Yeh finish the job in Rhoserchan. The Twelve Steps. Yeh do the first six in nick.

The fly gets bored and decides to check out Sion's head instead. Gets bored of that as well and drones away.

—He's told us all this before, Ben, says Sionie.

Benny blows smoke in the air and nods. —Jes checkin, that's all. Making sure his memory's holding up under all-a pills he's been taking.

I laugh. —Sod off, Benny. He gives me a wee wink and has a drink. Me hands feel useless, flopping about like without anything in them, an I don't want another smoke so I just bury them in me pockets. There's a tingling in the soles of me feet.

—Was it good, anyway?

—What, the pill? It was shite. Just told yeh.

—No, the rave stroke party thing. Was gunna go but we were otherwise engaged, weren't we Sion?

—Aye. Women.

In my ankles now. Creeping up. —Wasn't a rave like they used to be. Just like, a fire and some music and a load of weed and these crappy little pills. And they even played 'Fluffy Little Clouds', believe that?

—In the twenty-first century?

—I know. And not in a, like, ironic or nostalgic way either. Arrested development in some of them people, no lie. Retro. It's in my knees, now, that tingle, and it stays there for a second or two before it rushes up through me body an into my head where it becomes words that I can't do anything to stop leaving me gob: – An I saw something. In the sky.

—Did yew? What kind of thing? Like a UFO?

—No, not like that. Benny's holding his drink to his chin so he can take quick little sips at it like a bird and Sion's kind of leaning in towards me, at the waist, his hands in his pockets like mine. The noise from the pub is a background blur and I can make out no individual words or voice or even types of sound. It's just here, around me. This beer garden, beer yard, beer square or whatever it is has become a bit too small. Too small for the three of us. I know that there's blue sky above me probably beginning to get a bit less blue now but that doesn't seem to be enough at the moment.

—A plane or something? One-a them jets?

—No, no.

—Paraglider, Sion says. —Get them on that mountain a lot. Cos-a the winds, see.

—No, it was nothing like that. It was a kind of shape, a a glow. Like a shape *inside* a glow.

—The sun, then.

Benny nudges Sion in the ribs with his elbow. He's smiling but not in a nasty way; I mean it's not a fuckin *smirk* or anythin. I don't really want to say anymore but it's like I can't help meself:

—It was like a woman.

—A woman?

—Floating in-a sky?

God I wish I had a drink to hide behind. I take the baccy out of me pocket and roll up.

Sion asks again: – A woman in the sky?

—Kind of, yeah. I can't really describe it any other way.

—What was she like, this woman? Fit, was she? Would you of?

I look up at Benny's smile and it's still not nasty. Sion laughs.

—An yew said-a E didn't work, says Benj. —An en yew talk about women floating in-a fuckin sky.

—Since when has MDMA been hallucinogenic like that?

—Well it wasn't MDMA then, was it? Yew ad some mild acid or something, didn't yew? Women in-a sky, mun. Don't be so daft.

All tingling gone, now. Gone, and what's this sudden sensation in me chest as if I'm missing it? What's going on here? Again, I wish I could drink. Wish I could drink like Benny and Sion and millions of others do, get happy-drunk for one night and drop a mild pill and enjoy meself and wake up with nothing but a hangover, just a grotty feeling and not an uncontrollable lust for fuckin mayhem. I really wish I could do that. There's a little urge to tell of how happy I felt when I saw that glow in the sky with the shape hanging in it, just a small urge, like the itch for a shot of strong coffee. But it soon goes.

—Women in-a sky, Benny says again. —What are yew like, mun?

I light up and suck smoke deep into me lungs. —I saw it, Benj.

—I'm sure yew did, mun. I have no doubt about that at all. Which is another reason why my favourite scwelsh ex-junkie nutbag is yew.

He ruffles my hair and gives a big grin. Obviously coming up on that pill. 'Mild', he said. Sion laughs again and announces that he needs a piss and goes inside.

—Did anyone else see her? Iss woman?

—Yeh.

—Who?

—Some girl called Emily or Emma or something. Pretty. Kind of a cat face.

—Lives in Trefechan? Got a kid?

—Don't know, I hadn't met her before. She's a mum, is she?

—One kid, aye. Little boy. Don't know her very well meself, like, just know of her. Know who you're talking about, I think. Got some stars here? He touches behind his ear.

—That's her. And she's got a kid, has she? Who to?

—Some crusty who passed through, few years ago. She's not with him now, like, he had to do one cos Black Jerry was gunner stab him, if I remember right.

—Who's Black Jerry?

—Before yewer time, mun. Black feller called Jerry. Did a bit-a dealin. Few years ago, iss was. And she took one-a ese pills as well, did she?

—Think so.

—There we are, then.

She's got a kid. She's a mother. Some crusty. Change the subject, Adam lad. —An some big fucker, dead sparky. He saw it too. Started on some students, he did, and taxed em for an iPod. He was there n all. Got a big red dragon tat on his neck.

Benny laughs loud. —Cowley, yew mean? Fuck sakes, boy, he'll see women floating in-a sky pills or no pills. God almighty! He knocks back what's left of his drink and puts the glass down on the wall. —So let's recap. A slapper an-a nutter an-a ex-junkie, smashin as he might be, all take a fuckin pill which is supposed to be ecko but is probably acid or somethin an then ey all see somethin floatin in-a sky. All three of ese people have a history of hard drug use. Iss sum it up? An ey all see iss thing in-a sky after stayin up all night on top of a mountain. No sleep. Right?

I can't help but return his grin. He's well up on that pill, now, and it's contagious. And behind him, over his shoulder, I see a small woman, not a dwarf or anything, I mean a small flat woman with blonde hair and wearing a bikini top rise up from behind the low wall that separates the beer garden from the alleyway. She rises up and speaks in Sion's voice gone spooky:

—Wooooowooooo! I have come for the one they call Adam! I am the floating woman of Pendam and I have come for him!

Benj spins, starts to laugh. Sionie stands up from behind the wall, all pleased with himself.

—Daft bastard, Sion.

He comes over the wall with the woman in his hand. He holds her up in front of me.

—Yur she is, Adlad. Your very own floating lady. Sexy one n all. Been looking for yew, she has.

One of them KP display board things that packets of peanuts are stapled to. Didn't know pubs still had them but this boozer's hardly bang up to date. Still got a bag of dry roasted over her fanny.

—Where'd you get her?

—Asked the barstaff. Had yew going, didn't I?

—Oi tort it was hurself, I say in a Father Ted voice.

—What yew gonna do wither now, then? asks Benji and Sion holds her up to, like, appraise. —Taker home, he says. Make a couple of holes in her.

—Dirty get.

He laughs. —Na, barman needser back. Only a lend, see. Apparently eyr collector's items now, so he says.

Without any warning a memory pounces; I shagged one such woman once, years back, a model for them KP boards, like. Well, she was probably a model for a lot of other things as well but that's how I met her, in a pub on the Wirral, when she was doing some promotional tour thing for the nuts. This was before I was using heavily and was drinking only like most people up there do. She came into the pub. We got talking. Went back to her hotel. And I don't remember much more, not Her name, not her skin, just that she was wearing denim hot pants and she was nice.

The sun goes down and it gets a bit colder so we go back inside. Sion returns the lady to the barman and they share a laugh. Twat-head 20 has gone, I'm relieved to see, and the telly is showing replays and punditry with the sound off. It finished two nil. It's all fucking up. Is the desire to put meself through this shite so strong? And why? Well, there's the dead grandad and the memory of sitting on his shoulder on the terraces, for one. It's one of them: if you need it explaining to you then you'll never understand.

—What can I get yew, Adlad? Ty Nant, is it? Or ey'll do yew a cup-a tea if yew ask nicely.

Benny's eyes are big and he's chewing his tongue a wee bit. The day in the pub has entered its third and final act, when the faces shine like the bottles arrayed on the gantry and the talk becomes darting and the body language becomes easily readable; you can tell, now, who's gunner kick off with who, who's gunner go home with who. That loud lad at the bar with the splashes of paint on his jumper is gunner get a smack from the feller in the lumberjack shirt, who in turn will, no doubt, get off with the overweight lady with the short purple hair who keeps putting her hand in his back pocket. The Brummy guy with the shaven head is gunner go home with the lad with the floppy white fringe who's admiring his ink. It's all a unique and lovely theatre which I'm on the outside of now. I'm just an observer of it all.

The glow.

—Nah, I say to Benji. I've had enough. I'm gunner get off.

—Yew sure?

—Yeh. I'm hungry.

—Can't tempt yew wither bagger nuts? Go on, go crazy. Pork scratchings. Go wild.

—I'll pick something up on the way home.

He hugs me tight, Ecstasy-tight. 'Mild', he said, but listen to him:

—What I said before, mun, yew being me favourite an that. I fuckin mean that. Truly fuckin do. Yewer one uv a best, boy. Never forget that aye? One-a the best. Yew and yewer floating woman.

—Aye, lad, alright. You n all. Now let me go yeh daft bastard cos yeh crushing me windpipe.

He does and I get squeezed by Sionie too and then I'm outside. There is the smell of frying onions and the noise of music, loud. At this top end of town the light is bright and the people are many, bare legs and pastel shirts gathered to smoke in the doorways. As if it's all inside a dome, the night sky over it all like a skin. It's alive and it's electric and I'm outside it all.

Temptation isn't so much everywhere as *everything*; lose two nil? Have a pint. Some dickhead with '20' on his back? Have several pints and get right in the cunt's face. And I know that 'Jacqueline' by Alabama 3, which I can hear from an open window somewhere, would sound even better and make me feel cool and strong with a bottle and a pipe or a line inside me. I know this as much as I know anything, as much as I know about abscesses and spewing blood and turning myself into a fuckin beast. This I know too and this I am entirely fuckin sure of.

Fuck it. None of this matters. Just the memory of that glow. And the knowing that the complexity of it all is a thing to be celebrated.

A bunch of burly boys dressed as cheerleaders spill out of the Academi. Welsh rugby boys dressed as women; someone's getting a broken jaw tonight.

I head homewards, through the people, through the glow from street lights and pub/club doorways. Humid night. On the way I go to the whistling hippy by the twenty-four-hour garage and pick up fish and chips and a sausage for Quilty who's on the bed when I get home, licking his balls. Wish I could do that. The old joke: give him a bit of your fish and he might let you. He rubs himself around me legs and purrs as I break the sausage up into his bowl and he bends to eat and arches his back when I stroke him. Little lion. Appeared at my window one day and didn't go away; decided he liked it here, with me. Chunky grey tabby with eyes like jewels and nicks in his ears. I remember twisting ticks out of his skin.

I sit on the bed to eat and watch the telly. Nowt on but *Match of the Day* or Graham Norton or a programme on Channel 5 called *When Animals Attack* – a more accurate title would be *When Humans Act Like Knobheads*. I watch Graham blethering to Tom Hiddleston for a bit until I'm sure that the lowlights are over and then I watch the rest of the footy. Turn it up a notch to drown out the revelry from outside. It's Sunday night but tomorrow's a bank holiday, hence all the fun. Well: fair play to em. Hope Benny and Sion are having a whale of a time.

# SLOOOOOOW RELEASE

WHAT AV BIN thinkin is that that E I yad was slow-release. Dead slow release type-a thing. Or thingy, whatsit, delayed reaction or whatever ey call it cos yur was nowt from it at-a time, jes kept me awake like is all, but see since then ... don't know what it is. Jes that since A came down off that fuckin mountain Av bin on one, like. On a fuckin roll. Jes do not feel like any fucker's worth it. I mean, iss is me – mellow. Jes-a mellow man, aye, that is what I yam. Jes like Popeye said.

I mean, see this: that brickie from Trawsfynydd or wherever-a fuck he's from, he makes some snide comment about me mix, asks if Av got any bread to mop it up with like, an en ee gives me iss fuckin look, iss smarmy fuckin smirk on is gob, an I do not no I do *not*, it im in that fuckin gob. Like a usually would, piss-takin twat: bang, aye, smirk *now*. An A mean iss is not like a question of control or anythin, no, it's jes that-a urge has gone away. Snot even there. Yur's nothin in me that's tellin me to it im; that part-a me is not workin today, same as it haven't been workin since A came down off that mountain. Jes gone, it has. All's I do now is give-a cunt a grin, like, jes show im me teeth an a nod an give iss little laugh like an ee looks at me more shocked than if I adder smacked im one inner gob. Fuck im an his stewpid games. I do not fuckin care. I feel pure mellow an I will not let no cunt stop iss feeling. Cos it's nice. Like a good spliff sept I yaven't smoked in a week. Delayed reaction from that E, mun, must be. Sloooow release, likes.

So I wash me hands n face in-a Portakabins an leave me boots an hard hat in me locker and put me trainies on an change me shirt an put me coat on an A leave-a site an head down inter town. Day off tomorrow. *Bouncing* on me feet I yam. I do a kebab in at-a bottom of-a 'Glais and get some cash from-a machine an double-back on meself to go-a Cooper's. Why ey don't av a cashie in iss part-a town is beyond me. Makin us walk alla way to-a square if we need spends and what if we wanna go-a Cwps or Scholars? Town planners, mun, must be fuckin stewpid. Banks n all. Makin everyone walk fuckin moren ey need to an wait longer for the pint ey deserve after mixin fuckin cement all fuckin day ... Oo the fuck ey think ey are. Selfish twats.

And Am thinkin iss stuff but me heart is normal. Me head feels normal. Am fuckin *right* in thinkin iss stuff but still Am mellow. Jes bouncing along. Money in me pocket. Jes roll with it. Stay like iss. All's yur is to it. Dead, dead easy. Tidy.

Bernie's already in-a pub, sitting right by-a door. His hair's getting long an A give it a rub with me hand an give im a little song: − For goodness sake ... I got the Bernie Bernie shITE!

Cunt's jes given me a dig in-a bollax. —The fuck was that for?

—Yew called me a Bernie Bernie.

—Aye cos that's yewer name innit? Get yewer bloody hair cut if yew don't like me takin-a piss. Yew can get-a bevvies in for that. Brains dark.

He goes to-a bar an I give me plums a rub. Sound feller, Bernie is. Only he can get away with-a odd dig, likes. Truth be told he's not all yur, in that noggin of his. Bit *penwan* as ey say. But he'll do for me.

I give his arse a pinch as I pass him on-a way to-a bog an he jumps in-a fuckin air. Barman gives a laugh. Me first squirt-a piss is black, like, with all-a muck from-a site. That's how dirty that fuckin site is; the muck even finds its way down yewer japper. Soon runs clear tho, or well, not clear, exactly − greeny, like. Yellowish like cider. Day off tomorrow an Al have a good lie in-a bath, I will. Unless *she* gets on at me to fuckin *do* somethin like she normally does, specially if she's started on-a fuckin cider with Jeremy Kyle like she normally does.

Am washin me hands at-a sinks when Aney Lavin comes in.

—Now then, Cowley, sor.

Least I fuckin *think* it's a Lavin. He's called Aney, A know that much. Probly is a Lavin cos-a McBrides tend to be ginger an iss feller's dark. I look at im in-a mirror an see the top of the tattoo on the back of is neck, the head of the fuckin goblin or whatever it is, the top of its pointy green hat. Saw it last summer when he was scrappin on-a south beach with Jason McBride an he took his top off: a fuckin elf thing in a green suit, bottle in one hand an a bomb in-a other, some words by it which A think said 'Fighting Irish'. All over is back, like. A pixie. Looked a prick, Aney did, standin yur on-a beach and roaring like a fuckin gorilla, punching with is fists at is own belly and boobs. Wobblin like custard. Made me feel a bit sick, it did. An im with that fuckin goblin thing on is back.

—How's yehself, Aney?

—Can't complain, butt. An no cunt'd listen if I did.

—True dat.

I see his back shake as he shakes off. The top of-a pointy green hat moves up and down. I look at the *ddraig* on me neck in-a mirror an Am thinkin that I've got by far the better ink, here: great big *ddraig goch*, mun, roaring on me neck. What kind-a knobhead gets a fuckin pixie on eyr back? Bomb or no fuckin bomb.

—Glad our paths have crossed.

—Oh aye? Why's that then?

—Got what ye might call a proposition for ye, sor.

He comes over to-a sinks. I can see all cement snots on me head in-a mirror so I start-a scrape em off with me fingers.

—An what might that be, Aney?

—Some Quinn cunt down Carmarthen way's after a straightener. An wants it yesterday. Now I'm out of action cos of the oul ribs, like, still knittin. An in fact the only feller in fightin form's our Frankie but ye know the like of him; boy's a lover as he says. Useless with the oul fists, him. A lover, if ye don't mind! Last thing I saw him push his prick towards was a crackhead down Swansea dock. Lover be fucked.

—Ah. Not interested right now, Aney butt.

—Hear me ou', tho. Yer purse would be to say the least sizeable. An this boy, this *Quinn*. He spits-a word out so's all spots-a slime go up-a mirror. —He's a fuckin pussy. He'll be sparko in two rounds, sor. Definite.

—An yewer family will okay this, will they? An outsider steppin in?

—If there's enough money in it they will. He grins at me in-a mirror an I can see his teeth. Look like fag ends, ey do. —Easy enough to get a bye out of the blood if there's enough zeroes at stake, ee says, rubbin the fingers an thumb of one hand together.

Christ, mun, ese fuckin pikeys. Money's all ey ever think about. Couple-a weeks ago I'd be up for this, like, I'd be getting-a time an-a place sorted right now. But tonight? Nah. I jes cannot be arsed. Slow release.

—Not interested right now, A say again. —Am in temporary retirement. Ask me in a couple-a weeks.

—There's money in it, shag. A lot of fuckin money. Sure an couldn't we all be using some of that right now?

—Yur's other things I can do to get it, tho, mun.

I press-a dryer button so's A can't hear what he says next an leave-a bog. Don't even dry me hands. Could-a done with stickin me head under-a hot air like cos A can feel ese wet spots on it where A rubbed off-a muck. Unless eyr from Aney's spit … Dirty bastard. Cos he's got hardly any fuckin teeth to keep is spit back in is gob, see. If he arsks me-a same thing next month A might very well say yes. Easy money; all-a Quinns I know of, none-a em can barney. An if Am rememberin right, Ikey Pritchard's in Cowbridge jail for breakin-a jaw of one-a em an then torching his caravan. An-a fire spread to-a pub where the cara was pitched, in-a car park like. But aye, it'd be easy to give a Quinn a few taps like an if he arsks me next month I might jes well say aye but now? Tonight? I am a mellow man tonight. Aney can sort out his own straightener. Got nowt to do with me.

Back in-a bar an Jack the Boy's with Bernie, now. No Jac the Bird as yet but she's probly onner way; fillin up on chips or somethin, rollin down-a road she'll be like a great big wheel-a lard. Got to line me stomach, she says, an all's she ever drinks is one glass-a wine. Line-a fuckin stomach! It'd take ten rolls-a wallpaper to do that.

—Jack.

—*Shwmae* Cow.

—Seen-a 'do on iss fucker? I ruffle Bernie's hair again.

—Aye. Bleedin mess. Glen Hoddle, '87.

—Glen who?

—Before yewer time, Bern. Footballer.

Bernie haven't got-a first clue what we're on about. Not that
he ever does. His home address is not on iss planet, no lie.

—Where's Jac?

—Onner way. Stopped off at KFC.

—So she'll be with us in about three hours then.

He doesn't laugh. To him, his Jac is Megan fuckin Fox. It's all
blind, innit? Sept he cannot see how to others his missis is a case
of roll her in flour an aim for-a wet patch. Fart and give us a
clue. Which is a question I will *not* be arskin tonight. If Am not
in-a mood for a paid scrap I am not in-a mood for *that*. No lie.

—She'll be needin-a energy, Bernie says, with-a daft drooly
grin on him. He smacks-a inside of is elbow with is hand an
pumps is fist in-a air. A look at Jack an he looks-a same as
Bern – pervy.

A jes shake me head an have a drink.

—Not tonight, Jack. Not with me, anyway.

—Eh? What yew sayin?

A jes shake me head an change-a subject. Or change it back,
like: – Seen-a urdu on iss twat? Larst time I saw anythin like
that it was bottom-feedin in-a harbour.

He's not havin this. —So what you sayin?

—Am sayin that Bernie's got a fuckin mullet on his head,
mun.

—No no. About Jac. *Well* into it larst month, yew were.

—When I was full-a billy, aye. Stick it in a hairy knothole
when Am full-a billy.

—Lucky A came prepared then, ay?

He puts a wrap on-a table. I flick it back off towards him,
with me finger. Bernie grabs it up an scarpers off to-a *ty bach*.

—What's wrong with yew, mun? Jac's expecting, she is.
Expectin another night like-a larst one. Been going on about
it ever since, she has. Says she's never felt so sexy.

—Jes not in-a mood tonight, butt.

26

—But it's yur on-a plate, boy! Fanny on-a fuckin plate! What kind-a bloke turns down-a offer of free fanny? What kind-a *normal* bloke, that is.

I give him hard fuckin eyes. He's very close yur to crossin-a line. —Don't, Jack. Jes fuckin don't. One warning, *dim ond*.

—But tell us why tho, Cow.

—Why? Cos it's all jes a bit fuckin sordid, innit?

—Sordid?

—Aye, y'know. Sleazy, likes.

—Sleazy?

—Aye, sleazy. Yew a fuckin parrot now? A deaf parrot? To tell-a God's honest I don't fancy yewer Jac anyway.

—An what's *that* got to do with anything? Christ, mun, it's just friction, innit?

—It's not, tho, is it?

—What?

—It's not jes anything. What it is is yew watchin an wankin in-a corner at two fellers, yewer mates like, spit-roastin yewer missis. Puts a bloke off is stride, that does.

—Didn't hear yew complaining larst month.

Twat sounds all sulky, like a kiddie told he can't go out to play. —Aye, cos I had-a speed horn, didn't I? *Duw*, coulda knocked nails in with-a hard-on I had on me. An it seemed like a good idea at-a time.

—An yew regret it now?

Daft twat looks like he's about-a cry. I can't help but take a bit-a pity: —No. It was a laugh. But I'm not in-a mood tonight, butt. Bernie is, tho. He's yewer man.

—Aye but-a two of yew. That's what made it. Never felt so needed, Jac says. The two of yew together was what made it so special, that's what she said.

—Well I'm jes not in-a fuckin mood tonight. I don't want-a have to tell yew that again.

He kind-a yelped like a dog, Jack the Boy did, when he came. In-a corner, like, as if he'd been sent yur for being naughty. He made an orrible yelping sound like a kicked dog when he came an en ee started-a cry an begged us to stop. An Jac the Bird, she told im to shut-a fuck up an ordered us to carry on an it was horrible but A shot me load anyway an had to get out-a there. Bernie jes carried on thrusting like a fuckin puppet or somethin, doin that stewpid brain-dead laugh ee does, all spit on is chin an drippin off onto-a top of Jac's head. And yer's Jack the Boy in-a corner, crying like, beggin Bernie to stop. I fucked off to-a kitchen, I did; I remember havin the idea that A needed to scrub me dick n balls with bleach. Couldn't find any bleach so A used washing-up liquid instead. Which was probably for the best, cos bleach woulda burnt.

And, ew, God. Not fuckin puttin meself through that again, not tonight, mate or no mate.

Bernie comes back, sniffin, eyes all shiny.

—That's set me up, that has. Raring to go already, boys, I am. He sits down and slips-a wrap back in Jack's pocket an en gives us a look, from me to Jack and en back again. —Oi oi. What's a do yer? Fuckin faces. Oo died?

—Arsk im. Jack nods at me an Am jest about getting fuckin fed up-a this.

—What's up with yew?

—Fuck all, Bern. It's him getting a fuckin strop on cos Am not in-a mood for porking his missis tonight, that's all. Daft twat that he is.

Bernie gives a shrug an sniffs a load-a snot back up his nose. It gurgles. —Suits me. All-a more for me, then, innit?

—Aye but it was-a two-a yew that made it special. Never felt so needed, she said.

—Oh for fuck's sakes Jack. Special be fucked. Shut yewer gob about it, now.

—Now now. All mates yur, boys. Bernie grabs me around-a waist an his hand clunks against the thing in me pocket.

—What's this? Baccy box?

—No. It's one-a these. A take it out to show him. —One-a them music things. Like a Walkman, aye? Plays music.

Jack ignores it all an goes off, to-a bar or-a bog. Fuck im.

—Aye-Pod ey call it.

Bernie picks it up an looks at it, holds it about an inch away from his face as if he's blind. Which he's not, jest thick.

—Where'd yew get this then?

—Up on-a mountain. That party last week, remember?

—Never went.

—No but yew heard about it. Yew were gonna come, remember? But *The Apprentice* was on.

—Did yew nick it?

—No. Found it on-a floor. In some plants.

—Oh aye. Bet yew nicked it.

—I found it on-a floor, mun, told yew.

He pokes at it with his fingers. God this boy has sheep shit for brains, honest-a God. From Tregaron, originally, see.

—How's it work? How'd yew use it?

—It stores songs.

—Aye but how'd yew then get them out?

He's jest poking at it, stabbin at it like with his fingers.

—Can I have it?

—No can yew fuck have it. An giz it back now before yew fuckin break-a bleedin thing.

I take it back off him and put it in me pocket. Tell-a truth I don't know how to use-a fuckin thing either but I'm not goin to tell Bernie that. An I know better than to jest peck at it with me fingers like Am a fuckin chicken.

He has a drink an wipes-a foam off his lip, spreading speed-snot all over his face. —Was it any good, then?

—What, mate?

—Iss rave yew went to.

—Wasn't really a rave. Jest a few people. Stew-dents mostly. Did an ecko which A at first thought was shite like but now Am not so sure. An I saw iss glowing thing.

Why am I telling him this? Them words jest bounced out. I saw a rising sun, that's all it was. No shape or anything, it was nowt but-a fucking glow in-a sky like-a sun.

—A glowin thing?

—In-a sky, aye.

—Probably jest the sun, mun.

He sniffs again. Could do with a line meself, really. Bernie seems happy on it, like. But then Ad end up with me dick in one-a Jac the Bird's holes an then Ad feel like a right dirty cunt in-a mornin.

—I slept on that mountain once.

—Did yew, Bern?

—I did.

—Why?

—I had to.

—Yeh but why?

—Got lost. Had to have a shit in a plastic bag. Ever tried that? Not easy.

—Why did yew have to av a shit in a plastic bag?

—Found it.

—Found what?

—The bag.

—Aye but why shit in it? Why not jest have a dump in-a grass or something?

—Didn't want-a leave a mess on-a mountain, did I? Nice up there, it is.

Oh Christ. See what Av got to deal with, yur? A boy all in-a sulk cos A won't spit-roast his missis with a retard from Tregaron an that retard from Tregaron who'd sooner have a shit in a plastic bag than leave it on-a mountain which is full-a shit anyway from sheep and cows an everything else. An a pikey tryna get me to fight his fuckin battles. How the fuck did I end up yur? I am a mellow man aye that is what I yam but how-a fuck am I? Still, A mean?

—Missed with most of it. Bit loose, I was, see, an it went all in me socks. Ad to fall asleep in me shitty socks, I did.

A Lavin scrum comes through-a door jest then, five-a them, dark boys all, all done up in eyr bling, fuckin gold ropes an rings, all eyr tats greased up an on show. Loud, ey are. Bunch-a wankers. Ey go straight parst me an Bern an parst-a bar to where Aney is sitting an A see Steve the barman give em iss look, like: *yewer not fuckin welcome in yur.* Most or if not all of em will be barred but who's gonna say anything? Stevie? Wither body on him liker corner flag? He'll have a pickaxe handle handy underneath-a bar like but that's no fuckin good against a crew-a Lavins. When it kicks off which A know it will soon he'll probably try an rope me in an I am not in-a mood tonight, mun. Not in-a mood for that at all. Iss is one mellow man yew have before yew an he is jest not in-a mood tonight.

—A thing to do is to wear it like a nappy, Bernie's sayin. —Put yewer legs through-a handles like an tuck yewer dick an balls in and it all just squirts right in.

Pictures in me head now of Bern on-a mountain with a bagger runny shite hanging down-a back of his legs like a horrible udder. Goin *squelch* with each step. An yur's sounds in me ear of Steve tellin-a Lavin boys to take eyr custom elsewhere an all-a them jeerin an shoutin, stampin on-a wooden floor. An no doubt if I went in-a bogs now all's I'd hear is Jack cryin in one-a the traps. Fuck all this.

—Trouble over yur, Cowley butt. Or gunna be.

A finish me pint. Never made me mind up so fast about anythin.

—It'll kick off soon, aye. I'm getting off.

—Yewer what?

—Getting off. Going home. Getting fed up of all this I yam, see.

—What about Jack tho?

A stand up. —Bird or boy?

—Both.

—Not my problem, Bernie. Al give yew a bell at-a weekend. Enjoy yewerself butt.

I pretend not to hear Steve callin me name as I leave-a pub. The Lavin boys go all quiet but I am out of there. Not fast, A mean a jest walk it, likes, cos it's not that Am fuckin *scared*, it's jest that Am not fuckin interested tonight. Let em sort out eyr own crappy little problems, which av got fuck-all to do with me. Not Cowley's problem, not his concern. It is jest not in me tonight, that feelin in-a belly that would burn me up if A did not let it out, or that feelin like Am being squeezed, crushed like, by a snake, a great big fuckin boa constrictor, getting tighter n tighter n crushin alla air from me lungs. Jest not in me, now. Or on me, wherever-a fuck it is. It is all daft and like little fuckin children in-a playground an A feel like Am lookin down on it all tonight. Mellow, man. Slooooooow release.

Outside-a pub A roll-a smoke under a street light. A picture on-a packet is that one where the feller's got iss horrible fuckin growth on his neck, a big pink horrible brainy growth. Av known hundreds-a smokers in me life an some-a em have died from lung cancer or bad hearts but Av never known anyone to die of cauliflower of the neck. Must think Am fuckin stewpid. A move away from-a pub so's A won't be able to hear it if it all kicks off an so's Jac the Bird won't see me if she comes down-a road all stinkin-a KFC and leavin a trail-a grease on-a pavement behind her which she probably will do any second now. Unless a-course she've stopped off for a bagger chips after her KFC. A go down Cambrian Street to avoid-a main road like an surprise meself by not chuckin-a brick through-a windows of-a chapel when A pass it. See? Not even that fuckin place can put a badness in me tonight. I jump in a cab by-a station. Front seat.

—How's it going, Cowley boy?

It's Stiff Richards. Hates being called that, he does, so that's exactly what A do: —Not bad, Stiff, not bad. Busy night?

Ee pulls out into-a road. —Steady. Ome, is it?

—Straight home, Stiff, aye.

—Not pubbin tonight then?

—Jest av been. Only the one. Early night for me.

—Not like yew. Yew feeling okay?

—Never better, Stiff.

We call him that cos he useta balance trainers on his hard-on at school. In-a changing rooms like, iss was. Standin yur with a shoe hanging off his stiffy. Useta experiment with different shoes, like; rugby boots and stuff. An army boot once, one-a them that Denny Jones useta wear all-a time. Said ey were his grandad's, from-a war. Wonder what an ex-soldier would think if he knew his boots were gunna one day be dangling from someone's bellend in public. Well, what did we fight-a war for, mun? Beat the Nazis for-a freedom to swing shoes from our dicks if we want to, didn't we?

We drive up through Trefechan an-a town opens all up below. Alla bright lights an-a library on-a hill opposite like a massive fuckin bunker an-a sea under-a moon. Looks nice, it does. Stiff drops me off an A pay him an go into me block an-a lift is fucked again so a take-a stairs an on-a floor below mine A see-a letter box go up on-a Morris's flat. Two eyes starin out. Ey see me an en a flap shuts again but A go over to it an lift it up with me fingers an shout through it:

—*Nos da*, Mr and Mrs Morris! *Cysgu da, cariads!*

Nosy pair-a ole twats. Fuck em anyway. In me own flat it's dark but-a telly's still on an it stinks-a fags an oven chips. *She's* conked out on-a couch, belly hangin out, empty cider bottles on-a floor around er. Snorin like a rhino. Er belly's all floppy an yellow and yer's some kind-a stuff, crust, around er gob and A don't wanna look at it so A go in-a bedroom an roll me weights out from under-a bed, dumb-bells like, an do a few curls. Jester few, like, each arm. No fuckin wonder she miscarried, aye? All em fags an cider an all em fuckin oven pizzas an chips an sausages she eats. No unborn babby is gonna survive all that shite fallin down on top-a it.

Am lookin out-a window an it's steamin up cos-a me pantin breath. Heavy bloody weights, ey are. A can see alla lights of-a town all kind-a blurred an it looks like yur's all mist outside but it's jest me breath on-a inside. The glass is warm. Gonna be a hot summer, iss is. An next month Av got to deck some Quinn cos-a fuckin Lavin's bust his ribs an cos A need to make some fuckin money an Av got to give a fat bird one up the trumper filled with fried chicken turds while her friggin hubby watches an wanks himself soft in-a corner. An why? Cos he's a mate. My fuckin life, mun. This is fuckin it. How did A get yur?

Anyway. That's all next month. Fucks to it all till then.

Even in-a bedroom A can hear her snorin so A get a blanket from-a wardrobe an go back in-a front room. Daft fat lazy cow but still she might get a chill. Still cold in-a night-time, it is, up yur on iss hill like, an-a damp's all through iss room an she'll catch her friggin death without a blanket an then Mister fuckin Muggins yur would have to do more than he usually does. Mix fuckin Lemsips an alla rest of it. So a put-a

33

blanket over her an tuck one side in. She makes a noise like a growly dog an turns onner side. A turn-a telly off an go to-a bathroom to give me teeth a brush. Got through another day, mun, aye.

# FUCK BUDDIES

THIS IS THE time when IT usually sets in, when I'm back home after dropping Tom off at the school. Around half nine. After I've dropped Tomos and I've walked home either through Penparcau or across the playing fields by the river like I did this morning, this is when IT starts to creep in – the usual feeling. Except it's not a feeling, really, not an emotion, more the *absence* of feeling – a kind of emptiness. No colour. As if I've been drained of everything. Without the Citalopram blocking it then maybe it'd turn into the thing they called Depression but which was more like constant terror; the medication's probably keeping that at bay, and I'd sooner the feeling of emptiness than *that* stinking black fucking thing. But isn't it strange the way the mind works cos gradually I realise that this morning, that nothing-feeling isn't there. There is the absence of an absence and it's, well, what? Just one thing: a good feeling. Cos it's A Feeling. It's alright.

Dig and bridge and wild.

Them words, them three words.

I'm standing at me front window with a cup of tea and looking out at the river, the Rheidol, flowing past, the new footbridge going over it, some people on it, a feller with a walking stick and a woman wearing some kind of uniform. The sun is out. The river is carrying a big branch out to the sea, into the harbour on me left. I heard recently that otters have returned to the river; it was in the *Cambrian News*. If I stand here long enough, I might see one. I would love to see an otter. That new bridge still looks flimsy to me and why people choose to use it instead of the old stone one I really don't know. I'm scared to use it and I've never once used it to cross the river; I'll walk the extra distance to the stronger stone one and cross into town by that. There's a word for this, the fear of crossing bridges, and I looked it up once: gephy-rophobia, although that probably refers to a fear of *all* bridges rather than just a specific one. I'm liking the taste of me tea and I think I might have a biscuit; there's some KitKats in the kitchen, a multipack cos they're one of Tom's favourites. I hope the postie brings the housing-benefit cheque and I hope the other benefits have gone into my account cos I'm fucked if they haven't. He needs some new shoes, Tom does, but his grandparents, my folks, have said they'll get him some and I need to go and see them soon but it's one bastard of a bus ride to Trefenter. I'll go shopping later. Lidl for vegetables. Pay the next instalments of the bills.

God, look at this: this is me, feeling, thinking. There's stuff going on inside me. I'm standing here at the window but today I am not hollow. Today there is a lot of stuff going on inside me. Thoughts and things. Emotions. This is the way I should be, a mixture of things; not always happy, not always sad, not always scared. A big mix of things. This is what it is to be normal.

And this is the way I've been feeling since that crap little rave thing. Since I came down off the mountain. Since I saw that glow in the sky with the figure inside it that was a woman. Three words I heard, but for some reason they weren't in a woman's voice, nor a man's, really, they were just in the air, and those words were 'dig' and 'bridge' and 'wild'. Don't know whether the other two, that nutter Cowley and that scouse lad, heard the words as well and I don't care if they did or didn't, but I do wonder how they're feeling now, since that morning – if they're feeling like me. Which is how? How am I feeling now? The only way I can describe it is: I now feel that the river that runs past the front of my house is there to be looked at. That's the only way I can explain it.

Doing the dishes in the kitchen I turn the radio news on and listen to some posh twat going on about cutting tax credits for single mothers and why should benefit claimants be able to live in houses that people in work can't afford? I explain to him, aloud like, that I moved into this house when I was working full-time and it wasn't my fault that the shop had to close and that maybe it'd still be open if rents had've been capped instead of now sitting empty with letters piling up behind the door. What does a man like that know about a woman like me? This I say aloud, and instead of anger and disgust – which is what I'd usually feel at the sound of this man's voice – I feel only lucky and grateful that I'm able to live in such a good place and bring Tomos up here, next to a river in which he might see an otter. God, what's wrong with me? No, fuck that, what's *right* with me? Look at the dishes, clean on the draining board. I flick the radio off, cutting that fucking voice off mid-whinge, and go upstairs to run the bath. This is not wrong. To be feeling like this can only be right.

Dig, bridge, wild. Three words which I've thought a lot about in recent days and the significance of two of them I think I might know but one remains a puzzle:

*Wild*.

I run the hot tap. Put in some bubbles, one of them mad new flavours they have: hibiscus weed and coriander root. Smells lovely.

*Dig*.

I take my clothes off in the bedroom. It still smells sleepy in here, that kind of milky whiff that bedrooms have in the morning. Slept well last night, I did; I sat talking with Tom until he nodded off and then I watched a bit of telly and then I went to bed and I put my head on the pillow and I fell asleep. I did *not* lie awake staring into the blackness and closing my eyes against the shapes in it, I did *not* sit up till dawn watching crap on the TV and going fucking mad. No, I slept and dreamt about lakes and submarines and I woke up feeling good.

I turn the hot tap off and run the cold, swish it around with my hand. I put Radio Wales on, just for the background noise; I don't really listen to the words or the music, it's just nice to have a friendly voice in the room. I get in the bath. It's perfect.

He called himself Weasel, Tom's dad did. Never did find out his proper name cos he said he didn't have one anymore cos he was really a weasel in human form. Otherkin. This he said because he was something of a dickhead, but he might've been right; I mean, he *was* a bit like a weasel, if

37

truth be told – sneaky, rodential. A New Age traveller and a novice smackhead. Self-deluded; the filth he lived in he saw as getting back to nature, which is what people like him call being bone fucking idle. People can be as *mochyn* as they want but don't dress it up as political protest. Had dreads, he did. Of course. A white boy with dreads and that should've been a warning sign in itself but what's done is done and sometimes the hole inside me gets too wide. Too fucking wide. So I shagged him at some outdoor party at Ynyslas sands and he knocked me up in the dunes. Didn't see him for a few months, and then I did, in town, and I told him I was preggers and he legged it altho someone told me that was because he was gonna get stabbed so he had to do one but about that I have my doubts.

But anyway: *dig* and *wild*. The weasel growing inside me.

Which is what I thought, that I had a little weasel forming inside my body. In bad moments this would scare me sick, and I'd have images of this little thrashing thing inside my body, all evil eyes and sharp teeth. In my good moments, which there weren't so many of then, this would please me; a wild and untamed thing inside that I wanted to stay inside cos as soon as it came out it would lose its wildness and the world would tame it the moment it took its first breath. But he is what he is, Tomos, my boy; bright and bloody brilliant. Has his dad's eyes, he does, that blue in the middle like a bullseye with the ring around it of darker blue, almost black.

So, aye, those two words; now I know what they mean. Or I *think* I know. They join together into a sort of instruction.

It's so quiet in here but I want it quieter so I reach and turn the radio off. The water dripping from the tap goes plink and ploik and I can hear a bird singing outside. Blackbird, I think. Bold, those birds, them and robins; there's one or two out in the garden that'll eat from my hand. The first time Tomos saw that when he was still a toddler he jumped up and down in delight. Literally jumped for joy, and scared the birds off, and then fell over; he hadn't developed a proper sense of balance by then. The joy in him, tho. And the feeling of the robin on my palm, barely there.

I run my hands down my calf and don't feel any stubble so the razor can stay where it is. Like a womb, this bath is. Chipped polish on me toes which I can neither be arsed cleaning off or redoing. No point, because who's gonner see? Only the Tomster and he doesn't care one way or the other. But being clean, the feel of scrubbed skin – that is nice. I soap meself all over and then lie back in the water to rinse the suds away. Close my eyes. Drift off. Slept well last night I did but I can feel meself drifting off, the way your thoughts start to go a bit weird, funny shapes and faces. And I've got stuff to do so I sit up quick and pour some cold water straight from the tap into my cupped hands and dip my face in it and then I pull the plug and get out. Sunlight comes in a slanty beam through the window and I stand in it to be warm as I dry meself. I feel so calm. Even tho I am full of things, thoughts and notions, full of things all whirling around I feel so calm and peaceful.

And there is a wildness inside you to which you must dig down. Not, like, unearth it; don't dig it up, or anything like that. Just recognise it is there and dig down to it and talk to it and let it guide you. Kind of like: the worm in the soil is more important than the car on the tarmac on top of the soil, on top of the worm. Like: long to go to South America to see a real jaguar rather than want to own a car named after it. The beetle and the spider, these things mean more than a bank account in the black or saving for a pension. And what they are is inside you as well because there is a part of you that has wings and claws and your time here is so short. You have no territory. You must live in the now, like cats do, or the bats that come out from under the bridge when the sun goes down. You leak – I mean you give out fluids, all kinds of gunk, and that means you're alive. Living things are smelly; living things stink. Your life is a miracle and you need to remember that every morning as soon as your eyes open. What you are told is meaningful means absolutely nothing, it's simply a way for the powerful to hold on to power and this is the most shameful

39

thing there is. It is one of the worst ways a human being can ever be. That prick on the radio earlier, he spoke about people who Do The Right Thing, like that, with capitals, by which he meant what he wants people to do which is work at a job they loathe for five decades and save for a pension and then quietly die. That is not me. Dig and wild, dig and wild. The boiling thing, the weasel, inside you. Inside me there is a wild thing and yet I feel so calm and peaceful. Otters have come back to live in the river. The lowest point of humanity is golf and a Mondeo in the drive that every Sunday afternoon you must wash in the smells of roasting meat.

The river is there to be looked at. This is what I think she meant by those words. Kind of. And God it's working. This peace and calm I'm feeling, I have never felt this way before or if I have then it was only for a brief moment and I forgot it in a second.

*The lowest point of humanity is golf and a Mondeo in the drive …* God that's funny. Made meself laugh, I have. But *bridge*, tho; that's puzzling me. I don't have a clue about that one. Well. Just trust. Just trust that stuff will be made clear and if it isn't then so what? No, that's not right. There's no 'so what' here anymore. Not since the woman floating in the glow and the three words she said in a different voice. 'So what' has gone now, after her.

I check me kitchen cupboards and fridge for flour and eggs and stuff then make a little list of what I need to buy to make T's *very* favourite biscuits, his bestest ever, the ones with the raisins and the oats, then I get proper dressed in the jeans and the Uggs and then I leave the house. I still remember, and probably always will, how this once made me recently feel, stepping out of the house and closing the door behind me – shaking with fucking fear. Not today, tho; today I can feel the way the jeans cling to me legs and hips and arse moving as I walk. Me hair's still wet and I can smell it all clean. I see two swans on the river, just drifting. I watch them sail past beneath me and as they do I see the way their feet move under the water, their orange flapping feet. So, what, graceful above the water but going ten to the dozen underneath it. Pretty birds, aye.

One found a month or so ago with a crossbow bolt through its neck but I'm not gonner think about that today. It's recovering anyway in the RSPCA. They removed the bolt and it's gonner be okay. Fuckin sicko tho whoever would do such a thing but I will not think about it today. I will not let it into my head. Except it's already there, innit? Well, then – push it out, woman.

I cross the old stone bridge and then I turn right when I'm over it and walk to Lidl, past the roundabout, past the train station. There are closer shops but none cheaper. I only need a few bits but I'm in a queue for ages so I let the swans drift into the space behind my eyes and I let meself enjoy the attentions of the older bloke in the queue opposite who keeps looking at me when his wife isn't looking at him. He's not a rapist, I tell meself, not a stalker; he's not gonner follow me home. There is no danger in him and there's no need to react as if there is. He's just a bloke, that's all. You've drawn his eye and that's all and that's alright.

Me phone goes outside. I check the screen: JOHNNY MOBILE. Thought I'd deleted him. Fuck. I answer it anyway:

—What?

—Ems, where are you?

—Lidl car park.

—Heading home?

—Yes.

—The kid at school?

—It's Thursday so yes he is. I tell him a bit of a fib to put him off: —I'm going home for a bath.

—Aw brilliant. You'll be all clean, then. I'll be round in a bit, yeah? Got you something, I yav.

—I'm gonner have a bath, Johnny. Just told you. Don't—

—See ya in a bit.

Bastard hangs up. Unbelievable. I call him back but it goes straight to voicemail. Fucking unbelievable. Not in the mood for him today, I'm not. Want to go home and bake biscuits and give my M and D a ring. Read a book or watch a film. In the mood just for my own company today and I do not want him in my house with his stupid fin haircut and needs. Should've ignored the call. God we make mistakes.

Dig and wild, dig and wild. That glow.

I buy a paper and go for a cup of tea in the little caff by the station. Take me time over it. Maybe he'll get fed up waiting and I can't see him outside my house when I'm crossing the bridge but soon as me key's in the door he appears from behind the riverside wall. Oh God. He's tipped the spikes of his hair white and he's wearing a sleeveless t-shirt to show off the tiger stripe and Celtic tats that every fuckin soup-for-brains idiot without a personality has got these days. Me heart sinks. How could I have ever shagged this man? God we make mistakes. And sometimes the holes within get too wide.

He's not smiling. —Where've you been?

—Shopping. Lidl. Told yeh.

—Thought you were having a bath?

—Just about to. This isn't a good time, Johnny. I'm dead busy.

He stands close to me and sniffs. —You've already had one. I can smell it, yeah?

Oh Christ. Dig and wild. I open the door and he follows me in and puts a bag of something on the table which clunks. He watches me as I put the shopping away.

—What's wrong, Ems?

—Nothing.

—What's the puddy for then?

—Just got a lot of stuff to do today, that's all. No puddy.

—You're not the only one with stuff to do, aye. But take twenty minutes off, yeah?

I've got my back to him cos I'm putting the sugar in the cupboard and then his hands are on me waist. Squeezing. His breath is behind my ear, on the stars. They turn him on, them stars. Every time he used to do me from behind he'd pull my hair back so he could see them. His breath is hot and kind of spicy, yick, and I feel meself go all shop window dummy.

—Come on, Em. Set ourselves up for the day, yeah? This is what we do, innit, me and you. Fuck buddies, Ems. You know the score.

I face him and take his hands off me and give him a bit of a push away. Just a gentle one, like, not a shove, enough to make him take a step back.

—Not today.

His voice goes all whiney. —Yeah but I'm going away tomorrow. Greece for a week, see?

—Greece?

—Aye. Dirt cheap over there at the mo, innit? Do anything for money over there they will at the mo. Me and my boys, we booked it online. Well not Ryan cos he's on tag, but the rest of us, like. Week in Greece.

He says 'Greece' as if it's got eight e's in the middle. Like a whine. He grabs me waist again.

—An I've got you a present n all.

—Show me it, I say, not because I want to see it particularly but to get some carpet between us both. He goes over to the table and takes something out of the plastic bag and he's kind of giggling as he does it. He holds it up for me to see.

—What the fuck, Johnny? A dildo?

—Not just any old dildo, babe. It's mine.

—What?

—Make-your-own dildo kit. It's *my* dick, see?

—You've made a model of your own dick?

—From a mould, aye. Company while I'm away, innit.

He throws it over to me and in the half-second or so that it's in the air I feel the wild thing inside me stand up and scream. It's a flash, like, just one bright flash in me brain, blinding white and with bared teeth. It makes me catch the dildo then instantly throw it back as hard as I fuckin can. It zooms like a bullet straight and perfect and the bellend goes thwock as it hits home, right between the eyes. Hell of a shot aye.

—FUCK!

Johnny goes down in a heap, his face in his hands. One hell of a shot, that was. Caught him a right crack.

—The fuck was *that* for you mad fuckin bitch?!

—Can't be modelled on yours, that. For a start it's all stiff. Fuck off out of my house, will yeh.

43

He's still on the floor but he takes his hands away from his face and I can see a swelling on his forehead starting to come up. Patch of skin starting to go purple.

—What's fuckin wrong with you? Mad fuckin sket, what's fuckin wrong with you? What did you do *that* for?

He stands up, a bit woozy. Feel like hitting him again, I mean a real clenched fist full in the face, like. But I don't.

—Think I'd *like* that, a plastic model of your dick? That your idea of a present, is it?

I start to shove him in the direction of the front door. He rocks back and bounces off the wall and he's looking at me with … well, I've heard it said that fear can be seen in people's eyes but this is the first time I've ever actually *seen* it. It's like a shadow in there. He's shouting but it's just a noise and the thing inside me, I can feel that it's pleased here, with me and what I'm doing. Like a glow of warmth in me guts. Approval; that's the word.

—Get the fuck out. Just get the fuck out my house.

I give him one last hard shove and his back hits the front door and makes it shudder in the frame. His eyes have gone hard now and I can see that he's turned his hands into fists so I take a few steps back to be out of his reach. Not that he's ever hit me before, but I wouldn't put it past him. He's been a bully in other ways so I'm sure that giving me a dig is not beyond him. All those times – the emotional blackmail, the violence in the sex after he'd been on hatefuck.com, all of that shite. The drinking and the passing out and then the being woken up with a bit of him rootling inside one of me holes. *Fuck buddies.* Plenty of one but not so much of the other in what we had. I've been tired of this dickhead for a long time now, aye.

—Oh God you're in trouble now, he says. Kind of a grin on his face.

—Am I? Fuck off, will yeh.

—Oh yes.

—Be just your style to beat up a woman, wouldn't it?

—I am not going to lay one finger on you, you horrible fuckin skank. But I am going to *fuck* up your life, yeah?

44

I think of the knife in the kitchen, wonder if I could run and grab it before he grabs me. Wonder what I'd do with it even if I could.

—I'm just thinking that the people in the job centre will be *very* interested to hear about that work you're doing on the side, wouldn't they? And all that money you get from your fuckin folks every time you go crying to them. *Oh, Tomos bach needs a new coat for the winter* ...

The last words are said in a kind of high-pitched screech that screws his face up into a horrible mask. Spit flies out of his gob. Then he does a high girly laugh and I find all of this far more disturbing than anything he's ever done or could ever do.

—*What* work on the side?

—Think I don't know? The shopping you do for the oldies in the flats? Small town, this, babes. He looks at me as he spikes his hair up with his fingertips.

Them teeth flash again inside me. —Aye cos the day centre's been shut down! The Homecare scheme has gone cos there's no funding anymore!

—Doesn't matter.

—What d'you expect them to do? And it's only a tenner a week anyway! Fuck's sake!

—Doesn't matter. Then there's all the money from your fuckin folks. Undeclared income, innit? I've got a good mate works in the jobbie, remember? Carlos? You fucked him as well. He was second when you went threes up at Iestyn's party that time. His face goes into the mask again, kind of all folds in on itself. —You dirty fuckin disgusting whoo-er.

Dig, now, *dig*—

Bite him fucking *bite* him with these sharp and shiny teeth. I notice that the swelling on his forehead now looks more or less exactly like the bellend that hit him. Some beads of blood on it. All of a sudden I want to laugh.

—Oh fuck off, Johnny. You're a true dickhead.

—I'm going, don't worry. He opens the door. Stops halfway through, turns to have the last word but I give him another

shove and slam the door in his fucking face. He shouts something then presses his face against the frosted glass and waves.
I stick the middle finger up then go into the front room and
sit on the couch and stare at the carpet until my breathing
has gone back to normal and my hands have stopped shaking
by which time I feel exhausted so I lie down sideways on
the couch but my head's like a storm so I go upstairs and
take half a diazepam and then lie down on the bed and I
suppose I fall asleep cos in an instant it's nearly time to go
and pick T up from school. I go downstairs and make the
biscuits I promised him and as I'm leaving the house I see
that stupid plastic prick on the floor underneath the table so
I chuck it into the river outside and watch as the current
takes it out to sea.

I only stop seething, even with the diazepam, when I see
Tomos at the school gates waiting for me and soon we're back
home on the couch, just me and him, eating warm biscuits
and drinking milk. Tom's watching the telly. I can smell the
outside coming off him, out of his hair, grassy. My little weasel.
I fetch the laptop from upstairs and put it on the coffee table
and make a blog entry while he watches CBBC and eats the
biscuits. My wee wild thing.

—Mam?

—What's up, *cariad*?

—How'd you make these biscuits?

I tell him and he looks puzzled. —But all that stuff's wet,
he says.

—Ey?

—The eggs and that and the milk. All that stuff's wet.

—Aye, so?

—Well how come these are all crunchy and nice?

—The heat in the oven does that.

—How, tho?

—Magic.

—No but. How does it?

—It's just magic, *cariad*.

He looks at the half-eaten biscuit in his hand. There's a
light graze on his cheek. Dig and wild. Dig and wild.

—They're dead nice anyway.

—Good. I'm glad.

—They're always nice.

I smile at him over the top of the computer. He doesn't smile back but he looks at me with them blue eyes before he turns to look back at the telly.

# MESSAGES

Llyn syfydrin pendam sunrise saw woman floating in sky no joke!!! for real!!WTF?!
Twitter.com/@EmmaMum1

Small entry while T, who you all know about, watches *OOglies* and eats his fave cookies. Just got to tell you about this thing I saw in the sky a few days ago as the sun come up. On the Pendam mountain at Llyn Syfydrin (use the online OS map to find out where it is). Misty morning and there was a woman floating in the sky and I wasn't the only one to see her either. There was three of us and all of us saw her. A woman floating in the sky. Kind of glowing too. No word of a lie. I heard her say three words – dig and bridge and wild. I think I know what two of them mean and watch this space for more on that but the 'bridge' I haven't got a clue. Why did she say that word? I don't know. Anyway just like to know if anyone out there has seen anything similar or can explain it or even just comment on it. Love to hear your thoughts.
Http://Emmamum.wordpress.com
TAGS: Emmamum, vision, dig, wild, bridge, cookies, OOglies
4:47 P.M.

6:02 P.M., 304 hits
6:56 P.M., 918 hits
7:20 P.M., 1,100 hits
8:00 P.M., 3,116 hits
8:50 P.M., 17,340 hits
Midnight: 471,886 hits

#RT floatingwomanWTF?! You said it girl. Tell us more @ EmmaMum1
#RT floatingwoman: gweledigaeth? Beth? Dweud mwya plis @EmmaMum1
#floatingwoman: too much to tweet check out blogpost Emmamum.wordpress.com/@EmmaMum1

# MEAT

THE SLATEY WATERS of Llyn Syfydrin give back no sun as yet, still rising as it is beyond the hump of Disgwylfa Fawr. Soon they will; when the lifting wisps of mist have been hauled up into airy blue, then the disc will be seen, hovering over the islet on which geese and moorhens nest. The dry sedge of that island and the crisped rye grass of the banks and shores: soon a single match could sweep all of this up into one abrupt rush of flame. A breath ruffles the lake's surface, strokes out from it foamy scrolls that tap at the pebble shore with the noise of a cat at a milk bowl. Used firepits crater this shore and a log once used as a bench moves with the rising and sinking of the sun between damp and dry, conditions of which the orange underlips of plate fungi have taken full and opportunistic advantage. Bogbean bows in the fleeting breeze, the ducking pinkness flashing its inside white. Little bombs of bilberries nod in the grasses. Yarrow galaxies slowly help to heal the acidulated standing pools that remain after the conifers have been cropped, the regulated ranks of them, ordered and uniform like the politicians who compelled their planting, ripped from the ridges and sides about. A rowan tree observes and maybe the hiss of air in its ferny leaves is a comment. Sand martins have returned to their warren in the powdery bank at the lake's eastern end and are feeding now, their sickle wings skimming the water, gulping gnat and midge and joined by their cousins the swifts and the swallows, a tribe of screech and speed forever and deeply wild although their travels obey utterly dictates laid in their brains when the rock up here flowed and was still halfway soft. Tonight, when the sun will be sinking behind Craig-y-Pistyll into the sea at the valley's end, Daubenton's bats will join them, bulleting too, white-breasted too, and chasing the same prey. Bird and mammal exulting both in flight and fright when the sun burns the sky scarlet and gold.

The Dolgamfa barrow, the Bwch a Llo stones, the mines on the valley floor. Nant yr Arian – see the silver. Transhumance and tumuli. Industry and burial and worship, all from five-fingered hands, have in parts of this high land shaped and stained it for millennia, mapping the movements of the night sky, other patterns brightly high. Stone cottages crumble into mounds of mouldy boulders. Tunnels capillary the hills. Dug-out dwellings marked by huge chunks of quartz. The simple water that flows. Malleable land that endures yet as the people pass, always the people pass, their things seen off by the hives of hornets or the tunnellings of moles or even the thin marks that migrating birds make through the clouds. The oldest narratives made by them. When these volcanoes were active and the sky was red-threaded black and worms writhed away from bigger worms and left ribbony traces in the rock that was then mud. Such stories up here. And such echoes. And with what do we de-code and assess? All there is is flesh, in this. Infinity in the joints of a millipede's legs. In the pulverised pearls on the wings of a moth. All the pallid empires of men ... In the husky mutes of the owls are tiny bones of paper, skulls breakable by a breath. The merlin leaves small pancakes of shit on the blocks where he has butchered little birds and they resemble the pats of lichen yet in that lichen lies a world which also eats and ejects. Five-fingers formed some humps and tilted mighty stones erect and tamed the trees into uniform files but the flicking and creeping and crawling that steadily makes them nothing but matter find voice in the call of the vanishing corncrake and cuckoo and its only words are fuck you. *Fuck* you.

And still the people return. Visions shimmer in the crackling air. Several of them, this early morning, on the shores of the lake, one wearing a clerical collar. Each isolate from the other as yet but they will talk and share, soon. Outfliers from the hive online, meat emissaries from the virtual world. One of them studies an OS map of this area, the lake and its surrounds, and points to a ridge and another follows his finger and speaks and these first words, although spoken low, do bounce back from the water and the encompassing hills:

—Do you think?

The figure with the map nods. Someone has lit a candle and balanced it on a rock. Some other is on his knees at the water's edge and has genuflected and now appears to be praying. The two who have spoken now wordlessly begin to ascend the ridge and the man in the collar starts after them.

On the road leading up to this lake, the road that serves the ridge hamlets of Llwyn Prysg and Penrhiwnewydd and the low-lying village of Penrhyncoch and then joins with the larger roads that feed the larger towns nearby, a lone man trudges up. Pine woods on one side of him and a drop on the other, steep, down to the valley floor on which he can see the roundish scar of the ancient settlement of Craig-y-Pistyll. Above this stretch hills, green fading to distant blue, some of them stippled with the skinny white mills of wind farms, their blades front-crawling above the crests. He trudges, this man, because the road is steep and the morning is warm, but the set of his shoulders and head, the fullness of him, somehow puts an elemental into his step, so much so that a line of cyclists, all Lycra and helmets and reflector shades, berth him widely as they pass, as if the strange stateliness of his carriage may be contagious. He stops and steps aside for them to freely pass. One of them thanks him. He walks on and where the road temporarily levels out he takes a left turn into the woods and down the valley side to Rhoserchan.

# CALON ONEST, CALON LÂN

USED TO HATE the sun, I did. Never felt it on me as a blessing, if I ever felt it at all. Aye I'd sit in it, surrounded by people in shorts and vests and I'd be fucking shivering in a jumper with me arms wrapped around meself, teeth chattering. And birds; I'd hear them of a morning wherever the fuck it was I'd woken up and I'd think to meself *shut the fuck up, there's notten to fuckin sing about.* Wanner shoot them, I would. But now I love it when they wake me up. I love it when I hear them sing. Walking up the mountain in the sunshine, listening to the birdies do their thing. Sweet moments, man.

I hear an *excuse me* behind me as a cyclist bozzes past, all done up in the gear like, the helmet and the tight shorts. I step aside and watch them go by, hoping one of them's a woman so I can blimp at her arse in the Lycra but no, they're all blokes – hairy legs and that kind of squareness to their arse cheeks that women don't have. They head on, up the mountain. Wonder if they're going to the lake. *My* lake, I mean. They're all sweaty determination and the gear on them, all the para- phernalia: pure obsession. Isn't it meant to be fun? Each and every one of them looked in pain, to me. Slow down, lads, listen to the birds and feel the sun on your arms. Nothing is so important that isn't, what, birth or death that means you have to strain yeh tripes out getting to.

Ah well. What floats yeh boat, I suppose.

Stop to get me breath back. Steep hill, this, and a warm morning. Gunner be another hot one. The trees form a cool and shady tunnel over me on the slope down to Rhos so I sit on a dry stump for a rest. Smells nice; pine and grass. I hear a bark and see, through the trees opposite, on the hillside, Ralphie the sniffer dog being exercised, chasing a ball. Can't see his handler, whoever it is today who's been given the job, cos they're down in the hollow somewhere. Always got on with Ralphie, I did; he used to thwap me legs with his waggy tail. I remember wondering if he could smell emotions as well as drugs; sadness and loss and desperation and regret. But he always seemed too happy for that. But then he was a dog. An I remember when I first came here, at the end of a wet and humid summer, that hill over there that Ralphie's bounding down was full of mushies, almost completely brown with them. Hundreds of thousands. All that free temptation ... sensory derangement on offer, just growing out of the ground like. Woke up one morning and pulled the curtains back and the hillside had about thirty, forty people on it, each one on all fours, just plucking and eating like grazing animals. That afternoon I was sent out with a bucket to harvest the sheep shit for the tomatoes like and all the mushies had gone, every last one. There were a couple of pools of puke, still with undigested stems in them like worms. Easy enough after seeing that to resist temptation. Or was it? Don't clearly recall. But I did, tho. I *did* resist. Learnt to make some cracking pasta sauces as well; the toms came out dead sweet.

I hear an engine and look to me left and see the blue minibus rumbling up the hill towards me. Even at this distance I recognise the driver cos of the mad ginger hair sticking up like a busby, or a hive as I used to think of it at times, and picture the thoughts and bits of advice and stuff leaving it like buzzing bees. I stand up and give a wave and the van stops and the window goes down and Ebi shouts in his Cofi accent:

—The boy! A *fock* yew up yur tewday for then?

Christ: the decibels. The man is incapable of speaking at anything less than a bellow. —Fancied a walk. Thought I'd drop in.

He gives me a look, and his light blue eyes go all kind of knifelike and watery. A sign that he's thinking.

—That's all? Yew-a sure now?

—Aye.

—Definitely definitely? Hand-on-heart promise?

—Aye, Ebi. Nice day and just fancied a bit of a walk, that's all. Stretch the ahl legs like.

He looks at my face and then gives a little nod. —There we are then. Am off to Llanilar to pick up some new chook-chooks.

—Ah. Fox again?

—Aye, fockin Reynard took another few last night, didn't he? Can't see how he've been getting into-a pens meself. Got em like Fort Knox I yav. Crafty cont, aye.

—Where was Ralphie?

—Ad im inside. Leave im outside and he've taken to woofin at every shadow, fock knows why. Spooked by somethin last week. Keeps everyone awake he does. Can't stop him, so he've been sleepin in-a laundry. He puts the van into gear and revs the engine. —Anyway, dinner in half an hour! Soup! Leek and *tatws*!

He gives me a salute and drives off. Kind of *roars* off, really. Nothing that man does is ever less than loud; he even snores like a jumbo taking off. He first came here in recovery, he told me, but he relapsed on release. Went back up north to the mountains, got a flat in Porthmadog with a mate, also in recovery, opened a bottle. Less than a month later his mate was dead; Ebi found his corpse. So he came back down to Rhos, cleaned up, and got a job here as general oddjobber. He's not a member of counselling staff or anything but he was hugely helpful in that way. I remember one night, a weekend night it was, we were all sitting around the barbecue pit and the stars were all shining and I had this feeling like I'd finally fuckin kicked it, finally learned to accept and not rage. And Ebi started singing. The firelight on his face and that head of hair of his all red and mad and his head tilted back, giving it laldy to the Milky Way. The song was 'Calon Lân'. He sang it in Welsh and then in English, kind of, cos the words then didn't really fit the tune, but I remember them clearly, in Ebi's translation, cos that night I wrote them down and I've still got them somewhere:

> I don't ask for a luxurious life
> the world's gold or its fine pearls
> I ask only for a happy heart
> an honest heart, a heart that's pure
> a pure heart full of goodness
> is fairer than the pretty lily

none but a pure heart can sing
sing in the day and sing in the night

Pure lovely, man. Except, except, how to keep a pure heart, out in the world when you're released, clean, into it only to find out that it's anything *but* pure? When it's governed by an infatuation with money, obsessed with money to the point that people with money enough to support them through a thousand generations are encouraged to make more, always more? So obsessed that it will be taken from the poor so that the already rich can have more. More than they could ever need. So obsessed that they will kill to make more, lay cities desolate so they can further insulate themselves from the world. Pure heart? And they'll say in public and totally without shame or irony that they are proud to belong to a Christian country. Christian? Under those cunts it's barely even fuckin civilised. Their podgy, unlined, never-known-struggle faces, their dead fucking eyes unlit by any imagination, their sober-suited insistence on Doing The Right Thing, their tax-avoiding Bullingdon Club restaurant-smashing fucking stinking hypocrisy, their fucking fucking fucking fuck—

The glow, Adam. Christ, man, remember that glow. And Ebi's face in the firelight as he sang those words. What takes root in your head is your choice only and nowt else. Pure heart.

I walk down to Rhos proper, to the buildings, like. It's cool in the trees and I can hear bees. The swallows zip and zoom through the shadows. The sun hits me, I mean it feels like a proper biff, when I leave the trees and come out behind the Second Stage house. Used to be a working farmhouse, it did. God, imagine living here, working these hills. Must've been a hard, hard life. The garden looks brilliant, all the colours; they're doing a good job with the upkeep. I wonder if them slow-worms still nest behind the compost heap. Probably: I mean I don't see why they'd move. Safe from the cats there, they are. But then nowhere's truly safe from a cat. I remember Quilty bringing back a dead bird that left my hands covered in soot when I took it off him; he'd been down a chimney to get it, the mad wee bugger. I put chicken wire behind the compost to protect the lizards from the Rhos cats but they dug beneath it so I had to dig it down, embed it deeper into the soil. So then they just reached their paws through. So then I had to get a smaller mesh. Don't know if it worked, if the lizards are still there or if the moggies (and the maggies) have wiped them all out. I hope they're still there. And no one can blame the cats for doing their thing. Funny, tho, how all the feral cats in these hills find Rhos, how they gravitate here. Cats have a knack for knowing which houses will take them in and look after them but I like the fact that the wild ones in this area would end up at Rhos, as if similar souls were acting like magnets to each other. And Christ how they were doted on ... people hiding the bacon from their breakfasts to feed them with. They'd arrive all skinny and bedraggled and in a couple of weeks they'd be porkers, like rugby balls covered in fur. I remember one, a real bruiser tom he was, big rip through his ear, scars all over his face, proper lion in miniature, kind of a bluey colour as if there was some real pedigree in him, there was this aura around him, the way he moved, prowled, the light in his eyes. He had a collar on so someone must've owned him, once. But the wild life called him with a loud voice I suppose and he could do nothing but listen. Wonder if he's still around. Cool animal he was; whenever I watched him walk that song would go through me head, 'Stray Cat Strut'. And then Quilty came out of the town at night-time just when I needed him; sitting on my bed I was one night crying and thinking, again, that to stop breathing once and for ever might be the better option and then there was this shape at the window, against the glass, grey-striped and ghostly with mad yellow eyes. I heard him miaowing behind the pane. It's the world, man; it sends you these gifts every now and again, usually when you're least expecting it. No, fuck that, cos you *never* expect it. But still they come.

I smell cooking as I pass the Second Stage house. I'm hungry but it can wait; first thing I want to do up here is see Sally. That's always the first thing I want to do up here so I circle the First Stage building and head towards the polytunnels and there she is, outside, sat on a chair, mug in one hand and thin roll-up in the other as always. I whistle and she looks up and her face breaks into a grin. There's a black cat at her feet, his legs tucked beneath him. He looks like a furry curling stone. He blinks.

—Look at *you*! Sally shouts, and I actually do; I look down at meself, see the clean jacket, the clean jeans over the abscess-free legs. —Aren't *you* looking smart?

I give her a great big hug. Small flowers caught in her hair and compost in her clothes.

—What brings you up here?

—Weather. Nice day. Fancied a walk.

—I'll put the kettle on.

I follow her into the polytunnel. Flowers here, young flowers which will be planted outside soon, and vegetables; tomatoes like Christmas baubles. Some thin vines across the curved placcy roof but there's no green on them and certainly no fruit.

—See the grapes haven't taken then.

—No, she says. —And they won't, either. Don't know what I was thinking of, hoping for grapes in Wales. Be better off growing laver.

She busies herself with making tea. The cat comes in and stretches and yawns and I see his pink tongue and his white teeth, the fangs like needles and the side ones, the carnassial teeth (aye, I read, these days) like a tiny mountain range. I tickle his head and then he slopes off behind a bag of compost. Multipurpose, it says on it, but I can think of only one thing that it might be used for.

—You haven't come to tell us you've won the lottery, then?

—I wish. But I don't even do the lottery. Why?

—Funding. Cuts are starting to bite. Same old story innit? Nothing changes. Except it gets worse, aye.

—Not a danger of going under tho, I say, and it's not really a question.

—What, closing down?

—Yeh.

She holds crossed fingers up on both hands. —Not yet. But God the struggle for money you wouldn't believe. And not just that; we've got to endlessly fucking justify the tiny bit of funding we *do* get. All the time, form after form after form. Cos we generate no money, that's what it is, although we save one fuck of a lot. A few quid spent on this place saves a few thousand in the NHS or the police service or whatever. Try telling *them* that, tho. See how far you get.

*Them*: I know exactly who she means by *them*. She gives me a mug of tea and leans against a bench full of salad pots and rolls another smoke. I get me own baccy out and do the same. Still got the packet that Benji gave me. Nice one that man.

—Economically it makes no fucking sense at all, she says. —I mean, just for a moment forget care and compassion and all that kind of stuff; just pretend that they don't matter and look at it from a purely economic perspective. We save money. We save *lots* of fuckin money. We're cheap as rehab goes anyway and we're successful with it; eighty-nine per cent are still clean two years after leaving here.

—I know that, Sal.

—Course you do, sweetheart. An the amount of money society has been saved from you alone. She licks her Rizla and lights up and blows out smoke in a snort. —No sense. Only in ideological terms does it make any sense. But we'll be alright when that 350 mil a week comes back, aye? Lying fuckers. Anyway. You haven't come all the way up here just to listen to me bang on. How've you been?

And how *have* I been? What can I say? —Alright.

—Staying clean? I know I shouldn't ask like but. Can't help worrying, can I?

I must hesitate for a split second because I see her facial expression react to fill the gap; the eyes kind of fill with something and the lips go upside down like an n. She just says: —Oh no, in a voice gone small, and instantly I go on the defensive but I must be honest at all times:

—No, no, listen, it's not what you're thinking. No smack or crack, nothing like that.

—You had a drink?

—Not even that, no.

—What then?

I tell her about the rave thing on the mountain by the lake. The white pill and how it did nothing but keep me awake so I'm guessing it was pure caffeine and nothing else.

—And you were disappointed?

—No. Can't say I was. More relieved than anything, to be honest.

—Yeah but where did the desire come from? I mean you weren't to know it was a dud when you necked it. Could've been anything. Dread to think what's passed off as E these days.

—Aye I know. But I felt … I don't know what I felt. Bored. Like I needed a reward or something. You know how the junkie mind works, Sal. I'll never do it again.

—Never say 'never'. Day to day, boy. Control is the key. And where was your sponsor?

—Off on holiday. And I saw something. In the sky.

Fuck. I've done it again. Without any conscious intention those words have just leapt out. Why is this? It's like them words, just them words and no others, are wild creatures inside and I can't control them or keep them in. They just spring out.

—What d'you mean?

—Like a shape in the sky, I say.

—A cloud?

—God no. I know what clouds look like, don't I?

—Kind of a UFO? There's been loads of them seen recently. Lights and discs and stuff. Giant white cigars, one person said on the *Cambo News* letters.

—Nothing like that. This was kind of like a woman.

—In the sky? A floating woman?

—Aye, yeah. We were up on this ridge like and the sun was coming up and it wasn't raining but the air was kind of wet? Know what I mean?

—*Awyr glas*, she says.

—What?

—Welsh for 'blue air'. That's what we say round here cos the air's nearly always saturated. Who's 'we'?

59

—What?

—You said 'we were on the ridge'. Who's the 'we'?

—Me and two others. Some big feller and a woman.

—What was her name?

—Who, the woman?

—Was she called Emma?

—How'd you know that?

—She's been blogging about this, she has. Have you not read it? It's 'trending on Twitter', as they say. I can hear the quote marks in her speech but I'm glad to see she doesn't do the fingers-in-the-air thing. —My Jess pointed it out to me.

I want to ask her how her daughter is but the other words won't let me, won't give me room. She jumps into my mind, tho, Jess does; last time I saw her she was on the prom, with her mates, late at night, massive heels on her feet and a tiny silver dress. She didn't see me, but I wanted her to.

—So what was it, this shape? I ask. —What're they saying online?

Sally stubs her smoke out in a plant-pot overflowing with dog ends and other rubbish. —Shadow or something. God knows. An atmospheric phenomena to do with a concentration of water molecules in the air. She smiles at me and then says: —That's what someone said online, anyway. I dunno, people see funny things all the time, Adam love. Overactive imaginations. You were sleep-deprived cos of the caffeine. You were dreaming awake.

—Hallucinating?

—Kind of. Not like when on acid or anything, you were just dreaming while awake. Or half awake. Your mind needs to sleep.

—Aye but all three of us saw it. How could we all have the same dream?

—Maybe you didn't. Maybe one of you saw it and mentioned it to the other two and now all three of you think you saw it. Or believe that you did. Power of suggestion.

—No, it wasn't like that, I say but I'm not entirely sure anymore.

—Or maybe it was just a shadow or something like I said. I doubt it was a ghost or anything.

—Who said anything about ghosts?

—I wouldn't worry about it, *cariad*. And get yourself up to the kitchen for some soup. I've got to go down to the stream for watercress.

—Shall I come with?

—No, no, go and see the others. I know they'd love to see you. Floating woman. Daft bugger, you.

She gives me a hug; that smell again of flowers and soil. I squeeze her very tight. In the same way that I never used to feel the sun I never used to feel people either; they were just things, objects, useful in only two ways: can I score off them? Can I rob off them? And that was it. Useless to me otherwise. Now, tho, I squeeze Sally until I feel her breath whoosh onto my neck.

—Ow!

—Sorry.

She lets me go. —Someone's had their Weetabix. Now go and have some soup. I'll see you soon.

I'm dismissed. I leave the polytunnel, back out into the sunshine. A breeze has sprung up now and is setting the polythene flapping with a rhythmic thumping sound. At the woodwork sheds I turn and see Sally heading down the valley side, away from me, with a bucket under her arm. The watercress grows wild down by the river. It was up here that I tasted the stuff for the first time and I've loved it ever since; on butties, with cheese and Marmite. It was not the kind of thing my folks would've recognised as food, mainly because it's not a spud, or meat. Me dad would've considered someone who ate leaves as highly suspicious and to be avoided. If not battered. To him, there was a direct link between a taste for salad and for taking it up the arse. Couldn't have one without the other. *You are what you eat*, that was one of his phrases, *so if you eat fruit* ... God almighty. Sometimes, when I think back, I'm amazed that I lasted as long as I did before becoming a junkie. Surprised I wasn't jacking up in me cot.

On the way back up to the Second Stage house I see a feller come out of First Stage and cup a flame in his hands to light up. Must be new cos I don't recognise him, but then, not being a rezzie meself anymore, I hardly ever do see the First Stagers; socialising with them is discouraged. They're taking the first steps towards relearning living skills and they're delicate, them steps are; it's so easy to stumble and fall over when taking them. Like learning to walk all over again. I look at this feller as I get closer to him and I see the shirt-sleeves buttoned up tight on the cuffs to cover, what, healing abscess holes, trackmarks still leaking maybe, any number of things. See the inky-dink tattoos on his neck and face and hands; notice that on one side, there's a bite taken out of his ear. It's healed in a scallop-shell shape. One of his eyes stays fixed; it could be false. And it's not as alive as the other one is, doesn't reflect the sky like the other one does.

He gives me a nod as I get close. I say hello to him and he goes *alright matey* but he's evidently a Brummie cos it comes out *mite-oiii*, like that.

—Yowr Adam, yeh?

—I am, yeh.

—Suki saw yow walkin past the window. Towld moy Oy should come and talk to yow.

—Did she? What about? And how is she?

—Shay's sound. Knows her stuff down't shay?

—Aye she does. What d'you wanner talk to me about?

He's still got the shakes a bit, this feller; the tip of his cigarette bobs about as he puts it to his face. Wounds on his hands still slightly scabby. When he speaks he does this funny kind of click in the back of his throat that sounds rusty; makes me think of a machine being started up for the first time in ages. I see that both of his eyes are moist, probably from the sun cos it's shining right in his face. *Both* of his eyes; not a falsie, then. Just a bit unanchored. Or would the ducts still work anyway? I don't know.

—Oy'm having troubles, he says. —Suki thinks yow moit be able to help.

—With the cravings, like? Them kind of troubles?

—No, not that. D'yow smoke?

He offers me his packet. —No ta. I smoke these, I say, and take me baccy out. Might as well roll another one while I've got it out of me pocket. —So, what, then?

—Ey?

—These troubles.

—Oy'm not craving anymore. Not physically, loike.

—You said that, mate. So what's the problem?

—It's in here. He bows his head to show me the top of his skull. He doesn't just tap it with his finger or anything, he does a kind of long nod so I can see his cranium. Aye, he's learning to walk again, sure enough, this bloke.

—I need a bit more to go on, feller. Which one of the millions of troubles inside yeh head are you talking about? I've been there before, mate, don't forget. I know what it's like.

He flicks his fag end away in the direction of the plant-pot ashtray and immediately lights another one. He studies the end of it, the tiny coal, as he blows smoke out of his nose.

—You can just say it, lad, I say. —Avver look at this. I pull the collar of my shirt away on the left side so he can see the date tattooed on me pec. —Got that done on me first year's clean. Whatever you wanner tell me, I'll know exactly what yeh talking about. I don't judge this stuff, man. Why would I?

His one good eye flicks sideways for a second to look at me. We're standing there, the two of us, on the slab path, smoking, and around us are the huge green hills. The breeze has died away now and the sun is hot.

—Oy down't know who Oy am, he says in a blurt and then looks down as if embarrassed. —Anymore. Oy can't talk about this in group. Oy should be aible to, Oy know that, but Oy just can't. Spoke to Suki about it last night. Speak to yow, she said.

So *this* is the step he's on; the one labelled IDENTITY REBUILD. Spent a fuck of a long time sitting on that step, I did. This is where the secondary addiction has to be dealt with (or maybe it's the primary addiction, even more urgent than the physical one, I sometimes think), the addiction to chaos, to intensity. I – and, evidently, this Brummie bloke too – used to define meself in opposition to the police, politicians, establishment people and anyone who seemed to be in their camp; the willing workers, either the happy or unhappy ones, stuck for five decades in a job they loathed and looking fowards to retirement when they could potter in the garden for a few decrepit years before death. From judges and ministers to people who put up NO TURNING signs in their drives, these were the kinds of people I knew I was not, and it was those people who sought to bleach my life of all thrills, who would put obstacles in the way of my experiencing anything intense or authentic. They were to blame for the chaos of my life; when I hurt others, it was ultimately the fault of *them*, not me. I now know that to be shite but I still identify meself in opposition to those fuckers and the forces they represent. I will never be like them. I will never Do The Right Thing, as they fucking see it. There's a glow in me now.

—Yeh don't know who yeh are, I say. —Yeh feel that you've lost yeh identity. Yeh not the feller yeh were, this is what yeh thinking. There's even a little voice somewhere inside telling yeh that you've what, fuckin surrendered, something like that, am I right? Given up, like.

He just nods.

—What was your thing, mate?

—Moy thing?

—Aye, y'know, smack, crack, booze, what? Actually no, don't tell me; it's not important. But it's gone now and so has the lifestyle that went with it and you're being normal now and that's a word yeh fucking hate. Right?

Another wee nod.

—Well, listen, man: fuck that. Fuck it. You're still the feller yeh were, but yeh getting rid of the shite and yeh rebuilding yehself around that, that core. Yeh have an identity still. *More* than before. You're here so you've done the first steps, you've accepted responsibility and accountability, and you've made amends, right? Or at least you've tried to. You're doing something useful with the guilt. Aren't yeh?

No nod this time, but he's listening. His Adam's apple moves as he swallows and it's like he's ingesting me words. My apple. *I'm* Adam.

—But look at these cunts; them who've already got massive amounts of money but who help themselves to the money of others, the poor people, the people who don't have much and what they do have they've worked their friggin arses off to get. Look at them coppers in the Met who tried to say that that cunt who killed Ian Tomlinson was a civilian in police uniform. Nothing's ever their fault. Or them who shot that Brazilian feller, or who lied about Hillsborough. Or the bankers, fuck. Them and their greed.

I raise me eyebrows to elicit a response. I don't say anything more until he looks at me and nods and then I'm on one, all of a sudden:

—You remember all this stuff, right? From before you came in here. The expenses scandal. Rupert fucking Murdoch. George Osborne and his fuckin inheritance. Brexit, Christ, remember that shitstorm? Fuckin Farage and fat Boris and that abortion Gove. Jeremy fuckin Hunt! I could go on all day naming names, all these cunts that do their best to defer blame, to fuckin weasel out of everything bad that they've done. Thousands of these pricks. They do everything they can to put it onto somebody else, don't they? Always. Always. They never accept that they're the ones at fault. But yeh, tho, you *have*, haven't yeh? You've accepted that you've behaved like a twat and hurt people and you've apologised and yeh trying to make it better and move on. So in that way you're still in opposition to them bastards. If this is a battle then morally you're the winner and what else is there, man? You're trying to clear yeh conscience; *they're* not, tho, fuck no. See what I mean? You and them, lad. It's still you and them. And it always fuckin will be. Yeah? yeh know what I'm talking about, don't yeh? The inner life, man.

I want to touch his chest with me finger, poke it like, but I know how averse to being touched First Stagers can be. —It's always more important than the shite going on outside. Knowmean?

I see him thinking; can almost hear the grinding of the mental gears, rusty and chipped from whatever substances he's not long stopped hammering. A small breeze has come down off the mountain around us and has caused a kind of low wee whirlwind and is blowing leaves and bits of litter in circles around our feet. As if we're the centre of a vortex. I like that thought.

He takes a last long drag and then again flicks the butt towards the plant pot. —Is this how yow foil now? he asks.

—Course it is. Wouldna said it otherwise, would I?

—Is it good?

—Is what good, mate?

—Y'know. To have it all behind yow.

—To be clean and sober?

He nods. And then the world brings a little gift again in the form of a ladybird that lands on my hand. The breeze brings it onto my hand and I show it to him.

—See that, I say, and it's not a question. —Look at it, man. I mean *really* look at it.

He leans in, this feller with the shakes and the bad eye and the mangled ear and the healing wounds and the memories, the darkness of which can only be guessed at, leans in until both his eyes are an inch away from the bright and tiny insect on me hand.

—See how fuckin amazing it is? I say. —Precious little thing, man. This is miles more important than our needs.

I blow gently on it and its shell opens and its wings come out and it flies away and we watch it go.

—Urroyt, he says.

—What is?

—Just urroyt, he says again, and it's enough, really. Got a long way to go, this bloke. He smiles at me and I smile back but I can't look directly at him because of the teeth.

—You going back inside now?

—No. Think Oy'll gow an sit in the bird hut for a bit.

—Ah yeah. Nice place. Spent hours in there, I did.

—When yow next up?

—Dunno. Next week maybe.

—Oyl see yow then, then.

He walks off in a kind of shuffle, favouring his left leg. In him I see carnage, smithereens like, beginning to form a shape

66

again. It's like at the end of *The Iron Giant* after the big robot's been blown up, and all the bits of him start to roll together and join up again; that's what the Brummie reminds me of. Welcome back to the world, feller. You need each other. Or *yow* need each other, down't yow? Bostin!

Now I'm *really* hungry. The hills around are beginning to seem insubstantial and dreamlike and I think I can hear drums from on top of the mountain, in the direction of my lake. Probably just my own heartbeat or some forestry machinery in the trees. I head up towards Second Stage. There's Suki waving at me from the kitchen window. I wave back and she raises an invisible spoon to her mouth in a question and I give her a thumbs up and she turns away from the window. Suki, Sally, Ebi, all the others – grand and lovely people. There was fuck all to lose with them around and freedom from addiction and despair to gain. That's what it said on the website. It—

And then the sky is filled with screaming. I stand still and put my face in a clench until the jet has passed and is further down the valley and the air throbs with the aftershock. Feel my heart and breath normalising again. They map the flight path over a place like this, where people with their nerves stretched to snapping point and yearning only for some kind of calm reside. Either they haven't even bothered to find out what Rhoserchan is or they have and they don't give a shit. I'm beginning to think it's the latter. The longer I spend out in the world, the more I get involved in it and its work-ings, the more I realise that the people with power truly do not care about those without. Same goes for the rich, who are nearly always the same people. They truly do not care. They care more about a scuff mark on their shoe than they do about the well-being of millions of people. This is the reality.

—God's sakes. Any lower and that would've taken the chim-neys off, Suki says as she meets me at the door. —Did you see that?

—See it? I could count the blackheads on the pilot's nose. How are you, Sooks?

—All the better for seeing you. Another hug; this one offers the smell of lavender soap and shampoo with a back note of stewed leeks. —Come and meet everyone.

—Any new arrivals since I was last up here?

—No.

—Then I've met em all already. I was up here last week, remember?

—Yeah well comen meet them again, then. Three've gone into town to pick up a bit of shopping and Alex is on a Reality Check.

—And that's in ... Swansea, right?

She smiles at me. Always like it when Suki smiles at me. —You've got the old memory back. He's in the Domino project now, did you know?

—Is he? Fair play to the man.

—Learning the guitar and everything, he is. He's getting pretty good.

I follow her into the kitchen. There's a good steamy smell hanging over the four people at the table who all look up at me and stop talking as I enter. They're eating from bowls and there's two loaves of bread on the table next to flowers in a vase and a spare bowl at the end closest to me.

—This for me?

—Dig in, Suki says, and goes to the galley kitchen and runs water into the sink. I say hello to everyone and start to eat. I'm so hungry that I'm drooling. And once I never felt people except just as objects to get things from but look at these four around the table, so very different and so very the same ... or, no, first thing, look at the room, the simple furniture, the grey carpet, all of it tidy, and the big windows looking onto the valley, the green V running down towards the sea which, today, twinkles in the distance cos of the sunshine. It was in this room that – wish I had the fuckin words for this – it was in this room thick and stinking with old sickness and sweat, kind of sweet, too, with the acetone; not sweet like flowers but sweet like the breath of a bad diabetic. And all the people quivering in this room. It was in here, among all those shaking people and the smells coming out of them, all them months ago now, that I first felt, what? It was in this room that I first felt, kind of *sensed*, that there was something at the end of the valley all them miles away by the sea that was moving towards me, not in a menacing way, more like a friend who you haven't seen for ages and who you've missed and they're coming towards you with their arms open for a hug. Like that. As if the horizon at the valley's end had a message for me and that message was telling me that there was something much, much bigger than me and it was good and it had me in its sights.

Aye. That's not bad. That'll do.

Soup's good but my tongue's accustomed to powerful tastes. —Can I have the salt and pepper?

A Chinese lady smiles and passes them down the table. She's like a doll; the specs and her black bob and the ever-present grin. Forgotten her name, but I remember being quite startled when I first heard her speak; this thick Glaswegian accent coming out of that tiny lady. Like slicing open an orange and finding it blue inside.

—Will Ah cut ye a piece, eh?

—Aye, go on then. Do us a thick one. I'm ravenous here.

—And go easy on the butter, Suki says from the sinks. — We're nearly out and no one's doing a proper shop till Friday.

—If it's butter we're out of just give a pint of milk to the Major there, the goth girl – Mary? – says. —He'll have it churned in no time.

The Major harrumphs but not in a grumpy way and holds his hand out above the table. It's a pure blur. —Steady as a rock, my girl. Steady as a dem rock.

Everyone laughs but the Major doesn't even smile. I've never seen him smile. He looks like the major off *Fawlty Towers*, that's how he got his name, and I'm wondering how the goth girl – May? – knows about that series cos she's young but then I remember that there's a DVD box set of it in the telly room. Harmless viewing, y'see, altho I do remember the cravings coming back strong when watching it; the chaos of Basil's life, how that could only be made bearable for me by a pipe or a spike. The Major – our Major, I mean, the feller here at the table – I've always found him the saddest one. The most desolate. I mean, he speaks dead posh, he always wears a tie even on a hot day like today, he never swears, his manners are impeccable, but Suki told me once that when he was first brought in he was half-naked and could hardly speak and he was caked in shite and he was as yellow as a banana. Like something from a nightmare, she said. And it's like he's followed, all his life, a set of rules governing behaviour and he was promised that if he abided by those rules he'd be happy and successful but all they did was steer him towards ruin. The sense of betrayal hangs over him like a cloud. I mean, most people who come through this place have a notion of the broken social contract when they're very young, the rank unfairness of it – like, if I'm provided with good education and housing and a fulfilling job with decent pay then I'll behave myself and obey the rule of law, yet *their* side of the contract was shattered long ago but I'm still expected to stick to mine, on pain of punishment. So, y'know, fuck em all. But the Major never had that, did he? He grew up with privilege and never with the feeling that he'd been shat on and shat on again. And in fact he had all the trappings of a successful life but inside him was this horrible despair. The good citizen that he was brought him only a nothingness. So his feeling of being let down must be the size of them fucking mountains that I can see through the window.

The Scottish Chinese lady holds out a slab of bread with butter on it spread so thin that it looks like she used a spray gun and I reach out over the table to take it. I wonder who made it. I'm about to ask when I notice that the goth girl – Moira? – isn't eating soup, she's eating a piece of bread and peanut butter with a knife and fork. Cutting it into dainty little squares.

—Didn't fancy the soup, no?

She shakes her head. —I'm vegan.

—It's leek-and-potato, aye?

—With milk in.

She gives a bit of a look to the other feller at the table next to the Major, a guy in specs with a thinning blond quiff and acne scars like tiny craters on his face.

—Anthony's apologised, Maria, Suki says from the kitchen.

—Thought it was soya, Anthony says.

—With a cow on the carton?

—Glad it wisnae, says the Chinese Glaswegian. —Soya milk in soup? Would've given me the boak, ay. Ah've hud some bad things in mah goab in mah time but no that.

She's right; soya milk in leek-and-spud soup sounds manky. Maria doesn't say anything else, she just puts a tiny square of bread into her black lips with the tips of her fork. Anthony gives her a bit of a worried glance. Some frisson between them? Maybe on his part, but not on hers, I don't think. She's skinny; not emaciated, I mean not catwalk-skinny like, but there are enough protruding bones to suggest that she's had recent problems with food as well as substances. The soya was just a convenient excuse probably.

Suki says my name from over by the sinks.

—What's up, Sooks?

—Since you've been in the town have you come across a feller with one arm? From your neck of the woods originally.

—Can't say I have, no.

—You sure?

—I think I'd remember a one-armed boy from Liverpool. How'd he lose it?

—The arm? Dunno, probably infection. Didn't ask him. Anyway we're bringing him up from Carmarthen this evening.

—Carmarthen?

—Yeh. He was in Afallon ward but they shipped him down to Carmarthen when that closed.

Anthony groans. —*Was* closed, Sooks, *was* closed. To save a few measly quid.

—*Was* closed, then, aye.

—What was he doing there? I ask.

—Where?

—Afallon.

—He lost it big time. Spectacularly was the word they used. He'd been in recovery for years and was doing well but he relapsed and charged into the ward one night ranting about

71

being hunted by gangsters or something. Said he needed locking up for his own safety. They sectioned him and he started rattling so he's coming here tonight. He's detoxed down in Carmarthen. Just thought you might've bumped into him, that's all.

Suki starts to scrub a pan. I blow on the soup in my spoon and as I do it turns into bubbling skag, brown fizz, the lump of spud in it like a ball of cotton wool. I close my eyes until the memory fades and then suck the soup out of the spoon and swallow it.

Surprised I'd never met the one-armed bloke at meetings. But then he might've done his steps somewhere else. Unless moving here was an attempt at a geographical cure. Which never works. I thought I knew every scouser in the town, but obviously not. For a small town it's got a fuck of a lot of secrets.

An engine rumbles outside. Suki says: —That'll be Ebi back with the chickens, and dries her hands. —You lot behave yourselves and play nice, she says with a smile and goes out the back door.

*Spectacularly*. There was a relapse of *spectacular* proportions. Already lost an arm, the feller must've already had a bad time of it but part of him was craving that horror back in his life. I'd imagine that for him the term 'rehab' makes no sense; it's 'hab' he needs, there's no 're' about it. He's never known normality so there's nothing for him to get back to. He's not relearning, he's *learning*, for the first time, like, in his life. The word '*re*hab', it's often meaningless, for many people. The general use of it shows how very little is understood about the ways in which people live their lives. The worlds they are born into.

But *spectacularly*, Suki said, and that word sends a shiver, like an electric shock, down my spine, from the base of my skull to the top of me arse. *Spectacular*. Like a great big firework display, like an eagle taking off. *Spectacular*. That's the way I'll go too, when I *do* fall. In mad fire, like a fucking comet. The fucking planet will tremble. The entire fucking—

Christ, what am I thinking about? *When* I fall? This is not a good thought, man. Not good. There was a glow in the sky and you saw it once. Pure, pure heart.

Anthony looks around him in a kind of conspiratorial way and leans in over the table. —What's it like, Adam? he says.

—What's what like?

—Out there. He nods at one of the windows.

—In the town, you mean?

—No, well, in the world, y'know. It's driving me nuts, no telly or Internet or newspapers. Need to know what's going on. Too cut off up here.

—Whit's gaun oan is thit ye've goat yir sleeve in yir soup, the Chinwegian lady says, and Anthony kind of yelps and his arm jerks up in the air. The Major harrumphs again and Maria goes 'Hoi!' cos some soup spots have landed on her bread. All of this makes me laugh and then as Anthony pulls his sleeve away from his wrist I see the pink scars there and instantly I want to weep. God, I'm not kidding; at this age, and sober, my heart has become as uncontrollable and unpredictable as my dick once was. No lie. It's like a wild animal.

—I can't eat this now!

The Major holds his hand out for Maria's plate. —I'll make you some more.

—*He* should do it.

—It was entirely an accident. Let me.

Maria hands her plate over and it's like a surrender. The Major transfers her half-eaten bread onto his own plate and cuts a new slice and puts that on Maria's plate and hands it over to her then picks up the butter dish and the jar of Sunpat and passes them over to her as well and all this is like an offering.

—There we go, he says. —No harm done.

—Except I'm not supposed to use any butter, am I? Suki said.

—Yir a vegan, pet, eh no?

Maria wrinkles her nose in a kind of scowl. Starts putting peanut butter on the bread.

—Look at me shirt, Anthony says. —It's soaked in soup.

—Aye well that's yir supper sorted oot. Just give yir shirt a good wring ovir the soup bowl, eh?

The Chinwegian gives me a wink and I give her a smile in return. How come I can't remember her name? I know why;

cos the word 'Chinwegian' took over. I invented it and liked it so not only did it stick but it absorbed the knowledge of her real name. Swallowed it up.

I scrape up the last smears of me soup then rub the bread around the bowl. Still a bit hungry. Don't want to have another bowl tho cos I'm not a resident anymore and I'd feel, what, rude. Cheek is good but not rudeness. Manners, man; for many years I never even knew what they were. And straight after that thought comes the memory that Anthony used to be a journalist, *before*, like, in his Before Times, which is why he asked me that question. Which I have't answered.

And what the fuck can I say, anyway? What's the world like, how do I respond to that? God almighty. I remain in this part of Wales not only to stay close to Rhos and people like Benji and Sion but because it's stayed halfway resistant to the darkness that's taken over much of the country yet even here I see it happening too. A cloud of enforced sameness. Should I tell these people that what is waiting for them is a widespread attitude, government-led and media-fed, that sees the treatment they are undergoing as a waste of time and money? That they'd better sort themselves out so quickly and completely that it must be miraculous because there's no help for them out there cos all services for the damaged and the vulnerable have been cut almost to extinction, that there's no help anywhere for the young and the sick? That what was once a welfare state now seems to see it as a duty *not* to give poor children enough to live on and that this attitude has come to be seen as good? Christ almighty. What can I say? I'll tell them that this morning I read about a woman in full-time work who was overjoyed when she found a fiver in the street because then she could feed her son for the two days til her next pay cheque, and a page later in the same paper I read that sales of wine costing over twenty quid a bottle increased so that the chief executive of Majestic Wine could be quoted as saying 'these are wines you can have a real conversation about'. Should I tell them that? These people around this table are not children and nor should they be treated as children. So I'll tell them that out there people are killing themselves, in this isolated, inward-looking, mean country that its populace voted for it to become; that as the support they need is eroded away so they fall out of life. I'll tell them that anyone who needs state support is now regarded as a scrounging parasite to be ostracised, and persecuted, to death if needs be. Anthony and the Chinwegian and Maria and the Major, when you all leave this centre with your selves rebuilt and the capacity for connectedness restored there will be no support for you, nothing in the world that will recognise the demons you have beaten, and with what bravery. You will have no money. Should you be lucky enough to be interviewed for a job, and you're asked – no, 'invited' – to explain the gaps in your employment history, you will come up against a collective mindset utterly without empathy cos this is the age of the snoop and the bigot in which no one sees the 'ex', all they see is the alky and the junkie and the never-to-be-trusted monster, the worthless piece of human waste. This is what I'll tell these people around the table. All of this I'll tell them. And I'll tell them too that, to fit in, to belong, they must never forget to celebrate, when they're instructed to do so, the particular scab of rock on which their genes happened to collide and crash land because that will make their suffering all worth it. It will give meaning to their lives. All of this I'll tell them.

—It's alright, I say to their expecting faces. —Has its moments, y'know. It's worth it, honest, that's all I can say.

This seems to please them, and I feel the death of something inside me. I think about Quilty the cat and glowing shapes in the sky. And I do not express the opinion that to remain here in Rhos for the rest of their lives would be the only option for these broken souls I'm eating soup with.

Suki comes back in. —Right, you three. Need some help with the chickens and then you've got Group. You stopping up for the afternoon, Adam love?

—No, I say. —Got a meeting in town at teatime. What are the new chickens like?

—Haven't met them yet. Ebi says they're a bit scrawny but apparently good layers.

75

Maria makes a gagging sound. —Aborted birds. Don't know how anyone could eat aborted birds.

—They're unfertilised, hen, Chinwegian says, then repeats the last word and laughs. Anthony joins in. The Major, all deadpan, says: —What an eggstraordinarily bad yolk.

—You can sit the job out, Maria, Suki says.

—No thanks. I like the chickens. Wanna see them. Just don't want to eat them, that's all, or their unborn babies.

—Fine then. We'll be seeing you soon, Ad, yeh?

I tell Suki I'll be back up in a few days and give her another hug and say goodbye to the others and leave. Sunshine and breeze again. Hot. I hear Suki's voice through the open window:

—Get some gloves on, everyone. Ebi says they're all peckers.

That makes me smile, the image of them four, the odd crew, chasing chickens around. The Major harrumphing, Chinwegian cackling her little doll-face off, the hens running frantic and bawking all mad. Funny image.

I walk away from Rhos, up into the trees again. It's a steep track up onto the Pendam road but after that it's all downhill into Penrhyncoch where I can catch a bus into town. I look up at the mountain crest, imagine the lake up there. Day like today there'll no doubt be some people up there, fishing, basking on the pebble beach, whatever. None of them will have the first clue of what I saw that morning. None of them will know. And in fact nor do I; what the fuck *did* I see? I can hear what sounds like drums again, from up there. Maybe the trees are being harvested.

A little bit above the buildings I stand on the path and look down on them. There's the wooden bridge that leads to the main building, the bridge you cross only twice as a resident, once to check in, and once to leave, freed. You don't have to be able to understand the symbolism to appreciate it. Like the Twelve Steps themselves; all you have to know is that they work. Most times. It's like baking a cake; into the oven goes a gloopy mess of eggs and butter and flour and sugar and stuff and half an hour or so later out comes a lovely fluffy sponge. You'd have to be a physicist, or Heston friggin Blumenthal, to explain how that works. Same with the system up here. Don't question, don't wonder – just accept. Like magic. It's the total opposite to jail; Fazakerly nick was like a turned-off oven. In went the gloopy mess and out came the same gloopy mess, with a manky little crust on top.

I follow the flight of a kite down the valley. He circles over the First Stage house then catches a thermal and rises then catches a high wind and is carried down the valley. Beautiful fucking birds, astonishing things. Stunning even in their savagery; aye this is a wonderful place, the hills and the animals and the birds and the plants, everything, but it's a place completely drenched in death. At night sometimes, in my room, I'd lie awake and listen to the night sounds, hear the owls call and screech, hear the squealings of small animals as they became food for bigger ones. I'd find corpses out on the hills when I was collecting the sheep shit, bones, ragged severed wings, skulls. I'd see sheep with their arse ends caked in cack and boiling with maggots. Sometimes their front legs would've rotted away to stumps. Horrible, aye, but I realised that the Reality Therapy was working when I stopped seeing all of this stuff as repellent and scary and just began to accept it as the way things are and, even, realise that I was a part of it, that the wildness of it all was in me and that I came from it and that I'd return to it when I die. At the root of my addiction was a fear of dying; inviting it on me each day, and cheating it, was a way, I once thought, of beating it. Accept the things you cannot change, is right, is right.

The Three Rs, that's what they said: realism, responsibility, and right-and-wrong. Not symptoms of a mental disorder, Reality Therapy maintains – and these words with their rhythm will be in my head forever – 'that the individual is suffering from a socially universal human condition rather than a mental illness'. Like a little song or poem. 'It is in the unsuccessful attainment of basic needs that a person's behaviour moves away from the norm.' A person's past has no relevance to Reality Therapy, it's all here and now, and an understanding of how what you do now will affect your future. Glasser, that was the name of the feller who developed it, William Glasser; he pointed out that it was too easy to label people as mentally sick and that problems of behaviour had a deep social component. *Involvement*, that was one of the key words, and *control*, and *focus on the present*, and *planning*. And like a mantra: *no excuses no punishment never give up*. The core of it was a need to understand that we must live in a world full of other people and that we must learn to satisy our own needs in a way that does not encroach upon anyone else's needs. In other words: be nice and don't act the cunt.

And it's bollox, really. I mean, get an army of RT counsellors into the Houses of fucking Parliament, then. Cos them cunts could do with a course of it. Or, or, maybe just build great big fucking walls around Eton and Westminster and Chipping bastard Norton, keep them isolated where they can do no harm to others. Sacrifice the odd fox or pheasant – old and ill ones – to them every now and again so that they can satisy their psychopathologies. Let the rest of us get on with the insane fucking job of just being alive.

'Social component', aye. It made me laugh when I heard the name 'Glasser' cos it made me think of that balloon-head on the estate where I was brought up, also called Glasser, Glasser Thompson, so called cos that was his favourite hobby; glassing people in the face. Man or woman, it didn't really matter, if Glasser had a gripe with them, and it must be said that the insults were usually imaginary ones, that'd be it; smash, ram, twist, screams, sirens and stitches. It was like a compulsion with him. Went to do it to me dad once but missed and got him in the neck, just missing the artery. Me old man made a few phone calls and that was it, no more Glasser Thompson, except in legend. Someone told me that they found one of his legs in the bin by the seesaw in the school playground but I don't know whether that's true.

But that's Reality: Glasser Thompson. And the soaring birds and the Brummie bloke trying to rebuild himself from fragments. Sally in her polytunnel, the feral mountain cats. This is all Reality and this is all Therapy. The abscess scars on me legs, the shadowy memories of what I've done. Ebi. Suki. Rhoserchan itself. All of this can be touched. It is all Real.

So where the fuck does a floating woman fit into this? A floating, glowing woman? Is *she*, or *it*, whatever, part of the Real? I could not touch or smell but I could see, and so, evidently, could the other two. And the way the sight of her put a lift inside me, bounced the heart out of me chest and put a buzz of, of what – joy? – at the base of me skull that hasn't yet gone away, and that, despite everything, is there when I fall asleep and is waiting for me when I wake up but might vanish for a moment when I read a paper or watch the news, is this Reality? I could not touch or smell or hear. A waking hallucination, said Sal. But where does this fit in?

God, God. Being alive. It's so fucking strange. More every sober day.

At the top of the Rhos track where it joins the Pendam road I stop to catch me breath and I see a big car coming towards me up the hill. Sunlight off its windows. I stand and watch it get bigger. It's a huge Merc or something, with tinted windows and dried mud-splashes up the sides. It stops by me and the back window slides down and the feller in the back seat looks out at me. He's sitting in the cool air con, I feel the fridgey wave, and he's got a curly white quiff and shades that cover half his face and a load of bling around his neck and he's wearing a blue Hawaiian shirt, flowers and boats on it, beneath a smart black suit jacket. He doesn't say anything, just looks out at me with the big black eyes of an insect.

—Help yeh, mate?

He shakes his head. —I don't know, he says in a deep and growly voice like he's been gargling with ground glass. So deep I feel it in me ribcage. —I certainly hope so, brother. Have you just come from the place?

—Where, Rhoserchan?

He nods. —Yeah.

—I have, aye.

—You a resident?

—Not any more. I *was*, tho. Just up here helping out, like. Clean and sober, now, me.

79

I can't see anything behind his shades. Might not have eyes at all for all I know. The idling engine stinks, sharp and sour in me nose. Should be low emission, a big posh car like this.

—Does it work?

—Does what work, feller?

—The, the treatment up here.

—Well it did for me. Nearly four years clean I am now.

Christ; it's not the car that pongs, it's this bloke's breath. A blast of booze both old and new, all kinds of booze, the main whiff being, if I'm remembering rightly, rum. Bloody hell. It's like a cloud. He's been giving it some, this geezer. —Think you need an appointment, tho, I say. —Not sure you can just turn up, like. Need to make arrangements first.

He gives a wee smile. —They'll take me in, my brother. They're expecting me.

I imagine that Suki would've told me if she was expecting another rez as well as the one-armed scouser but I don't say anything about that.

—Everyone's expecting me, the guy says. —The whole world is waiting for me.

I can't help smiling. —Is that right?

—Hunnerd per cent. *Hunnerd* per cent.

—Good luck to yeh, then.

A hand chunky with rings comes out of the window. I shake it and it gets pulled back in.

—Thank you, my brother. God shine his light upon you.

This makes me laugh. A voice from the driver's seat says: —We go down, Mr Larry? and the window slides up and the car pulls away and turns left onto the track and is swallowed by the trees. What the fuck was that? *Who* the fuck was that? Had to be a rock star. Could only be a rock star, with that Christ fixation. I imagine the Major's reaction when that guy turns up … but then, if it's working with the Major, as it seems to be doing, he'll just accept. No doubt he'll just give a little cough and a whiffle of breath. And if he was wearing the monocle that, really, he *should* be wearing, it'll leap off his face in astonishment.

I head down the hill. From up here, the valley opens out below, the massive and deep green V of it towards the sea and the town there, which looks like a model from this distance and height, Monopoly houses like, with the castle tower sticking up. It looks all baked. There's a big walk ahead of me but it's all downhill and anyway I feel up for it, bit of exercise, fresh air. Get the heart going a bit. Madder every day. Ladybirds and rock stars. Reality Therapy, man. Pure fucking heart.

# FIVE BIG WHITE UPSIDE DOWN YS IN A LINE

BLOODY HELL FIRE! A come out of-a bog and *she's* standin yur, on-a landin, right outside-a door. Hell of a fright, mun. Near shit meself *again*, I did.

—Christ, woman! What yew doin yur? *Lur*-kin.

—Am not *lur*-kin. Am dying to go. Been knockin for ages, I yav.

—Give it ten minutes, then, A say, waftin me hand at me nose.

—Didn't yew spray?

—Aye, course A did, cider shite all up-a walls.

—A meant with air freshener. Fuckin *mochyn*.

A ignore this and go down-a stairs, laughin to meself as a hear her gaggin in-a bathroom. Sounds like a backed-up drain. Well, if she fed me at least once in-a while with stuff that wasn't fish fuckin fingers or baked bastard beans from Lidl, maybe ad produce somethin from me arse that didn't look an smell like rotten cawl left in-a airing cupboard for a month, mun.

Fair dos, tho, she've left me a tea and two bits-a toast next to-a telly. Only marge on-a toast, like, an A coulda done with a bit-a jam or somethin but still, fair dos. Spose A could go in-a back an fetch a jam meself like but Am gunner need me energy if Am gunner be workin on that fuckin bridge all day. Blows-a fuckin gale down yur, it does, close to-a sea. Paintin, they said, an bolt-tightenin. Tightenin bolts! On a bridge! I ask yew! Shoulda been me on-a team that put-a bastard thing up in-a first place like but the fuckin foreman was a right girl, he was. Wouldn't take a tellin. Got all sulky, got this fuckin art-itude on him. Well bollax. Workin on his fuckin bridge now, arn I? No wonder-a bolts are coming loose if it was put up by Poles. Fuck does he expect? Still be tight as a nun's cunt if Welshmen adder done-a job, see.

News is on. Some twat with too many chins in a tie. Politicians these days, what is it with them an their chins? Ey've either got too many or none at all. Lissen to this one: *it's morally wrong to pay someone cash in hand.* Morally wrong! Makes me spill me tea all over me toast, makin it go all floppy. Ruined it. Be fucked if Am makin another piece tho so A eat it as it is. Well, kind-a *slurp* it, like. Drink it. These fuckin politicians, mun, ey just don't have a clue. Not a first fuckin clue. If his policy was to make me avter take me brekkie through a fuckin straw, then he got that right. Nowt else, tho. Cash in hand. Morally wrong. Fuck me.

Got to fuckin move it now, tho, as well. Not a bad payer, this bridge job, an-a boss is okay, like, least compared to some-a em, so Am not gunner be late on me first day. *She* comes down as Am lookin in-a kitchen drawer for me cream.

—What yew doing?

—A need me cream.

—What cream?

—That stuff for me disco eczema.

—*Discoid* eczema.

—Whatever-a fuck it's called, where is it? I left it in yur. Now it's gone.

All kinds-a shite in iss drawer, fuckin Sellotape and light bulbs but no fuckin cream.

—Wharrav yew done with it? It's gone.

—I haven't touched it.

-Must-a been Mrs Jones from next door, then. Snucked in in-a night she did and nicked me disco cream. A terror for doin that, she is. Remember that time she snucked in an smoked all me ganj?

—Stop bein daft. Yew put some on last night, in-a bath-room. I remember yew doing it.

I go back upstairs. Exhaustin meself before Av even left-a fuckin house. A bog is stinkin, my shite *and* hers, horrible, but yur's me cream on-a cistern. A squeeze some out onto me finger an roll up-a leg-a me jeans an rub-a cream in. Four spots, purple round things like, look like bullet holes. *Discoid.* Suppose she'd know, havin once been a nurse like. Before they closed-a ward an mader redundant cos of-a cuts. Well, *and* because she hadder good sideline raidin-a medicine cabinet for-a boys in town. Not that I blame her; support a kid on a nurse's wage? Fucks. An that idle twat of a dad … lazy fuckin junkie. Allergic to work, him. So no A can't blamer for makin a bit on-a side like but God she used to whinge about it, getting sacked, like, she did. Not fuckin half. Me, tho, A don't say nowt about her having a kid to *that* waste-a space when she can't have one to me. No, *his* useless spunk produces a smashin little girl, but mine ends up as bloody gunk in-a toilet bowl. Where's-a justice?

All creamed up A go back down-a stairs.

—Yew find it?

A nod.

—*Told* yew, didn't I?

Smug cow. A ignore this remark.

—What yew got lined up for today, then? A usual White Lightning and Jeremy Kyle is it?

She blows fag smoke at-a telly screen. Some other chinny twat in a suit on there now, looks just-a same as-a other one sept he've got a different-coloured tie on.

—Am seeing Shawna, she says. —Got an afternoon with her today I yav.

—So that's yew off to Cardigan then, is it?

She nods.

—Do us a favour while yewer down there, then. Tell Shawna's dad to fuck off and die from me, will yew?

—Aye, will do.

—Tell him I hope he gets that AIDS and dies on his own, yeah?

—Aye.

A leave-a flat. A Morris's letter box goes up. Without lookin A give it-a fingers, nosy pair-a cunts, an go down-a stairs an out of-a block. Sa bright mornin. Bin bags all over-a pavement, burst like, all kinds-a cack leakin out of em an-a load-a seagulls flap away squawkin. Messy bastards. An-a dog an all, that fuckin pitbull thing of them scruffy cunts live on-a next avenue, the

84

Jenkinseseses, be a fuckin danger that mutt would if it weren't so bleedin scrawny. One of em gulls could take it, mun. It looks at me an tries to do a snarl but A aim a boot at it an it runs away for a bit then turns an does a snarl again, showin its horrible yellow teeth. A walk away from it, leave it to-a rubbish for its breakfast, KFC bones an pizza crusts an whatever other shite a people on this estate live on.

A roll up a smoke for the walk. It's im again, on-a packet – old cauliflower neck. Three times in a row. What're the odds? A few people on iss estate who av jobs are goin-a work, gettin into eyr cars, waitin at-a bus stops, walkin along with eyr butty-boxes an wearin eyr dirty clothes, overalls n stuff. Not many of em, like; most windows still av eyr curtains drawn. Few kids headin across to-a underpass. Some new words, painted like, on-a garages: FOXY IS A DEAD MAN. Ooer fuck's Foxy? Don't know any Foxy. Maybe some chickens wrote it up yer. Maybe eyv formed eyr own, what's it called, vigilanty gang. Some windows av pale faces lookin out-a em, people who've been up all night, party boys an girls an mad boys an girls, *penwan*, em ones who A hear screamin in-a night-times when Am tryin-a get to sleep. Iss is where A live, with ese people, up yur on-a hill always in-a clouds.

But-a view from up yur, tho. A library up on-a hill on-a other side uv-a valley an-a town below me feet an-a sea on-a left. People pay for views like iss, mun. A jes stand an look at it an av me smoke. My town, likes. Am not feelin like A did jes after A came down off-a mountain after that rave thing like, that E feelin's gone now, a slow-release thing A was talkin about, but Am not feelin like A normally do either. A mean, like – yur's me, avin me first smoke uv-a day, enjoyin-a view. Appreciatin-a view. Fuck's sakes. Somethin's changed, see. For good or bad A don't really know yet but something's changed, it has.

Town wakes up down in-a valley. See-a railway going up Consti, see-a uni, a library, all-a town kind of like *cwtched* together down yer. A can hear it, as well; all-a cars an stuff, a train honkin. A siren n all, iss early of-a mornin; wonder who's in trouble. Probly some farmer boy out in-a hills, got is arm stuck up a sheep's minge. Or is knob. It's gunner be a nice day, iss. Way away A can see a edge of-a land, way up yur where-a Gogs live, humps of it stickin out into-a sea. What is it, a Llyn? Bardsey, can that be seen from yur? All them saints. Find thousands-a saints in Gogland? Shite. Jes fuckin stories. Land-a singers an gobshites. And, ese days, land-a fuckin Poles and Liths an Lats, cabbage-suckers, mun, thousands of-a cunts all swarmin in. An how can I not be fuckin pissed off by iss cos, see, *I* can lay bricks, *I* can put slates on someone's fuckin roof, do a bit-a chippyin, bit-a sparkin, bit-a fuckin plumbin even, but all em east Europeans have them jobs now. No room for-a natives, fuck no; all's we've got left is mixin fuckin cement and paintin a bridge that is gettin a bit fuckin dodgy cos Poles put-a bastard up in-a first place. Not fuckin fair. Need a plumber, these days? Look under Z in-a Yellow Pages. Not for long, tho, not for long, now we've said tara to fuckin Ewrop. Doubt anythin'll change, tho – stuck like this, it is. Or fuckin *I* am, me, labourin for a minimum wage, no kid an a fat drunken whoor of a lazy missus, Housing Association flat all damp an mouldy, dopey fuckin bollax me still sloggin is bastard tripes out jes so he can pay-a bills. If my mam was alive now she'd be spinnin in her grave. But she's not, aye, an who gives a shite? Not fuckin Cowley, mun. Some fuckin mam she was, aye … *The Reverend Williams would never do such a thing! Horrible boys! Stop telling lies!* Smack, smack, one for me an one for Rhys; then locked in-a fuckin bedroom for two days, no food or drink, just the fuckin Bible. *Sick in the head!*, that's what she'd say. Or *scream*, likes. Us! *Sick in the head! You have the Devil in you and you are no sons of mine!* Smack, smack, out with-a fuckin stick or-a poker from-a fire. Me n Rhys tryin-a hide, fuckin Dad spineless bastard behind is fuckin paper … cunts, em both, an that fuckin Williams … sick fucker mun aye … any fuckin wonder I—

Breathe, Cowley, breathe, mun. Eyr dead an buried in-a ground, boy. Probly Williams an all. Let em rot. Ey can't fuckin bother yew no more. An yur was a glow in-a sky, wasn't yur? Remember *that*, mun. Even if it *was* jester rising fuckin sun.

Aye but I yavter sit on-a bench opposite-a caravan park for a bit. Me head's all spinnin an me heart's goin like fuckin mad an A feel like A can't breathe. Calm, Cow, calm. In an out, boy, at's all yur is to it. All in-a past, it is. Tonight yew can go round-a Bernie's and get him to email Rhys down in Cardiff. Ask him how he is. That always makes yew feel better.

A start-a calm down a bit an A roll another smoke but when A light it A look out again at-a town an it all looks so fuckin dirty, mun. It all looks so fuckin sleazy to me. A see a steeple-a St Michael's an it makes me think of horrible things, what it looks like, all stickin up, stickin out. Right down in me guts Am feelin fuckin sick an A get that feelin in the skin-a me hands an A think about bein in-a Cwps the other night when A left after all em Lavin boys came in an what A should've done is, A shoulda asked Steve for his fuckin pickaxe handle. That's what I should've done. Cos now ey must all be thinkin that am a bottlin twat. Callin me all-a bottlin cunts under-a sun, that's what ey'll be doing now.

Me breathin starts-a go all funny again and me skin goes all tingly but then, what's this, a minibus stops right by me. In a second Am on me feet like but then A see five big white upside-down Ys in a line squashed up against-a windows of-a bus an A can hear all this laughin, this ladies' laughin. ABER WRUFC it says on-a side of-a bus and five of-a team are givin me-a moons. A burst out laughin. An then ey turn around an pull eyr tops up and squash eyr tits up against-a glass and it's like ten massive eyes lookin at me. Iss is dead funny. Then yer's faces pressed against-a window and the bus pulls off and some hands come out of-a windows an wave an A can hear em all laughin again as ey drive away. Am laughin as well. Jes what I needed, mun. Fuckin medicine, that. Five big moons an ten starin eyes, that is jes what I fuckin needed. Glimpse-a bush n all. Oi!

Am still smilin about it as A walk down into Trefechan. Good girls. Not bad arses on one or two of em either; tight little cracks, like, not too hairy. Wish A could say-a same thing for Jac the Bird; she's like a fuckin yardbrush down yur, she is. Got to part the thicket with me hands before A slide him in, likes. Jack the Boy, he told me once that all the hairs had knotted together into a kind of net across her hole so every time she had to shite it came out like long chips. I didn't ask him how he knew this, likes; didn't want-a know. He said he had to get down yur with a pair-a scissors an snip it all away likes, which gave me pictures in me head that a didn't need an which gave me fuckin bad dreams, mun, for a few nights. Still shudder about it now, I do.

But them rugby girls ... made my bloody mornin. That was brilliant. Made me feel alright so to celebrate A go into-a Londis opposite a fire station an get meself a Twix an a can-a Coke. Bit of a sugar hit, likes, that'll do. Good girls, good girls. Funny fuckin things around, mun. Jes hang around an ey come to yew.

Outside-a shop A can see some smoke comin up round-a side-a Pen Dinas, on-a south beach, like; a pikeys have eyr sites yur, both-a Lavins and-a McBrides, close, even tho ey can't stand each other. Probly cookin brekkies. A pass-a Fountain Inn an am glad it's closed cos if it was open an A got that smell through-a door, that pub smell like, then A know it'd be *fuck* work, mun, giz a Guinness an a whisky chaser. Resistance is fuckin futile.

A finish me Twix on-a bridge, the old stone one, like, where, surprise sur-fuckin-prise, it's not blowin-a gale; gunner be a nice day, this. A look over-a side an up the river to the other bridge an see a few blokes on it in white overalls an two of em in hard hats. A watch these two sit in ese sling things, ese kind-a harnesses that ey tie around themselves, an en ey climb over-a railings an swing down underneath. Like great big horrible fuckin spiders under-a bridge in eyr webs. What is it that lives under bridges? Trolls, that's it. That's what aye are – trolls. Waitin for-a Billy Goats Gruff.

A go onto Glanrafon Terrace. Trefechan, this. Land-a Turks, ey used to call it; all-a people lived yur useta get called Turks, probly cos ey all useta wear rags wrapped round eyr heads cos ey all worked in-a lime kilns that aren't yur anymore. Protect emselves from-a sparks, like. Or maybe cos Turks – A mean, people from Turkey, like – set up a community yur, once, off-a ships, when iss useta be a workin port. No more, tho. Still plenty-a Turks, oh aye; oo else would yew get yewer kebabs from? Unless ey all get sent back soon. Useta be a poor area, ese houses along-a edge of-a river, ese terraces; now every cunt wants-a live by-a water so ese av all *shot* up in price. Cost-a fuckin fortune now, ey do. Second homes, some of em; empty for most of-a year. Ow's a poor cunt like me meant to buy a house in-a town where he was born? Fetch me my fuckin petrol bomb, mun.

A bridge bounces a bit beneath me feet. Wobbles, like, cos it's a suspension bridge. Feels a bit like bein on a boat. Not that Av ever been on a boat, sept for that time me an some of-a boys screwed that yacht in-a harbour, an that wasn't exactly on-a open sea. Still not on-a ground, tho, still floatin, like, an it felt like iss bridge feels now. Wobbly. An, *Duw*, that fuckin yacht ... plush, mun, it was. No other word for it. Bigger than my fuckin house. Jewellery, crates-a wine, ornaments, bottles-a whisky that probly cost moren a week's fuckin wage ... Set me up for about three months, that job did. Got clean away, n all. Coppers had no clew. Still remember-a name of-a boat, I do: *Cash Flow*, it was called. Next to another one called *Liquid Assets*, if I remember right. *Asking* for it, mun. Jes fuckin askin for it, yew call yewer boat that.

—Cow! Over yur, boy!

A give a bit of a wave. Want-a stand yur for a few more minutes, like. Jes listen to-a river goin past under-a bridge an watch-a ducks an-a swans. Them ducks sound like eyr laughin. that noise ey make. Wack-wack-wack. Got some babies down yur, ey av. Fluffy litttle buggers. Pike'll av them soon. Or-a otters.

—Today would be good, Cow!

*Art*-itude on that twat.

But he's-a man with-a money, inny? An that makes him-a boss. A bounce over to him. Doesn't feel a hundred per cent safe, iss bridge, if yew ask me. Sure it's not supposed to bounce *this* fuckin much. Poles, see. Shoddy workmanship.

—That feel alright to yew?

—What?

I jump up n down a bit an-a bridge shakes an I hear some shouting from underneath it. Ad forgotten about them trolls.

—Stop doing that, Cow. None-a yewer concern anyway.

—It will be if it snaps an A go down into-a fuckin river.

Ee jes gives me a look. Shakes his head a bit en points at some stuff on-a planks; tins-a paint an creosote, wire brushes, white spirit. Tells me that Am to put-a lick-a creosote on-a wooden bits an-a lick-a paint on-a metal bits. As if Am fuckin stupid.

—An make sure yew put it on thick around-a bolts an welds, he says, as if Am *really* fuckin stupid. —An give it all a good scrubdown first, ee says. —Yew know how important prep is, an if he keeps speakin-a me like Am jes out-a fuckin nursery he's goin over-a side, he is, into-a fuckin river.

He've got a big ginger beard, he has, but ee still looks as if ee should be still in school. Looks about fifteen. No wonder ey call him Pinkbits. I hear iss funny language comin up from-a planks beneath me feet. Time for a wind-up.

—I want-a go under yur, I say, pointin down. —Ey said a could go under yur.

—Oo did?

—Em cunts in-a agency, like.

—Not gunner happen, Cow.

—Why not, like? Can only go under if yewer a Pole or a Lat, is that it? Only they can be trusted with-a big jobs, is that what's goin on?

—Don't be daft, mun. Yewer not insured or trained. They are. And anyway eyr from Estonia.

—Estonia? Ewrop, like? What they still doing over yur, then? Shouldn't ey have left by now?

He ignores this. An fuck sakes, mun; not enough Poles an Lats over yur? Ship a shedload-a fuckin Stonians over an all. Must still be *some* decent jobs that we can take away from-a locals.

That's *my* mood fucked. All-a nudey ladies' arses and glowin things in-a sky in an entire fuckin world cannot lift me out-a this, mun. Slike Am in a fuckin lift, goin straight fuckin down. An anyway all's it was was a rising fuckin sun. A saw nowt. An what-a fuck did we vote Leave for?

—Al be back around lunchtime, see how it's gettin on. Got to go an put up a new postbox now in Llanilar cos the old one got crushed.

A don't say anythin. Jes look down at-a planks. A can see glimpses-a white ovie between em an hear a funny language.

Pinky gives me another look. He'll be fuckin Blackn*blue*bits if he don't stop givin me them looks.

—Alright, he says. —Al see yew later.

God al-bleedin-mighty. Someone's tied bits-a ribbon to-a bars an planks on-a bridge at-a parts where ey need me to scrub an paint so A get me wire brushes an start work. Scrape-a rust off, a mould stuff, whatever it's called, a manky bits. A monkey could do iss job. Fuckin *Bernie* could do iss job. An what gets me, what really fuckin pisses me right off right down in me guts like, is that ese are-a kind-a jobs I started out doin, twenty fuckin years ago. I'd mitch off fuckin school to do ese jobs, I would. I was a fuckin *boy* when A started doin iss kind-a work. An I can lay bricks an tiles an fix someone's wiring an stop eyr fuckin leaks, I can lay concrete, I can *plaster* for fuck's sakes. An all that stuff Av learnt meself, no course or nothin, picked it all up meself A did jes through watchin others an lissnin to em an learnin from em, for twenty fuckin years mun, an what's it fuckin got me? It's gotten me a job scrapin rust an mould off a fuckin wobbly bridge. A mean, fuck's sakes. Doin work that a fuckin chimp could do while-a skilled stuff goes to Stony-hands or Poles.

Aye but it's money. A need-a fuckin money, mun. An Al take whatever A can get. No fuckin choice.

Already me back's complainin. A stand up, stretchin it, feelin-a muscles slippin back into place. It's a relief. A hear clangin sounds from-a direction of-a Fountain an A look over at it an a can jes about see its roof from yur. Must be openin time, or thereabouts. Barrel delivery. Soon av enough spends for a Leo in that pub, I will. Which is summin-a look forwards to, and that lifts me mood, makes me feel better, lets me switch off an jes get to work with-a wire brush. Almost start enjoyin it, even, all-a rust comin off, makin clean patches that A can stick-a bit-a white on, make it all clean-lookin again. Not bad work, iss, really. An it'll give me-a money to put towards goin on a Leo, won't it? Sept yur's that fuckin gas bill. That's what-a dosh from iss job's supposed to be for, a gas bill. Aye, well. Some things are more important.

Coupla hours later an me belly's rumblin. A down tools an go back to a shop over-a bridge an get a cheese bun an a bag-a Monster Munch. A av me dinner on-a bench by-a river an watch-a ducks an-a geese an en A go back to-a bridge an A see that them slings, them straps that the Stony-hands av been sittin in, are jes lyin yur on-a planks. Must-a gone for eyr dinner, them boys. Wonder where ey'll get cabbage an pig's-arse soup in Aber. Pinkbits is gunner be back soonish but fuck im. What-a fuck does he expect, mun? A temptation's too big. Resistance is futile, as they say.

A step into one of-a slings. It goes up around me back an under me legs an A tie it tight in-a clips around me waist to make a kind-a seat. A step through-a railings so's Am standin on-a outside of-a bridge, holdin on likes, a river goin past under me feet. How deep is it, yur, in-a middle? An-a current's strong. Stew-dent fell off is bridge last summer an his body got washed up in Ireland months later. Iss sling – will it take me weight? Em Stony-hands, ey looked like big fellers. Got to be safe, iss, or ey wouldn't be allowed to do it. If it snaps A could get to-a bank-a silt in a middle, easy. Be dead easy. Only one way to find out, Cow. Let fuckin go.

A do. Well, a bit; A hold me weight up with me right arm an kind of ease down off-a bridge so that Am swingin out over-a water. Me fuckin heart's goin like mad. A can see under-a bridge, now, see-a web-a ropes that will take me under-a bridge if A let go. A seat thing Am in will jes be taken under-a bridge. If it's strong enough, like. Let fuckin *go*.

A do. Iss time A do. A feel meself swing under, me body jes gets kind-a sucked under, like, an A expect yer to be some jerk but those twats must know what eyr doin cos when A open me eyes again Am under-a bridge, jes hangin yur, swingin a bit. Me knuckles are dead white around-a rope but after about a minute A realise that it's safe an me heart goes back to normal an A let go of-a rope an yur A am, yur's me, jes floatin in-a air underneath-a bridge. An it's a fuckin buzz, mun. A thought it'd be all cold but it's not. A sunlight comes down between-a boards in slices an lands on-a runnin water under me danglin feet. Spiderman, I yam. Fuckin superhero. Iss is one big fuckin *buzz*. A water makes a nice sound an-a sling makes a creakin sound but that's all yur is, no other noise. Can't hear anythin, jes a lovely sound of-a water. A don't think Av tied-a sling on proper cos it's diggin into me bollax a bit but it's not too bad. Not bad enough to make me want-a go back up, anyway, onto-a surface. A *surface*? Aye, that's what it feels like; like Am under-a sea. It's like Am a fish, like A can breathe underwater. Fuck mun iss is one fuckin *good* buzz.

Everythin goin away, an me jes danglin yur. Gas bills, pikeys, still doin shitty jobs after twenty years' education … It's all gone away. A feel meself driftin off, not asleep, more like Av jes smoked a fat spliff a size of-a fuckin pool cue. Like Am yur but *not* yur. Bit like A felt after A came down off-a mountain likes, after that party. After that glowing thing an after Ad found that eye-pod or whatever it is, a thought of which reminds me to pat me top pocket to check it's still yur, where A keep it, to see that it hasn't fallen out; it's still in yur. A feel it over me heart, which makes me think of them soldiers who were saved from bullets by silver ciggie boxes or Bibles n stuff – they'd be in eyr pockets an stop-a bullets from hittin eyr hearts an keep em alive. Don't know why it makes me think-a this, A mean A don't even know how to use-a fuckin thing, but it's like A need to carry it round with me now. Snot like A feel fuckin *safe* with it or anythin like that. Jes like a habit Av fallen into. Fuck knows why.

Fuckin lovely, mun. Fuckin amazin, iss. Like Am floatin. Slike Av never been born. A could easy fuckin spend me days under yur, mun, jes hangin yur, someone bringin me food n stuff every now an again, keepin me alive, alive an pure jes fuckin happy. Iss is … what's-a word? A don't know. Bliss, is it?

An en a hear footsteps, on-a bridge. Ey kind of go boom, an eyr gettin louder, an A start-a bounce a bit in me sling. A look up. See-a shadow fallin through-a boards, cut up, like a strobe in-a disco or somethin. Ey stop right above me, cuttin off-a sunlight, makin it in a split fuckin second all cold an dark.

Pinkbits's voice goes: —How's it goin under yer? An where's Cowley?

Fuck. What would a Stony-hand say? How-a fuck do ey talk?

—Yah, A say. —Iss all go very gut.

—Cowley? Is that *yew* under yer?

Aw fuck.

—Fuck's sakes mun! Gerrout! Av told yew, yewer not fuckin insured! Gerrout!

Iss fuckin *boy* tellin me what to do. Fuck im.

—*Fuck* yew playin at mun? Am haulin yew out.

A feel meself movin along-a ropes, out from under-a bridge, bein dragged into-a light. It's gunner hurt me eyes. Iss is like some nasty bastard is wakin me up from me favourite dream as a kid, iss is. An fuckin Pinkbits is goin on as he drags me back out into-a light again, freakin fuckin out ee is, tellin me off, tellin *me* off as if *I'm* the fuckin *boy* yur ...

—Fuck's sakes Cowley mun! A *told* yew not to go under yur! Didn't I say?

Am grabbin onto-a boards but yur's nothin I can do to stay under. *He's* at the controls. And ow, the light's like salt fuckin water in me eyes, an now yur's another one who's gunner get a smack at some point in-a future. Yur's a tap waitin for *yew* soon, Pinkbits, too fuckin right yur is. Draggin me back, mun, bollax. Out of me fuckin buzz. Let me stay under yur, yew cunt. Jes let me fuckin stay.

# DO ONE, MOTHER NATURE

HE DIDN'T EVEN cry, Tomos, when he came out of me. *I* did – I blubbed enough to fill Cardigan Bay, I did – but he just looked around without any expression on his tiny wrinkled face and when the midwife placed him on my tummy he just lay there not making any sound and just calmly looking around at everything and she said: Well, *he's* been here before. And he looked up at my face with them eyes like blue targets. On the spot where he lay, just above the belly button, the cord all curled around it, I have his DOB tattooed and his name. One lad once said it reminded him of the carvings on a gravestone and I said yeh, except it's the date of birth, *dur*, not death. *He* didn't last long.

Period pains always make me think of that, they do – Tom's birth, I mean. All crampy and bloated and irritable and it's like: do one, Mother Nature, I've already propagated the bloody species, haven't I? Go bother someone childless. And super-market shopping when I'm feeling like this ... just horrible. There's an old Doris at the bread shelves, squeezing every fucking loaf in the rack, prodding and poking, tutting away. Christ! Hurry up! I just need some bastard bread! I reach over her and pick up a loaf, the Brace's white sliced that Mr Humphreys likes, and she gives me daggers. What does she expect me to do, stand here patiently waiting while she squeezes every last loaf in the entire fuckin shop? I've got stuff to do! As I move away, I see her start on the crumpets and muffins – the poking and the tutting. Good God.

Eggs and bacon, a tin of tomatoes and the bread for Mr Humphreys. Choobs, yoghurt, bottles of water and crisps for Tom's sarnies; rolls and Dairylea. This is all I need. Oh and a few tins for the food-bank trolley. Some co-codamol. And a litre bottle of Smirnoff blue but I don't buy that. Doesn't mean I don't need it, tho, aye. Best painkiller, especially when mixed with the aspirin. Just lie on the couch and drift away ...

Down the condiments aisle I see Bas checking out the jam, which is fitting and which makes me laugh because I've never seen a human being who looks more like an ant. Might be hard to imagine, that, but honest to God, he does; the man is antish. I ask him how he's doing and he tells me that his wife, Sandra, is pregnant again and I think to meself: *Yeah, with eggs.*

—Congratulations, I say. —That'll be what, the third?

—Fourth! He says; shouts, almost. —Turning into a right little army. How old's yours now?

—Year 2. Just gone six.

—And he's well?

—He is, yeh. Doing great.

—My eldest starts school soon. End of the summer.

We blather on for a bit about schools and that and I get quickly bored so I tell him I'll see him around and go to move away.

—I've been reading your blog, he says. —Interesting stuff it is.

—Yeh?

—What's all this about a woman in the sky?

—Ah. I don't want to talk about this, now; it's early in the day, I'm tired, and I've got stuff to do. Mr Humphreys will be needing his brekkie. And I'm feeling irritable enough as it is. —I'll update later on today, I say.

—Yeh but what was it, like? Causing a bit of a fuss online it is. What did you see?

—I explained it all in the blog. I'll write more later, yeh? Got to go now.

I scoot off before he can ask me more questions or squirt some formic acid on me or something. It's not something I want to talk about at the moment. I think about it a lot and I see her, sometimes, when I'm falling asleep and I think all the time about those three words I heard her say but it's become like something that I just don't want to talk to anybody else about. Chucking words out into cyberspace is different; alone in the house at the computer screen, I can say whatever I want to say, but to have to answer questions and see the reactions in people's faces, see their expressions change as they think, that's not something I want to do. Can't think of anything worse, to be honest, at the moment. Don't know why that should be but it just is.

Dig and wild. Alright, I get them. But bridge. *Bridge.*

I don't know. Maybe it was just the wind in the reeds. I mean, bridge? At this time? When what we're building mostly is walls?

At the tills I see the bread-botherer handing a load of vouchers and coupons to the checkout lad so I go to another one. Some hippy here, with his smock and smirk. I put me stuff on the belt. The hippy, I notice, and I'm surprised to see, is a bit of a hottie; what I took to be some crappy tie-dyed shawl is a big old coat splattered with paint and what I thought were crappy white-boy dreads (like Weasel's, aye, fuckin shudder at the memory) is a bandana knotted so that a tail of it hangs down his back. Some kind of artist, maybe, he is. Or just a painter and decorator like. Whatever he is he's got a good smile and fiery stubble on his face. Few years older than me, I think.

—Great boobs, he says.

—What?

—Fruit Choobs. He nods down at my stuff. God my hearing must be going. —The healthy option, is it?

—They're for my son, I say, then wish I hadn't, and then feel slightly ashamed. —He likes them in his lunchbox. Got to be a few vitamins in them aye?

He gives me a little smile and a nod and goes away with his shopping. Looked as if it contained pity, that smile did. Why? What did he see in my face?

Dig. Wild. Dig. Wild.

I bag me stuff and leave the supermarket, dropping some tins in the food-bank trolley. Might well be picking them up again soon, for meself, aye. It's going to be another warm day; the sky is like the opening of *The Simpsons*. The heat has already settled down here, at the bottom of this valley, the hills around looking all hazy. Up one of them go the Penparcau estates, like something spilled, and on the other one opposite I can see the National Library, massive, like a castle. The supermarket is at the bottom of a kind of bowl in the hills so it traps the heat in the summer; later on today the tarmac of the big car park will be all shimmery. A couple of summers ago, when another heatwave hit, the tarmac went all squidgy in parts and a mobility scooter got stuck in it; I remember it clearly, the great big fat feller on the scooter bellowing as the wheels sunk slowly down into the melty tarmac. Made me think of that picture of the mastodons in the tar pit in one of Tom's books. Couldn't help but piss me knickers laughing.

I'd like to sit here for a while, I would, on a bench by the river, with the insects buzzing over the water and feel the sun on my face, but I've got stuff to do. There's *always* stuff to do. At least I can walk back into Trefechan alongside the river, tho, and that's just what I do, listening to the rippling water and the birds. The shopping's quite heavy and the straps on the bags are digging into me fingers but I can ignore that, with all these distractions, the dragonflies and butterflies and the fast birds that skim the water, zipping low with their forked tails. Swallows, they're called. Summer birds. They'll be around for another few months yet. I like to see them, knowing that they've come back. All the way from Africa. And this walking relieves the cramps a bit.

Fucking periods. Should be able to *choose* the menopause. I mean I'm happy with the one kid so I should just be able to say: right, that's it, time to turn the body clock off. Get an operation on the NHS. It's just pointless, this – making me miserable for a week every month. Biology is daft. Mother Nature hasn't got the first fucking clue what she's doing when it comes to women.

I can see a supermarket trolley in the river, close to the bank. Looks like a skeleton of some river creature rotted down to the bones, which makes me think again of the otters; I imagine one swimming into the trolley, that graceful, oily movement they have, and playing in it, just rolling around in the water like they do, chasing his tail like a cat. Love to see an otter in the wild, I would. Love to see one with Tomos.

He loves animals, that boy; that time I fed the robin out of my hand and he jumped up and down and fell over, so happy he was. I love my boy. Love him more than anything. He lay on my tummy making no sound, just looking around at everything with those big blue eyes of his, taking it all in, and I remember thinking: *I need never be alone again.*

God it's warm. Good summer so far, this. And one that I'm aware that I'll always remember, for as long as I live – that shape in the sky. The summer of the floating woman and the three words she spoke.

It was the rising sun and the wind in the reeds.

In this heat, and with the damp spring just gone, the plants are going mad; over this part of the path the branches have grown on each side to touch each other over my head and form a kind of tunnel so, for a bit, I'm walking in the shade and it's nice and cool. Japanese knotweed is running riot. My dad told me once about that stuff; it was taking over his garden in Trefenter and killing everything else, strangling it, and he had to call somebody in to get rid of it properly. Had to use some kind of acid. Rich Victorians brought it over here, he said; they saw it on their travels and liked the look of it so they brought it back for their gardens without any thought of how it would effect the native ecosystem. Typical. Rich bastards, aye; they ruin everything. They're locusts.

Anyway. Dig and wild and fuck em all.

I see the new bridge coming up. I feel a little, what, throb of worry inside, every time I see that bridge. Never trusted it. Even though I can see my house at the other end of it, on the other side of the river like, I've never trusted that bridge. It wobbles too much when you walk on it. They've been doing some work on it recently; saw them from my window, fellers in overalls and hard hats, swinging underneath it in harnesses. Which suggests to me that there was something wrong with it. So I'm not gonna cross it. I'll walk further down to the old stone one.

Tired. It's warm and the shopping's heavy and I need a little rest so I sit meself down on a bench. Sunlight on the water, the ridge of gravelly soil in the middle of the river like a backbone and the old tree caught on it. Like the neck of Nessie. So good, this, just sitting here.

And it is good. It *is* good. Ever since I came down off the mountain ... the absence of the absence. Ever since then. Whether it was just the rising sun and the wind in the reeds I don't know, and, I'm beginning to think, I don't care, cos, I mean, why should I? Whatever it was I saw made me feel like I'm feeling, which is, what, full of feelings, and there's nothing wrong in that. Nothing gets me down since I came off the mountain; or, at least, nothing gets me *really* down, I mean I get angry and frustrated and all that shit but those emotions don't last. I think about the Tomster and that's all I need. *He's* all I need. Dig and wild. My little weasel. I notice that there are words carved into the wood of the bench: ALI IS A SLAG, really hacked in, as if with real disgust and hatred. That's the kind of thing that used to really get me down, but now? Nah. I mean, there's no doubt it was carved into the wood by a bloke, who, probably, got rejected by this Ali, some red-faced little prick sitting here on his own and nursing his resentment with a bottle of White Lightning. And this word 'slag' ... how many times have I heard that, been called that? Slag, whore, slut, skank, sket, slapper, bury you in a Y-shaped coffin, hang-out, split-horse ... Just men and their little needs. They all wanted to be the best fuck I'd ever had, wanted me to need them, often so's they could reject me and feed this stupid little notion of themselves as being a playa, a stud. They just couldn't stand the fact that all I wanted them for was to fill a gap; they couldn't stand to be used in the same way that they were using me. How did we get to this?

Well. Doesn't matter. Strange, tho, all of it. And for a moment I remember, in the Ynyslas dunes, Weasel's pointy face going all slack above me in the firelight when he came and I instantly felt a click inside, as if two pieces had slotted neatly together, and, even drunk as I was, I thought to meself: *oo that's the one.* I just *knew* I was up the duff. And knew that I'd never see Weasel again, not that I wanted to, like; white boy with dreads, calling himself Otherkin – for God's sakes, I was *hoping* I'd never see him again, to be honest. The void in me was too big, as it often is – *was* – and God wasn't it filled that night ... the sand in me crack, the sperm meeting the egg and becoming Tomos. My little Tomos. All I need is him.

Anyway. Mr Humpf will be wanting his brekkie. Enough of the reveries. One last thought, tho, one last wonder; that hottie in the supermarket ... what would it feel like if he touched me? That's easy to answer, this much you know; it would feel like electricity. Like a brilliant shock. What would his chest smell like as it pumped above my face? The muscles on him, the angles and planes. His dick. Inside me. All the new discoveries.

Which brings another question; I wonder if Johnny's still got that dick-lump on his head. Like a bellend. Hell of a shot, that was. Thunk. Quite proud of that one, I am. Should've been a darts player or something.

Carry on walking. Past the new bridge, which I'm sure I hear groan as I pass it. Sure it's just the girders settling or something but it makes me think of metal fatigue, weakness. Don't trust it. I cross the river over the old stone bridge further down by the winebar and enter Trefechan. Past the shop where I used to work, empty now, abandoned, piles of letters behind the door, nothing in the window now but dead flies. It's next door to Pets n Brews, which is the best combination for a shop I could ever imagine; small animals and alcohol. I'll have a kitten and a bottle of gin, please. A budgie, no cage, and three bottles of wine so both of us can go flying at the same time.

The curve of houses around the green, next to the old lime kiln; it's a nice place where Mr Humphreys lives. I see the curtain twitch on his living-room window as I'm approaching and then the door opens and Anne, the morning carer, is standing on the step. Sour-faced sod, her, sometimes, and she is now. No one really enjoys getting randy old fellers bathed and dressed of a morning but so fucking what? It's her job. Which is to make what's left of a life a bit better before it ends. Christ, give me her job and I'd do it with better grace, tell yeh that. But as if they would on the Hire and Fire scheme. Dogsbody is all you'll ever get. Christ, one time they sacked me by text.

—You're late, she says. As I knew she fuckin would.
Jobsworth, in that white nurse's smock that she always wears
even though she doesn't have to. Must make her feel important,
or something; Nurse fuckin Ratched.

—You told me to get the shopping in, I say.

—Tamping for his breakfast in there he is.

—Yeh, which I'll make him. Couldn't make it without the
ingredients, could I?

I hold up the shopping for her to see. She snarls at it.

—He's in a right puddy this morning. Right grump.

—Is he?

She nods. —He's all yours, now.

And that's it. She makes to move away.

—Wait.

—What?

—Well, where are you up to? He's been washed and all that?

She sneers. —That's what I'm paid to do.

—Yeh but is there anything I need to know? I mean—

—One egg one bacon one tomato tinned. That's everything.
And look out for the bugger's hands.

And she frigs off. I don't get it; sure she doesn't like her
job, who does, but she's pastoral care; she's supposed to make
old people's last days on the planet a bit easier. Can't do that
if you go about it with a face like a smacked arse. And it comes
from the inside, not from the words on a letter of contract.
I mean it shouldn't be a duty; it's not about yourself.

Ah well. My turn now. And I like Mr Humpf. And he
likes me; the way the lights come on in his cute tortoisey face
when I go into his living room.

—My very favourite! he says, all croaky. —This, this *jewel*
in my eye!

—How are you today, Mr Humphreys?

—All the better now, Emma *fach*. He pats his knee. —Comen
sit by yur.

—Not till you've been fed.

I go into the kitchen and put a frying pan on the hob and
a saucepan next to it. Oil in the fryer, a single tomato from
the tin in the other. Looks like a haemorrhoid.

I hear the Humpf hum as I cook. 'Bread of Heaven', which trails off into a low mumble. Then 'Myfanwy'. He used to be a great tenor, I've been told; was in the local male voice. You can still hear traces of it in his voice when he sings. Bet he was one hell of a boy in his time, him.

I get his favourite plate, the one with the ships on it, and arrange his food: egg on the left, tomato on the right, rasher underneath like a smile. Tea in a mug. I take it all through on a tray.

—Here y'go, *bach*.

—Oh my lovely girl. Famished yur I am.

I put the tray on his knee and he gives me a great big gummy smile ... The light in his watery eyes, the deep lines in his face, the way his cheeks have sunk in cos he hasn't put his teeth in yet. All the slow collapse and decay, but God there's so much life, still, in his face. I can see the little boy in this old feller's ancient face.

—Look at that, now, *DuwDuw. Perffaith*.

He's talking about the egg, gently prodding the crisp edges of it with the point of his knife.

—Never a better fried egg. Bloody *perffaith*.

I watch his shaking hands as he builds a forkful of food, a tiny bit each of egg and bacon and tomato. All so delicate and dainty; cos he's old, aye, but also because I reckon that he just has it in him, the appreciation of detail like, this intense pleasure in tiny things.

I notice a silence in the room. The canary; there's no twittering. I look and see the empty cage over by the telly.

—Where's Delia?

He looks up, chewing. —Bloody cat got her. What's her name, just left?

—Anne?

—Anne. Cleaned the cage out last week she did and forgot to close the bloody door. Yellow feathers everywhere, *DuwDuw*. Cat, see.

—Ate her?

He nods. —All's I found was her little legs. And a bit of beak. Not one bloody word of apology either out of that one.

—Who, the cat?

He laughs; a brilliant sound.

—Oh aye! He's a cat, mun! It's what he's supposed to do, isn't it? Doesn't know any better, him, see.

Nice of Anne to keep me up to date.

—So what'll you do, get another?

He thinks about this, chewing. I see the Adam's apple move in his throat.

—Too old now. Na, we're fine, me and the cat. Us two. Poor Delia. Sad for the bird *fach* but that's the cat's job. Doesn't know any better.

He gives me another smile. Yolk at each corner of his mouth. I smile back at him, thinking about how daft it is to get both a cat and a bird as pets, which is what a lot of old people seem to do, and then complain when the one eats the other. I mean, what do they expect? Might as well get a great white shark and a seal. A whale and some plankton. An anteater and a load of ants.

I take his cleared plate back out into the kitchen and wash it up as he starts to hum again. 'Calon Lân'. I smell his pipe smoke wafting in, nice, reminds me of my *taid*. I make his coffee, tepid, lots of sugar, the way he likes it. And the way I loathe it. He shouts something at me in Welsh.

—What was that?

I put his coffee on the arm of his chair.

—I asked how the Cymraeg was coming along.

—Tomos is getting good.

—Is he now? At the school is it?

—Year 2.

—You'd best brush up, then. Or he'll be having a secret language with his butties, see.

His face disappears behind a cloud of smoke. There's a directive which says we should discourage the clients from smoking around us; when we're in their houses, it's our place of work. But it's his house, innit?

He wafts the smoke away with a hand.

—Iceland, he says. I know what's coming; I've heard it before, many times. But I let him speak. —That's where I woke up, aye. Three days in the water I was, see. Torpedo. Still remember it, I can, me and Bob Pratchett, putting the life jackets on, jumping in. *DuwDuw!* Pouf! Soon's we hit the water we were out. So *cold*, it was, see.

Another cloud of smoke. When his face reappears it's like it's more lively, younger, as if in some kind of magic trick.

—Woke up in Iceland, we did. Hospital. Hear the nurses speaking and I look over at Bob in the next bed, blue he was, blue. Aye-aye. We're in Germany here, boy, he says to me. We're in bloody Germany. Cos of the language, see. Didn't have a clue *what* they were speaking. Thought we'd been captured.

He thinks for a bit. Or *pretends* to think, I reckon, cos this story follows a pattern, the way he tells it – it's a performance. Has a good sense of theatre, does Mr Humpf.

—But they thought *we* were the Germams, you see. Scared of us they were. Cos of the language! We were speaking the Cymraeg!

He wheezes with laughter. I join in.

—And what happened then? I ask, although I know the answer.

—Just started speaking the Saesneg and we all got along fine. But we couldn't walk, see, me and Bob – the ice, the water, well it'd got our legs. Froze em up. So every day they carried us down to the hot spring, the nurses did. Big girls, they were, built like bloody props. Carried us down to the hot spring every day and put us in. Sorted us out, it did. We were back walking in two weeks.

This old man, here, smoking his pipe in his chair. With his sparse white hair and ratty old cardy and his slippers with the toes gone out. The threadbare knees on his trousers and the pictures on the mantelpiece and the empty canary cage and God, what things have his watery blue eyes seen. The memories in his old head. All the stuff he knows, still, at this end, *the* end, of his life.

—He's gone now, Bob, he says as he picks up his coffee. —Same year as my Lily. That was …

He blows on his coffee, I don't know why cos he takes it almost cold anyway, and it's like he blows on it too hard and kind of blows the mug out of his hand; it falls onto his feet and spills and his slippers and the old feet in them get soaked.

—Oh bugger! Look at that! Oh I'm sorry *cariad*.

*He's* apologising to *me*. —Don't worry *bachgern*. This is nothing to worry about. Not burning is it?

I bend to take his slippers off.

—*DuwDuw* no.

—*Yma*, let's get you cleared up, then.

On my knees I take his soaking slippers off and his green and baggy socks. His old man's feet; the veins and the callouses and the thin, long toes like a chimp's and the rusty toenails like a kind of armour plating or something. Skin on the joints and heels like rind.

—You're wet through, Mr Humphreys. Let's get you cleaned up and dried off.

I take his socks and slippers through to the kitchen and put them in the wash basket where the afternoon carer should see them and put them in the machine. I fill the washing-up bowl with warm water from the tap and take it back through with a tea towel.

—Ah, now that's how I like to see a woman. On her knees, see.

—Now now.

Well ... he's an old man. And this is different to them words hacked into the bench. This is different from Johnny's face all twisted into a mask.

I lift the old feet and put them into the bowl. Roll the cuffs of the trousers up on the skinny white legs.

—Swish em about a bit. Wriggle your toes.

He does. Creatures from the deep sea that've never known sunlight.

—There we are, then. That'll do.

I lift his feet back out of the bowl and onto the towel. Fold the cloth around them and rub them dry. He leans and strokes my hair and I can't help but flinch.

—That's enough now, Mr Humphreys.

He takes his hand away. —Sorry Emma *fach*.

—That's alright.

I dry between his long toes; make sure there's no dampness left in there so no fungus can grow. *Ych y fi* – fungus.

—How's that feel?

He doesn't answer so I look up at him and ask him again:

—How's that feel, Mr Humphreys?

—I hope you never see a war, *cariad*, he says.

—So do I. How do your feet feel? Are they dry enough?

—And now we're turning away from our friends.

—In Europe, you mean? Looks that way. Are your feet dry enough?

He wriggles his toes again. —Aye.

—Do you have any clean socks?

—Upstairs in the drawer. Top drawer. I'll fetch em.

He makes to stand up and I protest but he insists so I help him to his feet. He's still nimble, if a bit doddery and I don't want to do *everything* for him and make him feel useless so I let him go. Hear his slow thumping up the stairs as I go into the kitchen and wash up the dishes. I hear him shuffling about up the stairs, opening and closing drawers.

From the kitchen window I can see the harbour, the new flats there. Empty except for a couple of months in the summer; holiday homes, see. I can see people out on the balconies, sitting in chairs. An umbrella is up on one of them and there's a fat bloke beneath it in a white floppy hat and sunglasses. I think he's naked, his belly's so big, but he moves in his chair and I notice his shorts; his stomach came down over them. Wonder how long it's been since he's seen his own dick. Or even his feet.

The sea's all glittery in the sun. On the horizon there's a ship, miles away. Iceland is over there. I think of a young Mr Humpf bobbing about among icebergs, a burning ship sinking behind him. A young man he was then. And dead brave. He fought in a war. Saw things and did things that most people alive now will never see or do. Lived so long that he's seen the people who tried to kill him become his friends and what did he say, 'now we're turning away'? There are times when it's easy to envy the old. They won't see what's coming. What's coming around again.

The light on the water bounces back into the air. Where the fuck are you. Please don't tell me you've gone.

Thump thump from above. I go to the foot of the stairs.

—All okay?

— *Perffaith, fach.* Strength in the legs yet.

He's wheezing a bit. He hands me a pair of woolly socks.

—Let's get them on you, then.

I take him into the sitting room and put him back in his chair and put his feet in the socks and there go the toes again, wriggling.

—How's that?

—Cosy. Lovely.

—There we are, then. Now is there anything else you need before I go? You've got your paper, aye? And tobacco?

He's beaming. Warm socks and his newspaper and his pipe; he's got everything he needs.

—I'm fine, *cariad*. Got it all right yur I have.

—And someone's coming round to make your dinner?

—Oh aye. A new girl. Smashin, she is. From Poland! Cheese on toast on a Tuesday.

—Good. D'you want the telly on?

— *DuwDuw* no. At this time of day? Telly be buggered. Radio.

There's an old-fashioned transistor on the mantelpiece. I turn it on. It's tuned to Radio Wales; someone's talking about the EU.

—That do you then?

He looks up at me and nods and smiles and looks so much like a little boy again … It's odd, the way we regress as we get older. Reminds me of that crap film, *Benjamin Button*; I always thought it chickened out, I did. I mean, taken to its logical conclusion, we would've seen Benjamin disappear back into his mother's fanny, all screaming and covered in blood and gunge, and we would've followed him inside, into the womb, back to foetus and embryo. And where would you stop? We'd follow him as a sperm back into the ball sack of his dad. God, he'd become a caveman, then an ape, then a fish. Where would it end?

—So you're all set?

He waves a hand at me. —You go on, Emma *fach*. Don't worry about me.

I get a strong urge to kiss him on the cheek, give him a hug, but you've got to maintain a professional distance, so I don't. I just say tara to him and leave his house with me shopping. Head home. Text the office to let them know that Mr Humphreys has been looked after for the morning and go back towards the old stone bridge and turn right onto my road. The postman's been; just one brown envelope. Looks ominous. There's never good news in a plain brown envelope.

I put the shopping away. Eat a bowl of cereal at the window, looking out at the river and that new bridge. People are crossing it as if they trust it. I imagine heads sticking out of the water, shouting for help and arms waving as the current carries them out to sea. I imagine Mr Humphreys in the ocean again, the burning ship and the icebergs all lit up. A cramp cripples me stomach and I suck air in over me teeth.

I finish me Cheerios and turn me computer on and check me emails and the air goes from me lungs. Then I check my blog and my Twitter and the air seems to leave the room; he wasn't kidding, Bas. The hits. The thousands of retweets. The links and the comments, my God, look at this, this is more viral than bubonic fucking plague.

What the fuck?

I can't sit still. This needs movement. Wash the dishes, God, wash them again. It feels as if the room is whirling around me. What the *fuck* have I started? Me belly's all churning and not only because of the period pains. What was it I wrote, a single paragraph? And I didn't even say much in it cos I didn't even know what to say, I didn't know what I'd seen or heard and now I'm starting to think that all I saw anyway was something to do with the light of the sun and all I heard was the wind in the reeds and Christ I hadn't slept all night and I'd dropped that crap pill which I don't even know what it was, I just know that it wasn't the fuckin MDMA it was sold to me as, and *now* look, *now* look. What the fuck is going on? Is this what it feels like, to be, what, to be at the centre of something big? Something important? *Love to hear your thoughts*, that's what I wrote in the blog. But Jesus Christ I didn't expect *this*.

Got to move. Or *keep* moving. Everything around me feels different in a way I can't describe and it's not completely pleasant, I mean it feels as if an anxiety attack is coming on, I start to sweat and me pulse starts to race so I leg it upstairs and down a diazepam. *Gulp* it. Feel it thud in the stomach. I go and sit on the edge of Tom's bed, breathing in, breathing out, trying to focus on that, just the breathing ... I can smell Tomos in here, my boy, the smell of him rising up out of the bedsheets ... my wonderful boy ... my little wild thing ...

I lie back on the bed. I put my face into Tom's pillow. It has a dinosaur on it, one with a spikey tail and a row of plates down its back. I can smell Tom's hair. I think of phoning my folks but decide not to. Maybe later.

Just breathe. In and out.

Dig. Wild. *Bridge*.

Fall asleep.

When I wake up the diazepam has done its lovely dopey stuff and it's nearly time to pick T up from the school. I wash me face and go downstairs. It's steady again. Calm. Nothing to worry about, aye. As I'm leaving the house I see the brown envelope on the table and I open it and skim the letter. Words:

'Under-occupancy'. 'Sanctions'. 'Possible legal action'.

And:

'Fraudulent'. 'Undeclared income'.

Oh, right, yes. *This* is the real world. *This* is what it's about. How could I have ever forgotten this?

The letter tells me that I must report to the job centre for a meeting on a certain date and in the meantime my benefits have been arrested. I put it back on the table and leave the house.

There was no floating woman and she said nothing. Everything that the world has and that is available to me can be contained in a plain brown envelope. There is nothing more than that, aye. Except for Tomos.

Long queue at the school gates, as there always is. The dads are off to one side and I am in no mood to talk to the mums about fucking washing powder. Her with the bob and the hefty muck-spreader at the back of her is giving me daggers as usual; it's the single-mum thing. It seems to wind some of the other mothers up. That, and she's jealous of my arse and body; well, get yourself to a Zumba class, porker.

The teacher at the gates calls out T's name and I step out of the queue. See him coming towards me with his brilliant smile. A pang twists through me again and I remember him, so tiny, silent on my belly and looking around at everything, taking it all in through them blue eyes. *He's been here before* the midwife said and now I remember that and now I think to meself: God, how tiring that would be. How fucking tiring, to have to go through all this, over and over again, the same old shit with no end to it ever. Then I'm squatting down and holding my boy and I'm thinking of nothing at all except how lovely he is.

# MESSAGES

#FLOATINGWOMAN @EmmaMum1 anyone seen what's happening up at #llynsyfydrin? What's going on?

#floatingwoman can't you tell? Don't you know? It's arrived. It's here #llynsyfydrin #itishere

RT Repent. Repent. The time has come #llynsyfydrin#floatingwoman#itishere #repent

RT you are wrong #repent. Rejoice. Judgment day #Madonna# BVM

From *Pobl Annwyl*, bilingual blogspot, Emyr Gwenallt Roberts, AKA Llewellyn Nesa, version saesneg.

Knock. Fatima. Lourdes. Now we can add to that list: Llyn Syfydrin, Ceredigion.

It's been a long time to wait. Since 1904, to be exact, when the sun danced in the sky. They saw that in Fatima too in 1917 but I'm talking about Wales, now. Three peasant children in both places. And the message: dig and bridge and wild (@EmmaMum1). These things are common to all such experiences and stretch all the way back to AD 40, to the Apostle James in Saragossa. I can give you more examples but one will suffice: 1981, Kibeho in Rwanda, and She warned of mass slaughter and we all know what happened there. Don't we, dear people?

We've been ignoring this, haven't we? And this is the most sacred of countries in ways most people will never understand. The very soil of this land is sacred. Nevern churchyard has a yew that bleeds which will cease to bleed only when all evil is expunged from the world (and yes, I know the sap is infected, but that in itself is a metaphor). On our maps are Bethesda, Bethlehem, Pisgah, Moriah. Get googling, dear people.

So tell me because I'm intrigued; what are you going to do now? All your certainties have fallen away. The man comes around. You have been kissing the feet of Mammon. Well, no longer, dear people. The time has come. The choice between

repent or rejoice has come at last but if you want my advice (and you wouldn't be reading this if you didn't) – do both. But repent first. And hurry up about it.
TAGS: Llewellyn Nesa, Llyn Syfydrin, sacred, Mammon, Wales, repent, rejoice

@ListenToDawkins #llewellynnesa shit. Utter shit. Why would an all-loving God make an imperfect world #evidence #llyn-syfydrin #BVMshit
#ListenToDawkins because there'd be no fucking point to you otherwise #llewellynnesa #paradisebuiltinhell
@ListenToDawkins primitive taffs this is 21st century bet you don't have broadband over offas dyke #llewellynnesa #poblan-nwyl what does that even mean? #BVMshit
@Enlightened #llewellynnesa get a life, a modern life. Proof. Evidence. Grow the fuck up #MadonnaBollocks #BVMshite #trigger50now #hurryupandLeave

Hits: 1,479,832

# MIST

OVERNIGHT, A VAST muffler of fog forms out on the Celtic Deeps and drifts eastwards. Pre-dawn it breaks silently over the sea-town and tendrils through the mostly sleeping streets, a twist of it curling like the tentacle of a phantom kraken around the pier and the twenty-four-hour bar there, the yellow lights of its windows aglow above the beach, a million sleeping starlings roosting on the struts rough with barnacles and crusted guano. Soon, people will wake to this, the town made dreamlike behind the fallen grey veil. It will enter the sleeping heads of some, the tang of it, its brine, and there will be broken dreams of drifting unmanned galleons and the teeth of sharks flashing in black fathoms. The fog rolls into the high backlands, into the hinter regions, through the scattered small settlements and even beyond them into further rises; blind grey worms probe at the windows of the cottages in the folds and gullies of these hills, places never touched by sun and so sodden, even in this stun of a summer, that it seems the wet lick of the sea-fret fronds must result in sudden damp collapse. Birds start to sing. Somewhere a rooster hollers. A light breeze lifts the mist further up, through the ranked pines which sway lightly, left to right, together, as if listening to the same sad song. Over Rhoserchan, its fevered sleeps and higher still as if drawn to the lakes on top of the mountain in elemental fraternity, the mist wisping apart now to disclose the landscape as more birds begin to wake and in all likelihood sing this high world into being. Under circling satellites whose lights like that of the stars wink out with the returning day yet whose clicks and pulses continue to relay data through airless wastes at last it is noiselessly broken into nothing at the eastern shore of Llyn Syfydrin where, in the reeds, a sign of slat on slat has been erected and which on the cross-beam reads:

*llyn y weledigaeth*
*croeso pawb*

This sign hammered into a quaggy splat in which simple proteins split and link, base pair to base pair. A spike of turquoise neon that is a dragonfly finds a spider in a petal-curl of an ox-eye daisy and takes it up into the middle of a carved O and bundles it into a ball and eats it and in full loud bloom, these flowers are, a bright rim of them linking the eastern lake-shore to the western, a thousand yellow eyes all turned toward the martin-warrened dirt-bank behind which the sun is rising and which will soon shake the sleepers on the shingle, some in tents and others simply bivvied on the bare pebbles. A slumbering lacustrine tribe around smouldering firepits and crude crosses hammered into the earth and lambeg drums awaiting a drummer and citronella candles balanced on flat rocks to deter midges and mosquitoes. Offerings, here and there: locks of hair, the clothes and relics of dead or sickening kin, prayer words chalked onto stone.

Something might be poised to happen here. An early hawk circles on a thermal out over the lake then returns again to wheel above the peopled shore as if in interest, as if drawn.

And there is one who has not slept. Or for no longer than a couple of hours, whimpering and twitching beneath a blanket in a sheep-scrape isolated from the main group, but he has been fully alert since long before daybreak and has located himself back onto the ridge from where he can watch the sun reappear and on where a weak but useable phone signal can be accessed. Which is not why this man is here, where he has sited himself every sunrise since he first trudged up from his bolthole in the town, this ridge where he clipped the collar around his neck for the first time in years, this ridge where he shudders and prays and sometimes grips the rocky ground beneath his knees so hard that buds of blood burst under his fingernails. This ridge that he read about online and which commanded him to come to as loudly as the jostling crowd of no-see-ums nearby commands the collared dove to come and feed. Delicate dove, resting atop a knee-high cairn built yesterday and topped with a baby's bib, still stained with something red.

# MAN OF THE CLOTH

IT FEELS TIGHT and choking and the symbol of that is not lost on me; not the collar itself but the constricting way it feels. Underneath it is mere flesh. Mere flesh always called weak but the demands it makes are so very strong, screaming for attention. It needs to eat and it never rests.

I was excused. The height of my calling justified the depth of my transgressions. What I did. In the shrieking demands of my flesh. Touched by a world fallen so far how could I not fold, how could I resist; my connection to a world so fallen, that was the reason why. Surrounded by the corruption of innocence and so connected to that how could I not be infected. Polluted. Corrupt and corrupting too, in need. I mean I saw them in Calais. I saw them sodden and without life on beaches. I saw them sold and used.

Yes but my crimes came earlier and under them all was doubt. Desperation. The things we do to distance ourselves from the terror of the absence of God and in what I did was my prayer: Look how much I am offending You, observe the cruelties of which I am, in your absconding, capable and if there is no intercession to prevent then that is proof of Your abandonment. If You will not heed even the crying out of children then surely You are nowhere at all.

Woodsmoke. On the beach below some small fires have been lit; I see the visitors awake now, tending them. All have come; the tattooed ones, those who have lost, those who are fearful of losing, the crippled, the old, the young ... a liver-spotted scalp next to another thick with adolescent curls and both of them bent over the same blackened pot. Rumours of a vision; nothing concrete, and yet here they are, the clans, gathered together as one next to the dark lake on top of this mountain. As I watch, some of them go in to bathe. Some plunge under. One woman carries a naked child into the water and I see the small white feet dangling over the crooked elbow and I hear and feel a crack inside me somewhere in the sternum region and I *have* to look away.

I recognise none of them, as yet. Not one from my gone flock. But in the long years of my isolation they will have changed as I have changed and I may not recognise them now nor they me. Perhaps I would know the pains of Christ if they did.

A hawk circles in the blue sky. I hear it squealing. A smaller bird, a dove I think, alights on a cairn nearby, a knee-high mound of shore pebbles topped with a baby's bib. A child lost or ailing. I watch this bird and it watches me. If this symbol of peace is a part of You then so too is that hunting hawk and the small lives it will soon destroy. In its claws. In the torn-apart animal. In each of the people on the shore below me or cleaning themselves in the dark water.

The coming day promises to be hot, again. I should, like the others, cleanse my morning body in the water of the lake but I feel like I have grown roots on this ridge. Was it from here that She was seen? Not much detail given on the blog post but this ridge alone of all the others seems likely. I don't know why.

And what if everything I was told is entirely and completely true? Then a broken and contrite heart will not be despised. But maybe I must flagellate, scar. Take barbed wire as a cilice. Never stop bleeding.

There is laughter from below. Some have gathered around a large pot and are dipping receptacles into whatever it contains. Two others, men, take toilet rolls into the trees where the latrine pit has been dug. The woman leads her child back onto the shore, the wet skin gleaming and sleek in the sun, so bright and unblemished. I *have* to look away.

All changed utterly. The very mountain I sit on has been moved in its foundations which reach into the core of the entire planet where the fire is and I can feel its heat in the rock. In the air itself. Inside me and unbearable there. The worst punishment that could ever be visited upon me is not to have been shown Her face. To not have been allowed to hear Her words.

But the flesh. The immense power of it. And why make it so weak in its resistance yet so mighty in its demands. Milton called You 'the Great Tempter' and I remember the names of two of them, the two most beautiful ones, and their names were Cowley and Lambert and if that is not temptation then what is? There they were in their innocence, the lamb and the cow, passive and gentle and there only for your sustenance. Do with them what you will. Enough. Never enough.

—Good morning, Father. A shadow falls over me. It is a young woman, flesh and bone, with a bowl. —I've brought you some breakfast.

The long red hair and the pale tones of the Irish. Her accent is local but her forebears no doubt came from over the Celtic Deeps.

—Thank you.

—I thought you looked hungry.

—Thank you.

Porridge. The people of these mountains sustained for millennia on not much more than what is in this bowl.

The woman moves past me, to the highest part of the ridge. She gathers her skirts beneath her and sits and studies her phone. Taps at it.

Utterly changed. The world yawns open.

And I must be like a god to them; when they close their eyes they still see only me. They'll be middle-aged now but in them there must still be the frightened little choirboy. There is nothing that does not remind them somehow of me. And that memory judges their lives. *I* judge their lives; what they have done with their lives since Me is mine to monitor and assess, so deeply and utterly have they been altered and affected by what I did to them. I *am* them. I am everywhere. I have read about cycles of abuse and about suicide and addictions and great psychic agonies. I fill worlds.

So weak, so weak. Tell me what to do.

—Ah Christ. That's really sad.

I look up from my bowl at the woman.

—Sorry, Father, she says, and comes down the slope in her long skirts and blazing hair towards me. —I've just checked out the local news. Something's happened in the town.

—Something's always happening in the town, I am surprised to hear myself say.

—I know, she says, and squats down next to me. She smells of woodsmoke and sweat. —But look at this. It's really sad, it is.

She tilts the handset away from the sun so that I can read the screen. The first word that appears to me out of the glare is BRIDGE.

# BRIDGE

HE IS TOLD by the newspaper that beyond his door lies danger. That out there in the world of unexpected noise and unpredictable movement, all is predatory; no one is what they seem, on the surface, to be; all, to the last, are out to scavenge and plunder, all are habituated to idleness and have constructed schemes of great deviousness and skullduggery to allow that idleness to continue. This he is told, every morning, and every morning the response in him is the same: his body releases gases, fumes of anger and fear, the vessels of his blood constrict, clotting agents enter his arteries in anticipation of injury. His heart and his lungs are forced to work harder. The cumulative effect of his daily world-data has impaired his memory and his thyroid gland has deteriorated in the efficacy of its immune response. His blood pressure has been elevated. The high hormone levels in his adrenal glands now show him suffering from acute levels of stress. The chronic has taken over.

And he's old. And there are the pains in his chest which he's been biopsied for, the results of which the postman will deliver probably today, if not tomorrow, but he knows what the pains signify; the smoking and the asbestos – there'll be tumours blooming like toadstools. And there's the blood in his motions and in the phlegm he hacks up into the sink every morning. The creaking decrepitude of his knees; to stand up from his chair, to get out of bed, these once-simple movements are now monumental applications of willed preparation. Add to this the hopelessness, the ever-present fear, the isolation now that the day centre has been closed and the nights spent sleepless and cowering, and he knows he's done. The wasting cannot be arrested. In a bleached world the young man he once long ago was is a tiny dot of colour, fading fast: remember me? I'm still here, just about. Don't let me fade completely.

Everything is done with pain. The washing of the cup, the combing of the hair, the knotting of the tie – this is all done in great pain. Needles in his joints, ground glass in each inhalation. As he's safety-pinning the fly of his trousers he pricks his thumb and raises it to his face. Look at that: no blood: there must only be dust inside.

He leaves the TV on. Bombs falling somewhere in the world. Riots. Plunging pound, economic ruin. Walls going up. Gnashing teeth on each side of each wall. Aye, well, let's see them issue a final demand *now*. He thinks of leaving the oven on too but decides against it; could cause a fire, harm the neighbours. He dials the speaking clock and places the receiver on the side table. At the third stroke, the voice says, and yes, he's had two; the last one on Christmas Eve. He does not take one final look around as he leaves the house but he does look around at the world outside the front door, the greyness of it, all washed out except for the glitter of the river at the end of his street. Walk, walk. The word is 'dodder'. How did he ever get this old. So fast.

Never trusted the new bridge, the footbridge, with its wood and wires and patches of rust. Fellows working on it recently, swinging in harnesses underneath. Perfectly good stone bridge not 500 yards away, stood firm for centuries, why they thought the river needed a new bridge across it … Waste of money. It bounces a little as he steps onto it; such a slight person, years taken all muscle, yet it bounces with the weight of him. Was right not to trust it.

He moves slowly, into the middle of the bridge, where a section of railings has been replaced by high-tensile wire. The water racing below, out to the anonymous sea. He leans against the wire. His thin body. A seagull alights nearby, on the wooden slats underfoot. *Bye, bird*, he says, and raises a foot. Or tries to. These knees, these knees. The pain. Like a knife blade, a terrible obstruction, set concrete in the joint, it's not a case of forcing a movement through the pain as encountering something immovable. Oh no. Oh no. He leans against the wire because maybe the forward weight of his trunk might tip him over, but the top rung of wire digs into his floating ribs.

This isn't going to work. This is ridiculous. It's farcical. Lean. *Lean*. He forces himself up onto tiptoes, the knees screaming, trying to create a top-heavy situation, God he can *smell* the sea. He leans with his arms held out over the onrushing river, its current working below, taking things out into the big wide sea. He leans and falls.

# SABOTAGE

AN YUR I am again, in iss fuckin room, an-a worst thing is, Av done fuck all to deserve it. Only thing A did was try an do a decent day's fuckin work-a put food in-a fridge. Cunts. Eyr using that word 'sabotage' again. Sabotage! A don't even know what-a fuckin word means.

—Told yew, A say. Again. Eyr not getting nowt out-a me, ese two twats. Not that er's anything to get out anyway. —Yew get Poles an Stony-hands to put-a fuckin bridge up an what jew expect? Only a matter-a time before a fuckin thing comes down, innit?

—That's by the by, the older one says – Totally irrelevant.

—And anyway. A younger cunt – A recognise him, went-a school with him, fucked if A can remember his name now tho – sits back an folds his arms all fuckin smug. —It was erected by a Bangor firm. I have the records here.

Ee taps a sheet-a paper on-a desk.

—Ah well, Gogs, A say. —Almost as bad.

—A Welsh firm, he says. —Not eastern Europeans.

—Aye but ey were working on it with me, mun. Em Stony-hands. Under it, ey were, in these swingy things. Already told yew this.

—We've spoken to *all* the guest workers, Mr Cowley. And to Mr Pinckney himself.

A laugh. —Pinckney? Is that his real name? Pinkbits, like? Learn something new every day, aye.

—And you're the only one with a criminal record.

A look at him, the younger one, like. Him from-a school. —*Now* who's being irrelevant? What's *that* got to do with anything? You tell me.

—Well …

—No, go on, tell me. Cos Av never been done for fuckin up a bridge, have I? Or of drowning some poor old feller.

123

A older one goes through some forms. Love forms, these fuckers do. —Vandalism. Vandalism again. Theft. Burglary. Grievous and actual bodily harm, twice. Vandalism a third time, these are serious offences, Mr Cowley.

—Aye, go on, son, carry on. Soon's yew get to-a word 'sabotage' Al hold me hands up and lock meself in-a cell meself. Or, or a fuckin custody suite, is it now?

—We're not charging you with anything, a younger one says. —We're after information, that's all. This is simply one avenue of inquiry we're exploring. One possibility, that's all it is.

—Aye well Av got another possibility for you. Another avenue of inquiry, like. You listening?

Both of em lift eyr eyebrows. Eyr like fuckin puppets.

—Shit happens, there yew are, A tell em. —Sometimes shit jest happens. Enquire about *that*, aye?

—A man has lost his life, the older one says. —Very probably. We've yet to find his body.

—Aye, very sad, A say. —Me art's all broken. But it's got fuck all to do with *me*.

—Well, then. Maybe you can tell us if it's got anythung to do with *this*.

A older one slides a latest edition of the *Cambo News* across-a table at me.

—With what?

Ee taps the paper with his finger. Well into his tap-tapping, he is, this twat. —Read it.

A shake me head. —Never read that in me life. Not gonna start now. Always had it in for me, it has. Won't have it in-a house unless Am out-a bog roll.

—Well read it now.

—No. A jest shake me head. Cunts can't make me do anything A don't want-a do.

—It's alright. The younger one takes-a paper back. Ee gives me iss look like he'd give to a raspberry ripple or something. Like he'd give me money if he saw me down Great Darkgate Street with me hand out an a scabby dog on a string.

—It concerns the gathering, erm, commune up at Llyn Syfydrin, ee says. —On top of Pendam. It's an article about that. Do you know about this?

Yer's a poster on-a wall behind him. On it is a woman with a black eye an a face like a smacked arse an some words an a load-a phone numbers an stuff. A horrible yellow light from a bulb is shining all around her head. Makes me think-a that rave thing an that E that wasn't an E. But it was jest-a rising sun. Something like that. An a only reason it made me feel all that fuckin happy way was cos-a that pill, whatever-a fuck it was. Slow release, like, that's all. An that's all fuckin gone now anyway. Could do with another one, very fuckin *quick* release iss time. Because A am getting fuckin annoyed, yur, A am.

—Got nothing to do with me, A say again.

—That's not what I asked. I asked if you were aware of it.

A shake me head.

—You don't read the paper?

—Jest told yew. No.

—Go online?

A jest shake me head again.

—So you can tell me nothing about this word 'bridge', then.

—What? How many times ...? For fuck, isn't that why yew brought me yur in-a first place? How many times do I have to tell yew? A did some paintin on-a fuckin thing, that's it. End of.

—And Mr Pinckney said he caught you underneath the bridge, a old twat pipes up. —In one of the harnesses. Where you were not permitted to be.

—And a little prick gave me a bollockin, A say, an A feel a bit-a hotness in me face which makes me fuckin angry which makes me go even hotter. Not yur, Cow, not yur. Don't lose it in yur. Hot n angry. Fuckin *angry*. Some cunt will—

Aye but A saw fuck all. Nowt but-a rising sun.

—Am I under arrest?

—You know you're not.

—Tara, then. A go to stand up.

—But you were there, tho, weren't you?

—Where?

—On the mountain. At the party. Which was technically an illegal gathering, by the way, but we don't intend to pursue that.

—A saw fuck all. An A heard fuck all. Am off.

This time A *do* stand up. —A remember yew, A say to-a younger one, an A really don't know why A say it.

Ee nods. —I'll see you out.

—Don't need a fuckin guide, mun.

—Aye you do, ee says, an holds up a bunch-a keys. Again; ey do it again. Ey can never get fed up of making yew feel small. Cunts, all of em. Every last one.

Outside-a room ee unlocks a door an we go through an ee locks it behind us. —A remember yew, A say again, an A still don't know why. An then it comes to me; ee was getting bullied behind-a gym by one of-a Wren brothers, a ugliest one. A gave him a tap. Broke-a cunt's jaw, as A recall. Not cos A liked-a victim, like, this copper cunt with-a keys, but cos A really fuckin hated that Wren brother. Hated em all, in fact, A did. An that was a good enough excuse. An it comes back to me, now, iss copper when ee was younger, like, crying his fuckin eyes out, all snot an blood up his face ... makes me feel a bit better, that does. Less angry. Bit bigger n all. Still don't remember-a twat's name, tho.

—Aye, he says, an goes to open another door. Puts a key in-a lock. —Listen, he says, but quiet, like. —That's all bullshit, that stuff about-a bridge.

—A know it is, A say.

—Jest an accident, that's all. Shit jest happens sometimes, in that right?

—That's what A said.

—But yur's an ASBO coming out for yew, Cow.

—What?

—An ASBO. Been complaints there has.

—Which fuckin cunt ...

—Ey, ey. Remember where yew are, mun, aye? An who yewer talking to. An yewer on camera so right now we're jest talking football or some shite, aye?

—Don't care. Just wanna know—

—No kickbacks now. Not one recrimination, yew hear me?

A jest nod, again, but Am promising fuck all.

—Some neighbours-a yours have made some complaints. Not gunner tell yew who, and I'm only telling yew this much cos I owe yew one. Oh, an-a DSS are onto yew n all.

—DSS? What?

—That bridge work. Ey know it was a hobbler.

—How'd ey know that?

—Someone's got flappin lips, mun, that's all Am gunner say. Am jest tellin yew so yew know. Ey'll be cutting yewer money off soon if ey haven't done so already so make arrangements, aye?

Yur we fucking go again. Fuckin rollercoaster ride, iss, mun.

—How fuckin, A say but ee shakes his head an unlocks-a door an waves me through.

—That's yew, boy. Mind how yew go now.

Ee locks-a door behind me. A stand yur for a bit an a copper behind-a reception counter thing gives me a look so A leave-a station. Sun's shining again. Gunner be another hot one. A sit on a bench an roll a smoke. Im again, with all-a vegetables on his neck.

Alright, alright. Yur's a way out-a this. Yur's a way to make iss better. Use yewer fuckin brains, Cowley man. Yur's always a way out.

A smoke me smoke. A riot wagon comes past an goes into-a yard behind-a station. Yur's rolls-a razor wire along-a top of-a wall. Behind it is Pen Dinas, dead big an green, an A imagine being on top-a it when-a sun's coming up. Maybe it'd put some fuckin shapes in-a air. At a bottom of Pen Dinas is south beach. An yur's also a field where-a pikeys live. That's where-a Lavins are.

Alright, alright. Use yewer skills, Cowley boy. Every last one. Cunts that they are.

# SANCTIONS

DREAMS ARE SO strange. Like, last night I met Cedric Davies from *The Wire*, of all people, and he was wearing sage green slacks which, he told me, only people who like celery are allowed to wear. I told him that I can't stand celery and he told me that, in that case, I couldn't wear the slacks. And the funny thing is, in the awake world, I *like* celery, especially dipped in hummus; Tomos does as well. We'll sit there watching the telly, the two of us, with celery and a tub of hummus, just snapping it off and dipping it in. Most small kids I know hate the stuff. But Cedric Davies, tho – what the fuck was *he* doing in my head? Strange things, dreams. And I've always fancied him so it was no surprise that I woke up with a wetty. Been a while since I woke up like that, a bit slippery down there. Was going to give the old bean a flick but I had to friggin come *here*, didn't I, straight after I'd got the Tomster to the school.

—Are you listening to me? You'd do well to pay attention. This is a very important matter.

Wish I was back in my dream. Wish I was anywhere but here ...

—Fraudulent claims are taken extremely seriously. *Extremely seriously.*

... having to listen to *him* bang on, this, this rancid little pissdrip of a man.

—I know. Just tell me what's going to happen, I tell him.

—We're going to get this sorted out, that's what's going to happen. We're going to get to the bottom of this.

—I mean with my benefits. The money we need to live on, me and my son. What's going to happen to us now.

Carlos – that's his name. Johnny's mate. I'd know his name anyway cos he's got it tattooed in swirly letters on the side of his neck. What kind of knobend ...? Maybe he needs to remember what he's called because he's so fucking thick. Has to look in the mirror to remember his own bleedin name, aye.

—Well, there's nothing I can do to stop the sanctions, I'm afraid. The wheels are in motion, as it were.

—I know, I say. —I read the letter. And I haven't eaten properly for two days.

—I'm sorry to hear that but that's a situation which, I must add, is entirely of your own making. You should've been well aware that any work, paid or unpaid, has to be declared, without exception. And if I take a look back at your records ...

He taps on his keyboard and looks at the screen. Raises his eyebrows, one of them with a nick in it. I blink, and in that instant of darkness I see wild white teeth flash and I know that somewhere inside me they're wanting to bite, fucking *bite* as hard as they can, but what's the point? What *is* the fucking point? It has come to this – that this smug little squirt sitting across the desk from me has the power to make me and my son go hungry. And there's fuck all I can do about it ey. He knows nothing about my life and cares even less. Behind him I can see the office, people clicking away at keyboards, other people sitting opposite them, separated by desks, hanging on what they say. It smells in here. The air is too warm and all kind of thick and heavy. Think they'd have air con in here but no. It's horrible and I hate it and I want to get out of here as quick as I fuckin can.

— ... there's an under-occupancy penalty on its way, too. Now, that's not really my department, but—

This shit never ends. When I leave this building I'll be filled with most of the negative emotions that a human being can feel: fear, anger, despair, hatred. What's going to happen to me? What's going to happen to Tom?

There's a spot on Carlos's shiny nose. It's got a small yellow head. Makes me think of that lump on Johnny's head that looked like a dick ... He'll be in Greece, now. Hope it's still there, that lump. He'll be trying it on with the Greek girls and they'll be saying: Scuse-ay, but you are sporting a big red penis on your head, innit?

—This is no laughing matter. You'd do well to take this seriously.

—Do you see me laughing?

—Are you listening to me? It's my job to clearly outline to you what will happen vis-à-vis your benefit claim and I feel that you should really be paying attention.

Vizza viz? Did he just say vizza viz?

—Of course you have the right to appeal. That's your right. I can—

Saturday tomorrow. I can take Tom to Trefenter. See the folks, aye. Take a walk across the moor. See the wild horses maybe. Try and forget about all this shit for a bit and there'll just be the four of us, my mam and dad and me and Tom. The lake—

Ah God, ah God. Where are you now. I close my eyes again, and hope to see those weasel teeth but there's nothing. Just a hole getting bigger. Swallowing everything and spreading a kind of numbness across my skin and everywhere inside.

And the old feller took a header off the bridge, or so it said in the *cambo*. *That* bridge. Is that what the word meant? Dig, wild, *bridge*? Is that what she was trying to tell me? And there's been no body found as yet. Out to sea. Pick pick pick. Or no bodies, plural, because I can feel mine vanishing; every time I look online and see all the words I feel more and more incomplete, cos bits of me are off there, in cyberspace. Pick pick pick. And in *this* world, here, my body, my skin and meat, the, the physical fuckin *fact* of me, how false it is starting to seem, a lie, a—

I get a blast of breath. It's warm, clammy like, and smells a bit of bacon. I open my eyes. Carlos is leaning across the desk at me, on his elbows. His face with its spot and its tattoo and its piggy breath is close to mine.

—I can't actually *stop* any of this, he's saying in a low voice. He's looking at my ear. —I mean, I don't have that power. Once the wheels are in motion, like, well. He shrugs. —But I might be able to do *some*thing.

—What kind of something? I say, and there's a tingling going on underneath me jaw. This is a place I've been before.

—Well, I can, I can slow things down, a bit. Put in a good word with the emergency fund. Arrange some sort of interim payment, maybe. Emergency loan, pull a few strings. I've got the power to do that.

—Oh aye?

—Aye, yeh. Cos, well, remember what we did? At Iestyn's party that time?

Oh yes, it comes to me now; apparently I've had this idiot's dick inside me. I remember Johnny saying something about it as that big red knob sprouted out of his head. I went threes up, that's what he said. I don't remember the first thing about it. I was probably off me head, for one thing, and shagging everything that moved, for another. How'm I supposed to remember this face, here, leaning across the desk and blowing gas at me? I try to picture it slack and loose above me but I can't.

And there it is, behind his looming leer – the desperation. Something pleading in the eyes, like. I could get something back here, couldn't I; some sort of revenge. Aye, I could, but it'd be empty and pitiful and the old feller would've drowned for nothing, if he *has* drowned (what? Where the fuck did *that* thought come from?) so instead I just get up and leave. Turn me back on the little turd and just walk out of the building, away from it and him and the clicking fucking screens and all the people and the things they need. Something opens wide inside me, outside in the heat, I feel it, not like a flower more like a hole. Familiar; the numbness spreading, like I've been given an epidural, and the thing inside me like one massive yawn. *He's been here before.* Oh yes I fucking well have. When the waves of no-feeling recede there'll be a feeling in me belly like I want to throw up, and all's I'd sick out would be black air. Fuck them all.

Do normal things, then. Dull things before the hole can start to suck everything in. It was just the breeze in the reeds and the rising sun and maybe that pill had some effect after all. I buy a local paper and go to a caff, order some tea and sit at the pavement tables outside. Do normal things. The cars and buses passing by. All the different people. The seagulls and the sounds they make. A woman walks past with a little dog and stops to let the dog sniff at a bin, at all the piss smells there that, to him, must be like reading the local paper. Which I look at. The old man feared drowned. Already read about this online. All the words. Bits of me drifting away, out to sea like him.

# TO TELL YOU THE TRUTH

OOF, A FACE on this fucker; got a horrible black-red gash from jaw to eyebrow.

—Fuck me, mun, what happened to-a face?

—Got it in Nam, he says.

—Nam?

—Chelten-nam. Gold Cup. Some bad boys there, sor. Some fuckin Londoner. Tried to put a Chelsea smile on me dial so he did.

—*Tried* to? Looks to me like he succeeded, butt.

—Aye, well. He would have been takin his jellied eels through a straw for a while after. Ee rubs at the 'tush on his lip an looks me up n down. —Anyway. What brings you here?

—Looking for Aney. He around, is he?

He nods.

—Tell him Cowley's yur, then.

Ee looks me up n down again. —I know who you are, chavvy. Wait here.

Ee fucks off, back into-a camp, like. A caravans. Dogs everywhere, little kiddies runnin around, a group-a older boys around a fire givin it-a full gyppo works; playing cards an wearin pork-pie hats an waistcoats an braces. Eyr nudging each other an givin me looks so I give em a little wave an turn me back on em an find a rock-a sit on, facing-a sea. Ireland somewhere over it. Must be funny for ese pikeys, like, livin yur in a different country an every day knowin that the place ey come from is jest over yur, over-a water. Sometimes ey must see-a Fishguard ferry goin over, back to eyr homeland. Must be funny that. Why'd ey come over yur in-a first place? Don't know. Not even pikeys know why pikeys do what pikeys do. An not all of em are Irish, even. Least, ey don't *sound* Irish, some-a em, like.

A roll a smoke. Some shite-hawks start hanging around. A gyppos eat ese fuckin things, ey do; put em in-a stews, like. Must taste like turds. It's a clear day an A can see down-a coast, the cliffs like, a towns down yur where-a cliffs join-a sea. A furthest one, that must be Cardigan, where *she* is. Soon as A told her about-a fuckin ASBO an-a fuckin jobbie stoppin me money that was it – offski. Back down to Cardigan, she says to see Shauna, and that was fuckin days ago. Haven't heard a word frommer since. Yur'll she be, with Shauna's useless fuckin dopey bollax junkie idle twat of a dad, suckin at a bottle of White Lightning in front-a the fuckin telly. An yur's Cowley on his Jack fuckin Jones. Again. Been here before, aye, many fuckin times. Dozen bother me. Al jest use what Av got. Know yewer skills, like, that's what it is.

On me right is Pen Dinas an on me left is another big hill, don't know what it's called. Know it was once some kind-a fort, like, ages n ages ago; ey told us that at-a school. Been forts n castles yur for fuckin ages, all over-a shop, an-a farmers are always ploughin up blades n bits-a weapons n plates n stuff. Ey all thought ey could come in yur n take over, turn us into slaves, like. A Romans and the English; pair-a cunts, both of em. Jest couldn't leave us alone, them wankers. What we'd do, we'd build our own places on top of-a big hills – easy to defend, see. So, ages ago, people lived on top-a ese hills, built eyr huts up yur, had little towns all-a way up yur, ey did. Must-a blown-a friggin gale all-a time, all that way up. But maybe, on days like today, when-a sun came up, like, maybe ey'd sometimes see things in-a sky. Things that glowed. Maybe that's what it is, yew need to be high up, on-a ridges like, cos when-a sun comes up—

Aye, an maybe yew jest need a fuckin pill. That's all yur was, *is*, to it. Fuck sakes. Fuckin tab-a ecko will do.

—Now then, Cowley boy.

Aney comes up, stands in front-a me. He's got no top on an is skin's al crawlin with tats. He've got that stewpid friggin pixie thing on his back, A know that cos Av seen it, when he laid into-a McBride that time. Down on-a beach yur.

—What can I do for you, sor? he says.

—That Quinn straightener still on, then, is it?

134

Aney gives a grin an A really fuckin wish he wouldn't. Them teeth, like.

—Ah, knew you'd come round. Easy money, it'll be, sor.

We make arrangements like, where and when he'll pick me up, all that stuff, an en we spit in our palms an shake hands. Got-a do that; pikeys won't settle on anything without it. Fuck knows why, but it's true. They probably don't know why emselves.

—And sure we'll drink on it, he says, an takes a hip flask out of-a pocket of a old suit kex he's got on. Unscrews it and takes a swig and gives it to me. Whiskey; feels fuckin tidy going down. Glowin.

—Oh aye, A say. —An Al be needing a sub.

Ee takes another swig an wipes his gob with-a back of his hand an puts his hip flask away. —Now?

—No, after the scrap. Of *course* now, Aney, that's what a sub is. Fuck sakes mun.

Ee looks at me, thinkin. A don't say anything, jest let him think. Am beggin for no cunt, no matter how bad A need the fuckin spends.

—How much?

—That's up to yew, butt. But yew know how it works, aye.

Ee thinks a bit more then nods an takes a roll-a notes out of his pocket, size of a bog roll. Must be thousands. Got the right idea, ese pikeys av, whatever-a fuck that idea is.

—Alright. Ee licks his thumb an peels off some notes. — That's yer halvers. Second half when that fuckin Quinn is swallowing his teeth, aye?

—Loud n clear, mun.

A go to put the wad in me top pocket where A can keep an eye on it but something's already in yur. Oh aye; Ad forgotten about that, probably cos it's always with me. Again, a don't know why – it jest is. A put the cash in me hip pocket like an Aney knocks a knuckle against the machine in me top bin.

—Mobile is it?

A take it out to show him. —No.

—What's that?

—It's one-a them Aye-Pod things. Got music inside it like. Found it, I did.

—Let's have a look at it.

A give it to him an he holds it up an looks at it. Pokes at it with his finger.

—What's it do?

—Jest told yew. Keeps music inside. Songs.

—How'd ye get them out?

—Dunno. Jest found it, like.

He looks at it some more, closer up. —I'll buy it off ye.

—No, A say, an take it back off him an put it back in me top pocket where it belongs. —A wanner keep it.

—Fair enough. Ee loses interest in half a second. —Al see ye tomorrow then, aye?

—Aye.

—Get on the bags, son. Ee holds his fists up boxer-style. —Can't *wait* to see that Quinn cunt go down. Lot of money riding on this, boy.

—Aye, you've said.

—Alright, well. Tomorrow.

A head off, towards-a town. The wad is already burning in me pocket. A can feel it. The heat. Am thinkin pub. Am thinkin charlie. But no, Al leave that for tomorrow, after Av buried that Quinn an yur's something-a celebrate. Al leave it til then.

Can't help thinkin, tho ... it's been a while since Av had to give out a tap. What if I – A mean what will fuckin happen if I fuckin—

No, fuck, don't think about it, mun. It'll come back to yew. Jest like riding a bike. An, *Duw*, A can feel it in me shoulders an fists already, like the burning from-a money is spreading through me, making bits-a me tingle. Almost like A felt after Ad seen that, that thing, after that pill had made the rising sun go all amazin. A feel a bit like that. Power. Tomorrow. To tell yew-a truth, A can't fuckin wait.

136

# CAMERA OBSCURA

I CAN STILL hear her begging – one kid on her knee, another holding her hand, another rolling around on the carpet, all of them grizzling and crying. *Please*, she said, *you can't do this to my children; let me starve, I don't care about that, but not my children*. She begged, right there in the middle of the fuckin office. I thought she was gonner offer herself to the guy on the other side of the desk, drop her joggers and bend over the computer terminal and whore herself out in the middle of the job centre. Would everyone just stare or look away, embarrassed? They'd probably just look down at their feet, understanding her desperation, altho I bet one or two would get their fuckin phones out. But that silent slumped demeanour that the beaten-into-resignation always have. Buckled under the sense of their own worthlessness. Drilled into them. Can't help but wonder – how will the memory of this affect them kids? They'll always remember their ma begging and pleading all snot-nosed in a public place. Horrible to think how that will work on them as they grow up. At least the guy on the other side of the desk from her – the assistant, like, the clerk, the Aspiration Aide or whatever the fuck they're being called these days – had the decency to get embarrassed for her; beamed a right reddener, he did. Still sanctioned her, of course – he's got his fuckin targets to meet if he wants to keep his job. I swear, tho, *my* feller gave a wee smirk when security took the woman and her kids away through a side door. Couldn't fuckin help himself, smirked all the way down to that stupid tattoo on his neck that said CARLOS in swirly letters. Thought it might've been his boyfriend's name at first, like, thought he might've been Colwyn Bay, but then I saw the same name on his ID badge. Dick'ed had his own name tattooed on his neck.

Anyway. The politicians blether on about the great new opportunities for Britain outside of the EU. Endless shite. And in all the fuckin job centres up and down the land not one thing changes. In all the bedsits, in all the pokey flats at extortionate rents, at all the foodbanks ... the same fuckin thing goes on. The crying and the pleading. The fucked up children. The fuckin air is thick with it.

I move the handle, the joystick thing, to the right and the screen below me swoops over the town and down to the harbour. Ace thing, this camera – it's like I'm a drone, a spy in the sky, a bird bozzing over the town. See all the sunbathers on the south beach and with better resolution and magnification I would close in on the babes in bikinis. This is a poor man's version of Google Earth sure enough but then I am a poor man. And besides, I like the control in the joystick; gives you a better sensation of flying than clicking on a mouse does. Swoop out to sea. There's a fishing boat. Back to the beach. Christ the shapes of women ... I seem to be appreciating that a hell of a lot more these days. Since that rave thing on the mountain. It's like my libido has returned with a vengeance. Take away the heroin and the hard-ons return, after a while. There's a dog chasing a ball into the ocean.

Smug cunt, that Carlos. Seemed to take pleasure in what he told me. I wasn't working up at Rhoserchan I said. No pay. Yes he said but while you were up there you weren't available for work were you? But I was doing voluntary stuff I said. It's classed as experience and looks good to any prospective employer. Yes he said, those potential employers who were waiting for you to contact them but instead you were incommunicado up at Rhoserchan.

His voice in one ear and the woman's voice begging in the other. I knew this was going to happen soon. That word 'sanction' in both ears. Should've prepared meself for it. I'm old enough to know how it works.

I pan back, away from the beach and hover over the railway station. There's a train in at the platform. Borth, Dyfi Junction, Machynlleth, Caersws, Welshpool, Newtown, Shrewsbury, Wellington, Telford Central, Wolverhampton, Birmingham. All the stops on the only rail route out of this edge town. I swing away. The dog bounds back into the sea again.

But how *can* you prepare yourself for this shite, tho, really? Aye, sobriety is a high in itself, that I understand. Involvement. Focus on the present. Planning, above all. No excuses no punishment never give up. I get it, aye, I get it in me bones. And then you see a woman forced into making a holy show of herself, in front of her kids. A wanker like Carlos with the authority to turn her into a pleading dribbling wreck. You hear the word 'sanction', you get told off – told off, at your age – for not taking your job search seriously and now what the fuck do you do? Where will that woman be now? What will she be saying to her kids? *I've no man*, she said repeatedly. *I'm on my own with my children.* Made me think of that time in the Moorfields job centre back in the late 80s when the feller came in, a baby under each arm, plonked em down on the counter and said: *you fucking look after them, then. You fucking feed them, and buy their nappies, cos I can't afford to*, and just walked out. Just left em there, screaming on the counter.

Christ. All those years ago and nothing has changed. You'd think that, eventually, they'd run out of shit to dump but no, the supply is evidently inexhaustible. Oh this brave new Britain. Standing tall in the world. Taking back control. Fuck off.

I make the camera eye hover.

That fucking sneer when I mentioned Rhoserchan. *Resident, were you?* he said. Some people just refuse to see the 'ex' in front of the 'junkie'. All they see is housing estate, scouser, thief, feral underclass, ghetto scum, and aye I was fucking wild, aye I ran fucking mad, and who do you think taught me to be that way? What do you think was inside me? Cunts, every day I saw and I see you behave exactly the same and it's just like the shite from my childhood: do as I say, not as I do. I *had to* understand, from a very early age that the most powerful tool in teaching was behaviour; compared to that, words barely mattered. They meant nothing, compared to models of behaviour. And so a dysfunctional upbringing is the model for social nurture. I mean, for fuck's sakes. I mean—

Swoop back over the train station. Over the footy field. Looks like someone's going over the white lines with one of them single-wheel things. Hover out over the river. Bits of yellow, ribbons like, across the new bridge; looks a bit like police tape.

Remember this:

> the individual is suffering from a socially universal human condition rather than a mental illness ... it is in the unsuccessful attainment of basic needs that a person's behaviour moves away from the norm.

Alright, alright. Like Glasser Thompson. Like Carlos. Like a mother forced to beg in public.

Aw man ... aw man ... The camera eye moves in a quick circle. Sunlight rebounds back off the bonnet of a silver car on the prom and I see a woman – that shape – walking past it and for a second she's caught in the flash and it's like she's glowing but then she walks out of it again because in this world people do not glow or float. And them words ... that was just that bloke with the dragon on his neck muttering to himself as he farted about with that iPod. Which he 'found in the reeds' my hairy drug-free hole; there's probably some student somewhere still nursing a sore jaw and hoping for a new iPod for Chrimbo. Hillbilly, that one. Not that I know him but ... if you can't fight it, fuck it: that's written all over him. The hillbilly motto.

And *now* look – who won't see the 'ex' now? What's the word – *essentialism*. Aye, I read, these days. I'm being an essentialising arse. This is what boredom does to your head.

That word hits me with a jolt – is that what I am, bored? Am I? Is that what this no-feeling feeling is? It's been a long time since I've felt this way and I've forgotten how horrible it is. All this cack about 'muddling through' ... that's at the hollow heart of it. *The British people will always muddle through*, that's what some cunt said on the radio this morning, and they're the same words that the guy said to the woman in the jobbie this morning when she asked him how she was supposed to feed her kids on no money: *you'll have to muddle through somehow*. Same fucking words they use about austerity, about Brexit, about everything that they won't suffer from and is this it, then?

Is this something to be proud of? This state of being a robot who doesn't rage or even question, just 'muddles through'? Is this all there is, for us?

*Be honest with yourself at all times.* More words that are inside me now. So do it, lad; is that *really* why you're bored? Is it? Be *dead* fucking honest. Pure heart.

I move the camera back to the promenade. And then I get another jolt as I twitch the handle to the left and see who's sitting at a bench outside the Glengower pub; I'd recognise that mad red hair from Mars. Looks like he's got a drink in front of him. I take me phone out but realise I don't have his number so I leave the building and, *fuck*, the sunlight knocks me back, makes me lean against the curved wall of the obscura while I get me shades out me pocket. I can't see clearly for a few seconds and I have to wait for the eyes to adjust. The next funicular down off the hill isn't for another fifteen minutes so I leg it down and when I get to the Glen I'm sweating and panting and I can hardly fucking speak and I have to just stand there with me hands on me knees feeling like I'm gunner be sick. Ebi speaks first anyway:

—Adam, boy. *Duw*, look like you could do with a drink. What you running for, then? Not fuckin good for you.

I stand up and swallow. Christ I'm so fucking unfit.

—Ebi ...

—Deep breaths, now.

—You're in a pub, man.

He looks around in mock surprise. —Is *that* what this is?

He's not shouting like he usually does. In fact, he's speaking very softly.

—The fuck you doing, tho, man? You're in a pub, I say again.

—Aye, well. Nowhere else to go is there? Getting next train up the coast, I am. Leaves in an hour. No Rhos anymore, see.

I sit down opposite him. His face, his face – there's something gone from it.

—So what you saying, that you've been sacked?

—No no. Place's been closed.

—What has?

—Rhos. Receivers came in this morning.

—You're fucking kidding me. Rhos closed down? You're fucking kidding me.

—Don't I fockin wish I was.

He tells me that all the funding was withdrawn. That the public funding went first, quickly followed by all the money from the private benefactors, or nearly all of it; what was left wouldn't support the chickens. The administrative staff fought long and hard and presented the relevant boards with all the stats and figures to prove that Rhos was cost-effective but that made no impression whatsoever and the money was gone. Overnight.

—So that's it, Ebi says. —Fuckin finito. Out on your arses. Austerity, boy. Brexit fuckin Britain. Taking back control, innit? Or covering your own hoop more like.

—All the rezzies. What's happened to them? Where've they gone?

—Can't tell you. Think they've been carted off to somewhere else, back over the border. I dunno, mun, I didn't stop to find out.

—Sally and Suki. What are they gonna do?

—I don't fockin know, mun, told you. Gave em a hug, said tara an I was on me way. Place's gunner be emptied soon – furniture, the lot. Tellin you, it's gonna cost one fock of a lot to reopen. If it ever does. They'll be takin the fockin works.

I look out at the sea, expecting to see it rising towards me in a giant fuckin wave just so this day could be made a bit worse. But no, no – how could it be made any worse? A great big fucking wave, smash everythung down, wash it clean. Start all over again.

I look back at Ebi. —And what the fuck are *you* gunner do now?

My hand moves out and picks up Ebi's glass with the greenish liquid in it. It gets raised to me nose.

—It's fockin J20, Ebi says. —Apple and kiwi fruit.

He takes it back.

—What, think Am running straight back to the fockin booze, aye? Think more of me than *that*, cont.

He's right, and I feel a twinge of shame.

—Sorry Ebs. Just worried is all.

He hides his face behind a swig at his drink. I get a whiff of it – the fruitiness. Even Ebi's hair, usually so mad and sticky-up, seems to have deflated and has flopped down over his forehead and over each ear like the ears of a spaniel or something.

—So what *are* yeh gunner do? Back up north, is it?

—I see no reason to stick around. One-way ticket back up to Cric. Take up me old job. See the old boys. It's what I know, innit? Got *some* family left who still wanna talk to me. Support up there if I need it, see.

I see him again, his head thrown back and lit by flames, offering the words about the pure heart to the night sky. And as sure as I've ever known anything I know that, back up there on the north coast, Ebi won't last a year. He'll drink, and either his body will collapse with the shock of it straight away or he'll punish it until it just gives up. I know it, I can see it; the yellows of his eyes in a year or so. Like Colman's mustard. Ruination for him up there.

—Come with me, boy, he says. —Stop at me mam's for a bit with me until we get set up in a flat, aye? Got some savings I yav. Get yew some site work or factory work or something. Serious, now; follow me up in a couple of days. I'll have a camp bed set up in the shed. Serious.

I shake me head. —Ebs, I can't even afford the fuckin train fare, lad. I'm fuckin skint. Got sanctioned this morning, didn't I? Y'know all them times I was up at Rhos? Cunts said I shouldna been there, that I shoulda been out looking for work. No fuckin tellin them, is there? Honest to God. And there's me cat.

Speaking these words I realise, properly, and for the first time today, the depth of the hole I'm in. I could ask Sion or Benj for a lend or see if anyone can help me out at AA but, realistically, I'm fucked. There's not even the polytunnel at Rhos to doss down in any more. Suppose I could track down Suki or Sally but the thought of doing that ... well, the idea makes me feel a bit sick; I mean, it's so close to bad memories, of scrounging and scamming, of using people, that it makes me feel a bit queasy inside. I'd never rip off Sal or Suki but just the act of asking them for help ... I'd be afraid of what might be set in motion. Pure heart. Keep it that way. You're on your fuckin own, man.

—Don't need the conts, boy. Fock em. Fock em. No fockin charity anymore. No fockin welfare state anymore. All gone.

He's holding a bundle of notes out over the table. A slight breeze has risen and the notes are slightly ruffling in his hand because he's holding them at one end and the other ends are loose like tongues. Like they're kind of talking.

—I can't take that, Ebi lad. You're gunner need it. Ta and everything like but—

He's stuffing the notes in the breast pocket of me shirt.

—Yew fockin well *can* take it an take it yew fockin well *will*. An yew'll settle what yew need to settle down here, you'll buy a carry box for the cat and you'll buy a ticket to Cricieth and that's where I'll meet yew in a few days. Alright? Hear me? I can spare it. Sure what have I been spending me wages on up at Rhos? Not one overhead I had. What was I gonner do with the money? Spend it in the pub?

—Ebi, man ...

—It's a fockin loan. You'll get off the train at Cric an walk straight into a job. There'll be one set up. Know a few builders up there whoer always on the lookout for a new pair of hands. You'll pay it me back. An if yew don't, I'll get some boys to break your legs with a cricket bat.

He laughs, and for a flash there's the old Ebi sitting across the table, the loud one, the constant firework burst of energy. But it lasts only a second.

—I'll need the number. For your moby.

He tells me his number and I store it in me phone. Then I stand and put a hand on the nape of his neck and press me face to his and I feel sharp bristles and I smell oil in his hair. I tell him that I'll see him very soon and he tells me that he knows I will and then I walk away along the promenade past the magistrate's court which has fellers in cheap short-sleeved shirts outside of it, standing, smoking, and all of them, *all* of them it looks like, has 'only God can judge me' inked into their necks or forearms. I feel something in the atmosphere, in the molecules of the air and in the body cells of the smokers and in my jawbone and in my fingernails and in the spit that has suddenly gone from my gob, and it is fear and it is anger and it is something as horrible and as destructive as shame. Up the coast, far away to the north, I see the distant headland jutting out into the sea, the peninsula on which Cricieth is. I remember one of the north Walians I used to know in Liverpool – Mad Ernie we called him. Used to inject Pernod into his big toe. He did this even when he was on trial with Tranmere, although obviously that didn't last long. I wonder what happened to him. Wonder if he's still got ten toes. I can't do anything. I don't know anything. Here I am, fucked again.

There's evidently someone in the town who fancies himself as a Welsh Banksy – a Bancsi – cos on the gable end of a terrace is a spray-painted stencil of a sheep holding a machine gun. As I'm standing there looking at it I get an incoming text that reads: **No c for time. U good? If u r thinkin it dont do it. Alwys here 4 u bruv**. It's from my sponsor. I turn the phone off. 'No c for time'. The man's a knob. Got 'clean and serene' tattooed on his neck. Fancies himself as a Hackney gangsta and he was born in fuckin Tre'r Ddol. I walk on, towards home.

It doesn't come on like need suddenly taken to an unbearable level. I mean, it doesn't *scream* inside. It's just a simple decision.

I'm hoping Quilty will be waiting for me in the flat but he's not, although he has left me a present on the bed; half a dead mouse. The arse half. Tiny pathetic feet. I wrap it in newspaper and put it in the bin. Take me clothes off and get in the shower. Wonder how long I'll have hot water for. Wonder how long I'll have a flat for.

I soap everywhere. Sole to scalp and every millimetre of skin in between.

No, it's not like it howls or shrieks. It's just a simple decision, no holy show, like I've calmly and objectively weighed up all the options, studied the balance sheets and reached a conclusion: *I will drink today.*

I dry meself and put on all the nice smells. Clean clothes.

And I'm surprised at how easy it is, really, how undramatic, or I would be surprised if my emotional state allowed for anything other than this massive acceptance. So big it fills the world, *is* the world; I will go out and I will get drunk like normal people do and then tomorrow I'll sit down and work out what to do. Buy me ticket up to Cricieth. Track down Suki and Sally and say goodbye. Sion and Benji too. Maybe have one last walk up to Rhoserchan, just to say goodbye to that as well. Even if it is only a building.

I put some food and water in Quilty's bowls. What would *you* do, Quilty, my marvellous cat? You'd lick yeh balls and go out in your mystery and kill something, that's what you'd do. I check myself for baccy and lighter and keys. Gulp some water from the tap cos my mouth is as dry as a desert. Simple decisions. I am in control. I take one last look around the tiny flat as if I'll never see it again and then I emit a horrible little vinegary *frimp* of a fart and I go out to the pub.

# TWO SHOCKS

THE BARMAID WEARS a knee-length skirt and a white vest top and these garments are tight and they highlight the curves and cambers of her body. She leaves the stout to pour into the glass and turns to the optics and the man at the bar sucks the shapes of her in through his eyes then, when she turns back to face him with the ball of molten gold in her hand, he turns his gaze inwards and finds himself regarding, with shock, a pool of black despair. He'd forgotten not the fact of it but its depth and its darkness and how unreflective is its surface.

The barmaid tells him what he owes her for the drinks. The height of the price startles him, the increase since he last bought alcohol, but he pays it nonetheless.

# THE LOWS

I SEE TOM look up all worried at the transmitter as we go through Blaenplwyf. Them blue eyes of his go all big and he starts licking his lips, which is what he does when he gets worried. Like dogs do. Strange little boy.

—You don't have to go up there, I tell him. —Don't worry. No one's going to make you.

He just can't forget the time he went on a school trip to Harlech and he ran away from the group, went up the steps and found himself on the battlements, dead high, and he couldn't move for the fear of falling off. His teacher had to carry him down. Had bad dreams about it for ages, he did.

—Why's it so high?

—Well it has to be. So it can transmit the radio signals over a wide area.

—What's transmit?

—Kind of, like, give out? It's cos of that tower that you can watch CBBC.

He turns his neck over his shoulder to watch the tower through the back window get smaller as the bus moves further away from it, down the coast.

—It's okay, I tell him. So many things to reassure this little boy about. —You're not going to go up anywhere high. There's no need to worry about the heights.

—I'm more worried about the lows.

I laugh. —Worried about the lows? Where'd you get that from?

—It's just what I think.

—Well it's alright. Where your *nain* and *taid* live, that's not up high, is it? It's safe there.

—There's the mountain.

—You don't have to go up it if you don't want to. Nothing to worry about. *Yma*, have a snack.

I take the Tupperware box out of the rucksack with the celery sticks and the tub of hummus in it. —Want some?

He shakes his head. —Not yet.

I put the box back in the sack. —Just let me know when you're hungry, then.

He does that thing where he kind of withdraws into himself. I've seen him do it so many times before; his eyebrows kind of come down and a glaze comes over him. He taps at his phone and I see the Angry Birds app come up on the screen. That wicky music starts.

—Put it on silent, *cariad*.

He doesn't hear me. Or he ignores me.

—Tomos. Put it on mute, I said.

—But it's not the same.

—I don't care, it's irritating for other people. Put it on silent and be a good boy.

He does. An old dear across on the other seats gives me a smile and I smile back. The ground falls away in a great big swoop on my side of the bus, down from the road and towards the sea, dead blue, bright, light blue at first then darker blue further out where it gets deeper. I see a boat way, way out, probably the Irish ferry from Fishguard, and closer in I see a kite just hanging in the air, his wing feathers all goldy-red in the sun, a couple of crows bothering him. I go to point this out to Tom but he's absorbed by his own angry birds. I see the kite turn on his side to flash his talons but the crows carry on harassing him and he zooms away, down the dingle and out over the ocean. The bus turns inland, towards Llangwyryfon. Fields, here. And hedges and trees and hills. It's all 10,000 shades of green. The bus goes over a little stone bridge above the Afon Wyre. I know this area, I do.

So that's it, then – the old feller probably drowned. That's what I read. The poor old boy taken out to sea and his body hasn't been found. I was worried that something like that would happen – that word 'bridge'. I'd been told, hadn't I? Warned, like. I should've pitched a camp on that bridge, to make sure no one crossed it. I should've become like the troll in the fairy tale and let no one across the bridge. That's what I thought, yesterday.

And it's not what I think today. It's all crap. The word 'bridge' – I mean, *what* fuckin bridge? Could've been *any* bridge. Tower Bridge, the Severn Bridge, Sydney bloody Harbour Bridge. The card game. Dental work. The metaphorical bridge this country's burnt with the continent. It was just a word which wasn't even a word it was just the sound of the breeze in the reeds because if it's all true – if what the nutters and the conspiracy theorists and the off-their-friggin-heads online ranters are all going on about – then why didn't she say more? Why didn't she say more, that morning after the rave, and why didn't she appear again? Dig and bridge and wild. Just three random words. That feller with the dragon on his neck kept farting about with that iPod and the sun was coming up and there was a breeze blowing in the reeds and I'd taken some kind of pill and I hadn't slept. And the old feller fell in the river and the world is full of coincidences. They mean nothing. The way the world is today, with everybody connected to everybody else, it'd be more fuckin amazing if coincidences *never* happened, wouldn't it? There's nothing going on, here. This is not a, a visitation from God. The voices online are just the sounds of people searching for meaning, aye. That's all they are.

Another bridge, now, an old stone one. This must be the Afon Beidog. I look down into the little river as we go over it. There are rocks in the water and tree branches hanging down. It's dead clear, the water is. I only get a glimpse of it, two seconds, three.

It's beautiful around here, I know that – the landscape, this is what they call 'beautiful', and I know it is, in my head like, but in my heart, in the bit where it counts, there's nothing. I could be anywhere; there could be anything outside the windows of the bus and I'd feel the same way. It's just the physical bits of the world. It's just, what, fuckin *green* – that's all it is. Things called flowers. Other things that are called trees. They mean nothing. An old man fell off a bridge. Once there was blackness in me and now there is this flatness without colour and recently there was what? When I came down off the mountain. What was it? Whatever it was, it allowed me to send Johnny out of my house with a penis sprouting out of his stupid head. Which I remember being brilliant. But then there was that cunt Carlos and now there's this.

—Mam.

Tomos is tugging at my sleeve. He's paused the game on the screen.

—What is it, *bachgern*?

—What's this place?

I realise that we're at a bus stop in a village.

—Llangwyryfon. Why?

—Is this where I went to church that time?

—What time?

—Think it was Easter time once.

I remember. Things repeat themselves. I can't help myself.

—I think so, aye.

—Will Taid take me to church again this time?

—I don't know. Why? D'you want to go to church again with your *taid*?

There's a man walking up the bus. I see his face beneath the peak of a baseball cap. He's wearing oily overalls, baggy except where the cloth is straining at his shoulders. He sees me looking at him then glances at Tomos by my side and sits down a few seats in front of me. I see the hair curl at the nape of his neck. The big hands on him. Things repeat themselves.

—Who's that man, Mam?

—What?

—That man.

—Just some man.

What were we talking about, me and my son? He just asked me a question. What was it? Or was it me who asked the question?

The bus rumbles and pulls away.

—Are you not playing your game anymore?

He's not, no; he's gazing out the window. There's a big dark church up on a hill. He looks at it then turns his blue eyes like lamps on me. Again, I know that his eyes are beautiful; but that's just a description, just a word.

—Mam.

Here it comes. —What, *cariad*?

—Why do people go to church? Why do they believe in God? Why does Taid believe in God?

—Don't you, then?

He doesn't answer, just looks down at the screen, but doesn't resume his game. The bird-balls are suspended, still, on the display.

—Well, people need things to believe in, I say. —Like, a power? Something bigger than them. A faith.

—A face?

—No, a faith. F-A-I-T-H. It's like, well, something to believe in, a bigger thing than them, it keeps them going. Like, gives them something to live for?

How do you explain this to a little boy?

—I mean, for some people it's the sea.

—People need to believe in the sea? And all the fishes?

Oh God.

—Well, yeh, sort of. Cos it's bigger than them. It's where life comes from.

—I came from the sea?

—Yes. Long, long time ago. Well, I mean, you came from me, and I came from your *nain* and *taid*, but. People. Humans, like us. Long long time ago we came from the sea.

The man in the overalls is texting on his phone. Who's he sending a message to? Wonder if he's married. Has a girlfriend. Or a boyfriend. Someone he grabs with them big hands.

—I came from you? I used to live inside you?

—When you were a tiny baby you did, aye. Before were born.

—Will people live inside me one day?

—No, cos you're a man. Well, you'll *be* a man, when you grow up.

He thinks about this.

—When I grow up, do I have to believe in God?

—You don't have to do anything. You'll be able to decide for yourself.

—I've been in the sea.

—You have.

—So have I been in God?

—Some people would say you have, yes. Because everything is God. The sea is God. So some people would say that you *have* been in God. And that God is still in you.

—God's in me?

He says this with a little bit of panic. My little boy.

—He's in everyone, not just you. Because he loves you and he wants to keep you safe. That's what some people would say.

—At school he's called Father. Is God my dad?

Soon this hole will be too deep to climb out of. —Some people would say he's everybody's dad. Like the sea. *Yma*, let's have some celery sticks, aye? And see if you can get to the next level of Angry Birds. You've never been on Level 3, have you?

Ah, there we are; soon as your child starts asking awkward questions, distract them with things that flash and bleep. Fuck's sakes.

I take the box out of the sack and take the lid off and dip a stick in the hummus and give it to Tom.

—Mmm, nice. You must be hungry. Hurry up now, cos we'll be getting off soon.

He licks the hummus off the celery stick like other kids would lick an ice cream and I press the button on his phone to start the game again and immediately he's absorbed. He's trying to play with the celery in his hand and hummus is getting smeared all over the handset. But he's distracted, and I should, really, be feeling a bit of shame here. But I feel nothing.

The man gets an incoming text. I watch him read it and I see him smile. He sends a reply. I can't imagine his life.

I suddenly remember the Mormons who called at my door last month; two of them, young smart fellers in suits, handsome, with sexy accents. *We can do jahbs for you, ma'am*. I'm sure you can, I remember thinking, and then getting a burning in my face. Thank God that heat didn't trickle down to my fanny.

He needs a dad, Tomos does. More than anything else in the world. As do I – not a dad, I mean I've got a dad. But the man who would be a dad to Tomos, my litle boy – that's what I need. I really, really need that.

And where are you? Where are you? That's what I said to myself, over and over again, looking out of Mr Humphreys' kitchen window. And I have no fuckin idea who I was talking to. Sometimes I feel like only Tomos is real to me.

Now there are wind farms – the thin white columns and the thin white blades. Seems to be a lot more of them than there was when I was last here. Mynydd Bach, the Little Mountain, altho to Tom it's fuckin huge. Cairns up there. Standing stones. Lakes – Llyn Eidowen and Ffynnon Drewi. I know this area, aye. It should feel like home, if anywhere should; I mean I went to school here. Formative years. But it's just a place, a handful of scattered houses in the hills, a chapel. Dull as fuck to a restless child. I remember being bored shitless up here, I do, but then I probably would've been bored anywhere. I *am* bored anywhere. Anywhere can bore the soul out of you, the same as anywhere can be exciting – it all depends on what you're carrying around inside. But if what you're carrying is fuckin Johnny and Carlos and the knowledge that you'll soon be thrown out of your house and, around it all, a giant big black fuckin hole, if that's the kind of stuff you're hauling around with you wherever you go

then

oh fuck it. I *know* what I need. It's Saturday; Tregaron will be heaving tonight. A burning in my skin and a weight on me and bodies to discover, scratch – like stepping off a plane in a country you've never visited before. Fill me.

—Yes!

I turn to Tomos. —What is it?

—Level 3!

—Good boy.

—Poo.

—What?

—I'm out.

—That was quick.

—It's hard. They go too fast.

I see the screen light up again. —Don't start another game, *cariad*. We're getting off at the next stop.

I gather up our stuff and take T's hand and lead him down the bus. I glance at the man in the overalls, see his phone tiny in his hands, get a faint whiff of the fields coming off him but he doesn't look up. Not even when I stand there at the side of the road as the bus pulls away. He's absorbed in his phone. I'll never, ever know.

It's hot. There are birds singing and I hear some sheep in the field behind me and somewhere down the valley I hear a power tool, a chainsaw or something. The sky is light blue and there are no clouds. I wait for something to come to me, some feeling, a sense of homecoming or something, even just some kind of remembrance, but nothing does.

—Why are we standing here? T asks, squinting up at me. I just give him a smile and we walk along the road, holding hands, over the little bridge, past the chapel. My mam is waiting for us there and her face lights up and Tomos runs to her and she opens the gate and squats down to give him a great big *cwtch*. Squats down, at her age; she's more bloody nimble than I am, aye.

—Oh *bachgern*. How happy I am to see you, she says.

We do the hugging and greeting thing and go into the kitchen. It's cool and shady and full of the smells of baking and Waldo the dog gets up all slow and waggy from his bed. I bend to pat his head.

—Careful with him, love. Had an operation on his hip last week, he did.

—What for? Is he alright?

—Something to do with his arthritis. Don't know what they did to it but it seems to have made him a bit happier. Back on his food now. Just getting old, he is, that's all.

I pat him again. —Where's Dad?

—Down in the garden. I'll shout him.

She goes to the kitchen door and screeches 'HYWEL!' so loud that it makes Waldo jump. I fuss him behind one ear and Tom fusses him behind the other and then he's had enough and he waddles back into his bed in the corner by the Aga.

Waldo the waddler. The waddling dog. I remember when he was a pup and he would bounce everywhere.

—You hungry? I've got some scones fresh out the oven.

—Na. Could go a *paned*, tho.

She puts the kettle on. Truth is that what I could really do with is not a cup of tea but a shower and a spruce and a taxi into Tregaron, all in the next five minutes. But she's my mam.

She sits at the table and starts drawing things with Tomos in a sketchbook and I go upstairs to the spare room and put the clothes I'll wear later on the bed to air, the vest top and the skirt. Want to get them on now, I do. Want to feel them all tight on my shapes. I go back downstairs and my dad's there and so there are more hugs and stuff and T wants to watch Tracy Beaker so my mam gets him settled in the front room with the telly on and then me and her and me dad sit at the table with our tea. I'm itching to get out and fuckin *do* something. Have something done to me. Feel something.

—So, my dad says. He laces his fingers together on the tabletop. They look old and bent and knobbly. —What's going on, *cariad*?

—With what, Dad?

—Your mother was speaking with Mrs Harrison the other day in the post office. Said that you're something of a name online now, according to her daughter.

—Oh, that. I sip me tea and it tastes of dust. —It's nothing. I wrote a blog and it—

—What's a blog?

—It's like a kind of online diary, Mam. And it—

—Is it private?

—Well no. It's online, so no. It's a public forum.

—So anyone can read it?

—Suppose so, aye. And comment on it like.

She looks at my dad then back to me. —What's the point of a diary if anyone can read it? People you don't even know, *DuwDuw*.

—Well, you don't write anything dead secret in it or anything like that. Or at least *I* don't. It's just a, a log of your life, kind of thing. What you've been up to. Just like, this is what I've been doing kind of stuff.

—And everybody has one of these, do they?

—Not everyone, no. But a lot of people do. And they tweet, as well.

—Tweet? My dad makes an exasperated noise. —I don't even want to know what that is. What's all this about a vision?

—A vision?

—This is what Mrs Harrison said. That you told everyone on your, your *blog*, that you saw something and it's caused this big palaver online. Everyone's going on about it, she said.

I drink me tea. Could do with a smoke to go with it. —It's nothing, really. A load of fuss about nothing. Sometimes this happens, y'know, you say one thing and it gets taken out of all proportion. What happened was—

—Have you been seeing things?

—I'm about to tell you, Mam. I was on top of a mountain and—

—Which one?

—Does it matter? Pendam.

Me dad nods.

—And it was in the morning and there'd been a party and I'd been up all night so I was dead tired. And, I don't know, I climbed onto a ridge and I saw this thing and I thought it was something it wasn't and that's it. I wrote about it online and it's took off, for some reason. Not much more to it.

It feels strange, saying these words to my folks. Like I'm talking about somebody else, or making up a story. Telling lies.

—I don't understand. What did you see?

—It was just like a, a shape in the sky. Looked a bit like a woman. But it was just a shadow in the clouds or something, that's all. Nothing to it, really. It's been blown up out of all proportion.

—So you *have* been seeing things.

—No, Mam. I'm not hallucinating. That's what you're worried about, isn't it?

157

—Weren't there some words? my dad says. —Mrs Harrison said there was something about some words.

—Now she's been *hearing* things too.

My mam looks at my dad with her eyes all huge. Like Tomos does when he sees a tall building.

I *thought* I heard some words, aye. But there was a feller messing around with an iPod and—

—A what?

—It's like a personal stereo. And I'd had no sleep and I was sort of dreaming but still awake. Like what happens when you're dead tired? It's nothing to worry about. That's what it's like, these days; online is like another world. Things take on a life of their own. To be honest with you I've lost interest in it all and I haven't even gone online recently. So I don't know what's being said now. Nothing happened. It's like when people see UFOs but it's just a bird or a plane. I shouldn't've said anything. It's a big fuss about nothing.

Me mam turns her big eyes on me. —Are you still taking the pills, *cariad*?

—Aw Mam. You don't have to worry about anything on that score. I'm okay, now.

Except someone came along when I was asleep and shoved a Hoover up me fanny and sucked out everything inside me. That's what I feel like. This fucking nothingness.

Christ almighty this *itch*. I am one gigantic itch. I need to get out.

—We think you should move back in, my mam says, kind of blurts, like, and immediately looks all guilty across the table at my dad who shakes his head at her then turns to me.

—We've been talking, Em. Your mam and I. We think it might be best for the two of you if you move back in with us for a little while.

—Really? And why's that, then, Dad?

—Just have a rest. Take some time off. Recuperate.

—From what?

He goes all serious. —*You* tell *us* from what, love.

I almost laugh. —Dad. There's nothing to worry about, honest. Tomos is doing great at the school.

Another blurt from my mam. —The boy needs a father, Emma.

My dad gives a big sigh.

—Mam, I say. —D'you think I don't know that? But unfortunately there's no good dad shop I can go to and pick one off the shelf, is there?

—What would be the harm?

—Of what, Dad?

—Moving back in here for a bit. Just for a bit.

—I have me own life, Dad. And I don't think it'd be good for T. What about the school?

—Summer holidays, is it not? You'd be back in Aber before term starts.

I shake me head. —There's not much for him to do out here. Least in Aber he's got his friends. And the beach n stuff. Imagine it? We'd drive each other up the wall after a few days. You know we would.

Me dad gives a little smile. Mam doesn't, tho.

—And anyway, that's where I'm going tonight. To meet a feller, I say.

—Here in Trefenter?

—No, Mam, in Tregaron. Met him online.

—So you haven't actually *met* him yet? Not even seen him?

—No. We've been talking online, like. Seems nice. From Cardiff he is.

I'm surprised at how easily these fibs are coming to me. As if I've rehearsed all this.

—So he could be an axe murderer or anything.

—Why would he want to kill axes? She doesn't smile.
—Don't worry, I'm meeting him in the Talbot. He's got two kids. It'll be fine.

—How do you know?

—I don't, do I? Not a hundred per cent, like. But at the first sign of anything dodgy I'll get a taxi straight back. It's nothing out of the ordinary these days, Mam, to meet people online. It's called Match dot com, the one I joined, but there's loads of them around. Dating websites. Everyone does it these days. Sure, where am I gonna meet a nice bloke in Aberystwyth? I've—

I snap me gob shut. Was about to say that I've already shagged anyone half decent in the town and many who were not decent in the slightest and Christ wouldn't *that* have been a bad thing to say. Got to watch meself. Control. Fibs take on a wild life, of their own. This is your mam and dad you're talking to here, woman. Don't forget that. Or yourself.

—You worry me so, my mam says, but I just turn to me dad.

—Has Tracey Tacsi still got her car?

He nods. —I'll give her a ring.

—Ta. Half an hour, tell her.

—Into Tregaron?

—The Talbot, aye.

He reaches over and gives my mam's hand a squeeze and I do the same and then I go upstairs and jump in the shower and wash everything. I take the loofah to me legs and belly and back and tits but the itching will not be scrubbed away. I put the smellies on and paint me toenails and then in me bra and knickers hang out the back window and smoke a fag. The hill rises up behind the house, up towards the lakes, and the sky is starting to go a bit pink as the sun sinks. One last chance, then. You've got one last chance to stop it happening. If you value me. If I mean anything to you. By the time I've smoked this cigarette.

Only the trees in silhouette. Night-time soon. So black out here, away from light pollution as it is. I let the filter fall. I put me clothes on and look at meself in the mirror. *I'd* fuck me. There's a double beep from outside so I put me coat and boots on and leg it downstairs. Great big hugs all round and a pat on the head for waddling Waldo and oh this fucking itch. Whatever's going off in the virtual world can stay there cos I am not interested. This is me. This is me. Burning fucking itch. There was no floating woman and there were no words. Coincidences have no deeper meaning. The itch is not in my cunt it's somewhere inside, above the womb, and at the back of my brain. Coming apart again.

Dig and bridge and wild. One of those words, I'll *make* it mean something, I will. Watch me.

# HOLY SHOW

HOLY SHOW

MADE BEAUTIFUL, THIS morning, by the hills remaking themselves within the gauzy mist. The land itself reaching towards self-awareness and flicking out from itself the flecks of life that sing and that fly. Even the men, here, loosely circled on gravelly edgeland to the east of Carmarthen town, even they, in their focus and containment, tall shapes in the mist, have something about them of the tree and the monolith, supported by nothing but shared purpose. That there are forces abroad and at work that can with a pen make wobbly and unsure the common sap and muscle in this scene seems, at this moment, entirely laughable.

Two of the men are without shirts and they are the circle's bullseye. Eye to eye they are. The smaller man has a galaxy of pimples across his back between the prominent scapulae and the other has a red dragon rampant inked into his neck, the looped and pointed tail of it crawling into the armpit clotted with sweat-clumped hair. Were they hawks, these men, they would be in yarak – the lines of their world drawn spider-leg fine. And on the signpost for the town, just over the low hill to the left, beneath where it declares Carmarthen to be 'WALES'S OLDEST TOWN', someone has painted, in white, the words 'AND SHITTEST'.

—Clean, says a short man in a bowler hat and white shirt and braces. He circles too. Circles within circles is how these men operate. —Just keep it clean, boys. No biting. Ye gunner shake?

Both men shake their heads.

—Oh yes ye are. And I don't mean yer fuckin heads.

Fists are begrudgingly bumped.

—Right so. Remember what ye are. Remember *who* ye are. Set to.

The movement is instant; the hatted man scurries away in reverse and the fighters roll their fists at chest height and circle and the larger circle around them moves also, a carousel and there are noises now, the scrape of boots on dusty gravel and voices:

—Up, Cow, sor. Block him. *Block* him.

—Easy, Quinny boy.

—Remember yer father, Quinn. He's with ye now.

—Yon's glass-jawed, Cowley. That ye know.

—Fuck ye, Aney Lavin, and double fuck that cunt of a Welshman ye've trained ferra dog.

—Civil tongues now! yells the bowler-hatted man and with that is flung the first fist, scooping air as the targeted jaw is turned away and exposing for a blip the left eye that fist had been shielding. And so it works in nano-seconds; in that blip that eye is shut by bunched knuckles.

—Follow on now Cowley!

—Ye've got him! He's fuckin yours now son!

Gigantic arm movements follow the reel and stagger. Grunts and thuds in the thinning mist, sound waves that split that mist into scraps that drift away. A splat when the bad eye is hit again and bursts at the brow. And the slam as a back impacts with the planet.

Faces leer and drool. Phone-faced figures lean in at the waist, and that's the fight done – some quick movements and some blood. Before he is dragged off, the man with the dragon tattoo gets in three stamps on the fallen face, seeing in it as he does the remembered overbite of a certain Reverend Williams, a man of slimy threats and promises; stamp one breaks that overbite, stamp two hits only earth, and the third makes the nose flat and a colour known intimately to nature. There are protestations and then the dragon-man is dragged away and sat on a tree stump and a lit cigarette is slipped in his lips. The loser is put floppy and unresponsive into the back of a van where some crude doctoring will take place.

—Knew this was a banker Cowley but I didn't expect *that*, sure. A man squats and grins. —Fuck me, sor, what was that, two minutes, less? Bang. Fuck me.

Cowley, barely out of breath but a bit adrenalin-trembly, applies his tongue to his bruised knuckles.

—I'll take the money now, Aney. Soon as yew like, mun.

—Aye, aye. Just give yer man time to collect it up, now.

Aney crumples into a cross-legged position on the scuffed ground. Signs of war in this bare earth; the stamped-flat discs of beer cans, the black pancakes of old fires. Buried bones beneath. Behind Aney is much human movement; some pushing and some shoving, arguing, the accompaniments to the collection of money. But here is a still centre – Cowley licking his knuckles on the tree stump, a join-the-dots puzzle of blood on one of his white pectorals. Aney importunate at his feet.

—Got some notes coming your way, chavvy.

—A know that.

—Sure there could be a lot more, too.

—Not at the moment, Aney. Gunner do some spending I yam.

—Aye, course, but listen. What you've just earned now, you can make ten times it in one go. Ten times, sor. At *least* ten times.

Cowley blows smoke out the side of his mouth and of course it looks, for a moment and if you fancy, as if the dragon on his neck has come alive and is doing what it's supposed to do.

—Gunner ask me how?

—If yew like. Go on then. Tell me how.

—It's a secret thing.

—Oh for fuck's sakes Aney.

—Kind of thing doesn't happen too many times. Twice a year, if that. Never that many takers so there's always a call for them that will.

Cowley grinds his cigarette out under his heel.

—Tell me, Aney.

—Location's always top fuckin secret till just before it goes off. Needs to be, see.

—A'm running out of patience now, butt.

Aney leans in. The grin has gone from him but it's left traces in his face, in the lines at his eyes, like the echoes of old earthworks in the hills roundabout; the henge-scars on the land.

—Death-fights, Cow.

—Death-fights?

—Aye, yeh. Topping-fights, sor. Fights to the death. Simple as that, chav; you kill some cunt.

—Fuck off, Aney.

—Swear down, sor. Not one word of a lie and that's all there is to it. Anything goes. I mean no weapons like, but ye know. This one time, didn't a throat get bitten out? Saw it for meself. Like a fuckin dog fight. Up by Bethesda, this was.

The day will be warm again; the sun is rising high and fast. There is a widespread sense of dust.

—Money enough for life, Cow. No lie. One fuckin fight, sor, an ye can fuckin retire. This is the truth. The stakes! Oh you wouldn't believe. Knew this one feller, from Offaly, he was.

—And he won, did he?

—Well no, he lost, and they had to sink him in a lake. But he staked up everything he had, is what I'm saying, everything he owned; carra, acres of farmland. That's sometimes how it works. You get the purse, the fuckin huge purse, and on top you get everything else. Set up for life, sor. No worries ever again.

Over Aney's shoulder is a noisy dispersal; vehicles moving away, a dust devil pursuing each one. Victoriously smiling men are approaching, one waving a fan of banknotes above his head.

—So?

—So what, Aney?

—So what d'ye say?

—A'll think about it.

—That means fuck all, sor. Need to know now. Get the ball rolling likes.

—It means A'll have a fuckin think about it is what it means.

Cowley reaches for his shirt. He puts it on and Aney watches him do so. Watches him pat the breast pocket to check that the little machine is still safely in there.

—But I've got to let the fellers know soon as. The big fellers, so's they can start setting it up like. They've already got their man lined up, see.

—Not my problem, boy, is it? Cowley stands up. Hitches his jeans up over his hips. —A've got fuckin money to spend. That's *my* fuckin priority.

The only target for Cowley's eyes is the man approaching with his money. In this natural bowl, in a hanging whiff of exhaust, metallic and heavy and soon to disperse, even without a wind to waft it. Shadows shorten as the sun climbs the sky.

HILL TOWNS DO their thing and in high summer they do it raw; their bamboozled inhabitants sit on the sweaty stone balustrades of river bridges in the hope of receiving a lifted cool from the water below, even crawling as it now is, the eddies smudged under gnats and syrupy in their coilings like semen. And around this particular town burps the bog, fetid in its soupy sumps and abuzz with insects and the regular plips and hiccups of bursting bubbles. It gives off salt and steady throbs of sweetish stinks. And all around its rancid reservoirs the sundews reach for the midge, their little deadly pearls of such ugly honey. Dragonflies, joined tail to tail, create lovehearts on the canary grass. The heather, the moor grass, deep purple and maroon – shades familiar to the spirits of sex and death. Polecats skulk for the moist caves beneath the boardwalk, there to curl and gasp. Old energies heave in the peat.

The small town exists in this desiccated haze; it lives in a dome of scorched and seething need. Inside the Talbot pub, a hen night is happening; pink fairy wings and a lot of thigh and belly. The lone woman at the bar leans into one of the hens as she's up ordering another round of Cheeky Vimtos.

—What's going on here, then? Don't get many hen dos in Tregaron. Don't get *any*.

—It's the bride. Her man's from yur. Leanna her name is. Might as well have-a do up yur as in Treorci aye?

This woman looks at the other woman's face. The tips of her gauze wings bob in pink on either side of her neck.

—You local then?

—Not far. Aberystwyth. Born here tho.

—There's nice. And look at yew all tarted up. Look lush yew do. Meeting someone, is it?

—Just having a drink. Dunno yet.

—Yew don't know?

—See what happens.

—Aye. Best way. Something nice might *ah*-pen if yew don't go looking for it.

The barman reaches over the pump handles to place glasses on the bar, each one filled with a deep purple goo.

—Where's-a tiny brollies, then? Cocktails, these are. Av a bit-a class, mun, ey?

He drops little paper parasols into the drinks.

—An-a sparklers. An some-a them cherry things. C'mon, mun, *siap alan*, hen night this is.

The barman shakes his head. —Twenty-one pound.

—Twenty-one pound! Bleedin half that in Treorci. Must be loaded up yur, yew.

The money is handed over. The woman sips at a drink. —Lush.

She takes her change. The barman asks her if she needs a tray.

—No ta, love, I've got enough to carry as it is. She winks at the other woman then turns back to the barman. —Aye, go on, I'll av a tray.

A shout: —Lisa! Urry up! Gaggin over yur we are!

—Giz a minute yew impatient cow! Going as fast's I can!

The drinks are placed on the tray. Scoops of deep space, and in each one a captured comet; trails shoot and quickly fade in the liquid thickness as they go from bartop, up briefly into the air, and onto the tray. The glasses touch, kind of shuffle closer together as if affrighted as the tray is raised aloft.

—Hope something nice happens to yew, love. Av a good one.

—You n all.

The hen stilts away with the drinks into whooping. The woman on the stool touches with the tip of her finger the tattooed stars behind her ear as if to check that they're still there. The barman looks at her and shakes his beardy head.

—You're gonner be busy tonight, the woman says.

—Aye well. He shakes his head again. —Could do with the custom to be honest, Em. Another one is it?

Em looks at her glass, the centimetre of vodka left in it. —Same again.

The fan on the shelf behind the bar turns her way then turns away again as if in disinterest but in that few seconds of regard is an instant of relief before the clamminess creeps in again.

—Been a bloody hot one this year. The barman gives Emma her drink. All cold, all the bergy beads running down. —*Poeth poeth*. Fire on the bog last week there was.

—A fire on the *bog*?

—Aye, yeh. Can't remember that ever happening. Should've seen the birds. How's your mam n dad?

—Good.

—This just a quick visit is it?

—Tomos likes his *nain* and *taid*.

—Always talking about him, they are, when they come in. Dote on him they do.

There would be more talk of children and such but the barman is called through to the other bar and Emma is left alone to look around the pub known to her. Unchanged since her first. Them gone years. The small town around, baked and isolate, the scattered amassings of people on this Saturday night crowding the beer gardens. Cars coming in from the hill farms. Cold drinks and companionship and manners of basking. Inside the pub Emma scans for eyes that might be regarding her because usually there are eyes that regard her and because there is a furnace in a void like the sun itself and she sees these eyes, in the eating area through the arched gap in the dividing wall; eyes in a male face. So starts the throb. Put wattage in the smile. The man smiles back then is distracted as the woman he's with draws his attention to the menu and his childen suck at straws and swing their small feet in their small shoes a foot above the floor.

If Emma reaches up and back to adjust her scrunchie, her vest top will be tugged taut across her torso, the ribcage and the tits. So draw back that gaze and pin it. Only here does a woman glow. Her skin. Her skin. And if she *sliiides* off the stool then her denim skirt will be pulled above her hold-ups and that skin will be shown for a second and then she can stand and kind of shimmy as she smooths the skirt back down over her thighs. Into the heart now, the blood that bumps and is bumped. Only in here does a woman glow. The route to the toilet – that gaze will be on her the entire way. Skewer the eyeballs. The hens have put One Direction on the fucking jukebox.

Corked-wine sour but cool in the toilet. Some liquid somewhere going plink ... plink. Two hens touching up their slap in the mirrors.

—Yew avin a piss?

—Yeh, Emma says, although she wasn't planning to. All she wanted to do was move in her muscles.

—Yur's no bog roll. One of the women delves into her handbag and brings out a napkin. —Swhy I always come prepared. She looks Emma up and down then goes back into her bag. —I'd better give yew two in case you've got a big *fah*-nee.

Emma thanks her and takes the napkins into a cubicle. She hears the women leave. There is gurgling in the cistern above her head. The coolness in here at a clash with the enkindling that has begun in many parts of what she is. All is wet and cool, trickling water, but the hot hills outside and the small dust devils on the crisped ridges, well, Emma is their avatar, she is all summer distilled. So far removed from both mirage and blood – lost, lost once more. And how to relocate but burst into bits – there is nothing known but that. Once there was something else but the sun has scorched that away, here in the cool toilet, quiet around cacophony. Dig and bridge and wild. Only one of those words rings off the dripping tiles. And *bridge* is not a noun. It is an instruction.

Cross it, then. Feet-first. Fanny-first. Plunge.

She flushes, leaves the cubicle and studies herself in the mirror above the sink, applies some tap water to her eyebrows and to a small curl of hair that has frizzed out over her ear like some kind of stinger. Outside the toilet the man, the gazer, is standing awkward with his hands clenching and unclenching at his hips. He's shorter than he seemed when sitting but his eyes appear no less intense even if they seem incapable of settling for long on Emma's face.

—You with the hens then? he says, kind of blurts.

Emma shakes her head. —Na. I'm just out for a drink on my own.

—I'm, erm, I'm with the cocks. He winces at his own words.

—Nah, listen, there's no need for any of that. Just don't bother with it. Can you get away from your family?

—I'm not with my family.

—The woman and the two kids.

—Sister and nephews.

—Aye right. What've I just said? There's no need for any of that bollox.

His eyes meet hers now and Emma can see that there's not a lot of light in them. Not that she cares particularly, but the urge to get this done with as soon as possible becomes stronger. And his eyes aren't looking at each other – there's that, at least.

—Where can we go?

—I'm not married.

Emma shakes her head, hard. —Don't *bother*, alright? Where can we go?

—I have a van outside.

—What kind of van?

—Well it's a Land Rover. Blue one.

—And where's it parked?

—Under the tree on the other side.

—What's the registration?

—Starts with a J and a L. Don't remember the rest. Got a 3 in it.

—That'll do. Meet me there.

The eyes all askitter. But there are two of them, and there's a nose, and the teeth aren't too green or gapped. There'll be sparks that spit.

—Make some excuse to the woman you're with, aye? Tell her you've forgotten your wallet or something. And you've got to nip home. Make something up, aye? And I'll meet you by the van.

—It's a Land Rover.

—The Land Rover, then. Alright? Be quick.

He moves like a robot; his hand comes up and closes around her elbow. Emma bites back the laughter that wants to erupt and pulls her arm away.

—No. Not here. Outside in the car park. Be quick, now.

She thinks about grabbing his crotch but dismisses that idea and takes all the pieces of her out into the car park where ripples of heat do soft shudders and where the vehicles that have been parked there the longest will, when driven away, leave four indentations in the blacktop. Her nostrils flare at a faint whiff of burning and her lower lip sags a little in the jackboot stamp of heat on her skull, and she stands like that, a cat in flamen, scanning the cars, the entire sky weighty on her. Behind the tint of singe is the gamey taint of the outlying bog. Even the earthworms are panting in the soil.

And once, and recently, it was: married man: police line: DO NOT CROSS. But look – that's all gone.

The Land Rover is caked in mud up the sills and the doors, even up onto some of the side windows; a lucky screening in that. On the dashboard are some of those nodding toy animals that sit on suckers like gastropods and have heads on small springs. They'll be nodding away like mad bastards soon, they will. Dive. Dig. She finds a cleanish patch at the front of the vehicle between the grille and the headlamp and the mass of the planet accelerates into her and pushes her hip into that space to lean, and to itch, and to wait.

LIKE ONE FOOT is in light and the other in shadow. Sun and shade. Time enough, space enough. There's always been enough of each in which to fuck everything up.

He's awake because he's thinking, even now, the brain basted in putrid broth. Bashed and battered yet behind the lids it spins and will not stint and he wills it all to stop. Better if he opens his eyes; because then the visual stimulus. Help him shut it down. He sees his naked torso, supine, the date inked into the skin of his chest; last night she asked him if it was the birthdate of a child and he is not a dad but that's no indication of how he responded. He is not a father but that's no indication. And she asked him what the scars were on his legs, the puckered craters, and he cannot remember if he told her the truth – that they are what abscesses leave behind once healed. And anyway what truth. Another murdered thing.

Other senses, now; sleep's milky whiff and the cloy of sweated drink. A soft snoring. Behind drawn curtains is a pinky-grey light that suggests early morning to him. Pictures on the walls. A dressing table. Clothes all over the place and a wardrobe with a mirror at the end of the bed that gives him back the shock of his own face and a messy head on the pillow next to his, blondeish, the face all hidden. That's all there is to be seen, just the tatty hair entirely one mask. Or, no, a bit of ear, when he turns his head to look; a white lobe with a blue stud in it. His first shag in ages. That tiny turning of the head really fucking hurt.

God, God. Half in, half out of the world. The blue fur that sprouts from rotting food, that's what he'd see if he looked in the mirror and opened his mouth. He gathers his will in a monumental steeling and in one movement he sits and swings his legs out onto the floor. The woman grumbles a little. He looks down at himself and sees a ring of calamari around the base of his dick. What? He plucks at it with a thumbnail, pulls it out and lets it twang back against the skin. It's the ring of rubber from a condom. He clearly remembers going in bareback. Now he wants to weep for them both, for himself and her, and for the terrible paleness of his own long toes. He removes the ring of rubber and flicks it onto the carpet. Here we fucking go again. Only this can be honed so sharp. Only this can burn so bright. Can float and glow like it does.

But there was only the drink, wasn't there? No rock, no powder. Only the drink and the things it brings. Stand up now.

He imagines opening the curtains onto the blasted red dunes of Mars but when he does all he sees is the backlands of Borth; the wide splat of the bog with its ring of distant hills. A faint taxi-memory returns. It is green out there and bright with a blue rumour anterior to the hills, a gauze of which they solidly shimmer within. There are cropping horses on the bog with their beautiful heads bowed at grass. A dark church on a plinthy rock. A bilious surge threatens to erupt but he swallows it back and slams a sphincter shut on it like the cap on an oilwell. A geyser of puke. Don't think. Get dressed.

It will be warm out there. The windowpane was toast against his face. What it should be, for his mood and the matter inside him, it should be a dank winter dawn, dreary and all a-drizzle; or it should be a starless dark. It should be of a piece with his jeans, the clam of them when he puts them on; did he piss himself? There's no urinous lift when he drags them over his cratered calves, but there is the vinegar of long-spilled drink. His legs feel horrible inside the denim, like sea-squirts that wish they were something else. His movements set off an internal commotion, liquidy grumbles inside, and a full sentence of farts is unleashed; a verb and a noun and a splattery cadence and he clenches his arse against a follow-through. The noise stirs the woman on the bed and his name emerges from that briar of hair:

—Adam?

—It's alright. I'm going to get some tea for us. Go back to sleep.

—What's that horrible smell?

—Must be the bog. I'll be back soon with some tea.

He stands, the moist jeans low on his hips, watching the woman, waiting for the shape of her body beneath the duvet to lift and recede again in sleep's breathing. When it does, and when small whiffles and sucks are sounding from beneath the hair, he quietly finishes dressing and looks around for the handbag, or the purse, and sees it on the floor at the side of the bed. On the side he slept on. He squats and unclasps the catch as softly as he can.

Money, first; a few notes and some change. He pockets the lot. A few keys on a fob, a wooden wide-eyed owl with I NEED A HUG on it. Tissue-balls, cosmetics. No phone. A photograph of two children; smiles and party hats. A boy and a girl, the girl in a pretty pink dress, the boy in a yellow t-shirt with a dinosaur on it. Caught in mid-laugh, they are; maybe the photographer made a joke. Or maybe there'd been some joyous surprise. Adam studies the picture for quite some time then returns it to the purse and returns the purse to the floor. Stands and leaves the room.

He is in a hallway, on the ground floor. Evidently a shared house; by the front door is a low table with a mess of letters on it, many different names on the envelopes. Amazing this, really, to blackout so soon into the binge; he cannot remember what he drank or who he drank it with or even for how long but the quantities of all must've been sizeable. That, and the old junk-damage, the general ruin; easy it is to tap back into the empty wells. There is little of the woman in the crawl of his recall; a neck-bruise, a garbled story of a fight with a boyfriend. Nothing of a meeting, or much conversational stuff, or emotional click, not even a flash of sex, if anything resemblng that had taken place although it must've because of the ring of rubber. Addicted from an early age, only hostages have ever been taken. And true there had been no rocks or powders but derangement brings about a levelling. All that is not 'I' is made same in that state and in a world never to be tamed or understood or managed in any degree but that which can, at the same time, be tucked into a pocket or concealed in a sock.

He shuffles through the letters, holds a few up to the light, but they all look like either bills or promises of easy credit, all the same thing, nothing that looks like, say, a birthday card. No treasure, no booty. He takes the cloud of himself outside into a cloudless day, already sowing heat. Over the sloping concrete sea defences, on the other side of the road, will be the sea, but there is nothing in there for him. Just wet and smelly it is. He takes his phone out of his jacket pocket but it is lifeless; battery dead, then. This is how it starts, the falling apart – with forgetting to charge your phone. Something so small. A necrotising microbe, and only when the meat starts to shear off the bones do you realise what's happening.

The sky above the sea remains flat and blue so he turns away from it and turns left, towards the train station. Here, low above the bog and borne from its weathers, some small clouds hang, buds of fluff that offer no faces or figures, no matter that he studies until the dry sting of his eyes forces him to blink and look away and cool his face in a cupped palm. No shining light, nothing hominid, neither a voice; not even a mutter of zephyr through the couch-grass, so breathless is the morning. Some birds, that's all. Maybe if he had've stolen that photograph. That of the happy children. Ripped it up and put the torn pieces back in the bag. Wiped his arse with it. Burned it. Drawn hideous—

His headshake is vigorous. He tightens the focus of himself around the needing core that he both orbits and emanates and takes his body onto the station platform. It is empty; only he stands on it, in his stinks. This morning should be dank. The sky should be full of angered shadows and spitting rain, but the summer shows no intention of decelerating its intensity and the planet and everything on it is pinned in seared space.

Jetsam:

A vegetable furl of sea lettuce and dulse and bladderwrack's grey grapes and a traffic cone and a plastic crate marked SALMON and a corpse. Some starfish going mushy, quick-rotting in the heat, the orange ocarina of an empty spider-crab carapace and this corpse. Here between the sea and the dunes in which once a little boy was made and next to the giant yam of a log is this body. Crabs at it, picking on the blood-pudding fingers and the black face. Sand-fleas flicking around this dead human shell. Gulls descend, the light from the sun in their reptile eyes, land and tuck and begin to bow and stab. They raise their curved beaks as they gulp. When the child scampers out of the dunes and disturbs them they rise and cry, those cries the keenings of shame for what they've just done, the big and bloodless wounds they've inflicted. For a moment a small shadow is cast over the carcass, laterally across the midriff bulbous and gravid with gases. Crabs raise their claws in defence.

—Mam! MAM!
—What, *cariad*? What is it?
Sounds of puking.
—Oh God! What is it? What's wrong?
—It's a man! It's a man! Stinks!
More retching. The crabs fold themselves down and resume their picking, or most of them do – a few scuttle off the body and scurry towards the vomit – their claws at delicate work, a harvesting of exquisite dimensions. The plates of their mouths plap moustachioed across each other, minuscule chunnering below the stalk-eyes.
—Come here. Stay with me. Come away. I'll call the police. The woman's voice getting fainter. —Police please … Ynyslas sands. There's a, there's a body …

Further words lost in the squabbling skrikes of the re-descending gulls. One, big and black-backed, rips a shred of scalp away, a frill of white hair attached and for an instant this bird gives itself a wispy goatee beard.

IT FEELS TO Cowley as if, at the peak of every thrust, his bell-end bangs against a half-digested Chicken McNugget; there's something gristly up there. He can feel it. He's aware of the urban legends about the sweetcorn kernel but he imagines something much worse when he withdraws. A chicken-skin hood: an onion ring: Jesus fuckin Christ, the horrible extrusion of a limp French fry like some kind of parasitic worm.

And plus there's Bernie's toothy leer opposite, at the other end of Jac the Bird's back. Biting his lower lip with them grey fangs, his hands buried in Jac's shoulders and oh Christ is he holding a fag in one of them? Cowley closes his eyes. Hears Jack the Boy somewhere behind him blosh over his own hand with a *heurgh* and then, after a bit of panting, the whining begins:

—That's enough now, boys *bach* ... let's leave it there now eh ...

Jac the Bird tilts her head back, away from Bernie's crotch, and words leave her in a screech:

—Shut the fuck up Jackie! Don't listen to him boys! Carry on! Give it—

Other words plugged as Bernie thrusts again. Cowley opens his eyes. Hears his own grunty breath. And there's also the telly on, what is it, must be *Stars in Their Eyes* or something because is that Harry Hill dressed as Morrissey? Singing 'Every Day is Like Sunday'. The air in the room thickened with salty smells and kind of gloopy as if they're all caught in a long-neglected goldfish bowl. Bernie goes a-*huh*, a-*huh*, and Jack the Boy starts to sob somewhere in the gloom. Here we go again; returned. The vile mud into which you hammer, way up inside, the grease and bits of gristle. Cowley closes his eyes. Just think of the friction. His hips slam forwards three times, bringing a loud *HO!* from Jac the Bird and Cowley catapults some slippery bit of himself up inside her and he pulls out and settles panting back on the heels of his trainers and he will not look down at himself but there is a lifting whiff. He doesn't look, he can't look, but he can feel Bernie's grin and thumbs-up at the other end of Jac's jerking back. Jack the Boy's voice comes out of the haze:

—Why do I do it ... I can't help meself ... why do I do this ...

Another a-*huh* from Bernie again. Welsh hillbilly Elvis. For an instant, in Cowley, it is all okay, it has worked – there is a level smoothness, a landscape for the birth of him and the death of him and the inevitability of both, released from any needs, from those that shriek most of all. This is detectable in the electric snowflakes that can be seen blizzarding on the insides of his eyelids but then he opens his eyes once more and he sees, on the screen, a figure appearing from light, obviously a man dressed as a woman because the shape is all kinds of wrong, a special sort of inaccurate, but there it is, the surrounding glow – a taunt and a haunt, both. *Tonight, Matthew, I'm going to be* ... gone away. Offski. Out of this fuckin place.

Cowley wipes his dick on the sheet and gets off the bed and pulls his jeans up. Jack the Boy is slumped forward in his seat, his face in his hands, muttering to himself. Bernie gives a holler, horrible to hear, and Cowley sees Jac the Bird rolling away and wiping her face with the back of her wrist. She finds half a spliff from somewhere and lights it. The satiated 8 of her Buddha-ing the bed. Whatever it is on the TV starts to sing 'Lady Marmalade'.

—A moment, Cow, says Jac the Bird.

—Na says Cowley and shakes his head, although whether her words were a request for him to stay a short while longer or just some kind of observation he does not know.

—This you off then, is it?

—Got something to do I have.

Jac the Bird blows out smoke. —See you next week then. Same time. And tidy, that was, by the way.

Bernie's hand rises from behind the bed, where he's collapsed, in a drained farewell. Cowley just leaves, without even checking his pockets for his things but he can feel the weight of them against him – the coins and the keys at his hips, the clunk of the song-machine against his left pectoral. Outside the house it is a humid night-time and the street lights' glow hangs syrupy-thick. Gulls call in the upper dark. Leaning against a van Cowley rolls a smoke, old bubble-neck again, what are the fucking odds. His thirst is massive. Distract: everything comes down to that. Maybe it always did. Even before.

This is the part of town, drenched in a molesting presence and arm-pitty in the heat, rows of close-packed terraces spoking around the church, that is big in Cowley's dreams, and he *does* dream, Cowley, badly at times, the size of him, the scars on him, brute back to boy sometimes just before dawn and all alone in bed whether *she* sleeps beside him or not. He has woken whimpering out of these streets down which he runs and the church which has loomed at him from fog. And the man in the cape like vampiric wings. The man with the everywhere-hands and the meaty bludgeon beneath his cape, the man gargantuan on the church roof. Always this dream; not every night but always to return. And too the hyperventilation condensing on the slick windows bordered by mildew, the bedroom high on the hill and forever kept damp by the shadows of Pen Dinas. Shame in that room, burning, and impotence. So deep that it has been known to bring vomit, in that deeper darkness just before dawn. In a silence torn by the yelps of vixens in the sharp tangle of the hillside's gorse.

At the doorway to the pub Cowley finishes his smoke and enters. Telly on in the corner above a small loud crowd at the horseshoe benches. Steve behind the bar.

—Brains Dark Cow?

Cowley nods.

—Can't, mun. It's off.

—Why bother fuckin asking me then? Feelin Foul.

Steve puts a glass beneath the Felinfoel pump. —Missed you the other night we did.

—Did yew?

—Them Lavins. It all kicked off just after you left.

Cowley gives a look around the small room. —I see no boards up, Steve.

—Na, well, it didn't go that far. But you were needed. Could've done with a bit of back-up like.

And there are some marks on Steve's face; a graze above the eye, a faint discoloration on a cheekbone. Nothing that cannot be forgotten about and dismissed with a snort.

—I was needed somewhere else. Cowley makes a big dent in the pint. Thinks of what he's just done, where he's not long had his dick and makes that dent bigger. —Another one, butt. This one's not touching the sides.

They're a loud bunch, beneath the TV. They'd fallen quiet when Cowley entered but now they're at it again, laughing loud and in that teeth-baring way of mockery. Four of them, one with hair the colour of copper. These four and Cowley and Steve in the small pub, nobody else. Ynyslas sands on the TV screen and a man looking serious at the camera:

—What's going on yur?

—Darts team from Llanbadarn. Night out. Well, *day* out. Been in here all afternoon, they have.

—Eh?

—Them four. Darts team from the Gog.

—Na, mun, on-a telly.

—Oh. Steve puts a full glass on the bar. —Body washed up at Borth. Some old feller. Reckon it's the same old boy that fell off Trefechan Bridge.

Cowley drinks. The word, or the sound of the word, out of the copper's gob – *sabotage* – flashes once in his mind, in pink bulbs. —Ey questioned me about that, ey did.

—Who did?

—Fuckin coppers did. Cos I worked on it for a bit, didn't I? Tightenin bolts n stuff. Cunts called me in for questionin.

—Why? What did it have to do with you?

—That's what *I* said. Tried to say I'd vandalised-a fuckin thing.

—Why would you do that?

—I said that as well. Arsked em what's a fuckin point. Told em it'd been put up fuckin shoddy in-a first place. Cunts.

That laughter again, a blurt of it. The red-headed one's voice has gotten louder and sloppier and he's leaning over the table in a gesture of quiet intimacy that is at odds with his volume:

—Fuckin insssssss*atiable*, boys. Four fuckin times, tellin yew. Fanny, gob, arse.

—That's only three.

—Did her arse twice.

And again the laughter. But somewhere in it now is sound audible only to Cowley, a sort of growl from somewhere. Probably his own lungs.

—If yew see her, dive in. She's taking on anyone. Drain yew dry she will.

—Can't go to Aberaeron, Rang. An I can't stand the shitty little place anyway.

—Aye but she lives here she does. Not even lying, she's fuckin on heat, that one. Probably even let *yew* have a go, Cordy.

Mirth again, aimed at the fat and ugly one of their group, acne a furious crust across his lower face.

—Course she would, this one says. —Few roofies in her WKD, *course* she'll let me have a go.

—Eyr alright, Cow, Steve says in Cowley's right ear. Cowley leaning now, his elbows back against the bar, his crotch and belly and face thrust out into the room. —Eyr just pissed. Been at it all afternoon.

—Bet she's a right fuckin munter. I've seen some of the dogs you've been up, Rang.

—Aye but she's not, that's the thing. She's dead fit. Honest. Got these stars behind her ear, tattooed in, like. Look out for em, Rang says, and touches himself in that place. —Can't miss her. Just follow the trail of fanny batter.

Steve picks up a remote and the news is replaced by football. —Swans, he says. —Friendly.

Cowley grunts. Ayew has a shot that knocks a pigeon off the Liberty Stand's roof.

—*And*. The red-headed one leaning forwards again to be heard by his mates as if the pub is full, or like intimacy is something he's yet to fully learn: – She's fuckin nuts. Woke me up, she did, talking in her sleep, like: *She's here!* That's what she said. Screamed it like. Rang's voice, in the two words, goes insectly shrill: – *She's here!* Fuckin freaked me out, it did. Kicked her out of the carra. Had to. Fuckin bunny-boiler, that one.

Cowley's lungs – they're at it again. There is a sign given off him in his stance or expression that Steve recognises: – Don't worry about em, Cow. Eyr okay boys. Just pissed.

But Cowley makes a noise, a kind of 'yamyamyam' sound. It is nonsensical, and loud, and it is designed to do one thing only. All four of them look over at that sound and Cowley leans at the waist towards them:

—What the fuck are *you* looking at?

Steve's hand on his shoulder. —*Peid, Cow, bois iawn. Bois siarad Cymraeg.*

Cowley looks at the fingers on his deltoid and then looks back at the four. —*Be'r* ffwc *wyt ti'n edrych ar? Be'r* ffwc?!

And that's the foreplay done with. The four are pushed back in their seats by the juggernaut rush of Cowley, the loom of his mayhem. A Magner's bottle goes up and then it comes down in a slam, that quick. Yells and shouts, the bottle does not break but causes a rapidly widening zip in the scalp beneath the coppery hair. Cowley hears nothing, for he has known greater flames. But for a swift detonation the glow in him becomes blaze.

There was no way to escape the blood and pain, that much was known to the four. As soon as the manslide came away from the bar … A roar leaves the TV as Llorente scores. Steve is pressing a bar towel to a skull. Words burble. The attacker has gone, out and abroad in the town, and everything that the four have done this day, up to this point, has gone with him; their confidence, the ways in which they carried themselves – replaced now by the shame of vanity. What *were* they thinking of.

Some words, now, with clarity, out of the choppy scene: – Is he dead? Fuck me, is he dead?

—Ambulance!

—Course he's not dead, Steve says, pressing the sopped towel. —But he's gonner need stitches. Get him up to Bronglais.

Rang utters words: —*Ow!* What did he do *that* for?

—Dunno who he was, Steve says. —Just some nutter came in off the street.

Cordy speaks into his phone. Blood flows. Steve winces; whoever the Swans are playing have just gone close. Clipped the bar from outside the area.

THE EMPTINESS OF the house is immediately obvious, but still she shouts, from just inside the door:

—Mam! Dad! Tomos!

She wonders why she did that: the house's hollowness was known to her even from the outside, and she wonders too why she stands and waits for a response because she knows one will not come.

She moves into the kitchen and drinks a glass of water – how cool it is, all pure – and even Waldo has gone; his empty bed by the stove with the blanket ruckled and his favourite toy, the red rabbit which once squeaked. There is a clicking from the boiler timer and that's the only sound. Not unfamiliar to her, this kitchen and the things in it, just somewhat vaguer, as if they're veiled to her, or she to them, or like they're after-images; like they have an internal light and she's stared at them then shut her eyes. The dresser and the crockery. The kettle and the toaster. The armchair by the window, the spider plant on the sill. The rug beneath the table on the slates and, on the table, a note – some words on paper underneath the paperweight of a cockle shell encased in perspex although where the breeze is supposed to come from with all the windows shut and locked like they are she does not know. The air in here has been baked and the roof must be buckling under the sun's dry tonnage.

WHERE ARE YOU? the note says, like that, in capitals big and bothered. YOUR PHONE IS OFF. TAKEN T TO FOLLY FARM TO TAKE HIS MIND OFF IT ALL. WE ARE *WORRIED SICK*. GET IN TOUCH. The familiarity of her mam's handwriting; known from birthday cards, Christmas cards, through decades of such stuff. Not seen for some time because of texting but as likely, still, to Emma as the blood vessels on the backs of her hands. She turns the page over and writes a reply. Makes something up; a job offer in Aberaeron. An interview to attend. Weighs it down again with the captured shell and wonders if perspex ever rots. Imagines a consciousness of sorts imprisoned like that, and the resultant insanity. Robbed of all stimulus for ever. Lunatic, lunatic. And yet there are striations in that small shell. Once it held a living thing.

Half in half out of the world. Shimmering woman she is. Upstairs, on the table in the room where she should be sleeping, with Tomos, her son, the laptop is closed clam-like. In it, she knows, and also in the phone unactivated in her handbag, she is living her real life. A duo-verse, one branch of it more real than the other, more solid, recovering its curious course in the world accessible through those things – the laptop and the phone. This is a dizzying feeling, and Emma takes her unreal half-self and positions it on the edge of the mattress. The window is open a crack for the freshness and she can hear birdsong. A distant tractor. The inbox, the retweets. The hits and the followers and the tens of thousands of queries, links, violently worded dismissals, all the swarm online of words without tongues which are more real than the things she can touch – the coverlet clutched in her fingers – or even taste, the hours-old cola. She must wait for the spinning to stop, there, on the edge of the bed in the small house in the big hills and all of the summer outside and its green seethe. There is a part of her that wants no part and needs to stay apart from the part of her that has become spectacle. Half in, half out. Needs the feel of water on her skin. Something physical to root her.

She undresses in the bathroom. Marks on the insides of her thighs that no soap will remove but will in a short time fade because they are bruises and that last man had pointy hip bones. Reminded Emma of a cow, them pelvic flats. He made no mention of the tattoo by her navel yet appeared to aim his come on it although that may not have been deliberate. She gently touches the inking on her tummy and thinks of the marks she's never seen, except in the reflection of a reflection; the stars behind her ear. Mere hours after she'd had them drilled in and they were still rawly raised she showed them to her mam who'd been on the Penderyn for some reason. One glance and then she turned her eyes away and poured more whisky. Spoke about when Emma was born and when she was an infant and the way her skin was then, so new, so perfect, and that bit of skin behind her ear that was then marked forever was softer than silk and smelt of milk. The purest part of her, a secret place that only her mother knew about, that only a mother could smell, and kiss, and now it would be always marked. And another inch of whisky left the bottle. And he had a hellish long tongue, that last man did, like a fucking anteater; Em remembers it wriggling, way up and wormy inside her. Felt like he was licking the back of her belly button. He said he felt the plates of his skull shift when she came, so fiercely did her thighs clamp, which makes her think now of fontanelle, the conical shape of T's skull when he appeared on the planet. *He's been here before.* It never stops, from dazzling, bloodied room to the oblong hole in the sloping hillside, it never fucking stops. Distract: *move.* Caulk the gap. One day this life will end.

A splayed star on the wall above the sink is a cranefly. Not many of his type seen this summer – too hot, maybe. Too dry. Positioning her hair back on top of her head in a scrunchie, he's a thing to talk to:

—Is that why you're hiding, then? Don't like the heat? There's many who'd say thank God for that because, and I hate to break it to you, feller, but you're ugly. You are, you're bloody ugly. Them legs and that face. But don't worry. You can't help it, can you? I'm not the type to kill things just cos they're ugly.

She takes it in a hand to the window – the feather-flicker of it, in her loosely balled fist – and lets it go. It drifts as if caught in a breeze yet there is no breeze but were there a wind that whistled around the world, that teased the mane, in an outer lane, of a stallion walking stately in the dust. Were there such a thing.

Everything gets washed in the shower, every inch of her from sole to scalp and as much of the internals as can be reached with the probe of a finger, quickly because she needs to be gone. Out of the house, elsewhere before they all come back, bringing what they will all need her to give them and which, then, she *will* give them and there is not enough of her for that, insubstantial as she is, the meat of her that has cast this shadow now snared in the laptop and her phone and rent by the minds remote in their many millions and the smithereens sent to shape this form, here, wet from the shower and small in the small house in the big hills. Nowhere near enough in the un-reborn form to give them what they want, the flesh of its flesh and the old companion dog. They would ask too much and she would give it all to them and then there would be nothing left. This is a world in which women never glow and one day it all will end.

Back in the bedroom she dresses before the mirror and bits of her are given back; the ribs, especially, and the twin tracks of muscle between them. A rapid loss, she sees, as if whatever embers there are within her that give off no light nevertheless smoulder with a heat intense enough to melt fat. There are creams and lotions and then the skinny jeans, the cork-soled wedges, a top that ties tight across the tits. Racks of clothes remain in her home up the coast but that place belongs to that other woman, now, that other Emma that somewhere shimmers. And also to the landlord who no doubt put an eviction notice in the post box as soon as he was informed of the sanctions, but the consequential horrors of that also belong to the more solid one, she that can endure elsewhere, casting a shadow, displacing air. Such things are part of the midden, the distant midden over the hills, in the next town, wherever – far enough away anyway to give off no discernible stink.

And she moves now. With urgency. Takes up her bag and leaves the house, blinking in the sun and empty lane, and even while she's waiting at the bus stop she is moving quickly, pacing, scratching, humming and muttering to herself, counting the daisies, putting up barriers against the mental amassing. Two cows at cud in the field over the road watch her as prey-species do, with a hazy vigilance sculpted down to one query: *Can I be hurt, here.* Emma watches them watching her. Their side-to-side champing and the deep brown orb-eyes. *Will you hurt me?*

Not her, no. But creatures like her will. The sun is ruthless. Even the bees are sluggards, exploring the calyxes with an air of disinterest as if they can't really be arsed, depite what they are. Just doing what's expected of them. The air vibrates with birdsong and behind Emma, were she to turn to look, she'd see a kingfisher scorch that wobbling air, on its way to the stream.

She feels tall and sexy in her cork platforms, the shapes of her in the curves of petals and the under-swoops of the leaves above and yet these things do not twitch or thrum: out of any breeze they hang, in the hard heat. Only the legs of this woman seem uncomfortable in the stillness; that which mimics their slopes, or is mimicked by them, can be completed and perfected by the invisible sap that flows inside.

She hears a rumble and a hiss of air-brakes somewhere in the hamlet's centre, such as it is; a war memorial and chapel. She digs in her bag for change. Way above her a chalky contrail scars the sky, hours old and feathering. A ripping, all the way up there, the plane that made it far gone. So far above this lone woman watched by cattle on this still summer day inside the relief-map of the hills, the arrayed green humps of them and the tiny trinkets of the shrivelling waters on some of their basin peaks.

The little bus appears chugging and Emma boards. The driver is an older feller, looks a bit like Neil Kinnock. Fading ostrich feathers tattooed on his forearm, blurred at their edges, something in them of the contrail, the dissolution of their pattern into the empty space around, skin or ozone both.

—Another scorcher aye.

—It is that. Emma puts some coins in the tray.
—Aberystwyth.

She tears off the ticket-tongue and moves down the bus. The three passengers already on it register to her as nothing but lumps at her periphery. The bus pulls away and movement brings a cooling breeze. In her rear-corner seat she digs her phone and earplugs out of her bag and turns the phone on and puts it on silent so that the pinging of incoming messages will not be heard and then she scrolls down to her music folder and clicks the silent mode off and inserts plugs. Music. Noise. Goat Girl's 'Country Sleaze' starts to swagger in her skull.

The bus trundles over the one-hump bridge that spans the river Wyre. Emma sees the old mine workings and the scars of industry in the earth, of the dig for ore, and too the tumbling pit-heads and sheds being absorbed by green in slow reclamation; the tendrils sprouting. She sees and feels all of the two, the one abrupt lift and drop of the bridge and the glyphs of the old dig. And the vile void of the unfinished list, un-whole. That's also to be borne.

And maybe she should engage with it all – the tweets and texts and emails. The whole teem of it is here, in her hand. A few prods of her finger and she could be in it, of it. She could access her home page too, see what's been going on in the world, how far to a new doom it has slid beyond the chambers she's been taken in lately, she's had to seek out lately, and the things in them with their grabbing hands and clutchings, their bristles and screaming needs and sometimes wives behind them and kids behind them and home lives and drudgeries and the sparks coming out of them in spurts. All the untamedness in the new discoveries. All that is not the dulling pulls of the world – that'd be like opening the brown envelopes which have no doubt piled up behind the door of her house on the banks of the Rheidol river to the north. All that she does *not* need is there. All that she can *not* bear is there, where there will be judgments leaving the mouths of men, where there will be absolutely no hope at all. Where nothing will glow, of that she is certain. Nothing will speak to her in that world. Yet it is all waiting for her further up the coast and after the bridge and the abandoned dig she has entered its purview and there is one thing missing with an absence that roars. Crude amputation. Not only limbs are taken by the men of that other place.

Fuck it. She needs the noise harder and the obviousness is not lost on her but still she does it anyway; she fills her head with 'Fuck the Pain Away' by Peaches and she is carried by the boiling bus down onto the coast road where the land hurtles down to meet the sea. There is a flash far away on the horizon's line; the Fishguard ferry possibly. The sun has set a ship on fire at the end of the world. She gets on 'Monkey 23' by The Kills, during which she scratches her shoulder three times with a thumbnail. Fat White Family's 'Bomb Disneyland', her mind leaping this way, a sand-flea in sudden brightness. She calls up Germano's 'Darkest Night of All' which in turn calls up an episode of *Homicide* and that is her past invading, her history hitting her, and she thinks that she might spew with sadness so she jumps into 'Junkyard'. Her insides sizzling. Garbage in the sack. She crams her head with noise and her body responds so that she churns in a biological boil – horripilation at her nape and arms, the pimpling of her skin. Booming heart. Her mouth dries up and her toes twitch in the cork platforms. There is a cauldron at the core of her that brews this demented physical speech. She feels the dampness at her joins. A keening scream gathers at her larynx and stays there and the fingers of both hands curl into clasping talons as if in reaction to an imperative that has been given no form.

The bus rests at Aberaeron to change drivers and Emma gets off. It's not really a conscious decision or anything, she just disembarks; a woman like her, in the state she's in, she can make anywhere thrashy and unexplored, untamed, and Emma – here, now – is *the* wildest woman. There is nothing of her that is not perfect in just what it is and she is the wildest thing in this small town at the edge of the land at the edge of Europe where cracks yawn. This is languid day's end, the sweat is beginning to dry and its salts are tugging skin taut and the gulls pant like dogs on the harbour walls and the boats in the marina seem glued down in gloop. There is a scrum outside the Celtic chippy. Way out in the sea where the blue becomes black great things loll and turn over. Giant flukes flash then dive. The face of Dylan Thomas peers at Emma from the posters in this year of something to do with him and there are guided groups about with cameras and notepads. None of this concerns her. None of it calls her in any way, her legs in the skin-tight denim and cork heels carrying her through all its insignificance. She moves with a smoothness an inch or so above the ground and people see her but she does not see them. Like she is all guided by laser and is locked on and will not deviate. She can't wait for the night-time to come. She enters the Cadwgan pub through a huddle of torpid drinkers and everything then picks up speed.

He calls himself Rang because he has red hair so at school they called him orangutang and it stuck and he's from Carmarthen and he's staying in a caravan on the site just outside town for a few days and it is in there that he fucks her and is startled and delighted by the ferocity of her hunger. No sooner has he withdrawn than she's sucking on him and this she does three times and his third orgasm is painful, something seeming to snap in his belly and force out a thin blip of grey semen. They sit outside on the caravan's step in the still night-time and smoke a spliff and they hear a heated vixen yelping in the darkness and the woman says something about it sounding like a prayer but she's wrecked and talking gibberish and Rang has already decided that she's fucking nuts anyway; out of her mind. Back in the caravan he tries to penetrate her arsehole but she won't let him on the grounds that she's still sore down there so he goes in vaginally again and cannot come despite the images he calls up and the friction becomes raw, raspy and she goes dry and then it becomes abrasive so he pulls out and she swoops down to suck him again but he's having none of it and then there is some sort of sleep from which he thinks he is half-aroused by the sound of sobbing, twice, and some whispered words. This woman is a brilliant shag but she's off her fucking head. He'll have to kick her out early doors because he's got to put some practice in for the darts tournament in Aberystwyth. Get her number first, tho; anyone who fucks like her needs to be kept in touch with. But when he wakes up properly, with the alarm, he's alone in the caravan and the smells of salty rot and gasses from burst bladderwrack have not wholly crept up from the sea.

Emma's at the bus stop when the man awakes. Her face all colours from the make-up smears and her hair an abandoned nest. The memory of the woman-shape that blazed in her dreams is fonder, and clearer, to her than the man's hands and physicality, his insisting-within, which things and the fleeting peace that follows – all fading already. As they always do. And, too, he had one of those pointy, nosy little penises and the brief sanctuary of it all is almost gone even before daylight has returned to the planet's flank. The need is creeping, even before the goo has dried properly to scale on the pink and ringing parts of her and she knows that what was promised was done so falsely. So soon, the disappointment, and so soon too in each increasing twitch and mutter does the manic jabber of her body re-begin. If only she'd never gone up that fucking mountain. She wonders if Tomos is still sleeping or whether he's woken fretting for his mother as she waits for the bus that will take her further away from him and closer to what was nothing more than the rising sun and the breeze in the reeds.

# MESSAGES

@Madonna kicking off #llynsyfydrin#paradisebuiltinhell#fl
oatingwoman
@Madonna#llynsyfydrin I'm going. Coachloads of us. Anyone
wanna join? RT#paradisebuiltinhell#BVM
@ListentoDawkins you are all stupid children #growup#enlig
htenment#21stcentury'#getalife@enlightened@BraveBritain
@Repent#ListentoDawkins the end is not nigh is already here
#rapture#Megiddo#endtimes'#Repent
@enlightened primitive fuckin Taffs rotfl #growup#getalife FFS
@ListentoDawkins too true @BraveBritain ha yes we are
leaving suck it up losers

From *Pobl Annwyl*, bilingual blogspot, Emyr Gwenallt Roberts,
AKA Llewellyn Nesa, version Saesneg

Listen, now, pobl. She has spoken. She has chosen one of us.
Drop your machines, turn away from drugs and pornography,
forget your bank balance and pay attention. The scales have
been lifted from your eyes. Dig and bridge and wild, she said;
these were Her words. You have lived your lives in ignorance
until now. Here is the power. Everything else is dust. This is
the final warning and if you do not listen this time then expect
rains of fire. Four horsemen. Repent and do it quickly. Turn
away from your toys. Article 50? Mere dust. Put it all aside.
Children no longer. Must I translate?

  Dig = work.
  Bridge = this is an INSTRUCTION, people. Make connections. Do not burn.
  Wild = well, okay, I confess to being stumped. But I know
  how to google and I know how to read and I know how to
  listen. Watch this space, pobl. And LISTEN. And LEARN. And
  REPENT. Now is the time. Must I repeat myself? Must SHE?

TAGS: llewllyn nesa, chosen, listen, dig, bridge, wild, rejoice, repent, tsunami, She

@Enlightened ha ha ha! LMFAO! Learn? You need to snowflake #Madonnabollocks#BVM shite have faith in Britain

@ListentoDawkins cdnt agree more read some books taff. Time to grow up #Madonnabollocks#BVMshite

@ownperson a pox on both yr houses you shd all just shut up who even cares lol #getajob#getalife

@paradisebuiltinhell worried? We shd be. All shd be. You think this will be tolerated? Check it out youtube.com/watch?v=mA9&Bp93uyz

@ownperson cdnt put it better myself #talksense #discipline #growingeconomy#takebackcontrol

@FreeThinker #ownperson totally agree dont these people have jobs? #discipline#lazy#scroungers

@FreeThinker men in skirts up there! Trannies! Seen it online! #debauchery

@TrustinBritain repetitive beat law not still on statutes? Prob abolished by EU #takebackcontrol

@ownperson @TrustinBritain yes clause 44 where is it? And bet will be illegals up there #takebackcontrol #ourownlaws

@FreeThinker burning effigies now of Trump and Farage disgusting #discipline

YouTube: http/:watch?v=mA9&Bp93uyz
Government spokesman on the Llyn Syfydrin 'commune'
uploaded 30 mins ago
Well of course we as a government like to see the great British people coming together in this way for purposes of, of celebration and the like if indeed that is what this is. I gather that there's been some kind of, of apparition of some sort. But the reasons behind this, this *commune* as you call it, ah, they're not really important to us, ah, not really important. What *is* important, what we should all be rather concerned about, is the, the litter, the mess that is being made of one of the most beautiful parts of our country. We're looking at the question, the issue of trespass but the more immediate concerns, is the, ah, what

one might call the lack of sanitation – the question of sewage disposal and the like and any possible health problems that might arise. There are young people up there, children, and their health and safety is a valid concern, paramount, as is the welfare of our wildlife. We believe that the beautiful British countryside should be open to and enjoyed by the great British public within the bounds of the law of course and I'm afraid to say that we've been getting reports of, well, to be frank, offensive smells. As I say there is no system of sanitation in place up there and with so many people in the one place, there is the question of waste where so many people gather in the one place. So yes we're looking into it. There are further issues too, of, of police resources and the like; the local police do not have experience in, with, such mobs so we will have to draft in operatives from elsewhere, most likely the Met, which will incur further burden on the public purse and the hard-working British taxpayer. And, and, at this historic time, this moment in our nation as we exit the EU and, and we take this bold and brave step, then it is right that every citizen of Great Britain pulls together to make a success of this venture. We will be taking back control and each and every one of us will have a responsibility. The Great British public have given us a clear mandate and we will make a success of this new moment in our history if everyone gets behind it. Plus there have been rumours, we have credible information that illegal immigrants may be using this, this commune to, to, to hide in and in that way avoid the law and take advantage of our generosity. This will be looked into, as will the matter of lost work hours and the like but our first priority is for the health and safety of the people up there, in particular the children. Thank you.

COMMENTS 10

**OwnPerson** happy to live in there own shit these ppl. Dignity? Go and live on a mountian top while the rest of us have to work for a living. Vision of the virgin mary? Don't make me laugh!!! just an excuse for a party methinks. Bring them all back down forcibly if necesary

15 mins ago

**FreeThinker** why are they allowed to do this? Not there mountain is it! What if ppl want to go up there for a nice walk or something! Bloody hippies spoiling it! Don't they have jobs! Are they allowed all this time off work! Selfish you ask me! Pat yourself on the back Katie H you tell it like it is #KatieH for PM! I'd vote! Burning effigies! Remoaners guilty of treason!
15 mins ago

**Jimbob** i love going up mountains and now therl be hippy shit up their selfish bastards get them off your right andrew the foreman
18 mins ago

**Rita** who do they think they are? Think they own the bloody place. What about the children they cant live in that filth. Spoiling our lovely British countryside like this. Its for everyone not just them
20 mins ago

**SimonLillico** just an excuse if you ask me. Social networking has arranged this and they've been rubbing their hands with glee at the thought of a few days off work. Just lazy. Bet most of them are dole scroungers anyway or illegals like he said. We'll get rid of them all when we've taken back control again and then we can put them all to work clearing up the mess they've made and when they've done that they can come and sweep my road too
23 mins ago

**Bob C** dirty cunts
24 mins ago

**Rita** it's the kiddies I worry about should they not be in school
25 mins ago

**AndrewtheForeman** anyone else think those people don't belomg up there? Not just the foreners I mean its not their mountain is it? Doesn't someone own it?
28 mins ago

**KatieH** another excuse to slack off. If they put as much thought into working as they do into avoiding it the country wouldn't be in this mess. After seeing this, any Remainiac should surely be done for treason. Unpatriotic!
29 mins ago

**KatieH** seethe
30 mins ago

# THIN AND GREY

IN THE TOP left corners of the screens are the figures AR100B, and next to them a date. The images below them are of a silver lake around which people-shapes press with faces whitened by the IR thermal imaging; later, when night rises, these faces will glow and froth on the grey screens as if internally lit, as if bags of white phosphorus have replaced the heads, as if they might be terrifying to look upon. The images are resolute, defined, if thin and grey; and beyond the lake and its tight and chalky huddle, on the roads and tracks that cross the mountain from the flat-lands around, more shapes of cars and vans move and converge and there are more of those burning figures on foot and all traffic is upwards-aimed. Here, in this bunker of screens and watching men, hands tap at keyboards and the images on the screens change. Zoom, and the white-faced shapes appear to be dancing; zoom, and around the froth of fires the shapes sit. With added magnification the screens might reveal the smaller glows and shapes in the trees, in the bracken, beneath branches and on branches: owl-shaped, with that radar face, mustelid-skulky, others with wings that spread and cloak. Later in the rise of night and when the thermal imaging becomes honed these smaller forms will show up on the screens; bumps and pulses of life, the light of such stuff, the various sheenings of breath and blood drawn to that high place and aglow, here, in this hidden room where all light is artificial and every colour is bleached and the faces that study the screens are coloured no shade at all.

# LICHEN

*CEN Y CERIG* – skin of the rock. Or *cen y coed* – of the wood.
The old language. Indicators of great antiquity, splotched harle-
quin libraries of data that bloom in places of pollution, in old
mining scars and on the banks of mineralised rivers. Hungry
for rock. Ersatz fur for a child's hand to stroke. Earth-tongues,
whitecaps, fairy gills – these names given by the great non-
symbiont, the great ransacker of the most complex of webs,
he who can name the moths elephant hawk and hummingbird
hawk and death's head hawk and also acidulate the air to
scorch and ruin the gorgeous wing.

Moon-blue and verdigris; the growth's colours enlarged in
the changing moods of the lake, olive at the shallower edges
and tinged umber by the peat through which the waters have
bled. In the rushes, neon damselflies thrum and zip; even the
dung flies belong and are needed and in the bulge of their
eyes is an inkling of infinity. Bolted foxgloves scope above the
ryegrass like the necks of alert ostriches and offer themselves
to the long tongues of the brimstones. Beetle-shucks snare the
sun in the fans of cobwebs and seem, for a moment, to shine
with a life long slurped away by the jewels that hang in the
silver strings. Square celandine leaves scoop at the sunbeams
and gather colours for the petals and there are mushrooms,
too, brindled like the breasts of owls. In a moorhen's nest in
the reeds eggs twitch and crack and that noise alerts the shore-
rats and sets them to skulk hungry and also the magpies and
rooks which drop down out of the blue and amongst all this
the people have gathered, circling fire pits which vibrate the
air and there is music from the hunched figure on the decks
and the amps mounted on the bed of a van and there are the
smells of food and some people are in the water to bathe or
play, mostly play, as they do on the shores and on the rising
ground; a clan-gathering, groups on logs and on stones around
fires in some of which the framework of effigies bends and

burns and the air wobbles with the flames' heat and up here everything blooms. Epochal upheavals in each crack of rock. Everything has caught some kind of fire. There is a new quality of seeing – the future hangs up here as well as the past and everything converses with everything else and even the dung flies, especially the dung flies, minute beads of shite on their finest hairs, belong. In the conifers, at the latrine trench, three people squat at intervals dictated by decency and then kick humus across their leavings and, given time, a cascade could happen here, at this place of waste, a trophic cascade as the apex eaters would appear behind the scavengers and so behaviour would, given time, lead even to the healing of the scabs on the moth's wings. Given time enough, what unexpected chains of remedy could occur. The stinking midden brings the rats which bring the stoats and the weasels and the foxes and the badgers and the hawks and each of these brings others, always others. If given time. Light in the small and hooded eyes.

And through and just above the moving heads the martins rocket. At the cooking pits other small birds gather; larger birds, too, the corvids, some gulls. Sparrows writhe in dust baths. Woodpeckers tattoo the trees. A child throws a ball for a dog to chase and the dog galumphs after it into the lake. Above, and unnoticed, a strange flier hovers, its one eye trained below. A fat, mechanical arachnid, small propellors at each corner, a camera hanging like a haemorrhoid. Symbols on one arm: AR100B. Emitting a slight whine – its brushless and gearless motors, a whine becoming a low drone. A low, whining, never-ceasing drone. It sees a lot, this flying thing, its eye never needing to blink or tear; it takes and transmits and that's all it does, turns all the faces below it one whiteness and all the colours around, the thousand greens, a single shade of tarmac-grey. A goshawk soars above it, assessing in the ancient folds and pathways of its brain and alien-ness, not size, is the thing's repellent. The raptor blinks before it catches its own shadow in its claws, wrecker of the lesser fetch, banks again and swoop-glides away down the valley side across which the shadow of a cloud is cast like a sudden wave of ink. The machine also banks, drops then rises again, slides to a site above the ridge on which several people have gathered to peck with their fingers at phones and it hovers there, pinned against the blue, safe from notice as the eyes below are pinned downwards to the screens. It hangs above and watches.

# MAN OF THE CLOTH

ONE FIGURE STAYS isolate, positioned on the highest ridge. A band of white encircles this figure's throat and mostly he kneels with his head covered, on the hard rock, unmoving, his hands gripping the earth. The fires do not draw him, nor the waters, nor the groups gathered around the cooking-pits; the DJ does not draw him either. There are times when this hooded figure must leave the ridge and enter the conifers to squat over the stinking trench and then stand and move deeper into the trees to lean for support against a trunk with his face in his hands and at such times he is observed – the smaller shapes in the firs and the sitka spruce and in the pockets of bracken just as hunched as him. Quick trips, these, that he makes before he re-sites himself on the ridge again. At night he curls up in a sheep-scrape to sleep but is back on the rocky ridge at dawn, his face covered but turned to the sun returned, before the other faces appear bleared and agog from under canvas or lean-to or even holes hacked and mattocked into the up-sloping earth. In this place where it seems everything has relearned how to talk to everything else this figure endures aloof and hooded, unassessed by the eye that flies with its capacity to turn all the other faces that move around this mostly fixed point one blinding white, all without feature.

God it is a thudding sun that has turned the two carriages of the train into one long hot-box. Adam feels the heat from its steel sides rippling out and it feels to him as if there is too much sky above him; there is a giddiness within him as if he might fall suddenly upwards, into the scorching blue. An hour earlier he'd woken with a jolt on the couch back at his flat, baggy of face and hag-rid, feeling like someone from Tregaron, all drool and pustules, and in the bath his battered guts released bad and shocking gases the stench of which has stayed on his skin in some kind of hellish homeopathy. Couldn't remember getting back to his flat and there are scrapes and bruises on him, on his face and elbows. A thumbnail grouted about with black blood. He'd stacked all the post on top of the fridge unopened and there it will remain. Nothing of any meaning or value to him in those envelopes. Not to the chambers of his lungs. Quilty hadn't been there and this had pained Adam but there had been signs of his uncontrollable passage; a mangled rat's tail beneath the TV. Might well have been Adam's final sleep in that flat; surely some of those envelopes contained eviction. He can envisage his furniture in the windows of Craft on the other platform there, over the tracks.

The people disembark. Most of the faces are boiled-looking, peeled raw by the summer. A young woman with a backpack and blonde dreads in a headband is looking worriedly back over her shoulder as she leaves the train and Adam sees why and would've done so even without Browne's alerting elbow to his ribs; two insanely inked guys are getting off, one with his face vertically divided by Maori-style tattoos from his hairline to his thrapple and the other, topless, with a red dragon rampant on his skinny torso with the snarling face drilled into his own face and curled around onto the scalp above the ear so that his own eye, leaden and tunnellish, works as the dragon's eye too. Adam hears Browne mutter *Jaysus fucken Chroist* behind him and hopes that those boys haven't heard it too, but they just give him a bit of a glare and move off, down the platform. All the heads snapping towards them then instantly snapping away again. One little girl stands staring at them as they go abroad into the town, the two of them, to move anywhere, to do anything.

Adam and Browne step up into the train, the swelter and whiff of it in the long tin. The Formica of the tables sweats. The first two aboard, Adam and Browne find a table with a window seat and already Adam can feel a stinky ick glooping into a pool behind his balls and in each little jungle of armpit. There's a nasty couple of hours ahead.

—See them two? says Browne, his green eyes both big. — Who in their right mind ... Crazy mixed-up kids.

—Aye, yeh. But it's relative, man.

—Is it?

—Course it is, yeh. And Adam takes in Browne, the oddness of the man across the table, the cicatrice cables raw in the stubble on his skull, the Indian-ink tats on the fingers, and, especially, the interesting railway-track scars up the inside of his left leg revealed by the clam-digger kex, where once he'd had his entire femoral artery removed after toxic clot occlusion. Strangely proud of this, Browne seems to be, showing it off like a trophy; it had been the first thing he'd drawn Adam's attention to when they first met in the pub two nights ago. With the accent, and then the mentions of the Shantallow Estate and RAAD and Buncrana not being far enough away from the Rah and the 32 County Sovereignty Committee, Adam had supposed a kneecapping but no, only the chalk in the skag had resulted in the operation. Just abscess, and, before that, the entirely predictable poison of hopelessness. Long-limbed enough to leap a sea.

Browne's mouth lolls open to reply and then curls into a kind of grin – an event of jaundiced, jostling teeth. Adam thinks, again, that Browne's already ingested something this morning, with the unique energies coming out of him, and this steers him towards his own needs, beginning to clamour as they are. He rubs at the window with the sleeve of his shirt but all the muck is on the outside.

—That's privatisation for ye, Browne says. —Privatisation so it is. Can't be fucked to clean. Fine in principle, the oul privatisation, but see if there's no competition? They can offer the worst fucken service and they can get away with it. Cos there's no fucken choice. Ye've got to use it. Cunts, man, Arriva. German-owned as well, d'ye know that? Bet the bog's already overflowing with shite. And where's the fuckin air con? Sweating cobs so I am. Cattle car, that's what this is.

He pulls the collar of his top away from his neck and Adam does the same. It cost over twenty fucking quid for the day return which was the cheapest ticket on offer. But Browne paid.

—We should've got the coach.

Browne shakes his head. —Takes twice as long. An A wanna get this over with quick as A can. Sooner it's done an the gear's on me person the sooner A can take it easy. Get me jollies booked – a summer in Shag-a-luf, that'll do me, aye it will, two months on the piss and the pull. That'll do me.

People get on. Hipster students with beards of daft luxury; overweight male middle-agers in shorts and flip-flops (*shameless*, says Adam, *just pure shameless*). A beautiful black woman in a blue dress makes to take the table seat across the gangway but then she sees Adam and Browne, the state of them with the scars and whatever flickers in their eyes and she moves away, further down the carriage. Adam and Browne raise their eyebrows at each other but nothing is said. A lad lumbers past with his cumbersome rucksack, holding it out in front of him like a battering ram, talking into his earpiece loudly:

—Fings happen for a reason, dude, member I told you dat? Member? So what did she say after you revealed all? She fucking. Did. Not. She did? No way. You know you've got to get rid, now, don't ya? Member what I told you? All*ow* it, man, just all*ow* it.

He and his bag move down the coach. Browne and Adam watch him go, see the number 20 on the back of his football shirt.

—*Him*, Adam says. —That *prick*. Fuckin wanker. That shirt must be fuckin minging by now.

—Ah, the oul 20, is it? They've overtaken youse now, haven't they? Oul green-eyed monster coming out, there, son.

—Shite. Utter shite. Sooner be a losing Liverpool fan than a victorious Manc one any-fuckin-day. I hate them cos they're just horrible, that's why. I'd hate them if they never won anything. I'd hate them if they didn't exist.

—Alright, man, calm down. Touched a nerve there aye? This is why ye should support someone like Cliftonville. No fuss around them like. It's a job to even get hold of the results, Browne says.

—'No fuss'? Except when thee play Linfield. Plenty of fuss *then*.

—Aye but that's different.

—It's the same. It's exactly the fuckin same.

—How is it the same? How is it?

And Browne says something, some words, a lot of words but Adam's a little distance away, because someone behind him has dropped something on a tabletop – a handful of coins, perhaps – and the rhythmic clink has taken him backwards across years and miles to a dark and smoke-layered dock-road pub where his grandad is playing the spoons, rippling them off his thighs, knees, grinning gummily down at him from his stool at the bar, running the spoons down the ladder of his stiffened and spread fingers, astounding to the little boy how such music can be coaxed from two bits of mere metal, the magic that lives in what he eats his Rice Krispies with each morning. He's back there, for a few seconds, Adam is. Looking up at his grandfather amid the smells of smoke and spirits.

Browne kicks his shin, not hard, beneath the table. Adam looks at Browne.

—Ye listening to me?

—Nah not really. I was miles away.

Browne takes a breath to fuel some more words but then his eyes focus on a place over Adam's shoulder. —Ah now. Here we go.

A man takes the table across the gangway. Sleeveless band t-shirt and the scrawled tats on his puny arms. The can of Spesh already on the go and the guy plonks stuff on the table; a plastic bag of clunking cans and a small portable cassette player. He looks at Adam and Browne looking at him and gives a nod and then sits down and takes a slurp at the Spesh. Adam licks his lips and swallows and Browne points a finger and says: – What's this?

—Cassette player, the guy says. —Eight pound from Craft. Just bought it now before I got on. Haven't seen one in ages. Back dahn sahf see now so I don't wanna get bored. Only fing is, tho, there was only two tapes cos who wants tapes these days? Well, I do. Old school, that's me. Can't beat it. Cassettes, man.

He takes a tape out of his rucksack. Browne watches him do this.

—They had the Pistols and the Insane Clown Posse but I grew out of the Pistols years ago.

—So, what, you bought the Posse one?

The guy puts the tape into the machine. Browne goes on:

—You grew *out* of the Sex Pistols and *into* the Insane Clown Posse, is that what you're telling me? You've got *that* all back-arsewards, haven't ye?

The guy presses play and there is a half-second of sound before Browne leans over across the gangway and presses stop. Adam looks on and he is amused. This is a distracting little playlet and he's watching with intrigue.

—Oi!

—Not gunner happen, son. See if I wanted sounds on this journey I would've brought me own. I am *not* gunner be forced to listen to yours. Now either sit there quiet like a good lad or fuck off to another carriage.

The guy looks at Browne, hears his blowtorch accent, sees the raised and naked ropes on the skull and the scar laddering up his leg like the track of a giant centipede. Everything about him that is a loud warning.

—Thought you looked a decent feller, that's all. Thought you'd know the score. Bit of entertainment on the journey, that's all. Fucking boring without. I must be the only one on this fucking train with a bit of fucking life to em, knowmean?

Browne and Adam laugh. Browne jerks a thumb down the carriage and shakes his head. —Get along with ye now. An put a scud on, aye?

With a mutter and a clink the guy does. There is a hiss and a swoosh as he goes through the door into the next car and then the recorded voice comes over the tannoy: *Welcome aboard ...*, and then the list of stations. It is a female voice, metallic, like that of a lady robot, a woman automaton culled from spare parts: Adam thinks of scurf curls for eyelashes, a fanbelt coloured scarlet and bent into an 8-shape for a mouth.

There is a shunt and a jerk in the world and the train groans into motion. The windows are turned into dust-streaked TV screens and the hanging thickness of the snared air is swirled into movement by a faint draught and some small level of coolness is released and it is a relief. The retail park slides past. The police station, the rugby field. On top of the hill to the left the big grey buildings castellate the sky; the national library and the university.

The journey is underway at last and a sigh of some sort seems apposite and so Browne takes out his vape. He takes a suck and passes it over to Browne who takes it with gratitude.

—Yick. What flavour is that?

—Think it's supposed to be apple.

—Tastes like fuckin shampoo.

But Adam draws again and some need is satisfied. Yet beneath that there is a zigzag crack a-widening: a breaking need. Adam forces his focus onto the strange chemical taste on his tongue and hands the pipe back.

—Thank Christ for vapes, man, eh?

Browne nods, sucking at the thing, the mist leaving his nostrils and the two sides of his mouth.

—True that. Used to have a crafty one in the jacks, me. Wet some bog roll, stick it up against the smoke detector so I did. Don't need to anymore tho. Brilliant things these are.

But there is always someone who must tut and stare, and such a one rises now above the seatbacks, scoping for the source of the vapour.

—It's a vape, Browne says to the upright man. —Totally fuckin legal son. Catch yerself on.

The man makes a noise and sits back down again. Adam laughs. —Hear that? Man actually harrumphed. Don't think I've ever heard that before, an actual harrumph.

—Ah sure there's always one begrudger so there is. Browne takes a lot of rapid little sucks at the mouthpiece without inhaling, builds up a fogbank in his face, and releases a great big rolling muffler of vapour down the carriage. One of those rollers they have in carwashes – it's like that, but made of fumes. A few seats away there's a theatrical cough under its tumble but nothing more.

Hills pass. There are sheep on them and houses and some of those hills have been baked bald on their crowns. Everything looks, is, parched. Adam sees three rabbits in a field on their hind legs observing the train as it blasts past. They stare, lollopy-eared and twitchy. What if it never rains again: these hills dunes of tan talcum and bestrewn with animals' bones. The water-courses dry and split, the angled shapes of their craquelure, something in them of the patterns on the unbelievable beasts that once towered on the grasslands and were called giraffes.

They pass a big field. Adam studies it for as long as he can because in it is one rock only and on that rock is a duck. And then they pass a building site; holes in the ground, men in yellow hats, diggers and bulldozer blades. Browne gives it a nod.

—Used to be a hospital, that did. Mental hospital, like. Sanatorium or whatever it is that it's called. Like that one on Queen's Road; that's been knocked down n all so it has. Got to wonder what they're hiding, man, don't ye? Why they see the need to knock it all down. Must be something going on.

Adam barks a laugh. —Hiding something? Lad, you've got that all wrong. It's the opposite of hiding – it's a fuckin decla-ration. It's out in the open, for everyone to see – *this* is what we think of your needs. We don't fuckin care, and we're saying so publicly.

—Ah, now. So much cynicism in one so young.

Adam laughs again, not as loud. —Call it that if yeh like, he says, and wants to say something about it all being as merciless as birth but he doesn't. Feels the need to speak a few words about unrelieved alone-ness, but he pulls that need back into his skull with a hard sniff. —Rhos'll be going the same way soon. Believe me. Or if they don't demolish it it'll be sold off. Some cunt's second home. Holiday flats or something.

—Aye and what a loss cos it fuckin worked, didn't it? A mean look at yerself. Fine example. Clean and serene, isn't that what you twelve-steppin boys say?

Adam's eyes harden. —Aye well. Something happened.

—*What* happened?

—Just something unexpected. You don't need to know. But it worked brilliantly for a bit, Rhos did. An, an, an anyway; I'm only using the booze, aren't I? Not touching anything else.

—Yeer not telling me that was only the drink inside ye the other night in the pub there.

—I am, yeh. That's *exactly* what I'm saying. I was just rat-arsed.

—Well it must've been some special fuckin bevvy, then, cos ye were pure buzzing so ye were. On another planet, sor.

Adam cannot wholly, nor clearly, recollect, but he can imagine; how it gets the human, that need, how it remains mightier than the attempts at relief. More: how the insane energies of it can concoct a stimulant from a depressant. The power of it, sometimes, the awful, awesome power.

Adam says: – An what about yehself? I must've missed that one of the twelve steps that tells yeh to goan score a loader beak off some gangsta in Wolverhampton.

—Whisht! Keep yeer fuckin voice down son! Browne zips his fingers across his lips and lowers his own voice. —Never know who's listening in so ye fuckin don't. An it's not for me own usage anyways.

—What isn't?

—The, the what you just called it, the stuff. Never touch it no more. But capital must be made.

—Thought you just said you were going to Magaluf on the proceeds?

—With some of it, aye. Rest of it, I'll be setting meself up in business.

—Business?

—Usury.

—Whatery?

—Usury. Moneylending, to the brainless and inattentive novice like yaself. Loan-sharking.

—Yeh not serious.

—Suren A fuckin am. An, c'mere and listen to me. Browne leans forwards over the table and beckons with his fingers for Adam to do the same but Adam keeps his back pressed to the seat.

—They were telling me about it, Marc and Griff an them pikeys who live by the south beach. Them head-the-balls. Ikey's buddies. Know Ikey?

—No. Heard of him but don't know him.

—Everyone's heard of oul Isaac. He's in Swansea nick now anyway but this is what ye do. This is what they told me. For one thing, see, it only carries a max twenty-four-month sentence so it's a safer option than dealing, *and* ye don't have to put up with junkies all the time *and* there'll be no temptation floating around ye. Just act like a bit of a bully, that's all you have to do. Even if yeer not one, all ye've got to do is pretend that ye are. Ye with me? Ye target them ones with no back-up – which, by the way, is exactly what the fuckin DWP are doing – and all's ye need is threats an, an, intimidation. Griff said he's never had to give out the digs once and he's been at it for years *and* he's fuckin rolling in it. Build up a hard rep and that's enough. I lend ye a hundred quid and then next week it's 'Where's that 200 quid ye owe me?' Ye see? Turn up at the house with a baseball bat and a big fuckin dog and guaranteed they'll pay up. Griff's made enough, d'ye know what he's doing with his profits? He's buying a house in Aberporth so's he can set up a weed farm. Why Aberporth, yeer thinking, aren't ye? Cos it's next door to the MOD place, so it is. Copper-choppers can't use the airspace so he'll be safe from the heat sensors. Browne taps his own temple, hard enough to make a noise. —Switched on, that mahn. He's been fuckin *thinking*, that he has.

And Adam is thinking too; trying to reconcile the two forces in the embattled man opposite him. It is not easy.

—So what d'ye say, son? Ye in?

—What?

—Am gunner need a right-hand man sure enough. Trustworthy feller like. Always more effective when two's up. Come in with me.

—Nah. It's not my thing, mate. I'm not the hurting kind.

—What have Ah just said? Ye don't fuckin *have* to be. Just got to *look* as if ye are. Sure isn't that what yeer gonna be doing today? Don't tell me I've invited the wrong mahn, here.

—It's different.

—How? How is it?

—I can scowl an snarl at some beak dealer but I can't do it to a, a single mother who's lost her benefits cos she was a minute late for her Jobsearch interview. Just couldn't do it. Just not in me, man.

—Aah, well. Browne sits back in his seat. —Ye need to toughen yeerself up, son. All's ye've got to do is *act* the part. Just fuckin pretend. Don't have to give anyone a dunt. Got to get yeerself hard for our bright new Brexit Britain. Ye'd better not let me down today, Ah'll tell ye that.

More rabbits, outside, in the field that whisks by; a scattering of them, grass-cropping, a few on their hind legs to watch the train. That those little animals might come to caper now around Adam; that there is the possibility of that happening, if only in his mind. As it is enough, or almost enough, to be aware that the most dangerous creature on the planet is a man who is terrified of being seen as a wimp. Yet somewhere in the world there must be things that are born and which live entirely and then die underground; worms, maybe, or some kind of mole. And even in the deepest of seas there are eels, oarfish, huffing noiselessly past with coxcomb crests and binlid eyes. And in those spans of life such creatures have the slightest of sight, if that, and the world is just touch or sound waves felt in the skin, vibrations in the aura, smells turned to taste and no need ever to scent the warnings brought on the wind or to have to know the sun.

Borth, and waiting on the platform is a trolley-dolly, someone who'll have alcohol for sale. Like a predator sensing the spillage of blood, the proximity of alcohol has Adam upright in his seat, alert. The train stops and the doors open and fresher air washes along the coach and Adam's arm-hairs sway like the cilia of anemones, plankton-searching, famished in their way. This craving in him, this thing inside. Not in the pipes perhaps, but somewhere a bug full of demands has set up insistent camp. Let there be a clink, soon. Let there be a hiss of a ring pull. This thirsty earth.

And there is Borth, outside. The sea on the left and on the right is the baked bog and the far blue hills and the hit of gym-knicker whiff from the weed in rot on the shore-shingle nearby. And there was a recent photograph here, wasn't there? A happy dinosaur on the yellow t-shirt of a happy little boy and his happy little sister beside. Some kind of key-fob too. He took all the money and he would've taken the phone had there been one in the bag and flogged it for a flim in some dingy pub. And there was a defacing urge, and he remembers that with a sore lurch and just for a few seconds he very nearly gets it, can almost see the source of that urge for what it truly was and is but then the dryness blares at the back of his tongue and fills most things. If only he'd never gone up that fucking mountain. If only he'd never taken that fucking pill. In them hills there, away over the bog, the baked expanse under which vapours pop and send clods in somersaults into the air. Some birds on it – geese, a few egrets blinding white – sluggish, slow, as if caught by the webs in the immense festering swelt.

The train tugs itself into motion again. Browne has found a *Metro* and is flicking through its pages. There is a clink of glass from somewhere further down the train and then another one louder and Adam is digging in his hip pocket for money. The cart is wrestled through the vestibule. He watches it come towards. Fears he might whimper, salivate.

—Ah, yer mahn. Time for a bit of the oul brekko, says Browne, and eyes Adam. —Ye drinking?

Ad nods. —Just a couple. Take the edge off, like.

—A few only. And eat something aye. Got to keep yer bap clear for Wolverhampton, ye hear me?

—Aye, yeh. Just a few, that's all. Take the edge off.

They buy four cans of tepid Stella from the cart and two miniature whiskies and some snack-bags and Browne buys a butty. Ad is into his first can in seconds, sucking at its warm and coppery thickness, the lump in his throat leaping with the gulps, all of what he is opening to receive it.

—Ey, now. Go easy I said.

Adam opens a whisky and pours it into his half-empty can. —Fuck me that's better.

—Aye well. Go fuckin easy. I'm not having me back-up all coggly, ye hear me?

Adam busies himself opening the packets along their side seams and arranging them platter-like on the table. —There ye go. Birkenhead tapas.

Browne, a lip curled in distaste, picks some limp green-ness out of his sarnie. Shows it to Adam.

—Seen this? Look at it, mahn. Cheese fuckin sanger I asked for. What's all *this* shite? A cheese sanger is a slice of cheese between two bits of bread. I never had, had *green* in me piece as a wean. Can't get anything simple these days. Some kind of grass or something in yeer cheese piece, Christ.

Adam laughs and eats a Cheddar. Sucks at the can – the sour cheap Scotch in the vegetable-soup lager. He long ago learnt to suppress his gag reflex when such a thing is called for. Alcoholic Cup-a-Soup, that's what it's like. Horrendous. But the work gets done.

At Dyfi Junction an osprey swoons from its nest, close to the train; unfurls its great and brindled wings and drops and then sheers outwards. Beats its pinions and is taken in by the haze. Nearby as it is, some passengers see it and make appreciative noises but when Adam turns his gaze out there the bird has gone, drawn deeper into the steely sheen of the air. Hills in that haze and aren't Adam's powers of recall hard at work this morning, even with the drink-damage, because as he sits and sips and stares he remembers how walking in those very hills, one spring day, he'd gotten off the train here at Dyfi Junction and just walked – water in his bag, a turkey roll and an apple, a book, and a pair of binoculars. He came across a farm high on one of those ridges half-erased now in the heat haze, a lofted smallholding – a cottage and some sagging outbuildings, dangling barbed loops and fertiliser bags half-submerged in slicks of slurry, which was everywhere: the overall feeling was of a faecal flood. There was a pervasive reek and an abrupt shadow came over all and turned the spring day darker and a scream had come from one of the tumbledown sheds, an outraged animal bellow, and no birds sang and the sun was veiled and Adam knew for certain that, in those rackety outhouses, pigs were hoisted up by their back legs and put to death with sledgehammers. A scabby dog had dragged itself out of a standing pool of liquid shit and slaveringly chased him away with much bearing of brown and broken fangs. A nightmare place it had been; visited before, yes, but only in the very worst of delirium — the kind that comes after a week on the brandy and the speed and the skunk. Demented.

A shake, a shudder goes through Adam and Browne asks him what's wrong and Adam says 'nothing' and Browne turns back to his *Metro* and the train slides into motion again and Adam thinks that he could get off at the next stop, Machynlleth, just get off and go over the platform and jump on the next Cambrian Coaster up to Cricieth and get off there and go and see Ebi. Stop the terrible hurtle. Call Ebi. Take the promised job. Aye but that all would hinge on two things: that Ebi himself has stayed sober, and that the better part of Adam was not left behind in the ocean, refusing to return and shuck its gills and fins.

The train turns inland. Ad crumples his empty can and immediately opens another and Browne raises an eyebrow.

—Easy now. Keep the bap clear I said.

—I will, man, I will. I'm just smoothing out the edges.

They pick at the food on the table and by Mach the packets are empty. A man clears them away, a man with the words TRAIN MAINTENANCE TEAM on the back of his tabard. Outside, there are pink ribbons tied around the railings and posts of the station platform and Adam genuflects with his can and will not dwell on what those ribbons signify — an abomination forced into the world and into some of the lives it contains. Whatever's inside Adam, whatever it is that crackles and cuts and is twisting him into such shapes as he has not welcomed nor even invited and what could with a certain level of accuracy be called *pain*, he offers it up so that the anguish of others may in turn and in however small a part be relieved. And then he takes a big, big suck at his can. And then he focuses on a blackbird on the roof of the public shelter; the golden beak haughtily cocked skywards. Such things sing.

The lady robot announces that at this station the train will adjoin two more carriages and you may experience a small jerk.

—Nothing new there, Ad says, and raises a smile from Browne. And there *is* a jerk, a double shunt, and organs move within, in their stabilising jellies, and hills pass by again. Cottages and hedgerows. Streams. And over it all the never-ceasing sun.

Browne stretches – a great big bone-cracking unfurling of his limbs. He stands up, his hands on his lower back, chest and belly out-thrust.

—Think I'm off for a wee daunder.

—A what?

—Wee daunder. Bit of a wee stroll.

—Where?

—Up and down the train, where'd ye think, mahn? Not good for ye to sit too long so it's not. Ye get that, that thing, what is it now, sounds like trombones.

—Thrombosis?

—That's the boy. Deep-vein thrombosis. Got to keep the blood flowing around ye.

—Giz a bang on that vape, then, before yeh go.

They each take a few tokes on the tube.

—Think I'll try for a shite as well. Been bound up for a few days so Ah have but it's that butty-grass – it's given me the skitters. No more bevvy after them, alright?

—Alright.

—I mean it now, d'ye hear me?

—I said alright, didn't I?

Browne taps a finger to his temple. —Hard bap, d'ye hear me? *Clear* bap keep it.

—Yes, lad, I *heard* yeh. Now goan have yer crap.

Adam watches Browne go. Watches his leg move around that blaring scar that serpents around from his shinbone to his calf and down into his sock. Trace fossil: first life-signs when that life's long gone. Marks in rock when rock was soft. Thrown out of the mad and ancient mix, out of the age of despair and its span.

Adam drains his can and cracks another. Swipes the *Metro* towards him across the sweaty Formica and starts to read; devils out there. Dementia in 140 characters. Some suit declaring again, again, that some event cannot be blamed on Brexit. Paragraphs of extinction, an obituary of the newly dead: drowned in the Med, welfare-reformed to death, shot or blown up or stabbed, and then a list of which women or girls have most recently been raped or abducted or killed. And then the entertainment pages; recipes, reviews. Something for his eyes to do and the nerves behind them and the fire in the synapses, the alcohol breeding these sparks like midges and like them they swarm and bite. So he drinks more. The elbow lifts and the throat dilates and the heart and its blades rest where they must and slice where they must and the train stripes across Wales towards England at the edge of the continent on the curve of the earth. The void almost close enough to touch, and smell, if smell it has at all.

The trolley man returns to the carriage and someone asks for tea. That drink: how serious the making of it was when Adam was a kid, as if it was a test of manhood – *crackin brew that, son. The boy's doing well, Viv.* Sooner that, tho, than the other shite that skirted his life and was to later roughly intrude. The dad he had. The damaged part of the world that he was born into. The passenger gets her tea and Adam raises his hand to the trolley man and buys more cans and miniatures. There's a slight raise of a judging eyebrow so Adam is effusive in his thanks, guessing that the sarcasm of that will be unrecognised. He can drink whatever, and whenever, he likes; he's an adult – he's a grown-up, now. But in truth, there was never, for him, in booze, that incredibility that there seemed to be for others; he never really experienced that immense and terrific seize of the blood that he discovered, later, in other drugs – the white rock and the brown powder. But in those lies calamity now and in any case it's not entirely about the hit. Not *entirely.* It's about the putting of him into the world in a condition of disassembly, all defences drowned, a declaration: there was an event that did *this* to me. Do not help me rebuild but look upon me in this awful vulnerability and see what powers I have felt and encountered and how bereft their passing has left me. Pray that you never know such visitation. And if you're asked to go up the mountain then never ever go.

The train gulps the country and shits it out behind, leaving a faint diesel tang and the rising scatter of birds, startled up from the fields by its blattering passage. The land passes, blasted, its usually watery parts inspissated down into thick and viscous slicks, gluey gloops in which amphibians pant their last. Adam looks out at it and he recollects, not long ago, it being under flood; rescue boats in the lanes, the lower hills become islands on the crowning humps of which groups of people sat and waved for help and animals stood dumb. On the news was a drowned land and now there is this drought, an escarpment of parch, all crisped and rusted and dehydration is dragging itself across places that have never known it. Sticklebacks lie curled and dried, caught halfway up the desiccated rushes and the fading fire of their bellies is the colour of alarm. It is a land in which it is fully understood that there are storms which arise from nowhere and uproot its inhabitants as they do trees and that such refugees need without question compassionate support. And toads burp their ultimate breaths in small salt pans; barren dry splats that were reed beds, not all that long ago.

At Newtown a beautiful woman boards and Adam guesses Polish; those Slavic features, the cheekbone peaks, the full jut of the lips drawing the jawline towards and into them. The slight snubbiness in the nose. She has hair dyed the colour of a fantastic thing, the red of a paradise bird, and she takes a seat further down the carriage from Adam on the other side of the aisle and she puts a phone to her ear and Adam strains to listen; hears the language and allows himself a satisfied nod. If not Poland then somewhere close. He gulps at the tepid beer. On the bubbles that pop in his brain they rise: Sion, Benji, Quilty the astonishing cat, Suki, Ebi, Sally. All those he met on his last trip up to Rhos and what will they do now, let go as they are, abandoned. The cat will be fine; feral soul, he'll steal and hunt and importune; his type can survive in any world. But the hominids: follow the wailing and the trails of blood. The lost shoes.

Someone gets on with a small dog. Adam clicks his tongue and winks and the dog regards him and thumps its tail and Adam asks it how it's doing and wishes Browne was here so he could set him a task; try talking to an animal without asking it a question. It can't be done. Where is Browne, anyway? His wee daunder up and down the train – he's been gone for an hour.

Forward motion again. Out of Newtown. He drinks and reads the paper. An interview with some bloke who blew most of his huge inheritance on drugs but saved himself finally by putting his last million into an import venture, shipping Harley Davidson bikes over from America. *I dared to dream*, he says. Adam swallows brassy saliva. Heat builds around his eyes. Because what it is – remove the need for money and it's all just a bit of dicking around. That's all it fucking is. The woman with the lapdog glances at Adam and he opens his mouth to speak then shuts it, quickly because no sober person has ever tried to engage a drunken stranger in conversation on a train. Money signifies, and in that dies value. Vixens in heat past midnight, the noises they make on the starlit hills – that sound is not in the junk, not in the hit because nothing is in the hit, but it is in the getting of money to get the hit. Only that shrieks. Don't have to fight to find it then all it is is poker for pennies. Adam must still be staring because the lady gives him a nervous kind of half-smile – the copse of cans and little bottles on his table – so he half smiles back then looks away. Out of the window, not back at the newsprint. He sees more hills pass and knows that power wants matter. Power needs to touch and manipulate and it has the means to do so. Him with the bikes, in his quest was a realisable endpoint that could be straddled and ridden and so it was not a quest at all yet power could make it seem so. All a thing, an object, another thing in a world of things. That he could afford to do. Adam drinks. The circumstances of his life could never entice him into the arena of games: never were his energies so squander-able. Oh the sordor around. He glances at the little dog which is curled up sleeping on the seat and thinks of Quilty, how he has never even half-belonged to him. Yowling apparition at his kitchen window that cold night and he was only ever semi-loaned from the wilds he slunk out of, the leopard-in-the-world that would happily feed on Adam's face if, when, all the human things crumble and collapse. Such is the antidote.

And no matter how far that feller may travel on one of his Harleys he'll always end up at the same place which is exactly where he started from.

That's better. That's a bit better. Oh the squalor. If you're invited up the mountain never fucking go unless you're prepared for what could possibly happen and no one ever is or ever could be.

The lady carries her small dog off at Welshpool and once out of that station Browne returns, rocking in his walk a bit as if aboard a boat. He retakes his seat and holds a hand out, over the cans and little bottles.

—Fuck's sakes, mahn! Ah told ye to go easy!

—Yeh well I was bored shitless, wasn't I? What took yeh?

—Drumming up some business so Ah was. Advance orders. Few fellers I know on board. Pissed and useless now, are ye?

—No. Adam stiffens a bit, camply affronted. —Not in the slightest. No lightweight me, lad.

Browne leans, sniffs and looks into Adam's eyes. Adam opens up his face, wide, juts his jaw, returns the stare. Three seconds, four, then Browne nods and sits back.

—But no more. That's yeer lot. We turn up with ye rolling all over the fuckin shop ... this could go bad for us, mahn. Ye've *got* to cover for me. Ah'm trusting ye here, now. Relying on ye to have me back. Right?

—There's two cans left. You have one. So I can't drink em both.

Adam opens a can and pushes it over the table at Browne who takes it up and drinks from it. —Ah. Hot day like today, hits the spot, that does, lovely bit of ice-cold lager. So refreshing. He winces. —Manky fuckin pish.

—Does the job, dunnit?

—Fuckin horrible so. Mushroom Cup-a-Soup with a wee bit of a kick.

They drink. The border approaches.

—How many orders did yeh get, anyway?

—A few. Not bad. More than me capital, anyway, let's put it that way. They all make good on em and Ah'm already seeing a profit. Shagaluf here I come.

They gaze out of the dirty window.

Into England, now. A proliferation of flags here, St George banners hanging limp in the gardens, Union flags tacked up on the sides of sheds. Shibboleths from a cult not close to these two moving men.

—What's with all the butcher's aprons?

—Heart of England innit says Adam. —And there's some fuckin thing going on, some royal bollox. Baby or a wedding or some such shite. I dunno. Birthday or something.

—Is there? Passed me by, that has.

—Something about it in the *Metro* there. Dunno, didn't read it, just saw the headline.

—Could've done with that when I had a shite just now. Two sheets left there was in the dispenser thing. Disgusting n all; bog full of bangers n mash. Made me fuckin heave so it did.

—Aw man.

—Telling ye, it's privatisation. This is what happens. Fuckin Brexit n all. Fucked everything up, or it will do. Rich government cunts raking it in even more.

The swells of Shropshire now, through the grey-streaked windows, the ruckles at the fringes of the central plain. The flags flop in the breezeless out-there and Adam sees the stasis of it all, how it unmoves, how it remains, and for one sickening second he gets it: the dull and diffuse docility punctuated by moments of state-approved mass distraction and intoxication. The heady hits of nostalgia. This, more than any other event in his recent past, makes him long for the needle, to dismantle the barrier between the stuff inside him and the stuff outside, violently and with bloodshed. It is this that makes him suck hard at his can and drain it as if it's an oxygen tank and he is slipping beneath brine. He cracks open the last one.

—No more after that, Browne says. —That's yeer lot. After we've done our thing we'll find a good boozer in the town, aye? Get as locked as we want to then, sure.

—Alright.

—Good mahn. We're nearly there anyway.

Shrewsbury, and beyond. Drawn deeper into the interior. Wellington and Telford stations are loud in their festoons. The union seems to be slipping out of favour, here, although a large crowd of people draped in that flag wave to the passing train from Cosford airfield. Waving their little flags on sticks. Browne regards them without expression and then mutters something inaudible.

—What?

—I said there's something fucking wrong with this country. Something not right. It's like a fucking madness or something. A psychosis.

—You know it, man. It's dead and it doesn't realise. It's just refusing to lie down and be buried and Brexit is just fucking digging up the corpse. Make Britain great again my hole. D'yeh know what it is? It just can't let go of the fucking empire. That's what it is.

—Who're ye telling? Don't have to tell a mahn of the Six Counties that. Tis a fact that I'm well aware of. Sure they use the word 'decline' but it's been fucking murdered, more accurately like, and it's never fuckin coming back. Look where we are now; Black Country. Factory of the world at one time so it was. Didn't me own granda used to get the boat over here to work, in the foundries n stuff? Sent money back in fuckin bricks, he did. *Now* look.

And Adam *does* look, and he sees a clogged canal beneath some concrete struts and a cluster of white flowers flown about by white butterflies, purity all heartbreak, and he would like to watch more of their exquisite air-jerks but he is of course carried past them yet that glimpse has reawakened in him – torrential recollect today – his visit to the Cwm Rheidol butterfly house a few months ago, the big blue wings spread on his wrists and the tiniest of tickles as the sugar syrup he'd smeared there was slurped off. Blue Morpho it was called. The size of a bird. The wings *beat* and did not flutter in a vivid blizzard around him and he needed nothing more, at that time and in that place. Oh, yes, and the violin mantis in its case; a thing of points and lines, unbelievable, of bladed triangles. And outside the jungly heat of the house, in the spring, with his cheese roll and his cup of tea from the caff and the steam rising up out of the sessile oaks on the valley sides, he watched a man go into the caff and ask for a bucket of hot water and there he washed his car in the car park while his wife and kids went in to see the stunning things that flew and crawled and could stay motionless in their startlings for hours. The man washed his fucking car.

Browne brings him back with a poke on the wrist.

—What?

—I said, d'ye know how many squaddies had Black Country accents? How many of them got sent over there, from this part of the country? To get their fuckin legs blown off? One feller, young feller, got caught by a bomb in a beer barrel. End of me road, this was. Walking past the pub yard and boom. The bhoys had been waiting nearby with their dogs and there's the feller, the squaddie like, only a young lad, torn to bits, still alive, and they set the fuckin dogs on him so they did. He's lying there, bits of him hanging off, and the fuckin hounds are tearing at him. The raw meat, see? Imagine that, mahn.

Adam drinks. —Did he survive?

—Far as I know he did, aye. Peelers and ambo came and the bhoys did a scarper with their dogs. I remember the paper saying that he'd survived. Bet there wasn't much left of him to send back to his mammy.

Ad's eyes seek out a hill but there aren't any. All is flat, the high parts now only buildings. The train begins to decelerate. The sun remains a flat weight.

—And now it might all start again, Browne says. —All this talk about hard borders. Last time I was over there I could feel it, so Ah could, this fucking *charge* in the air. People getting antsy. Unsure, see? They don't know what's gunner happen. Fought for thirty fuckin years, all that fuckin misery, just started to learn to live with each other and then fuckin Brexit comes along. Did one of them cunts ever give one second's thought to the Six Counties? Yer mahn Johnson, Gove, them cunts. That sicko fuckin Farage. Did it ever cross their tiny fuckin minds?

Adam shakes his head. —Course it didn't, feller. To people like them, it *never* fuckin did. Ever. Why would it? Why would they care?

Browne blasts air out through his mouth and rasps a palm over his skull. The scars there now maroon. Big brick warehouse outside, greenery in its gutterings, a yard filled only with broken pallets. Jeremy Clarkson's face on a billboard.

—This cunt, look.

—Who? says Browne. —Yer mahn Clarkson there?

—Aye, him. He's an English thing, inny? Like Farage.

—Well, aye. He's from England.

—No, I mean, what he *is*, like. What he stands for. Worrying about yer car. Sooner wash yer fucking car than go and look at mad butterflies.

—Ah, ye've lost me there, so ye have. How'd ye get onto butterflies?

—Yeah but. The concept is a clot in Adam's throat. Somehow it is linked, this is what he wants to say, all of it is linked but in ways that he cannot understand much less articulate. Gristle from a cheap and dirty burger, that's how it feels – that an obsession with cars is seen as an achievement, as doing something unique and interesting with your only life. Like losing sleep over the fact that someone somewhere might be getting something that you're not. Desperation; an awful lack, and then the crash in the world and the eye-searing flash and the slaver and the tearing teeth. How to explain all this … Orange Barred Sulphur. Painted Jezebel. And the flower mantis looked like a flower; it had evolved to do that. Ambush predator, miraculous, stone-still in blooms with its scalpels mounted on a lightning bolt. The car has to shine.

—Anyway. We're getting off now. Our stop sure.

Big station. A platform lined with waiting people. Adam and Browne disembark, climb the stairs, cross the footbridge, the booze heavy and sloshy in Adam's belly. Heat from the sky and up from the concrete and this is the Midlands and outside the station there is a dusty grumble of cars and taxis. The stream of people leaving the station meets the counterflow of people going in and they break around each other smoothly in shoals. A zephyr arrives from somewhere, brief half-relief, brings up a fine grit of track-cinders, gravel detritus and pulverised precursors, forebears now tough talcum that are crunched between the teeth and Browne and Adam move towards the taxi rank and climb in the back of one and the Sikh driver asks *Where to, boss?*, and Browne takes a scrap of paper out of his pocket and reads out the address that is scribbled thereon and the cab turns left into the city and things move fast, very fast.

Happening, now. A captured thump going through Adam, the drink and the adrenaline and the heat. Something is about to occur.

Browne speaks into his phone: – Ey, Sameer. It's me, mahn. Browne … on me way, aye. In a cab. Be with ye in a wee bit sure.

Trucks and buses slide through the streets, steel hills in a landslip. Knives of sunlight thrown from their chrome and glass. People, people.

Browne elbows Adam. —How ye feeling?

—Alright. Sound.

—Don't say anything. Browne drops his voice. —A mean when we get there. Just stand behind me and don't say anything. Leave all the talking to me. It'll be grand.

Ring road, the wide traffic-way all heat-speed and boiled hate. A big dark church that bakes and the bulk of the university and the vast waspy feat of Molineux, gold and black, a glimpse of the turf through the barred gate – an instant of mint in the flash of pampered grass. Sweat. Behind the stadium, down onto the Newhampton Road and its tight terraces. The bricks blackened over sooty centuries. It is here that the taxi stops. Sweat.

—This is yow, boss.

Browne pays the driver and they get out. This is Adam, temulent in the heat and the strangeness. He looks up at the roofscape – the blinding tiles and the ariel ideograms. The sun high and beneath it nothing fantastic will appear amongst the black chimneys.

—Thirty-six, Browne says, and his eyes scan. All those net-curtained windows and the wheelie bins, some windows tinned up and scrawled on: WANDERERS on one, and, below it, BAGGIES SCUM. Hot, hot. Touch that steel and there'd be a hiss and a blistering. —There. At me shoulder, now, Adam son. Stay at me shoulder. Don't speak.

They cross the road. Browne raps his knuckle on a door. Adam stands at Browne's right shoulder and then takes a step to the left and he has no idea why he does so. The door is red and with three long, thin, vertical frosted windows in it, behind which there is blurred and scumbled movement and then the door is opened by a short Asian guy.

—Sameer, yeh? Browne.

Browne holds out his hand. Sameer drops his eyes to Browne's lower leg. —There's the scar, he says. —*Knew* it'd be yow, robbing Irish cunt, and then Browne is yanked by the hand into the house and a big hand reaches out from behind the door and clamps around Adam's nape and then there is a hallway and the pissy stink of skunk going past and a green carpet with brown swirls and some sort of magnetic vice and then there is a kitchen and there is a fridge which Adam is hurled at and bounced off and things leap in his vision, black commas and ticks flickering and sharp, a whirl of animal impulses that rave and snap. Only three words can rise: – What the *fuck*?

—Down't spake, says a local voice. —Or Oy'll hurt yow. Really fuckin bad.

The senses snatching at stimulus before shutdown: the glass phials on the worktop and the scorch-sided saucepans on the cooker. The walls with stains on. Bare lightbulb. Stuff everywhere, tools and clutter. It's like, it's like—

—Who the fuck *are* yow? Matey's supposed to be on his own.

And a man. There's a man, here, in the gulping senses: the home-made tats on the face and neck and hands and the reddish stubble and the one eye that appears unnaturally fixed while the other one circles. The scoop taken out of the ear. Such a face. A kind of click in the voice, too, the voice that comes out of that face. Big before Adam, all details enlarged; pores like craters and the lip-cracks trenches. That ear; it's been bitten. There are four smaller scoops within the larger scoop where teeth once met and held and tore.

—Oy said: who the fuck are yow?

Adam's dad would've hurricaned, would've grabbed at tools, furniture. Adam says: — I'm, I'm fuckin no one, mate. Don't even know Browne. Just along for the ride. Only met him a couple of days ago, honest. In a pub.

*He comes at you with a knife, son, you go at him with an axe. An if he comes at you with an axe, you—*

—So why are yow here?

—Just told yeh, I don't really know. Browne asked me to come along, that's all. Bit of support, like. Few quid. Whatever's goin on with him is fuck all to do with me.

A noise from elsewhere in the house; a kind of yelp. Adam hears himself blink; two damp clicks. —What's happening to him?

The man curls a lip. —Nothing good. There's bad blood.

Reach out and grab. This is a *big* man, a big scarred man, a big fucking violent man, shove him, shove him hard and he'll stumble and go down and then you can stamp on his fucking face, stamp—

—It is, innit. It's fuckin *yow*.

—What?

—It's *yow*, innit? Oy fuckin knew it. *Knew* there was a reason why yow were still fuckin conscious.

—Ey?

—Little fuckin voice in moy head there was. Soon as Oy saw yow at the door.

*Now*, the fucker's rambling, now, do it now, the stiff fingers in the eyes, blind the cunt, lunge and—

The man drags a chair to him and sits.

—Down't recognise me, no?

Something, something outside, shakes Adam's head for him; it reaches down from the yellowy ceiling and makes his head move. —I don't, mate, no. When did I meet yeh?

The man just looks. There's even what appears to be a small smile on the wreck of his face. The one good eye kind of roves over Adam's face, taking in the details, while the other one remains fixed to a place on Adam's thorax.

—Yow don't remember. Yow don't remember the little thing. Now the man, bafflingly, tickles the back of one inked hand with a finger of the other. A secret sign or something. Kind of Masonic. —Little spotted thing, no?

—No, mate. You've got me scoobied. Sorry.

And who knows why the mind recalls what it does and by what strange routes. The thud of Adam's heart now retreats from his skull.

—Yow towld me things, before it was clowsed down. Oy met yow. Yam were going to the kitchen. Yow towld me things but they clowsed it down an here Oy am but Oym still not using. This is just work. Mun-aye. Are yow?

A flicker, now – a tiny twitch in the recall. Something about identity, yes, but other, bigger things get in the way, as they've started to do. Of everything that is not them. —No. Just drink.

—Glad to hear it. Clean as a fucking whistle, Oy am. Still.

That eye takes it all in. Then it closes, briefly, and the man rubs a hand over his face and there is another anguished cry from somewhere in the house and the man points to the back door.

—Gow out there, there's a ginnel. Turn left onto the rowd, go round the Molineux and yow'll be back in the town. Easy. Alroyt? Someone up there's looking out for yow, must be. Oy'll tell Sameer yow did a runner. Get away with yow, now. Quickquick.

And then Adam is outside in a small yard full of junk and then he's through a gate and in an alleyway and then there's the stadium and then there's a scrawled underpass and then there's a pub and over it all is the heat, always the heat. Then there is drink. There is a jumbling in the brain and everywhere else. Browne has gone, out of the world that Adam is in now and he is looking at his face in the mirror behind the bar and he is imagining it inked, tattooed, say with a skull, or decorated as if the skin has been peeled away and the muscles bared in glistening maroon sheets, or, or, just the one word CUNT on his forehead because maybe *then* it would come back, the inferno found within him, these eating flames. Because it's not about the display of disarray or not wholly – there is immolation, too. The Vietnamese monk, unmoving in the agony, only here it is raucous; it must riot and roar. This plea of his must deafen.

231

There is drink – lager and whisky nips, again and again. There is a woman reaching past Adam to take her bottle of BrewDog from the barman and there are words, more ink, on the inside of her pale arm, cursive: *what doesn't kill me makes me stronger.*

—I know some paraplegics who'd disagree with that, a voice is saying. —Or this feller I met once who got blinded by a rubber bullet. Or this other feller with no artery in his leg. None of them are dead but they're a fuck of a lot *weaker* than they were. It's, it's all just plat. Platitudes.

—Ah. That's nice, bab, the woman says. She has ear-rings like tiny chandeliers.

—Yeh, an, *and*, y'know the feller, even the feller who wrote them words? He had a breakdown, he did, ended up in a fuckin asylum. Did *that* make him stronger?

—Who, Kanye? Rubbish. He's playing at the NEC next month. I'm off to see him, chick. Got tickets.

—It's like, it's like ... things happen for a reason. This shite that people come out with all the time. Things happen for a reason they say. Oh do they? the voice is saying, all slurred. —A mean, fuckin *do* they? What reasons might there be? The rape and murder of children. What fuckin reason can there be? *What*? Platitudes. Bollox. Fucking meaningless, all of it.

—Let go of me arm.

—Oi. Stop bothering my regulars, you. I'm gonna have to ask you to leave.

And then there are street lights in a humid night and there are many moths around those yellow bulbs. There is a train station in the haze, and far people who move like zombies, under the lights, between the buildings. And they must see him in the street-shine and haze moving like the bones have been taken from him but the water in the booze and the oxygen in the boiled air – oh the toothsome metabolic components of the still-here, still breathing and moving, if brokenly, around. Better not to think, just let machines take you to wherever you need to go. Drink.

The question of what-will-spring-out: the unknowability of it. Hard, already, and craning; or maybe limp and sad. Clean and soapy or thickly cheddary, putrid in the pastes. Clean-shaven or thicketed; pendulous of gizzardy bollock or sprouted out from a wrinkled and seemingly empty skin-fold. Roped with veins or smooth as a sliced potato. In this beats being. An attractor, her, these things drawn by her very biomass; that and the smile she gives out and the availability in her limbs' open arrangements. And something like the accessibility always in desperation, too, in the eyes that would seek an eternity in the crust of dried semen between her breasts, a forever in that instant when the eyes roll back in the head. Her dark matter; she bends the light. Some circumcised, some not: the hoopy nodules of gristle. Twists of fluff on some that must be picked off. Ones that swing like clubs; others, like Rang's, that poke and prod rudely, without manners. And always behind these never-duplicated things the needy flesh-engines that fade into shadow, that pant back in the distance somewhere, pushing out hands to grab her shoulders or hair or tits or her throat. Astonishing, really, all of it, but briefly so; agonisingly briefly so. There will be sparks, in the things that move on two legs towards her; in this meat you may meet me, or something very like it – that is the promise that is its own scourge. That scoops itself out. But they tend to come at her from light – out of the gantries behind bars or the doorways of illuminated rooms or from windows where they've been standing, those framed holes into the wider world where nothing glows in this season, the big sun making only the smallest trickles of shade that puddle at shoes like the piss of the incontinent.

She'd been half expecting her belongings to be stacked on the pavement outside her house but that hasn't happened and she's surprised to feel relief: rather a bit more than half, then. But other things are as she imagined; the yellow-and-black police tape that bars entry to the bridge, the brackish indifference of the river, and the knoll of mail that means she must put her shoulder to the front door and *shove*. She enters and tramples the envelopes under her cork platforms. This is some other woman's house. It is not familiar to her. Somewhere in it is the phantom of her and a smaller acompanying one. She bends, scoops the post up into her arms, carries it like a baby into the kitchen and dumps it onto the table. Do not open. Like the tape outside says: DO *NOT* CROSS. Disobey and soon you'll be bloated on a beach, picked over by crustacea and carrion birds.

There are things she must do: shower, change. Just, what, refamiliarise herself with the place where she is supposed to live. She reaches out and flicks the switch on the wall and makes light; not disconnected yet, then. She flicks the switch off again and picks the phone out of its cradle and puts it to her ear; a dialling tone, broken with no doubt many stored voicemails. Minor fucking miracles. She can hear herself breathing.

Men with eyes that change colour, according to their moods, and can even, in certain types of light, be golden. Men whose smiles are abrupt and joyless. One, recently – how many days ago – who screamed at her when she accidentally knocked over the wine. The last bottle, and at 3 a.m. She'd mopped it up with a sock and he'd wrung it out into his glass and drank it. An episode in which no one covered themselves in glory, including the sock. Sometimes the stubble seems to change colour, too, octopus-like with mood; fiery red, the white of age or concealment from sunlight like an axolotl, in the facial folds. Where no lights ever probe.

She moves to the window. A few dead flies on the sill. The houseplants withered and under dust. A spider in her web in the corner; Emma blows, very gently, towards her and she spins and scurries into the safety of her crevice. Out there, two swans drift upriver; Emma gets their feet, beating, beneath the stately grace. Sea-pinks out there, thrifts. A large log on the central spine of silt, a kind of neck and head it has like Nessie. The hole in the bridge. He drowned. The poor old man. The police tape brightly coloured like a venomous snake. Upstairs, directly above where Emma's now standing, she would read stories aloud every night about an I Love You Bear. The How Do You Do books. No alpha in that little boy; he told her once that *trophies can be quite heavy* so he'd prefer not to win any. And on his first day back from school: *it was okay, but I don't think I'll be going again.* And yet each night there'd be a different dinosaur, a new thing to haunt, happily, his hypnogogia: pronunciation gore-go-SAW-russ meaning 'monster lizard'. Carnosaur type. Upper Cretaceous 90 million years ago over 4.2 metres long and 4.5 metres high. Bigger than this house. Food: meat. Found in North America and western Asia but never in Wales, no. And it would take a very very *very* long time to count to 90 million.

Her hand crawls up beneath her top, her sexy, white, tie-across-the-tits top. One tie is half ripped away, now, hanging loose, because that one in the baseball cap, him with the teardrop tattoo, just would not fucking wait, would he? But it was less out of impatience and more out of control – that she knows. And it is her body; hers, and the quest she carries within it, even criss-crossed with scratches as it is, now, on the neck and back and hips and belly, as if something has tried to erase her as a mistake. *Her* limbs; *her* organs. The wildest fucking woman. You tug the cloth down over the hips and it all tumbles out and boings upwards and God the variety spins the head and to know that it could never all be experienced exhaustively unless that head be shattered like a shot vase. All to know of immortality. Short ones, long ones. Hairy, hairless. And oh the colours! No tropical reef could know such a rainbow. She remembers once, in her unwellness, talking to a therapist about cognitive behavioural therapy and then going home and googling CBT with the safe search off. God almighty: nailed to blocks of wood, they were. Foreskins stitched shut. Blowtorches, for Christ's sake. The variety without end.

With her fingertips she traces the place where she knows the tattooed legend is and she touches the thin crimp of stretch marks that in some lights look pink and in others seem silver. Signs of life. Out there is the world. In here is her. And the way things wrongly echo, as if she's a traveller through time returned to alter a calamitous present that here is future and needing to wrestle against some powerful and reactionary and preventative cosmological force: do *not* open the envelopes. This wildest woman smoulders in her skin and then a very, very interesting thing happens, lovely in its way, a startling coincidence of events; she rubs the inside of her right forearm against that of her left, probably to rid herself of an itch, and at the very instant she does so the landline rings and it is like stridulation, as if she has coaxed the trilling from her own needy skin. The caller ID reads MUM and Emma moves away from the phone quickly as if it might pounce. Up the stairs she goes, towards hot water and things that smell nice. Get clean to get dirty. This body is hers. Things speed up.

He waits a while in the betting-shop doorway; the length of three cigarettes. No neck-growth on this one, just a corpse in ghostly blue light. The minds that thought up these things – the opposite: always do that. They preach frugality, you waste every penny. Self-discipline? Shed every shred. Temperance and moderation – well, watch what happens *now*. They come and go in groups, to the cashpoint over the road, some of them studenty, others workmates on a night out, some right fucking 'roidy-boys because Carmarthen are in town to play Aber FC. 3–1 to Aber so the pill-heads will be out for revenge. Cowley stares at them from the little cave of his hoodie and remembers Carmarthen and the judder in his shoulder and he wills them to make eye contact but they don't seem to see him, half hidden as he is inside the shit-brown hoodie in the doorway.

There, now: a guy on his own, youngish, rucksack. Cowley is over the road in four bounds and very close at his back:

—Do not turn around, mun. Stay looking at the screen I SAID DO NOT FUCKIN TURN AROUND! Yew don't need-a see what I look like, twat. A balance. Get a fuckin balance on-a screen. Feel that? That's a fuckin blade. Go right in yewer fuckn kidney it will. Ba-*lance*, I said. Rich cunts, yew stew-dents, these days I SAID DON'T FUCKIN LOOK AT ME! Hurry-a fuck up! Maximum. Three ton, I know what it fuckin is. Do not fuck about .... I am gunner walk away backwards an if I see yew try an look at me I'm gunner blind yew in both eyes.

Cowley snatches the flap of money out of the machine and legs it around the nearby corner and down onto the hanging steps, that pissy dank passage down which men and women were once marched to the gibbet on the shore and there he removes the hoodie and drops it in a corner and then he leaves the passage and goes onto the promenade at an amble, nothing suspicious here, just a bloke taking the air. There is a bouncy castle and the smell of onions and some bikers standing around next to their machines. In the heat there is much skin bared and Cowley watches the legs of the girls and their midriffs too and their cleavages where and when possible. And he eyes the male torsos, sees either the puniness or the overdevelopment shielding the internal timidity that, Cowley knows, would not take much effort to reveal, to drag dribbling out into the light. And that there is in such men with the urge to dominate the equivalent counter-urge to submit, to roll over when the real alpha comes along, Cowley has always known this; even in the sacristy, behind and within the shrieking in his held-down head, he had that knowledge. Maybe that's where it began, in fact – where it was actually born.

He takes a left up Pier Street, at the top end of which the robbed guy is talking to two coppers by the town clock. Botherless, Cowley walks past them and heads down Bridge Street and turns left at the end of it. There is a small weight in his pocket which causes him to list away from the Trefechan Bridge on which, if he looked upriver, he'd be able to see the new bridge under which he once swung so weightless. He has a couple of pints in the Mill. Quiet; just a couple of old guys at the bar and a large woman watching the telly. No Carmarthen fans. Down, then, to the bus stops, where Cowley stares at the timetables for a minute and then turns to a woman with two kids licking ice lollies.

—D'yew understand these things, love?

—Where is it you're wanting to go?

—I'm needing the time of the next Traws. Down to Cardiff, like.

The two children look up at Cowley. Sticky pinkness all over their chins.

—Let me see. Cowley looks at the woman looking at the marks, the numbers and the codes which might as well, to him, be animal-tracks, swirls in the sand or mud. One of the children, the boy, points at Cowley's neck and says:

—Dragon.

Cowley smiles. —That's right, *bach*. Big red dragon.

—Looks like you're in luck, the woman says. —This says that the next one leaves in half an hour.

—Where from?

—Here. Thirty minutes. The TX to Bristol.

—*Diolch*.

And he's away, at a jog, down towards Wetherspoon's. Half an hour. Better work fast, faster.

They look cool and attractive, Reservoir Dogsy – white men in a group in black suits and shades. She squeezes in next to one of them at the end of the bar.

—You all in a band?

—A band? *DuwDuw* no. Funeral.

—Ah who died?

—Friend. Doubt you'd know him.

—I might do. It's a small town.

—Owen Lambert. Ring any bells?

Emma pretends to think. —No. How'd he go?

—What?

—How'd he die? If you don't mind me asking.

—Suicide. Hanging.

And the man takes a bite at his pint.

—Ah. That's awful.

The man doesn't answer. Doesn't look at Emma, either. She orders a large gin and tonic and drinks half of it back, hoists herself up onto a bar stool and arranges herself so that the man is kind of wedged between her legs, her right knee a blind behind which she can squeeze his thigh.

—Ey now. Enough of that. I've just come from a funeral.

—Take your mind off it, then. Life goes on.

—And I'm happily married. Got two kids I have.

Emma almost splutters. —Does that matter?

—To me it does, aye. A lot. And he slides out from between her knees and takes his pint off to join the other mourners, wherever they might be, probably at the buffet that's been laid on, in the back room; there are smells coming from that direction, sausage roll and quichey.

Emma puts one leg over the other. Her toenails, chipped; she'd neglected to touch them up, or remove the last flecks. Looks a bit skanky, if truth be told. She starts to pick at her big toe with a thumbnail and kind of loses herself in that before she catches herself on and sits straight, back upright, with both feet in their cork platforms on the rung of the barstool. Gets a faint whiff from down below but thinks that might just be in her mind; she'd showered, after all, but did she feminise? Douche? She puts her chin on her chest and takes a big sniff.

—You okay, love?

—What?

—Not crying, are you?

Emma smiles at the barman. —No. Just having a sniff.

—Thought you might've been with the mourners. Not that you look like you're in mourning, I mean.

He lifts and lowers a big hand above the bar top to indicate what he can see of Emma, the white top with the snapped tie and the valley of flesh behind it: no widow's weeds, here, on her. She smiles at him. He smiles back, and is then called away by a feller waving a tenner at the other end of the bar. Emma appraises – not a bad arse on him. Christ this never-ending fucking *noise*. She finishes her drink and crunches ice. Thoughts of crustiness crowd in, of stepping so far outside of something that there could never be any way back, not even when you realised that the place you'd stepped into was desirous of your wreckage and, even, before the final cremation, intent on making you regret every moment of your life hitherto, from birth, from conception, if *this* is what it leads to. Such horrors crowd in. Her tonsils burn in the ice-freeze.

And she re-enters herself with a jolt. Small jolt, and all she can smell now is juniper. And the scruffy toenails, well, who's going to be looking down at her feet? Although there was that Bristolian recently, wasn't there, on his hands and knees, kissing them … kind of worshipping. Grunting as he was down there. She could see the double-crown of him, the red backs of his ears, the doughy rolls of his nape, when she looked impassively down.

The barman returns. —Sorry about that. What can I get you? She asks for the same again and raises her empty glass.

He gets off all of a sweat and a thirst but train-ness remains within him – the unstoppable forward motion, the slamming clatter, the occasional warning wail and sideways lurch. Such noise. A pint in the station's Wetherspoon's to reignite his buzz, there to look up at the blueness above through the glass roof, beyond the anti-pigeon mesh.

Drink drunk, buzz back, into the town. A notion in him that he should return to his flat, just to make sure his stuff isn't piled up on the pavement outside. And maybe Quilty ... Quilty, that wondrous animal, who once licked his eyeball and sent a ferocious shudder through his whole body that was not entirely unsexual. But, well, he's a survivor, now. He's returned from his quest still whole, un-holed, and he will not think of where Browne might be now, in that skunk-fumed terrace and in awful pain and fear or maybe even shoved into an adjacent actuality, no, he will not think of that, only that there's cause for celebration – his continuing-in-the-airness. Plus there is this mad momentum in the noise, Christ, the endless noise.

Only a pub. The downstairs room of a pub empty, nearly, because upstairs is an open-mic night and the drinking is soundtracked by muffled declamatory voices from above which are in turn punctuated by bursts of applause, diluted: a thunderclap with an L-plate. Adam drinks away the recall of the scoop-eared man in the kitchen and whatever details there may be of him in some secret niche of the mind. Just luck, that's all. Drown everything else in alcohol.

People troop downstairs. The poets, their audience. Adam is a hunched and drunken man at a large table which is soon occupied as are all other seats and indeed much standing room too. Two tiers at the bar and Adam has just an inch left in his glass and he is snarling. Needs a refill but fuck just *look* at the bar. It'd take ages. Sion and Benji. Are they wondering where he is. Browne. In what state is he. All organs unanchored in Adam's body, it feels like – unbecalmed. Under and in the crackling sun and the storms go on raging, registering on no gauge or map.

The guy on Adam's left; beardy bastard. And on his right; beardy bastard too, and in some kind of stupid smock. Between them is an overweight girl in glasses and another man, older, in a waistcoat of self-aware flamboyance. Also bloody beardy. Boiling amongst is Adam and his extreme weathers. They know nothing of the day he's had, of the charred things he's seen, nor to even for one instant think about shapes in the sky that hover and bring messages and other things, things that cannot be named but which leave devastation behind, snapped trees and seared earths.

Blurdle blurdle. That's the sound they make. Their talk. Then Beardy Left wipes beer foam from his whiskers with the back of his hand and says: – Well, I'll be famous when I'm dead.

Adam barks. A leapt laugh. And now they notice him, in wary regard.

—You okay, man?

—Aye, sound. Adam feels the tip of his tongue slicing the inside of his cheeks. —Famous when you're dead. Another one. World's fuckin fuller yiz.

The overweight girl stands and is absorbed by the pub.

—I mean, right, this is what I mean. Adam leans in. —So d'yeh think your, your poetry will benefit the world, then? Heal wounds? Think it'll make the world a better place? Well, a writer of any worth knows full fuckin well that the words are more important than the person who wrote them. Right? So why don't you fuckin top yerself? Cos, cos, I mean, you've obviously got all this brilliant stuff lying around that will benefit, fuck, might even *save* the world when you're dead. That's what you're saying, innit? So huury up and die. Let the world have its cure. Tell yeh what, I'll even supply the means; wait here for a bit and I'll go and score a load of temazzies, enough to kill a fuckin bull. Sit with yeh when you take em. Sing you a lullaby as you die. Alright? And then we can all read your poetry and be saved. Go on, lad, you can be a hero, here. This is your chance. Kill yerself and save the world. Be, be Jesus.

Beardy Right laughs. Beardy Waistcoat shakes his head and Beardy Left hisses and says: – God almighty. What a cock.

Adam leaves the bar. Wants gone. His is a clumsy, un-grand departure, with the need to stand up and kind of *sidle* around the table and the Three Beards, but it is achieved without too much stumbling and staggering and sniggering and then he is outside, on the pavement, one hip against a car as he rolls a cigarette. The sun has slid down behind a roof yet with the warmth in the air it seems as if shadows should be cast but when Adam looks down at the ground he sees none, not even his own, and he feels as if it has been robbed from him and he wonders, with some small sadness, where it has gone and what has become of it. Probably nothing good.

The last time Cowley hitched down to the capital he'd acquired a lift as far as Llangurig and then one from there to just outside Rhayader where he stood in the pissing rain for three hours until a milk-tanker took him to Brecon. And there he'd stood with his thumb out like a dickhead, two hours or more, half-empty vans ignoring him, some faces openly jeering, pointing, giving the wanker sign, and him there boiling inside sending the wet rage off himself in rising vapour. Some bear of a bloke had taken pity and stopped for him but then put his hand on his knee on the outskirts of Merthyr and then there'd been a red splatter on the dashboard and Cowley had then to crash in a garden shed before dragging himself in the morning up to the motorway again where some rugby fans heading down to the Millennium Stadium had stopped for him and put a spliff and a tinny in his hand and dropped him off at the castle, smack in the city centre, so it turned out okay in the end but the shite leading up to that was not to be repeated, ever. Two days to reach the capital; would've been quicker on a horse and fucking cart. Four hours and a fortune on the train and the barriers are unjumpable these days. Free movement: the passage of bodies. With restrictions, in this country, chains pulled ever tighter. And so the lived-in flesh crumples and draws in upon itself and all the worlds it does contain.

He makes a kind of wee encampment for himself at the back of the bus, a *cwtch* in the furthest corner; coat on the seat as a barrier, a shop-bought butty and a half-bottle of voddy. Coast road, turn off at Aberaeron, veer away from where *she* will be, her and that waster fucking junkie and that lovely little girl. Hills and churches – the steeples, the way they can be seen above everything; each one a painful probe into a shame-hole, a corroded place inside. Imagine them all in flames. Lampeter. Students from the university get on. The accents – a couple of American, most English. Cooing over the land-scape. Cowley nips at the burn of the vodka and wants to tell them that there is nothing out there, that it's just empty. That *this* is ancient Cymru, here, in the furthest corner of the bus, and all of it that you've never seen so why the fuck wouldn't you want to gawp? Yet behind his shades his eyes are often closed, and when they're open they stare out at the emptiness, dry in the heat and so many people unclothed in any kind of light except the sun's ceaseless sear. Fuck it all. Imagine every-thing on fire. Doze.

And then Carmarthen. Ten-minute break. Cowley hauls himself off the bus to stand leaning against its exhaust-reeking and heated steel and smoke. The driver, smoking too, makes an attempt at conversation, asks him what he's heading to Cardiff for, but Cowley does not hear, gone as he is in recall; easiest purse ever, not far from here and recently, the toppling McBride, that remembered rapist in the form of his face, stamp, three breakages. Had to be dragged off, didn't he? Would've killed the cunt. And *money enough for life* is what Aney said. *No money worries ever again, sor.* Take every belonging – house, car, the lot. Get a private car down to Cardiff. Limo. Or do what every other fucker with a lot of money and some Welsh ancestry does and buy a flat in fucking Pontcanna. Or emigrate to Patagonia. Or just fucking London, where you can sit in the bar of the Welsh Centre and whinge about *hiraeth* and the old soil when you can be standing on it again two hours out of Paddington. *Hiraeth*, bollax; that's what the Great Western is for. It's just another thing to enrich the sense of self. How can the world retain its shape, not crumple like an empty chip wrapper, when it is made up of more hole than substance?

The bus rumbles against Cowley's back. He re-boards. Re-snuggles himself in his nest, re-nips at the vodka. Keeps his eyes behind his shades and, as the bus shudders again into motion, takes the little machine out of his pocket and cradles it in his hands, doesn't examine it, just feels the small weight of it in his palm. Then he returns it, to the safety of the pocket over his heart. A few quid in the Cash Converters. But there are other ways of getting money.

A couple of years ago he was with Llŷr in Llŷr's van going, where, he can't remember now, Tenby it might've been for a weekend on the piss, and on this road out of Carmarthen they'd hit a sheep. Well, not much bigger than a lamb, although it'd left a big bloody dent in the wing panel. Llŷr had stopped the van and they'd gotten out and gone over to the animal, lying broken at the roadside. Squatted down next to it. Its breath – how shocking loud that'd been, and how fast, the quick rips of it, the ribs going in and out, the eyes clouded over already but the bellows of the breath, frantic, and then everything had just stopped. In a nanosecond, from one state to the other, and so great the breach between the two seemed – eyes to pebbles in one quick trip of the heart. They'd carried the carcass into the van and Llŷr had taken it to a farmer boy he knew outside Saundersfoot and they'd had free Sunday roasts for ages.

Doze. He wakes, finishes what's left of the vodka, dozes again. And when he next wakes there is a strong sense of conurbation, of heavy traffic and big buildings nearby; it's Merthyr, he thinks, but there is somehow a sense of looming – not only in the velocity of traffic, the torrent of which the bus now joins, but in the sense of some largeness pressing up against the sky, slipping now from blue to a darker blue. A feeling that whatever's on the ground nearby is thickening the sky. Through Cowley's half-awakeness two faces drift; the girl with the tattooed stars behind her ear and the skinny lad with the scouse accent. Unclear shapes, just noses and eyes and lips. Where are they now and what have they been doing since.

So much traffic outside. It was a *whomping* sound that the lamb made, not very loud, when it hit the van; not a sound of lethality, really. And the ease of transitioning that followed ... pantpantpant then nothing. That easy; no fuss or bother. And think of free lamb roasts for the rest of your life or, rather, having so much fucking money that they might as well be free. You could pay people just to stand there, in front of a light like a searchlight while you just stood and looked. Women, like; get that shape outlined. And the freedom of the body. Free to not be shunted and controlled. Free to not be chipped at so that the struggle to hold on to any kind of reliable structure in it becomes something to which every fucking second and every remaining cell must be devoted. *Whomp* – just once. It'd be *that* fucking easy.

At Swansea, Cowley is fully awake, and there is a hunger in the way he now sits upright. Taking everything in. By the time the Millennium Stadium is in sight, the lofted struts of it all lit up sharp and a-shimmer in the haze of evening, he is thirsty again.


Need calls to need. Microscopically precise. Close as it is to a vortex that calls it grasps for hostage or if not that then just the co-doomed. Like proteins call to proteins in the gutweed on a shore; the chains such sugars are called to form. In both there is growth, of a sort.

Adam smells the burning; it is brought to him not by any breeze, because there is none, and the heat stamps on his head like the heel of a boot, but still he smells it – something aflame on the beach. A suggestion of a party. He makes to stand up from the bench on which he's sitting but in doing so his knees go puddingy and he falls back, hard, an *oof* leaving him, the drunk's innate gimble letting the bottle in his hand trace his movements so that not one drop is spilt. He spreads himself on the bench. In front of him is the sea and its far red ridge. See them all outside the Glengower, in their couples and crowds, every shaded face turned to the blaze. Trade route, once, out there. High eyes on the hills on watch for the boats coming from Ireland. Some contemporary commentators calling it the avatar of the Internet, he read that not too long ago, when he was reading, before.

—And it's shite. Bollox. Fucking bollox.

Some strolling people stare at him.

—It's cack. They just don't fucking get it. It's *new*, man. We've never had anything like it before. That's what they just can't understand.

All the legs quicken. Adam notices hairless male legs, a kind of white scale at the ankle bone, so sharp in his vision; the senses heightened before the shutdown. Is he talking aloud? He takes a pull at the wine bottle. Sour, sour. He has been the crust on the crotch of kex discarded. He has been the fly, spoilt for choice. And God he's been a zombie and he is that zombie. The disconnect from the soul – look into the O of the bottle's neck. Put it to your eye and have a good look in.

—Mam what's that man doing?

—Nothing now come away.

Adam looks up. The woman has back-flaps of flesh that hang over her belt and her child is bright blue and holding a shield. A boy; he looks back at Adam over his blue shoulder and then is tugged away again by his mum.

—Why've yeh gone that colour, lad? Why are yeh blue?

A sharper tug. They cross the road where, outside the old courthouse, they meet another plump woman and another tiny smurf.

Kids' fancy-dress party. That's what it must be. Or some kind of environmental protest because some of the adults are blue too. And holding placards. The Na'vi – that's what they're meant to be. Some gurgle leaves Adam which could be taken to be a sort of laugh. There were people dressed like that when he went to see *Avatar*, with that mad woman from St Helens; they dropped some mild acid beforehand but all he got was irritated. And in the cinema bar, following the film, he'd cornered one of them and told him about how there were people *here*, on *this* planet, suffering, being shat on, and there's this prick painted blue getting all emotional about pixels. The St Helens woman had been laughing hysterically. The information world has become more real than the world of sense, that's what he'd said. He's all for ecology and liberation and all that nice stuff but these twats, these humourless, pious blue bastards which don't even exist – go on, the baddies! Blast the shite out of Hometree! He'd still been ranting when he'd been ejected from the multiplex. Carried on ranting in the pub over the sliproad. Never stopped, really.

And yes he's been the gnat that whines in your ear when you're falling into sleep. He can smell something burning on the beach.

It's a lovely sound that the waves make, a soft sigh and collapse. A lull. Each suck of water back into the sea, across the tinkling shingle, he feels something of him get tugged back with it, a small and fluid part of him taken back into a vast absorption and it is not bad. He drinks, and in that way makes himself more fluid – to give the sea more to take. Dissolve the body for the soul needs no flesh. Offer it all up. No fear, just deliquescence, and the shore is awash with it, in the dead creatures, in the reefs of bleached weed. Laughable, really, that thing about eternal life in the optimum physical state when dissolution is the aim and that we were sure of up until recently. Until power and its props became valued above all. Oh the squalor.

He hears the unmistakable sound of happy young women, a lit-up sound but it puts the hairs on his nape and forearms into horripilation. He hides the bottle beneath his jacket and arranges himself roughly sober – arms folded, back straight. The nice noise nears. Voices that shine and a glistening laughter. Please let it not be Jess and her friends. He keeps his eyes low as the women pass and God he sees the skin of their legs and feet, honey, and the *shapes*, he burns, and the scissoring shadows and he will not watch as they move away from him, further up the promenade. Will not watch their arses and backs for he understands that there is no room in their vision for the sight of him or if there is it would be only to assess for threat. Which is the way it is. The way it must be. If he had looked up as they passed they would've been between his eyes and the sunset and Christ they would've glowed. All of them, surrounded by the blaze. But they might've seen the direction of his stare and ruin would've come.

That there needs to be some level of shame: he gets that. He knows that, always has, and he accepts. But there is a level of murder that has come about and a sickness in the hate of the weak, of the vulnerable. Rhos has closed down. There will be boards nailed to its windows. And there is a fawning infatuation with such. Were he upright the sickness of this, an instant glimpsed, would no doubt knock him back down again, but because he sits he just takes the bottle out of its hiding place and raises it to his lips. Sour. But it is wine. Which does its thing.

Stronger, now, that burning smell. He counts to five then surges to a stand, steadies himself with a hand on the back of the bench then very carefully moves over to the gap in the railings and descends the stone steps to the beach. Tide long out and the weed on the steps has baked to a crust so there is no danger of slippage but it is a crippled descent that he makes, putting both feet on each step like a child. A sweetish smell rises and there is a group of them at the foot of the steps, spliffs on the go, talking in the one accent that can be pinpointed to no locale.

—Ah, now, fuck, here yis are. Students. Look at yis.

He stands amongst them. *Sways* amongst them. The bottle clasped by the neck between two fingers and swinging like a pendulum.

—This is it, lads, innit? Don't tell me, don't tell me. This is your fuckin chance, innit? This is your time. It's come.

He's not even sure if he's talking out loud — he's not really sure of anything. They're mostly not even regarding him, just silently looking down at the stones on which they sit.

—I know you. I've met yis a thousand fuckin times. And you've always been the same, you have. You've always envied people who, to you, to you have led more, more fuckin, *realer* lives, haven't yeh? Yis, yis've always fuckin wished you were poor. Jarvis Cocker. When you hear 'Common People' you're not the, the Greek girl, are yeh? He burps, hugely. —You're the singer in that song. In your fucking tiny minds.

A lad with white spikes for hair looks at a lad in a beanie hat. —Jarvis what?

—Aye, yeh. You're the fuckin singer. Now, tho, *now*, the time has come that yeh don't have to hide. Hide yer fuckin sheltered and your, your fuckin privilege anymore cos, fuck, you're encouraged to fuckin *flaunt* it. Aren't yeh? Look at me, I can *afford* nine fuckin grand a year to spend on me education. Or, or, or Mummy and fuckin Daddy can. Doesn't bother me, no. Sitting here on the beach with yer weed. Nine grand a year man. An yeh know what?

For effect, Adam takes a big pull at the bottle and swallows with a noise.

—Yer still wankers. Even more now than you've ever been. Pamp, pampered bastards. Mummy and Daddy will always think the world of their little fuckin rays of sunshine. What you think youse know, you don't. You really fuckin don't. None of you have ever seen what I've seen.

He thumps the bottle twice against his chest. The drama.

—Predictable, yis are. Boring. For all your fuckin money. You'll never. Never burn inside.

He moves away. Did he just say all that out loud? Behind him he hears a mutter and a burst of several laughters. There is the sea and the sinking sun in its distant sear and there is the sea wall which he stays close to as if famished for shadow and because he can steady himself with a hand on its stones. Further up the beach, he can see some small flames beneath the jetty; in the darkness under the wooden slats, a small fire flickers. He can smell it and he can see it.

The music is dumph-dumph-dumph shite and the back room of the pub is too bright, no interesting shadowing going on, but at the core of it is her and she's incredible; not because of what she's made of but because of what she's *made* of what she's made of. She moves sinuous, joyous in her skin, her face aglitter with rings and bolts, a swoosh of inky hair down over one eye, the tattoos crawling across her bare arms and the spangly maroon dress tight to all her swells. Her cleavage is a creamy fold and above it a raven has spread its drilled-in wings.

Emma cannot take her eyes off her: the confidence, the pleasure declaimed in being here, in all of her zinging skin, in this overlit too-warm back room of this pub. A tattooed sheela-na-gig in a tight sparkly dress.

And Emma's not the only one to gawp. People dance around the woman and there are many eyes turned her way over shoulders and through hair. Emma necks her Cheeky Vimto and puts the empty glass on a sticky tabletop and sways over to the woman.

—I love watching you. You're cool as fuck.

—Thanks.

The woman's hand, chunky with rings, clamps on Emma's skinny hip. The fingers dig in and Emma wonders if they now blister, if the woman wants to instantly jerk her hand away because of the scald. She looks at Emma's face.

—Are you not going to dance with me?

—What? Oh.

Emma's been standing still, while the brilliant woman serpented around her. Again this has happened; she's realised she's been statuesque when it's seemed she's been in motion, twitching and scratching and nodding her head. So she dances; she mirrors the woman, her opposite hand on the opposite hip and God how small it looks, there, clutching like that. With each step Emma smarts a little down there – that barman had been rough and she hadn't really been ready for him but the bar could not be left unmanned for long – but that doesn't matter and she feels the eyes on her and her partner, all the different eyes and the histories etched in them, but soon she feels no eyes on her at all; very quickly there's just her and the otherness held between her hands, the fact of it, all its charged knowledge, and it would not matter if there were no other people or even no music. Just this yielding warmth in each of her pressing palms, and they *do* press, as if they need to meet through the flesh that separates them. So the body between them writhes all the more. Like an accordion.

A time goes by. Then the woman whooshes air upwards through her fig-coloured lips and the swoosh of hair jumps for a moment and reveals her black-rimmed eye and falls back down to conceal again.

—I need a drink. Let's get a drink.

She takes Emma's hand and leads her across the dance floor and through the people who part. Some will is being done. In a damp cave a squirt of oxytocin lights it all up. The hand in Emma's shrinks and for a moment takes on the dimensions of Tomos's but then the bar is there and Emma needs to hold on to the lip of it. The woman orders two Lady Di cocktails.

—What's in one of them?

—You don't need to know. She has a great and unusual half-smile, this woman, the top lip curving to show just a chip of tooth. —They get the job done and that's all that counts, amma right?

The drinks are two half-pint glasses brimming with foamy blood. The woman clinks her glass against Emma's. —Down in one.

And it doesn't burn it hums behind the sweet redness. Finds Emma's belly in a rolling rush and then scoots upwards to her head.

—Just to be sure that I'm reading the signs right. The woman engulfs a piece of Emma in a large-ish hand and squeezes and in her glare is a warning allure: this is a new land. —You want this, don't you?

—Yes. Emma's not entirely certain if she's spoken aloud so she nods her head to be certain. And then says it again, or for the first time: – Fuck yes.

—Good. I thought so. Follow me to the bog, then. And we've got to be quick cos my man's on his way.

If Emma is observed there is no way she could know because the world has shrunk to the woman's back and another inking there, what is it, Emma blinks twice, a yellow circle of some sort with wavy lines around it to indicate heat or radiance. Emma wants to touch it. Which she will, and very soon. She'll fuckin lick it, nibble at it and at other places with the teeth of a weasel.

Fuelled by driftwood blue shoots and green thumbs sprout within the fire's red wrestle. It has turned the space beneath the jetty into a hearth-side which could be described as cosy, in another actuality. The people gathered here like jetsam. Their limbs.

The bottle of sherry comes Adam's way again, handed to him by a topless, skinny guy with the crappest tattoos Adam has ever seen – inky-dinks, needled in with the point of a compass, six-inch nails, with soot for ink. Adam accepts the bottle and bows his head in thanks and takes a gulp. Sour, so sour, but it is sherry. A film all over the inside of his face; the drink seems to draw mucus out of the ducts and glands that produce such stuff. He passes the bottle to the figure on his right, long beard and woolly hat, even in the heat, browny-reddish the beard with springs of white. Not old, yet he appears to be trying to look old.

—Ah thankee.

—What?

—Ah said ah thankee.

A strange accent.

—Where you from, mate?

—What?

—Where you from?

The man pokes the bottle into his beard and tilts his head back. The fading light sliced by the boards above into three stripes across his face. His eyes close as he gulps. Then he passes the bottle to his right.

—Whoy might you need to know?

—No *need* about it, mate. Just wondering, that's all.

—Ask me no questions. None. Hoy do *not* care where *you* are from after all.

Adam had forgotten this about such gatherings, such clusters – the paranoia, the simmer. The enclosure of the self, that smith-ereened thing, in an armour so fragile that the steps from small talk to hospitalisation seem to stem from a kind of logic. He'd forgotten it, yes, but he's always *known* it lies in places like this.

The skinny guy on Adam's left nudges him in the ribs.

—Pay him no mind. He's harmless if you don't speak to him. Most of the time. Just pretend he's not there.

Adam nods. The bottle travels around the fire clockwise, through the people who sit and squat, six of them, no, seven;

there is a figure lying down and covered entirely by an over-coat, except for two small red trainers. The bottle is passed over this person. There is a smell under here, briney, on the edge of rancid; probably just the general shore-reek but Adam cannot stop himself from thinking of the armpits of these people, their groins, their feet, their breath.

—I'm Darren by the way.

—Adam.

—Alright man.

They talk in a whisper. Everyone here does, excepting the guy to Adam's right who says nothing, does nothing, just gazes into the small burning.

—Who's everyone else?

Darren shakes his head. —They come and go. Weather like this, you can kip on the beach.

Which is no kind of answer. —Who's under the coat?

—A doll-woman. Tiny *twt* of a thing. Thought she was a midget at first but she's just way tiny. A right *twt* she is. Scottish lady like but she's Chinese. From Glasgow.

A spark leaves the fire, drifts like a seed towards Adam's face but then, as if snagged, veers vertically up towards the jetty boards against which it dunts and dies. The bottle comes round again. Adam drinks and passes it on wordlessly. Feels a lurch inside himself, an abrupt shift in his fathom; he will soon be unable to stand. Soon he will fall flat back on the shingle and know nothing at all for several hours.

—*Yma*, Adam. Eat these.

—Eat what?

Darren takes one of Adam's hands and puts two pink pills in the palm.

—Get em down. I can see you about to go.

Adam laps the pills up, crunches to bitter chalk, swallows. And then he asks what he's just eaten.

—Dexies. Got me script today I did. Could see your eyes going. Figured you could do with a boost. This is not the place you wanner fall asleep, shag.

So that's it: another boundary breached. He imagines a sapling stamped back into dirt. And he never thought it'd be dexedrine, prescription as it is, unadulterated; he thought that, when, if, he ever did regress, it'd be a swooning back into that which his soul called out for; mounds of dirty speed, cut with all kinds of filth and the ensuing vileness of the comedown with the sick and suicidal thoughts and the horrible marathon wanking sessions, the frantic friction taking his dick, and his mind, into a state raw and bloodied. The dirtiest of drugs, that's what he'd always imagined; a resignation without hope. It is shame that he needs, only shame. It is a craving. It's always been that way, with him. Even more so now.

—They'll sort you out, shagger. Quarter of an hour and you'll be throwing some shapes, guarantee it. And I don't need a thank you.

—Sorry man. Big thanks.

Darren gives him a smile. God his tats really are bad; like he'd been infected with burrowing insects and then painted himself with blue ink and then took a shower. Vermiform traces all over him; stickmen and truncated words.

Adam looks into the fire, already a bit less drunk. An arrangement of wood collapses into two, the crosspiece burning in the middle but unlit at each end, just slightly blackened. In one sudden movement the man to Adam's right leans with a grunt and takes this piece up in his right hand and begins to smack it into the palm of his left, repeatedly, a swarm of sparks instantly busying the darkening space beneath the boards.

—Aw fuck. Darren grabs Adam's arm. —Time to move, man. Now.

Adam is pulled upright and out onto the beach and up the steps onto the promenade. Quick, quick. Half aware of the people moving around him and the rest of the life up here, in the proper world, the noises from the amusement arcade and the smell of chips and the lights in the buildings over the road, the Chinese takeaways and the rooms above them. Darren pulls a long piece of cloth out of his jeans pocket like a magician and it becomes a shirt which he starts to pull on.

—Just in time, that. Close one.

—To what? What were we close to?

Darren buttons his shirt across his torso's smudges and angles.
—Nothing good, I'll tell you that.

An echo. Bouncing off the chambers in Adam's beginning-to-buzz skull.

—You feeling them dexies?

—Aye, yeh. Think so.

—Good boy. Got a party to go to, me. Wanna join? Know a boy just bought a bag of rocks down from Rhyl the size of my head.

Darren rolls the sleeves of his shirt up with quite precise movements, neat folds, each arm, up tight to his elbows. Tucks himself in. —Be a laugh, shag. Town's been clean for months, so. Celebration, like. What else you gonna do?

And the question is a good one. What else other than accept. Let the wave take you. Deposit you smashed on whatever shore except *shore* is the wrong word. Perhaps because catastrophe itself is its own anchor, a ruination self-willed is just a holed boat when everything is sinking anyway and oh the thrill of the plummet, the deepening of the colours from green to blue to black. What does the jumper see between the twentieth floor and the ground? In those seconds, what choirs are heard in the whistling zoom of the air? Now there is a boom in Adam's chest. Just step off because there is nothing up here. Nor is there anything down there but the space between the two is fuller than forever. You'll be able to scream so fucking loud; you'll be permitted, in that compressed universe of unrule, to see everything hidden. Just step off. Be true to yourself at all times. And if there is to be any disappointment in the recognition that the plea repeated in reverie and entreaty to *do it all over again* could've possibly been referring to this, *this*, well, the roar and frenzy of that shortest of journeys will be all the distraction that could ever be required. Enough, even, to reduce the crash and splatter of terminus to just a small tinnitus in the ear.

It's all in there, amongst the roofs of this small town by the sea in this summer of scorch. In this small town with the mountains behind it the frazzled peaks of which hold lakes so cold and blue.

—Alright, Adam says into Darren's waiting face. —Take me with yeh.

And step off. But someone is calling his name; he can pick out his name amongst the general jabber of the promenade.

—Who's that?

He looks and sees a car at the kerb. And someone is leaning out of it and calling his name.

—Adam! ADAM! What-a fuck yew doing with him, mun? Get-in a car! Aw Christ. Look at-a fucking state of yew.

Cowley nods at the figure on the settee but it's no kind of a hello.

—Ooer fuck's him?

The man looks up, over the top of his iPad. Raises an eyebrow.

—Lodger, brar, says Rhys.

—Didn't tell me yew had a lodger.

—An yew needed to know, did yew? I need the fuckin money, mun. Fuckin bedroom tax innit.

—Does he speak?

The man smiles. —Fluently. Like a proper grown-up and everything.

Rhys sits, takes a half-smoked thing up from the ashtray and relights it. —Be nice, brar.

—I *am* being nice, Cowley says. —And what's this fucking 'brar'?

—It's just what they say.

—Not what *I* say. It's what women keep eyr tits in. Yewer not from Cardiff, Rhys. Talk like yewer fuckin meant to.

—Jesus, mun, what's up with yew? Me only fuckin brother, haven't seen yew in ages and yew come in havin a go. Sit down, have a can. Chill out, fuck's sakes.

There's a spare chair at the end of the couch. There'd be room on the couch itself if that *lodger* wasn't spread out across it like the shite of a moor-dwelling crone, smiling and swiping his finger across the screen; little finger, as well, and that in itself puts a tight circle around Cowley's neck, constricting. Grinning to himself he is like there's a great big joke going on that only he understands.

Cowley sits. It's a kitchen chair, hard and uncomfortable, and after the hard and uncomfortable bus seat for hours. Rhys leans to one side, straightens up with a can in his hand, passes it through the fuming air of the small room to his brother.

—Have a drink.

Horrible fur in Cowley's mouth. Over his tongue and between his teeth, a grout of grot. He swills it away with warm lager. The beginnings of a headache appear, between his eyes.

—How'd you get down, bus?

—Aye. Four fucking hours.

The lodger looks over the top of his screen. —Four hours? From where?

Rhys answers for his brother. —Aberystwyth, brar. Home town like.

—Aberystwyth. The finger pecks at the screen and swipes. *X Factor* is on the telly in the corner but the sound is low and Cowell is making his tongue move around the outside of his mouth. The main ambient noise enters through the window, open in the heat, admitting the hard city summer in all its clottedness; and all the sounds of traffic, both mechanical and human – a siren, of course, and revelry. All exhaust. And the smells of Splott, curry spices behind the overnote of civic whiff, bronze coins touched by a thousand hands. Cowley drinks. Magazines are on the floor and on the cover of each is a massively developed man pulling a pose; cable veins and pumpkin muscles. Cowley points.

—What's all this gay stuff?

—Gay stuff? It's bodybuilding, brar. Supplements and exercises and that. Been hitting-a gym, I yav.

And a certain inflation of Rhys seems to have occurred since last the brothers met, Cowley can now see; the puffed-up neck and the rise of the pectorals in the V of the jumper.

—What 'roids yew pumping in?

—'Roids? Fuck off, this is protein shakes, that's all. An loadser red meat. Steaks. Don't need 'roids, just fuckin diet. 'Sall it is. Protein.

—Yew don't get that big that quick without steroids, Rhys. Bet yewer dick's like an acorn now.

Rhys laughs. —Don't yew wish. Cos then yew'd feel less inadequate, innit.

—Inadequate? I'm not-a one livin in-a fuckin gym. An calling everyone 'brar'.

—Yew wanner try it.

—Don't think so, *brar.* I'd sound like a twat.

—I mean the gym, dopey bollax. Works wonders, it does. In-a head, I mean.

Cowley finishes his can and holds his hand out for another. —In-a head?

Rhys nods. —Yew know what Am talking about.

—Do I? News to me.

—Yew do. Cos-a last time I got out of-a hospital with me fuckin knee held together with pins I knew I had to do fuckin something. Eating me up it was. Yew know what I'm talking about, mun.

The warm lager goes down. Cowley wonders why he came all this way on the hard-seat bus, for a headache and a sermon from his pumped-up brother. No one glows anywhere. *Set up for life* said Aney Lavin.

—I haven't got-a first fuckin clue what yewer on about, Rhys.

—You've got to let it go, brar.

—I didn't come all-a way down yur for this.

—This what?

Cowley just drinks. —I came yur to see what's left-a me fuckin family. Wanted a break that's all. Don't need this shite. And stop calling me 'brar'.

Rhys shakes his head sadly with a kind of quarter-smile on his face and at that, if he wasn't blood, that's what there'd be: lots of it and suddenly, all up the walls. Cowley watches his brother drop the dimp of whatever he's smoking into a beer can and hears a tiny hiss.

—Don't yew fuckin ...

—What?

With his flat in the capital and his new body. With his fuckin *lodger,* dicking about on his screen. —Just fuckin don't, Rhys.

—How can I not do what I don't know what the fuck yewer tellin me not to do?

—Yew know.

—Here we go again. Why-a fuck—

A loud voice bursts from behind the iPad. —Oi! Like the fuckin Gallaghers, you two! The lodger turns the screen to face them. —Stop squabbling and have a look at this.

—What is it?

There's like a party on the screen. People dancing, and music, and much movement amid the rise of high peaks.

—This is on YouTube. This thing going on up in Aber. You not heard about this?

The question is aimed at Cowley who doesn't answer, just leans in to see the small screen. He asks again: – What is it?

—This great big party on top of a mountain outside Aber. Been going on for ages, it has. All over the web. It's like a big gathering. Not heard about it up there, no?

And again Cowley does not answer. He sees people; he sees a crowd. He sees a ridge that he recognises on which shapes and forms of women stand and he sees the sheen of a lake that he has seen before. The noise of the scene that leaves the screen is loud laughter, mostly, and music, and chatter, heightened and excited; faces that look happy appear on the screen then move away and are replaced by similar others. A laughing man holds up a small child. Behind him a stick is thrown into the lake and a dog leaps in after it. Some words appear beneath.

—What does that say? Can't read it from here.

—Llyn Syfydrin, says the lodger, using the 'l' and not the 'll' sound. —That's the name of the lake. I've been following it. Apparently it all kicked off when some girl saw something on that ridge, there.

—What girl? What something?

—Dunno, some girl. She blogged about it and it went mad. Viral. All over world, judging by the comments like.

—Aye but what did she see? This girl?

—Said it was like a kind of floating woman. In the blog, like. A woman floating in the air and she spoke to her. Or that's what she said.

The people still. End of footage.

—It was just-a sun coming up, says Cowley.

—Well that's what some people are saying yeah but everyone's going up there anyway. It's become this, this big party place. Thinking of going up meself next week. You don't know about this, being from Aber and everything, no?

Cowley shakes his head. —What else is there?

—You mean from the lake? God, there's loads of stuff. Everyone's posting. Here's something, look.

He swipes, and a talking head appears. Uncreased features and neat hair. Rhys and Cowley lean in and the lodger makes a space with his forearm on the coffee table and arranges the screen upright, angled a bit so that he can see it too. The man on the screen is earnest.

—Oo's this cunt?

—Some government prick, looks like, Rhys says. —Looks the type. Now *whisht*, brar, I wanner listen.

—Can't hear a word. Turn it up.

The lodger does. *They've been told to remove themselves civilly, and with respect,* the man on the screen says. *And I have to say that, ah, that this polite request, from our police force who were simply doing their job, just doing the right thing, this polite request was met with the foulest of abuse. These people were warned, moreover, that if they do not remove themselves voluntarily then, well, force may have to be used. It is private property that they are squatting on and as they know, as they SHOULD know, such behaviour constitutes a criminal offence.*

—Squatting? On a fucking mountain? What's he on about?

No one answers Cowley, not that he was seeking an answer anyway.

*Many of these people have left their jobs to form this, this commune, jobs that many others would be grateful to have. And in doing so they are jeopardising the economic recovery which this government has worked so diligently to bring about. Not only that, but their presence is making a demand on the public purse which the hard-working British taxpayer is paying for, and this at a time when we need everyone in this country to get behind the government to make a success of leaving the European Union. We all need to pull together on this. And the, the site has been earmarked for wind-farm expansion, for investment, and these people are trespassers on that land. If they do not leave of their own accord and out of their own goodwill, and with the good grace that they have been allowed the opportunity to, ah, to show, then I'm afraid there will be an, there will have to be an eviction and that's the very last thing we want to do.*

The buffering circle turns in centre-screen.

—What's going on? Why's he stopped?

—It's buffering.

—What's that?

He tries not to smirk, the lodger, but Cowley sees the small wrinkle in his lip. —It's loading. Give it a few seconds.

*There are designated places for this kind of thing – Glastonbury and the like. What we are seeing in west Wales at the moment is simply illegal. The gathering itself is a breach of the law and we have it on good authority that illegal drugs are in use and, even, the sheltering of illegal immigrants might be taking place, of those who do not have the right to be in this country. It's impossible to say for certain that this is not going on.*

He appears to be pinkening, the man, his cheeks getting gammoner, more shiny.

—Goes on a bit, dunny.

—That he does, brar. Government, innit.

*Society, to function properly, needs structure. It needs the rules of social contract, mutually beneficial to all involved. This, ah, this gathering; well, this kind of thing, if left unchecked, could usher in the very breakdown of that. We will have a dispersal, make no mistake about that. They are*

The spinning circle. Then:

*breaking the laws of the land and not only that but the unwritten laws of social contract and mutual respect. I dread to think how many man-hours have been lost to the workforce, have been denied to the economy which this government has worked so hard to restore to a position of health and growth, by this, this commune. These people are the enemies of progress and growth, pure and simple. A religious gathering? It is hedonism, and criminality, pure and simple. These people think they can, can do whatever they please and trespass on private land and, and, do whatever it is they're doing up there while those who do the right thing and work hard and look after their families have to foot the bill. We as a government will not let that happen. If we learnt anything from the, the lawlessness of 2011 it is the need to*

And then the circle that spins again. The man's face is frozen in mid-snarl, a glint of blunt grey tooth.

*nip this type of thing in the bud. Stop the rot before it spreads. We have no desire to witness a repeat of such, such, such shocking scenes.*

The man's mouth closes and he nods firmly and turns slightly to the side as if to move away and indeed he does take one little step before he turns back again, kind of pirouettes back to re-face the camera:

*And another thing; the 12th of August is fast approaching. Parts of that land have been set aside, are, are used and have been for a long time, have been traditionally CONSERVED as a grouse moor. If those people are still up there on the 12th, when the season begins, then I shudder to think of what will happen. There are children up there. We need to get these people off the mountain and back in work and we need that to happen as soon as possible. This is a time for unity. Thank you.*

And the man's face freezes and stops.

—Look at this, the lodger says. —This is what's got him so worked up. Funny as fuck it is.

He taps at the screen and more footage appears; the same landscape, with the ridge and the lake, all of it upland, and this time the crowd not dancing, amassed instead on the pebbly shore of that lake and looking not out over the water or up at the ridges but towards a line of policemen in hi-vis and some other figures in sober suits. One of these raises a loud-hailer to his mouth. A voice comes from behind the footage, slightly apart from the image, evidently the voice of the filmer, that of a young man: *Uh oh. He's not happy.*

—Watch this now, the lodger says, and repeats: – This is funny as fuck.

Mostly distorted to inaudibility through the megaphone and by the openness of the landscape out into which the voice is thrown, only certain words of the suited man's speech can be discerned: *trespassing* is one, repeated, and *disperse*, and *fair warning*. You can see the crowd listening, mainly still, some flags aloft of crosses and dragons and the EU stars, and when the megaphone

262

is lowered those at the front, as if at a prearranged signal, turn and drop their trousers or lift their skirts. Loud laughter, footage ends, and words ticker-tape across Cowley's inner eye: *all them white upside-down Ys in a line.*

—Ha! The lodger barks and snaps his iPad shut. —Have that, man! That's what we think of your fucking threats. And rules. Telling you, I have got to get myself up there. Got to.

—What are you doing? Cowley says.

—What?

—You turned it off. I wanna see more. Show me more.

—But there's loads. I don't—

—I wanner see more from that lake.

Rhys cracks another can. —Show him a bit more, brar.

—But there's fuckin loads of it. What's he wanner see?

—Just show him some stuff.

Without looking at Cowley the lodger erects the screen again. Taps and swipes. Two men in armchairs now appear.

—What's this shit? Where's the lake?

—They're talking about what that girl saw.

—What girl?

—Up at the lake. That floating shape thing that she blogged about. I've just told you. They're talking about what it might've been and why it all kicked off. There's loads of this stuff online.

Cowley leans in, elbows on his knees, the dragon on his neck livid in the low-hanging light. A horn honks outside. The machine in his breast pocket, its weight falls forwards and down in this leaning position and gravity tugs it floorwards, causes Cowley's shirt on the left side to protrude pointedly like a moob.

—Wanner see the lake, Cowley says, yet he leans, still, leans in listening.

*It's not a particularly rare phenomenon*, one of the men is saying, on the screen. *Indeed, it's rather common in that part of Wales. The prevailing conditions in that area and at that time were perfect for this sort of, ah, apparition if you like, phenomenon to occur.*

Another voice asks, off-screen: *Atmospheric conditions, you mean?*

*Yes, atmospheric conditions. And the discussions concerning this that are occurring on social media and the, erm, the gathering, the commune that has been generated by this ... well, the sociological issues are intriguing, to do, perhaps, with societal atomisation and the like, or, or, the contemporary need for something transcendent, to believe in. To offer meaning in uncertain and turbulent times. To have a reason to come together.*

—What's he talking about? Why are you showing me this? I wanner see-a fucking lake, mun.

—Hold on a sec, the lodger says, and holds up an infuriating finger. Cowley looks at that finger. Knows the sound it would make if bent very far back.

*Such matters are not my field, but there are many educated and astute minds out there that are studying these things. What we are seeing, in effect, fundamentally, from a scientific point of view, is a hysterical reaction to a Brocken spectre; an easily explainable atmospheric event. As I say, the, ah, the hysteria, well that's not my field, but I can tell you all about water droplets and convection and the confusion of depth perception and the other scientific reasons behind the apparition. The optical illusion, which is all that it is, essentially. It's just physics. Let me quote, if I may, Johann Silberschlag, who, as far back as 1780 wrote*

—Get this twat off, says, almost shouts, Cowley. —Can hardly understand a fuckin word he's on about mun. Get this shite off.

The lodger raises an eyebrow at Rhys who gives him a firm, small nod and the little finger is reset to swish.

—The fuck yew show me that for? An what's a fuckin Broken spector?

The lodger laughs. —Broken spector? It's not a what, it's a who.

—What?

—It's a *who's* a Spector. Record producer, he was. Is, if he's still alive. Mad feller, mad hair. Shot his wife. Phil Spector.

—Don't act the cunt, brar, Rhys says, in a voice lower than his own ankles. —No need for a wind-up.

—I'm just messing with yeh. A spectre is like a phantom. A ghost.

—A ghost?

—Aye, yeh.

—So why didn't he just say that, then? A broken ghost. That's what she saw. Fuckin big words these twats use. An he can't even say em proper. English cunt, can't even use his own fuckin language in-a right way. An it wasn't even a broken ghost either. Doesn't know what he's on about.

—Alright, brar. Have another can.

Cowley accepts the tinnie and opens it. —Broken ghost be fucked. A ghost! Eyr like, like fuckin kids, ese twats are. What did yew make me watch that shit for?

The lodger has folded his iPad away and placed it on the sofa next to him. On the TV now a lad in a baseball cap is placing a hand over his heart. Nearby, outside, the eastern border is a land border, mapped, a smooth tectonic enmeshing. Yet it is on it where – just as at the spiked grykes and sea-cliff serrations of the western endlands – uncaringly carved and jagged edges rip and make us bleed.

There is a sear in Cowley's stare. The rapid rise and fall of his chest and the snorting in his nose. Rhys says his brother's name, twice, but elicits no response. The lodger looks at the can he raises to his mouth and fakes a noisy gulp out of.

—Slurping, now, Cowley says. —Can you not drink that proper like a normal cunt? D'yew have to make such an horrible fuckin racket?

Rhys sighs and rubs his face with a hand. Repeats his brother's name. Feels the air in the room hum and he knows, fully, if he knows nothing else, what will soon happen; what cannot be stopped from happening, now. What has its origins behind heavy drapery in a mote-mad sacristy in a small coastal town to the north, a four-hour journey away by bus, as do the muscles and fleshy swellings that now just flop uselessly against Rhys's bones.

He's waiting outside the bog; Emma stiffens when she opens the door and sees him in his abrupt tallness, the eyes slanted down towards her and the whitening lips turning back over the long teeth. In a nanosecond she knows who he is and she's aware of her own grin as she looks up at him. Her grin and what's in it.

—My *war*-man in yur? he asks. Accent strong Swansea. —Yew been in yur with my *war*-man? Someone said yew av.

—I don't know, Emma says. —You tell me, and she raises herself on the tippy-toes of her cork platforms, gains a few more inches, sufficient so that she can lick the man's lips, swipe her tired tongue twice across them. —That taste like her, does it? Anything in that you recognise?

The man rubs the back of his hand across his face. SCFC on the knuckles. —Fuckin lezza. Fuckin rug-muncher.

He puts Emma to one side and breaks his way into the toilet and the door swings shut behind him and Emma hears him shout: – Meg? Meg! Where yew fuckin to?

Meg. So that's her name. Nice name. And Emma's knees are wet because she knelt on the pissy floor and the taste on her tongue is herby so she drinks whisky at the bar, one double shot, two, and with the second the barman gives her a napkin.

—What's this for, then?

—To wipe your face with. He puts a fingertip on her chin. —Here. A kind of black stuff.

She wipes and looks and, yes, the napkin comes away black-smeared. It has the greasy clog of lipstick and there was, very recently, a mouth so adorned that snapped and sucked. To get away from the toilet behind her and whatever might come out of it Emma takes a third whisky around the other side of the bar into the furthest and busiest room. Obviously alone as she is Emma is touched in this room, hands on her hips and arse as she sways through, prowing with her chest. How they want to touch her, these days; to contact the crackling sparks. God how Emma burns. How the muscles shear in her legs and flanks and back and the smells of her, the stickiness of her, the imprint of clutching fingers at her nape. Encrustations, seepages. The living body leaks and reeks and moves like this – like a thing aware of the displaced air. She orders a drink, lager, at the bar with which to chase the spirits and when she goes to pay a voice in her ear says *I'll get this* and a hand gives a note to the barmaid. Emma looks, sees hair cropped very short like copper filings, a dressing steri-stripped to the skull on the right-hand side above the ear.

—Hello.

Emma can only smile.

—Don't remember me, no?

Electrics do ignite in Emma's head but the connections made are minimal. So many faces recently; so many hands. The faces above her and the hands below, often in a half-light, and through a blur of booze and blaze – the fires that carry her. And those faces loose, in the semi-light above hers, or buried between her spread legs and the crowns conveyed across her vision like a choice of toupees.

—Can't say I do.

—No? Aberaeron caravan park not ring any bells?

Emma hides behind her drink.

—Had my head shaved since then. Cos of this.

He inclines his head and points to the bandage.

—What's that?

—Seven stitches. Got bottled by some fuckin gorilla. Pardon my language.

—What for?

—Ey?

—What did he bottle yeh for?

—Don't really know. Not that it matters anyway. Just some fuckin psycho, that's all. Mind if I just check something?

And he reaches out and lifts Emma's hair behind her ear, where the stars are; just lifts it out of the way for a moment so he can see. He nods. —Thought so.

—What was that about?

—Just had to be absolutely sure about something. Comen have a drink with me and my boys, yeah? Won the darts so we're flush, we are. Drinks on us.

Where he touched her, where his skin brushed against hers, there is heat; it is like the stars there have become real, spheres of flaming gas and their awful scorch. Suns. At that very faintest of touches. Need, need. Emma was on her knees. The roots of her tongue ache. And then there is a hand on her hip, steering.

A brontosaur is Cowley from the doorway of Dorothy's chippy, his big surge and stumble. The drunk and hungry queuers part for him and once beyond them he leans back against a wall in a half-squat, his tray of chicken curry chips in his left palm. The knuckles of his right hand, well, he gives them a little lick; like a cat he draws his tongue across the gashes made in them by the lodger's teeth. Only the one punch before Rhys was on his brother's back like a chimpanzee and dragging him off but one punch was all it took, one mighty moment to block out that smirk and that swishing finger and the *intrusion* of it all. Him taking up all of the couch like he did. Back on there now he'll be, spitting blood into a bowl, crying over his screen-machine.

Caroline Street around. Spicy stinks and the people in a shifting lattice, boys in their shirts and girls with their legs and heels, the stiffish way such stilts make them walk. All the noise. The planet spun into a greasy night-time, the capital's hoard of heat belched back and made slippery through the film of hot hanging oil in which bits of birds have been boiled.

The saliva soothes, on the cut knuckles. Forgotten to pick up one of them little two-pronged wooden forks and not being arsed to go back in, Cowley fists the food into his mouth, the turmeric in the sauce yellowing his whole hand. It stings. He sees he is being stared at; four boys in t-shirts gawping. Cowley says something. The boys laugh.

What did you say?

Cowley forces the food down, gulps massively. —I said what the fuck are yew looking at?

More laughter. —Oh you *do* surprise me, son.

—Look like a fuckin pig, man, you do. D'you have to eat like a fuckin pig?

More food stuffed in. Cowley chews like a dog with a toffee, all visible tongue and teeth and rolling bolus.

—For fuck's sake. From Newport, is it? Gotter be from Newport. Where's your fuckin manners at?

Cowley barks: – Manners!, and shovels more food in. The curry sauce is smarting inside not just the cuts on his knuckles and the bared red beds under the nails he's recently bitten raw but also in the very skin of his chin; it stings there like sunburn.

—Making me sick to look at you, boy.

This one, the last to speak; he'll be the one to get the hot food in his face. He's the one closest and is standing slightly side on, to present a smaller target, his fingers beginning to curl up into the palms, the head tilted back a bit.

—Well stop fuckin looking, then. What's wrong with yew? Wanner give me one, aye? Look away, mun, now.

The hot food will be slammed into the face followed by a boot to the balls and then fists to the face. Less than two seconds of ferocity – and it *must* be ferocious – and the others'll back off, one of them will pick his fallen comrade up and they'll retreat, probably shouting something. The want of this throbs in Cowley's forearms and behind the wide balls of his eyes that have seen *such* things.

—I said fuckin look away from me, mun. Now.

—Chopsin fuckin prick, the man says but there's still a small shift in his feet, a tiny movement backwards; probably didn't even notice he was doing it. But Cowley did.

—Don't bother with him, says another boy and puts his hand on the main man's shoulder. —Look at him. He's fuckin redneck. He's fuckin beyond.

—His head's gone, says another and the movement begins now, away from Cowley, a backing-off. The fingers are pointed:

—You're fucking lucky. *Lucky.*

Cowley laughs and licks the now-empty tray.

—Fuckin pig. Get back to the farmyard where you fuckin belong. Mingin twat.

A few more steps away now. Further down Caroline Street and its human zoo some chanting goes up, the kind of thing that declares Stag Do, and one of the lads says:

—Here we go, boys. I can smell fuckin English, I can.

There's a bit more pointing, a few more words, and then they're gone, into the crowd. Cowley drops the tray to the floor. Licks his knuckles again. He looks around him at all the people in their busy fun, at the women wobbly as foals, at the pumped-up boys. He sees eyes that stare. He sees the hint of hunt in it all and he just can't be arsed. He's had enough of it. Wants out of it, away from it – that's his need, now. He is eaten by a titanic tiredness. One colossal yawn.

He moves, in the direction of the bus station. Around him the city bangs and boils over. Of course there are puddles of putridity underfoot and berms of garbage in the gutters and types of sordid underbellying. Of course there is the lilac lightning of ambulance and cop car. Of course there is the clog of spice and fume, of course people fight in the streets and grope in doorways, and of course there are the pigeons, always the pigeons, one of which squalls away from Cowley's feet and he watches it rise and fly to be lost in the great eruption of the Millennium Stadium, there to roost among the beams and struts, some topped with stars. They soar static through the emptiness, these giant slanting rafters, through the endless black that hangs above this. Tiny man, the pointless dust of him below the unlit forever. An unbearable weight comes down to buckle his knees. He wobbles and would sit, were there anywhere to do so; the wide window ledges of the big buildings nearby are stippled with stubby spikes. He stares. An iron maiden, this. Disciplinary. A public space designed to repel the public. Some of the spikes shine with what looks like bile. Cowley moves away from them and wishes hard that he'd laid into those boys down Caroline Street; that he'd crushed and stamped. Because the heat that rises from his feet to spit and sizzle in his face cannot be borne.

He sways to the left, through people, crosses the road. Bus station. No traffic out of it at this hour but from here and soon he can begin his movement back to the north. Shining eyes become dull pebbles in one quick trip of the heart. Easy, easy. Set up for life said Aney. Just hit harder than he hit the Quinn. Cowley curls around himself in the doorway of Marks & Spencer. He takes his tobacco out and there he is again, him with the bumfluff moustache and the neck-vegetables. Cowley stares. A couple of hours, just, before the first buses start to leave the city. Unbearable weight. Set up for life said Aney.

Benny's turned around in the passenger seat, twisted at the waist:

—Where the fuck've yew *been?* We've been calling yew and calling yew and yewer phone's never on. Dropped off the radar, yew. And what the fuck are yew doing with Darren the Pipe?

—Yew back using? asks Sion, driving. Doesn't turn around. Adam regards the back of his head, the shirt collar, a kink at the side of it that makes him think of Elvis Presley's upper lip.

—And look at the fuckin state of yew. When was-a last time yew ate? Or slept? And yew fuckin stink. When did yew last av-a bath, man? Fuck's sakes.

Adam can feel his jaws, in the dexedrine surge, doing an ungulate thing, a gurning, and that might be because there's some ersatz gabbling taking place – the maxillo busy-ness standing in for the tongue that needs to flap and form words but which a small sober section of the brain will not permit to do so, aware as it is of what such sounds will convey: sorrow and shame and guilt. He forces his eyes to meet Benji's.

—The fuck are yew on, mun? Yew've been on the pipe. Haven't yew?

—No.

—Then what's with all this fuckin tongue-chewing? An yew smell like a fuckin brewery.

—Dexies.

—Dexies?

—Just dexies. And the bevvy. And you're not me dad.

Benny barks a laugh. —Hear that, Sionie? Says I'm not his dad.

Sionie laughs too. —Just dexies and the drink. Not just a quick snifter, tho, is it? Yew've been hitting it since we last saw yew.

—Yeah, and? That's pissing youse off cos of why?

Benny shakes his head. —Jesus, Adam. *This* is what it does to yew. That was all one great big waste-a time, was it, in Rhoserchan? All for fuck all, all that effort, the drying out?

They drive through the town, the windows down and the warm night wafting in. Lights out there, people moving through the hot clog, cars, taxis, faces behind bus windows. Adam sees a man in a shop doorway, a dog curled up on his lap. Behind the backs of the buildings on Adam's left is the place where he used to live, could still live, he does not know; does not know whether he's been evicted, whether his belongings have been flogged off for pennies at a tawdry auction somewhere. In a heated pocket behind his eyes he sees Quilty on a window-sill, mewing; sees him broken on a kerbstone. His mangled little body.

—Where are we going? Where are you taking me?

Benji is now facing front. The backs of two heads before Adam. Coconuts on a sty.

—Away from the crackhouse, says Sion. —And the pub.

—Yeah but to where? Where are we going?

—Yew can get out whenever yew want, Benny says. —Yewer not being kidnapped, yew fucking idyit. But to answer the question we're going up Pendam.

—Pendam? The mountain? Why?

—D'yew not know what's going on up there?

—What's going on? What d'yeh mean?

Sion and Benny exchange a look. —Christ, mun, where've yew been? It's this big thing.

—What is? Speak to me, lads.

Benny twists around again. —Remember-a last time we saw yew, yew'd been to that party at-a lake? Yew'd necked a pill. Yew an two others. That mad-head Cowley and that woman from Trefechan. An yew were going on about seeing this, this fuckin *vision* thing in-a sky. Remember it? Like some, some fuckin floating woman or something yew said it was. Not remember this, no?

Adam hears a distant roaring in his ears, as of a Tube train on a branch line two tunnels away. His lips are sandpaper. So are his eyes. The dexedrine and *lots* of other things.

Benny repeats: – Do yew not remember?

—Course he doesn't, Sion says. —Boy's been on one. Be surprised if he can remember his name, me.

—What about it, anyway? says Adam, and then thinks he might weep, because drifting through his recall as if blown across there by a wind is, again, the small boy in the dinosaur t-shirt and the small girl in the pretty pink dress. The wooden owl that needed a hug. And all the mayhem of the latter days and Ebi maybe dead, alone amongst the northern mountains

272

and how hot it has been, still is, washing humid through the car as they climb Penglais, past the hospital and the national library and the university, the shape of a woman up there on the footbridge and Adam wishes that the moon was behind her so that she'd be in silhouette, and he turns his head so that he might regard her longer, that eloquent shape which is quickly hidden by the crest of the hill and when he turns around again Benny is looking at him and seems to be awaiting a response.

—What?

Benny laughs. —'What'? Is that it? Have yew heard one word of what I've just said? D'yew hear that, Sionie? Fucking 'what', he says.

—Well. He'll find out for himself soon enough.

—Find out *what* for meself? Will yis tell me what the *fuck* is going on?

—Ah, Adlad. Benny reaches through the gap between the front seats and tweaks the end of Adam's nose. —Don't worry about it. You'll see. Bottom line is, we're going up Pendam mountain cos there's a big party going on up yur and you're coming with us. Alright? If not we can drop yew off yur and yew can hoof it back into town. Downhill all-a way. Alright?

—Alright.

—To what? Coming with us or getting out the car?

—Coming with. Might as well, mean.

—Good man. There we are, then. An yew might as well have a top-up, aye?

Benny delves between his feet and comes back up with a can of cider which he passes back to Adam. Sion snorts.

—Boy's already pissed, Benji says. —One more's not gunner send him back to rehab.

Adam takes the can and cracks it and slurps. Warm and sweet. Horrible, really, but there is the burn in the windpipe and the gleam in the guts. Oh this need to liquefy; to drink until the ooze within him that *is* him pushes apart his bones and leaves an empty packet of skin behind. To be the rain that has not fallen for so long, to become the sea that laps at the baked land. There is another rush from the dexedrine, this one a lot milder than its predecessor. Adam gulps back half the can. One of his feet starts to twitch in the footwell. He is returning. He is being taken back up the mountain and that knowledge alone calls for alcohol. His genitals shrivel. Other organs, inside, squirt stuff and throb. The car swings into the hinterland and ahead of him Adam sees black bursts of trees and as he is lurched over the railway bridge he sees the moon, searing light, and he feels that it is new, as in never seen: an unfamiliar, startling ball, perfect sphere of shocking rock. And this summons something in him, a thing like a power, a thing the mad explosion of which needs to be arrested with alcohol before it can stun and terrify. So he drinks.

—Bit dry back here, boys.

—Already?

—C'mon, lads. I'm drinking. Giz another can. Pay the ferryman.

Sionie almost splutters: – *You're* the ferryman? Who's the one driving the bastard car?

Benji hands back a can.

—Ta B.

—Don't take this the wrong way or anything butt, but see when we get up to the lake, give yewrself a going over with a wet wipe or have a dip in the lake or something. Honest, mun, yew fucking pong.

—Nothing wrong with being a bit whiffy, man. Good honest sweat.

—Aye but it's not that, tho, is it? Yew smell *bad*. Yew smell like yew've pissed yewrself. *Have* yew?

—Not in the car, no. Adam smiles but whether that is returned by Benny he does not know because Benny is facing front again. Adam leans a bit, bows his head and takes three rapid sniffs and, dog-like, takes in an entire library of olfactory information, no item of which he feels, particularly, inspired to explore. So he sits back, moving his face away from the lifted niff of himself and the recent history of his span on the planet. The warm cider goes down. The sweat on his throat cools.

The grassland research station goes past. They enter Penrhyncoch. —Look at this, says Sion as he turns left at the war memorial and slows; around that white cross, and around the general store behind it, a group has gathered, lining the walls and benches. The people appear happily animated, engaged with each other. No one looks at the car.

—What's going on here?

—They're all going up the mountain. This is what we've been trying to tell yew, Ad, it's this big party thing. Everyone's going up yur. Yew not been online recently? Think it was on the news n all.

Adam does not hear, absorbed as he is at the surging crowd heading up through the village, some with buggies, some on bikes, some bent under bulky backpacks. One or two with children on their shoulders, others using sticks. All types. All ages. Agog is the word for Adam.

—Coppers, says Sion and slows a little and sure enough there is a police presence outside the football club; two cars, a van, several standing uniforms. A dog. They're talking to a group of youngish people, one of them with his arms outstretched to facilitate a patting down. Eyes under a peak follow the car as it passes.

—The fuck do *they* want? says Sion, his eyes fixed firmly ahead.

—*Duw*, I'd be surprised if there *weren't* any busies around, says Benji. —They're wound up about this, they are. Worried it's all gunner kick off. Not seen the politicians going on about it? All-a fucking time, mun. Shitting themselves. Criminal Justice Act and trespass and all that bollax. On-a telly and everything. Saw another one last night on YouTube going on about unlawful gatherings or some such shite. His voice goes all Tim-Nice-But-Dim: – Yah, if we larnt one thing about the riots of 2011 … crim-in-ahl-ity, pure and bladdy simple, yah yah. Fuckin wanker.

The crowd thins out until, at the bus depot – the sleeping coaches motionless and white, a school of belugas – theirs is the only presence on the road, climbing out of the village and towards the bulb of the moon. The dexedrine leaves Adam completely in an abrupt rushing-away and the booze takes over and instantly he is drunk, sloppily and groggily so. He feels the urge to sing and his jaw hangs down to do so but then

275

another thought blurts in and he says one word and then repeats it, lower, as if it carries a spell:

—Rhoserchan. Rhoserchan.

—What?

—Wanner go see Rhoserchan.

—It's closed down, Adlad. Empty. Nothing there to see, now, butt.

—Don't care. Wanner see it.

—What for?

—Just wanner see it.

Benny looks at Sion. —Whatjer think? Got time for a quick detour? Keep him happy?

—Aye, yeh. Might do him good.

—Stop at Rhoserchan.

—We're *going* to stop at Rhoserchan, mun. Stop saying the word.

Up, up. Between trees, familiar to Adam, this vegetation and contours, this camber of the land. Memories come to him in broken flashes; all the times he trudged up here. Ebi and Sally and Suki, Ralphie the sniffer dog, all the cats gone feral that would be drawn. I don't ask for a luxurious life. The hillside humming with psilocybin. *The whole world's expecting me* said the man with the quiff in the Hawaiian shirt and the cloud of rum and Ebi told the stars that *only the pure heart can sing* but that they already knew, have always known. Be honest with yourself at all times. All the dark parts. Even the slime. Not just a disease of the spirit and there is perpetually something more.

And even further up. The car's headlights catch the low lope of a polecat, the robber's mask of his face scoping the car in a second before he is taken by the ryegrass and bilberries, there to leave the musk and scat of himself, the wing-cases of beetles to draw blue bits of the moon down into curls of shit. And the rowans, up here, sprouting through the tops of the old beeches, their seeds freighted there in the mutes of birds. No one speaks in the car; Benji and Sion face front and Adam, head lolling loosely, casts glances left to right in a kind of visual hunger. Moths tumble across the front screen. Bats spin and hairpin. A tumult of smells rolls into the car, the vanilla of the gorse, the pine's turpentine, all the boiled saps and it is all of a gallivant, torrid, night-blue. Through a thick and sloppy fog Adam knows, in some sunken chest of himself, that there is permanence, importance, there are things that matter in this high place; and, for the years in which he didn't know that, there rises in him now a tug of sadness at irredeemable waste. So he raises the can to his mouth. Then wipes a slick of cider from his chin with his sleeve.

—Might've cordoned it off, says Sion. —The driveway like.

—Then we'll just park it up and hoof it down.

—And hoof it back up? To the car? Fuck that, man. Near fuckin vertical that path. And I wanner get up to the party.

—Well then we'll have to sack it off.

—Laughing boy in-a back won't be pleased.

—Aye well. He'll be sleeping boy soon enough.

But there is no cordon across the track and the car swings left to descend. Inside it the three men lurch and rock. Sionie drops the gears. A cobweb spanning the track appears for an instant like taut silver wire.

—Let me out.

—In a sec, Adam. Car's still fuckin moving.

Buildings around, now. Angular, lightless lumps in the dark. A KEEP OUT sign is ignored and Sion parks next to it and Adam is out the door before the engine is off.

—Best go with him, Sion says to Benny. —I'll stay yur with the car. Case yur's a night watchie or something.

Benny gets out and follows Adam across the bridge. Adam stops halfway over and peers over the edge as if looking into a river yet no water runs beneath and he holds his face for a moment and then walks on. The night-time has a rhythm, a steady thump-thump; Adam looks in the direction of the noise and sees the top of the mountain, lit up a little with regular flashes. There is something going on up there; there are those flashing lights and there is music. Adam moves in a shambling half-run, around the dark and hollow Second Stage house, followed by Benji. The polytunnels look like nothing more than big, discarded plastic bags, branches and leaves pressed up against the murky material of their curved sides but the impression is less of a healthy hothouse and more of a mound of clippings left to rot down in the heat.

Adam stops. Benny comes to stand beside him. Here, the noise of distant drums, fainter, somehow accentuates the quiet of the night; seems to deepen the hush. There is no lick of wind.

—Yew alright boy?

Adam does not answer. Just continues to stare at the wreck of the polytunnel and Benny takes in the shape of him, the clothes sagging on the bones, the heavy lids of his eyes and the jut of the lower lip. There is an urge to touch him. To hold him. And then there is a noise from the tangle that has surged up at the polytunnel's entrance, a voice from a throat of some kind and it puts a start in Benji because there is a cow-sized felid that still stalks in the species-memory and in the nerve-cluster at the base of his skull and hairs rise on arms and nape but Adam drops into a squat and holds his hands out, palms up, towards the shape that has detached itself from the shadows and moved uncertainly towards them:

—Is that you? Aw, man. Is this you?

At Adam's voice all tentativeness leaves the low shape's movements and it becomes a cat which strides, tail erect, ears high, towards Adam. That body, and the potential shapes within it; never a bad one, could such a body make. Never contort itself at an ugly angle to insult the air.

—Aw man. Quilty. Quilty.

The cat makes noises, all Ms and Rs, and Adam's arms. Adam falls back onto his arse and holds the cat to him and starts to make strange noises himself.

—Aw you. I'm so sorry. So fucking sorry.

—Yew alright, butt? That yewer cat, is it?

Adam says something but his words are muffled because his face is buried in fur. He makes more noises and Benny recognises them as sobs.

—Ey now. Ey now. C'mon, now. He crouches at Adam's side and puts a hand on his shoulder. —It's alright, boy. Look at him; that's one happy cat, he is. All the freedom up yur. All-a things he can hunt up yur. Look how healthy he is. He've been having-a time of his life, he has.

Adam weeps and squeezes. The cat writhes so Adam lets him go and he drops to the floor then spins and bunts against Adam's knee.

—Good puss. Good puss, Quilty. My tomcat.

The cat arches his back up against Adam's stroke, leans into his touch.

—Can we come back for him, Benj?

—Come back for him? On our way back down, like?

Adam just nods. His drenched eyes gleam in the moonlight and he sniffs snot back up his nose and Benny re-feels the need to embrace.

—Course we can, mun. Or, tell yew what, Sionie can drop us off yur and we'll look for the cat while he goes off to-a vet's and comes back with a carry-box. How's that sound? Sound good, does it? Best to av a carry-box, in a car like, innit?

Adam nods. Quilty bunts his fist one more time then turns, all fluid and mighty, and becomes a shadow amongst shadows again.

—That's a healthy cat, that, Adam boy. Prime specimen, him. Bet he's got a, a fuckin ha-*reem* up yur, he have, loads-a little kittens all over-a place looking just like him.

—He's been neutered.

—Ah. Well he'll be king of-a cats then, he will. A boss-cat likes. Tellin yew, perfect place for a tomcat, up yur. *Purr*-fect, see?

Adam smiles tinily and at the patheticness of it Benny feels the urge, odd but strong, to harm himself; to knock out his own front teeth. And then a car horn toots once and turns the entire situation into something else. One honk in the muggy night that bounces back from the far valley flank.

—That's Sionie. He's tamping for his party. Come on, feller.

Benny offers a hand and Adam takes it and lets Benny hoist him to his feet.

—I'm fucking tired, Benj. So, so tired.

—Have a kip in-a car, then, yeh? No probs, jes get yewer head down for a bit in-a back of-a car.

279

They move away from the polytunnel and whatever glorious beasts it might now harbour and the crunch and scrape of gravel under their shoes sounds out a rhythm to which the libretto *no excuses no punishment never give up* perhaps fits. A fragment of memory comes again: an ear, bitten in a half-moon. The toot of the horn again.

—Impatient fucker, ey? Yew okay to walk? Bit unsteady on the old pegs, there, Adlad.

—I can walk.

—There we are then.

And they do, across the bridge and towards the car that will take them all up, further up the mountain in the direction of the drumming and the flashing lights.


The barman leans over to collect the empties and in this position he can whisper into Emma's ear:

—Don't leave your drink unattended here.

Emma turns her head. It grinds slowly on her neck: – What?

—One word: roofies, says the barman, and goes back inside the pub.

One of the bleary faces around her takes on a frowning form: – What did he just say? Did he just say something about fucking roofies?

Emma shakes her head.

—Know him, do yew?

Emma shakes her head again and uses her drink to hide her face behind. On each side of her sits a man and they vice her between them and opposite her is another man, leaning across the table into her space, if the very concept of personal space had not been wrenched wide open by her. Out in the night at this table on the small square of cobbles and surrounded by smokers and passed by reeling groups walking and cars with music leaping from the open windows. A hand on each of her thighs, the toecap of a shoe abrading her shin beneath the table. The guy on her left, him with the dressing on his head, takes a half-bottle of vodka out of his pocket and glugs some of it into Emma's glass.

—Top yew up, lovely. Happy days, eh?

The hands squeeze harder. One moves up towards her crotch so she shifts on the wooden seat to dislodge it: not here, on display, even if the summer's steams have been absorbed into her own microclimate, the smoky stuff going on in the crannies formed of her flesh. Even if, drunk as she is, she stays gravid with something, her body throbbing visibly with its requirements. Like when Tomos was inside her and she'd watch her belly with awe as it rippled with his kicks and punches, his impatience to be out of her, to be in the world. Tomos. Tomos.

—So you're coming back with us then? To this party.

It's the one to the left of her, speaking hotly into her ear. She jerks her head out of its nod. —Where is it?

—At his. A finger is pointed to the man across the table who grins. He has pointed sideburns.

—Gotta be at his, see, cos he's on tag. He's not back in his house in ten minutes and he'll be getting a knock from Plod, innat right, Rye?

Rye nods. —You know it is.

The hand again, creeping up. Emma knocks it off with a knuckle and it slithers back in half a second.

—Got some charlie and a few bottles of ouzo. The Greek stuff? It'll be a laugh.

—Who else is gunner be there?

—Oh, loads. This is met with a snigger from the man on Emma's right. —Loadser people going. We'll have a wild time, ey boys?

—Too right we will.

*Wild.* That word makes Emma bite at her drink, whatever it is, falling fiery down into the lightless deeps of her. It never ends. Nothing she has done has made it quiet, nor stilled; this thrash inside. That place to which any bridge built must quickly crumble and to which any dig shortly falls in on itself. All mud, all dirt. All of a dreadful stink, the stench of an entire species' epochal demise and her, spotlit at its heart, just one glowing woman floating alone in a mayhem void, never to be reached but to be sought in such dark pits. Dig, bridge, *wild.* The slithering hand now starts to stab with rigid fingers. Emma reaches down and grabs a bulge and rubs and makes that bulge bulge further. A panting in her ear.

—Yes. *Yes*. Faster.

An ambulance blazes past, over the bridge and into Trefechan. Something about an old man drowning, there, recently. The siren loud enough to fill the townscape, to nullify all lullabies. Hidden fingers probe and a memory arises of an old man's feet, of cleaning the feet of an old man. Her hand works harder, faster, and there is a twitch and rapid pulse beneath her fingers and a small yelp in her ear. The eyes on the man opposite – Rye? – go very wide,

—Jesus Christ. Did she just …

—She did. Heavy breath in Emma's right ear. —She really fuckin did.

—Fuck, man. Fuckin intense.

—Right. The bandaged man stands abruptly up. —Drink up all. I can't wait any longer.

Drinks are necked. Emma's shoots right through her, from gullet to urethra, bypassing the entire wet network of her guts.

—Need a pee first.

—Na, c'mon, it's only five minutes away. You can have one at Rye's.

—I want one now. Bursting.

—Oh fer fuck … alright. Be quick.

She stands, steadies herself with a hand on the tabletop and then enters the pub. Her vision not so much swimming as *trying* to swim: floundering. She finds her way to the toilet, enters a cubicle, sits and squirts. This is where Meg sat. Emma fancies she can see dinges in the tiles between her feet, made by her own knees. These flames inside. Meg sat here with her knees apart; she had a teddy bear tattooed on the inside of a thigh. A yellow teddy bear with Xs for eyes. Emma lets out a laugh then stands and wipes and flushes and then is caught by some invisible thing strong enough to shove her back against the cubicle door, strong enough to set her shoulders shaking, to put her face in her hands. Above the cistern, someone has gouged the word HELP into the paint, and someone has written the word NO beneath it.

Back into the bar. The heat, the closeness. Everything sliding away from itself, away from its own mooring referent. The planet itself is spinning the wrong way. The barman sees her standing, staring about herself, and comes from behind the bar to put his hand on her shoulder.

—Listen, he is saying. Words leaving his mouth. —Stay away from them boys. I don't know what you're doing with them but they're bad fucking news. That one, Ryan? He's been done for rape. On bail. He's tagged up. They're not safe to be around, *cariad*. Are you hearing me?

This man's face is big in Emma's eyes. The light from the gantry behind him is forming a glow around his head. He looks so terribly worried that Emma can only laugh.

—It's not funny. Honest. Don't put yourself in danger with these pricks. Stay well away.

—Emma? You alright?

Another man has appeared, out of the shine. He has a face that is familiar.

—Ey. Antman.

—What?

—You know this one, Bas?

—Aye, yeh. She's called Emma. What's going on? She alright?

Bas and the barman talk to each other, just wak-wak-wak to Emma. Her eyes flit between the two as if she's watching tennis and there is a tendon working in the barman's neck and Emma knows how that would feel between nibbling teeth, how the stubble on his face would feel as it rasped against her skin. They look very serious, the two men, which hits Emma as funny.

—See? She's shit-faced, Bas. Look after her, yeh? Keep her away from that twat Rang and his mates. She needs looking after.

—With fuckin pleasure. She's going nowhere near them while I'm around.

—Good man. And use the back door.

The barman moves away and Bas holds Emma's elbow. — Come with me, Ems, yeh?

She falls against him. She's drunk, she's rambling; she's saying something about thousands of eggs and carrying leaves. He steers her through the pub.

—Where you taking me? Where's them boys?

—You don't wanner go anywhere with them. I'll take you somewhere interesting.

—Interesting? Where?

Out the back door and again into the night-time, the blue humidity from the gigantic electric tree above. Into the car park. Bas holds out a key fob and nearby a car flashes its lights.

—Where we going?

—Up the mountain. Fancy it?

—Up the mountain? What for, up the mountain?

—You'll see. There's something interesting going on up there. Something that you started.

—I started? What did I do?

Bas opens the passenger door and gently arranges Emma on the seat. Passive, she is now; rag-doll. Bas secures the seat belt across her. Her eyes are closing, her lower jaw drooping. Bas sees her prettiness; how even now, in this big relinquishing, her facial form stays one that lifts the lungs.

—That blog you wrote. The floating woman. I haven't been up there yet but I keep meaning to so might as well go now, yeh? With you, like. The one who started it all. Plus I've got the night off.

Pointless to talk to her; she can't understand, nor probably even hear, the state she's in. But like talking to a pet he does it anyway, and then closes the door and rounds the car and gets in and starts the engine.

—Don't …

—Don't what, Ems?

—Don't squirt acid on me, will yeh?

—Don't squirt acid on yeh? Like, like Katie Piper? Don't have the first clue what you're talking about *cariad*. I'm not gonner hurt you. Let's just go and see what all the fuss is about, aye?

The car starts to move. Bas glances left at Emma's bonelessly nodding head. It seems to him, just for a moment, that he is ferrying not just a drunken woman but a thing appallingly fragile yet immense in scope, the embodiment of a sorrow so vast, of a need so great that the mountain he's aiming for is nothing but a blackhead next to it. It is all he can do to stop himself from touching her, from putting a fingertip to her slack face, just to check that she is what she seems to be – just skin, and beneath that, meat. Her chin slumps to touch her collarbone. Before the car has started the climb up Penglais hill she is snoring, making noises similar in sound to disappointed groans.

This taste in his mouth – metallic, sharp, like raw meat. It is the taste that has always invaded his face just before his muscles lock and the weight of him gets anchored in his right leg because it is from there that all of his power will very soon be let loose. Funnelled through the web of muscle that joins his right foot to his leg and chest and deltoid and arm and fist and that will splash everything he is out into and all over this stinking pit into which he did not ask to be thrown. He clicks his tongue against that taste then gets out of the van and slaps the side of it twice and it moves away towards the industrial estate at Glan-yr-Afon. He'd struck a seam of luck, down there in Cardiff, seeing that mate of Pinkbit's come out of the M&S in the bus station with a bagful of sarnies for the drive up north. *I know you*, Cowley had said, *and that fuckin mate of yours owes me one*, and that was all it took to secure a free and comfy journey back home; told the bloke to stop at the garage outside Merthyr so's he could pick up a half-bottle – the man had his prawn butty, Cowley needed sustenance as well. Not much more than two hours ago, did they leave Cardiff; fair dos, the boy put his fuckin foot down. Anyone else would've been glad of the company but this boy, this mate of Pinkbit's, he hardly said a word; just stuck his earphones in and did the driving. Which suited Cowley fine. At one point he thought of asking the boy to show him how his own machine worked, the eye-Pod thing in his pocket, how to get the music out of it, but he didn't bother, not with the bottle sowing songs in his head anyway. He passed the place where he'd watched the sheep die; remembered the ease with which the life leapt.

Outside Carmarthen, Cowley recalled in his flesh the sounds of thump and whuff that led to the feel of the notes bundled and heavy in his pocket which led to the heaviness in his fists and this taste, well, nothing led to this; it has always been there, filling his face with fizz. Or nearly always, at least; in truth it has recently returned after a short vacation but that fact only illuminates that it never goes away. That pale grasping hand in the sacristy's floating motes. Pain and shame.

Pen Dinas is glassy in the heat-haze. The monument atop it shimmers, seems to break apart at atomic level and then reassemble again. The tip of Cowley's tongue goes rootling between his teeth. The face of his brother suggests itself in the hanging steamy static around him but then dissolves and, unlike the monument, does not re-form. Such a taste, this – like he's been sucking on an exhaust pipe. If he looked to his left he'd see the roofs of the estate where he'd start to wonder if he still lived; emptied flat, mildew taking over, turning it into a chain-smoker's lung. No need to wonder if *she'll* be there because she won't be; down the coast she'll be, scrunched up around a bottle of cider that has never seen an apple. And if he walked to the south beach by way of the river he'd pass the bridge under which he hung like a bat like a monkey like something not him. Above the running water. So this is the way to go – down Park Avenue. Keep the estate and the cop shop behind, which is always the best place for it to be. Sabotage, they said. Fuckin idiots. And like a spider he hung.

Almost jaunty, now; a thing like a spring in the step. Sprightly, despite or because of the alcohol amassed in his arteries and the sleep-lack and the abrasion against the world, energy given off by a turning dynamo and, too, this movement towards a clear goal; to get set up for life. The banishing of all worry, all need. In such a lively way does the body respond – like predator to prey. At the building site, where the day centre was demolished to make room for the Tesco, a big man is working low on some scaffolding, doing something with a drill, and as he passes beneath him Cowley imagines how he'd kill the man; with one massive blow to the throat, one windpipe-shattering impact either from knuckles or boot. It'd take mere seconds.

There wouldn't even need to be any blood; that stuff would stay inside and blurt into the lungs. The light would go just as it does when a switch is flicked. The batter of the big drill fills Cowley for a few seconds as he walks and for a moment he can taste only brick dust and then that too is gone.

Never been so in the world. In such a haze as this humming summer, in which everything appeared to be lost and refound swiftly and repeatedly, the body feels full and, as a consequence, apart. Cowley can feel not just the movements of his muscles but all of the organs inside, all the coils of them and the ichors they leak. He folds the fingers of his right hand over his eyes and he sees the cuts in the knuckles and smells curry sauce. His gait is that of an acrobat on a trapeze, above it all, swinging, net-less underneath. He alone in the blood-blast of decision and it is just his. He lifts his eyes to take in the glow of the sun but it sears, sore, as of course it fucking would because it's the sun and the sun burns.

Some little brown birds are thrashing in a puddle of dust. Cowley wonders why they do that, as he has on rare occasions wondered before about the things with which he shares the world: the mangy dogs of the estate, the stabbing gulls with their stupid eyes. He wonders how he would be, *could* be, if he would, *could*, wonder about them more – whether there might be something apart from the dull frustration and numb anger. He passes the Mill pub where he takes a deep sniff but can smell no yeast and at the foot of Trefechan Bridge he stops in the beating heat of the sun to roll and smoke a cigarette before he crosses the bridge because, all of a rupturing sudden, that bridge seems so very long; it unravels before him and becomes the bridge over the Severn, not the Rheidol; to cross it will need a huge effort of will. It spans not a small river but an abyss. From it there'd be, on the right, the glare of the open sea and on the left, upstream, the newer bridge under which he once hung. That calmness. Nothing of that at all on the journey over the bridge to the south beach and the Lavins: a desert trek that will be, sweat-soaked and parched, with a screeching emptiness beneath the bridge and above it only a blue void without end and of a terrible silence.

He turns away, leans his elbows on the low parapet, makes a face mask of his right hand. The dragon on his neck seems to throb. These surges in him a sensation not unknown, as of something leaving him and scraping bits of him out with it, both a birth and a death, of sorts, and accompanied by some of the necessary pain; a rasp on every nerve-ending. Its last invasion had occurred fairly recently, a few months or so ago, at around four on a starless morning in that damp flat up on the hill; it had pulled him gasping out of sleep and put him in a rank pool of sweat on the cushions of his couch. Then, he'd put it down to the binge he'd been on, all the booze and reeking speed but now, here at the sump of the summer, the pressure of it flattening him, little man beneath the savage weight, he knows not the provenance but is aware of the solution; just say *aye* to Aney Lavin. And get it arranged as soon as he possibly can; tomorrow, today, within the fucking hour. One massive trauma to the throat. Because it is not shame yet it adds to shame. It extracts from him a thing he'd wish to keep if the choice was his. It nubs his penis, wizens his balls to dried peas. The sweat he seeps smells sour. Detritus-man, scum washed up by the river, something deemed garbage. Yes, yes – big blunt force to the throat, feel the bones crack, see the light leave, plunder the stuff for yourself; capture it in a fist and bring it to the lips and slurp it down deep.

Urgency. He spins himself away from the wall and there is a taxi smoothing over the bridge towards him. He hails it. The urgency. He sees the driver shake his head and hold a denying palm out above the steering wheel and then he refutes himself by pulling into the kerb alongside Cowley.

—Cow! Yew alright boy?

Cowley leans at the waist. —Stiff!

—Yew alright, mun? Look like yewer about to be sick.

Cowley gets in the cab. —South beach.

Stiff shakes his head. —Jes been there. Dropped off three McBrides. Trouble in-a air, yew ask me. Am not going back yur now.

—What?

288

—A said Am not going back-a south beach. Am off-a clock, I am. Am going up-a mountain.

—Up-a mountain?

—Aye, up-a mountain.

—What mountain?

—Av got to move. Stiff Richards looks in the rear-view mirror and sure enough there is a toot from behind him. He sets the car moving, heads straight for the castle ruins and the sea beyond.

—What mountain, Stiff?

—Pendam. Al drop yew off by-a castle an yew can walk to south beach from yur. What d'yew want south beach for?

—Lavins. Need to see um.

—Ah, business, is it? A wouldn't bother at-a mo, like, if I was yew. Them McBrides were not fuckin happy. Heard um clank when they got out, y'know under eyr coats like? In this weather! Overcoats! Hiding something, see. Ad stay away, Cow, for-a time being.

—What d'yew want Pendam for? Everyone seems to be going up yur.

—D'yew not know?

—Know what?

—What's going on up there? On-a mountain? *Yma*, I'll show yew. Have a look at this.

Stiff pulls over, on the promenade. An area clogged with skin – moving legs and faces under hats and behind shades. Bellies, backs. Things rise from the beach; frisbees, balls of different sizes, leaping dogs. Cooked, it all is, and the meat smells that come into the car could as well be not from the burger vans parked up but from the human bodies themselves, crisped and grilled, flash-fried in the ocean's dazzle. The wide whoosh of the bay here has, it appears, kept down the seething ire that the heatwave has produced elsewhere; here there is laughter and hoisted spirits and musics.

And Cowley can feel it inside him: a levelling, like this tiny part of the world has lifted the gnarled tangle of him and snapped it smooth. He needs drink – water or something, not

289

booze. How swift this change, abrupt and utter, a jerk calling some words up from Cowley's choral past – epiphany, intercession – which he bites his tongue hard to distract himself from and what will follow them: the blood-bolstered battering ram bobbing from the parted cloth-folds. Refuse to let it in. Yet in it already is.

—Get on this, butt. Check *this* out.

Stiff has called up film on his phone. Cowley looks and re-sees it all; the ridge, the lake, the people. Hears fuzzy noise.

—Saw this last night in Cardiff. Someone showed me.

—Yew were down in Cardiff last night? That'll explain the curry smell then. Caroline Street was it? Got to be chicken curry chips from Dorothy's, right?

Cowley does not respond. Studies the screen instead. And what a window it is; the footage is the same as that fucking *lodger* showed him last night but the compression of the thing that's going on atop Pendam mountain into this palm-sized oblong; all the human traffic, here, touchable with a hand held out the window, seems shrunken next to the entire universe captured inside the phone. In it they await – there is an availability. Cowley too could be on that screen; he, too, could, and soon, be in the palm of the hand of someone he'll never know or even meet. New Zealand. Las Vegas. And perhaps it's just the bounce of the sunlight back off the screen but around the images there seems to be a light of some kind, a glow. Cowley watches the shape of a woman dance sinuously on a rock and her snaking arms do shimmer; her beanie'd head seems to beam.

—Av seen this, Cowley says. —Show me more.

Stiff starts swiping the screen. With his index finger. —Yew won't have seen this, he says. —Only uploaded an hour ago.

He hands the machine to Cowley and starts the car.

—What yew doing?

—Eh? Going up-a mountain. Jes told yew. Yewer coming with? Might as well see it in real life not just on-a phone, aye? Let's get up yur, see what's happening. Ad give-a Lavins a miss at the mo if I was yew.

—I don't know how to work this. What do I do?

—What, the smartphone? Don't need to do anything. Jes watch it, like, that's all. Let it do its thing.

Stiff U-turns. Beyond the peopled jetty, and over the harbour busy with masts, Allt Wen rises. Whatever's going on at the foot of it, on the south beach, is far apart from the window that Cowley holds tight in his hand and which he gazes at as he is ferried through the hotly hectic town and away from the sea and up, further up. Towards the crackling static of the sun and the elevated circus baked beneath it. High above the flatlands. Cowley in his smells.

# MESSAGES

@ThinBlueLine#battleofbeanfield#orgreave self-fulfilling prophecy! Lets bring um down boyz

@KatieH#ThinBlueLine go get em lads! Do us proud!

@ThinBlueLine#battleofbeanfield#orgreave#2011riots & still they didn't learn! Scum!

@PeopleofBritain#ThinBlueLine do it proper this time! Teach em a lesson! TRAITORS!!! No holding back

@KatieH#ThinBlueLine#PeopleofBritain to quote one of there hero's BY ANY MEANS NECESSARY #leftielibtards

@PeopleofBritain dont forget dale farm! DO IT RIGHT THIS TIME TEACH EM A LESSON ONCE FOR ALL LADS #dousproud

@Dionysus#lightindarkness#antifash fuck off @KatieH@ PeopleofBritain ignore ignore! Come and join! All welcome! Funfunfun! No bigots allowed #mynyddicariad

See the face, and so many see the face:
YouTube:http/:watch?m=pA7&Cc41xab
Government spokesman on the Llyn Syfydrin 'commune'
uploaded 5 min ago
As I said last night, as I think we're all aware, our, ah, the polite request that these people voluntarily remove themselves from what is essentially, what is lawful, ah, private property, well I'm sorry to say that this was met with abuse of the crudest sort. These people unfortunately will not listen to reason, I'm afraid to say. It was explained to them, clearly and civilly, that what they are doing constitutes a squatting offence and a breach of the law and moreover a safety hazard – not only in the issues of inadequate hygiene facilities and sanitation but the shooting season is soon to begin. The footage that has been released, that we've all seen, well that is the basest propaganda that shows nothing of the, the conditions up there, the filth, the neglect of children, the drugs and the violence of which we

have confirmed reports. Not to mention the more, ah, intangible concerns of lost man-hours and economic inactivity. It's criminality, pure and simple. It's betrayal; the will of the British people is that we leave the EU and it is every Briton's duty to ensure that we make a success of that. It is sabotage. And, and there is to be wind farm expansion in partnership with our new trading partners in the Far East and as I believe I've already said we need the work to begin on that as soon as possible to help us realise our long-term economic plan and satisfy our new global trading partners. Whatever police actions are called for will have to be paid for by the hard-working British taxpayer. Obviously Her Majesty's Government will do the utmost to keep the costs as low as possible which is why we do not wish to prolong this, this episode any longer. In answer to your question I do think there'll be an eviction, yes. The public mood is in favour of such, such an action. It's the last thing we want but frankly, unfortunately we have been left with no other option. The government's hand has been forced. It goes without saying that we will endeavour to achieve this as peacefully as possible and the sooner we get those people off the mountain and back into work the better, every right-thinking person would agree with that. Now if you'll excuse me.

COMMENTS 4

**KatieH** Took the words right out of my mouth!
1 min ago

**PeopleofBritain** Bunch of whingers/hypocrites/parasites/libtards. Bet theyll be Remoaners. Get them down NOW. No happiness without order. Impose it if we have to. Traitors must lose all rights!!!!!
2 mins ago

**Free Thinker** well said sir!!! The sooner the better!!!!! Tomorrow there's gona be some people who wish they'd never seen Lord of the Rings methinks
3 mins ago

**Bob C** dirty cunts
4 mins ago

From *Pobl Annwyl*, bilingual blogspot, Emyr Gwenallt Roberts, AKA Llewellyn Nesa, version Saesneg

I've followed my own advice and this is what I've found: a slut and a junkie and a thug. Yes, these are our witnesses; we are meant to believe that these are the vessels of prophecy. I searched and I read and I asked and that is what I was told: a slut and a junkie and a thug. And these three are our Lucia and Jacinta and Francisco? Our innocent peasants? No, I do not think so. Where, in these three, is the Immaculate Heart? In EmmaMum1? In my enquiries I lost count of the number of men who told me they had, in their godless idiom, 'been there' or 'been up it'; and, well, I cannot ignore that. I've never met EmmaMum1 but I will wager that her skin is red.

And so it comes again: the disappointment. What's happening on top of Pendam, that is no *seiat*, and this heatwave is only a consequence of man-made global warming, it is not the Massabielle Spring. Richard Owen spoke of 'a whole country aflame for God' but I have to accept that the country is aflame for nothing more than pornography and toys (and remember the burning bog at Tregaron? Those were literal flames, too, as we have been told time and time again they would be). I agree, now, with the Reverend Peter Price and Ambrose Bebb; that this so-called 'apparition' is nothing but 'a wind of emotionalism'. A 'product of fleshly, not heavenly fire'. Don't know to what I refer? Then play with your toys. Go to Google and feed the greedy.

So what is our 'divine resource'? (Evan Philips: Go to your toys again.) The drug-induced hallucination of a loose woman? A single mother, neglectful of her child? Or merely a Brocken spectre, and so nothing more than a meteorological phenomenon? This is no awakening. You are all still asleep and having nightmares. Of course Pendam would not be chosen as the new Blaenannerch. How foolish you have been. Little children begging for guidance. Grow up.

I take leave of the blog, now. It all seems so pointless. I may return to it at some future point but you will not hear from me for a while; I'm taking a sabbatical from sending parts of my soul out into the ether. She said 'dig', and so I dug, and I found filth. 'Bridge', and I put a match to it. And 'wild'? Well, I'm angry. Can't you tell? Again I have been let down. How many more times must this happen? Well, perhaps this is the last time because this is the Last Time. For now I must fall silent.

*Wrth ei draed cymerwch eich codwm yn deidi yn awr.*

# CYSLLT

# ADAM

Aw MAN. Aw man.

I know where I am. Which in itself is a small fuckin miracle, given the places I've been waking up recently, an the states I've been in when I've done it. An I know how I got here. Which, y'know, is in itself a small etc., etc. An then comes a third thought – I know what to do. And this time it's *not* to reach out for the nearest bottle or can an slurp down whatever slime might be in it.

Music: 'Dream Baby Dream' by Suicide. Haven't heard this in aaaages. An there's light, flashing lights around. I'm all folded in half on the back seat of Sionie's car and I go through, quickquick, the recent events; the jetty and the dexies and that lad with all them crappy tats on his body. The feeling of something about to happen. Something bad. Then Benji and Sion telling me off. Driving up the mountain, and Rhos, all closed an dark an empty, and, fuck, Quilty – oh Quilty – oh my little tiger tomcat. I'll be back for you, feller. An then falling asleep and now, now, waking up again. I wait, tensed, for the hangover to come on all horrible but it doesn't. It just doesn't hit. Must've slept it off. Which means I must've slept for about three fucking days in the back of this car and it feels like that, in me body like – every joint aches. Me knees feel like iron hinges all rusted shut.

I sit up. An I don't *throw* up, which is a fuckin wonder. I stretch me arms and me legs, as much as I can in the cramped space, and all the joints go *crack*. A bit *blurgh*, aye, who wouldn't be, but there's no pain; no headache, no boily belly. Maybe I'm still half pissed. The car stinks of sweat an stale booze even with the windows open but there's also other smells and there is the noise of music an lots of people an all the lights are flashing an I rub me eyes an look out at where I am.

Aw man. It's fuckin amazing. I know I'm on Pendam mountain but, God, look at it ... last time I was up here there were some people asleep on the beach and there was me an that nutter with the big dragon on his neck and that girl with the sexy arse and that, that shape in the sky but now? It's like some kind of heaven-place. Ahead of me is a line of parked cars going towards the pebble beach an the ridge at the far end of the lake an there are fires and lights an people everywhere and the movement of it all, an the sounds of it, is just, just … I can feel it all coming into me. It's like me body's absorbing it. To me left is the lake all dark like oil. On the right is the boggy bit with the ruined houses. A little boat drifts through the moonlight on the lake, the people in it singing 'Row, Row, Row Your Boat'. There's music an lights. God almighty … what's happening up here? This looks fuckin brilliant.

The music changes to 'Take This Job And Shove It'. I just sit there and listen, the knees doing a little jig. And then I give a little laugh cos The Geto Boyz comes on, 'Damn It Feels Good To Be A Gangsta', and I fuckin love this song and it's another one I haven't heard for ages. Through the windscreen, I see a figure in a big hat, like a sombrero, coming towards the car. I lean out the window. I haven't got the first friggin clue of what I'm gonna say to him but what comes out is this:

—Ey, mate. Is this the *Office Space* soundtrack?

—What?

—This music. Is it the soundtrack to that film *Office Space*?

His face in the shadow beneath the brim of his mad hat. All I can see are his teeth.

—Dunno, he says. —Never seen it. Sounds are good, tho. He knows his stuff, that feller. He's been at it for days.

—Who, the DJ?

—Yeh. Well, some bloke on the decks, aye. Set up a jenny on a truck. What, you just arrived, have you?

I give him a nod. —Who is it?

—The DJ?

—Yeh.

—Dunno. No one does. I've asked around. He just turned up and set up his decks one day. Never know what he's gunner play next.

He doesn't say anything and I think he's just looking down at me but I can't really tell because his face is all in shadow. Then he says: —It's fuckin great up here, it is, and he walks away, away from the lake, like, and into the trees behind me.

I sit back. The phrase *getting my bearings* goes through me head but I don't know why; I mean, there are no bearings to be got – I know where I am and I know how I got here. But it's all this, this stuff, it's all what's going on up here … I don't wanner go out into it just yet. Feel a little bit nervous, to tell the truth. There's so fuckin *much* going on.

I find a bottle of water in the footwell and a packet of tobacco in me jacket pocket. Smoke, rehydrate. The music changes to 'Leave Me Alone' by Calypso Rose and me knees start to jiggle. Not the *Office Space* soundtrack, then, but that feller in the hat was right – I wouldn't've expected this, after the Geto Boyz, but it somehow seems to fit. A big white bird whooshes across the bonnet of the car and I think it's a barn owl and then I remember the wooden owl that needed a hug and I take smoke as deep into me lungs as I possibly can. Think about stubbing the end out on me arm but I don't.

The urge to piss. Can't remember the last time I had a piss but then why would I? A group of people pass the car and they're talking all, like, excitedly, heading towards the lights, and they've got them kind of annoying studenty voices half-posh and I hear one of them saying:

—I know, I know, I'm just so impulsive, like I saw it online and I was like you know what? Time to go up there. Time to see for myself? Spur of the moment but that's just what I'm like.

God, them voices. I get another flash of memory – being on the beach in Aber – but it only lasts a split second. Don't know why that voice should bring it up but it does.

And what have you been doing, lad. What the *fuck* have you been at. Why did you fucking … it had been years, *years*. You were settled. 'Happy' is not the right word, no, but you weren't a fuckin wreck, were yeh? You'd rebuilt yerself. You were a thing, a person, in your skin, with emotions, and thoughts, and, and, fuckin empathy, or something like it. You were seeing the complexity as something wonderful. And you shat on it all. You fucked it all up. That's what yeh did.

Spiritualised, now: 'Do It All Over Again', and somehow the DJ blends the two songs seamlessly, which is impressive, the way he finds the echoes between the two beats and rhythms; definitely not something I could've done, meself. An I fuckin love this song. I close me eyes and just focus on it an then before I know it I'm out of the car and walking towards the lights and can smell all kinds of, what, *good* things, the smells of leaves and flowers and stuff and a kind of coolness, how can that be experienced in the nose, but it is and I suppose it must be coming off the lake. I walk down the row of cars. People pass, on foot. They overtake me cos I'm walking slow. Some say hello to me. I know that things are moving through the air above me – birds an moths an bats. I see a sign, a home-made wooden sign like, with candles on it to light up the words painted on:

*llyn y weledigaeth*
*croseo pawb*

Around it stand three shapes, lit up by the candles and lanterns and by the lights from the shore behind them and I see their silhouettes and know that they are women; them *shapes*, man. They're standing an talking and laughing and those sounds, mingling with the music – I feel the urge to *run* towards the lights and the flames. But I don't cos I'd look a bit of a dick.

—Adam.

Was that my name? The woman-shapes have gone quiet and seem to be looking at me although I can't tell properly cos the main light is behind them so they're in shadow. The candles and lanterns show up bits of their bodies but I can't see their faces.

—Ey, Adam.

One of them is saying my name. I stop. I make a shelf of my hand over my eyes as if that's gonner help me see any better.

—It's Jess. Sally's girl.

That voice out of the face in shadow. I see black curls and then some jewellery glinting as a hand raises a bottle up towards them curls.

—Ey, Jess. You just got here?

—Na. Been here a few days, we have. It's am-*ay*-zin. You just arrived?

Jess. Sally's daughter. Last time I saw her was at a pro-EU / anti-austerity rally in the town; she was standing by a shopping trolley full of cans for the food bank. Had a placard which she told me she'd made herself; drawings of Johnson and Rees-Mogg all bent over to snuffle at a trough. It was good. Left-wing politics in a miniskirt; nothing sexier, man.

—Last time I saw you, she says, and a finger with lots of rings on it comes out of the shadows to poke me lightly on the chest, —you were flat out on the prom. On a bench, like.

The fires are in me face. I'm glad it's night-time. I want to run, again, but for a different reason now.

—I must've been asleep.

—Na, you were pissed. Clinging onto a bottle, you were.

Aw Christ. What the *fuck* have you been at, lad.

—But you're alright now, aye?

She leans forwards, at the waist. The other two don't, they remain shadowed, but Jess puts her face into the lightness between us and the fires are orange on one side of her face, on the cheek-bulge beneath her eye, and the one dimple I can see is deep enough to hide in. Aw fuck. She asks again:

—You're alright?

—I think so, I hear meself say. Twice Jess's age, I am, but I feel half of it, now. Half her age and half her size.

—Don't worry about it, hun. You'll be alright up here. It's am-*ay*-zin, it is. My mam's somewhere over yur, on the beach, last I saw. She'd love to see you, she would. Been talking about you.

—Alright. Ta.

And then I'm moving away from Jess and towards the brighter lights. I can see it all more clearly now; the fires and the people around them, the flatbed truck with the decks and speakers on, the oil drums burning, dogs leaping across the flames. Hear it all, too; the track now is one I don't recognise but it's got a brilliant lifting beat and behind it all is laughter, a lot of laughter, and shouting and yelling, completely without aggression. Lots of people – hundreds. Must be. They are scattered up the bank and the ridge and above the ridge is the big moon. A flock of birds flies across it. I move closer towards it all and it feels like I'm, what, *shedding* things, leaving them behind, like a snake with its skin; dropping stuff off meself to leave in a trail behind me. I hear Jess and her mates burst into sudden laughter and, God, this is the mountain I'm on top of; *the* mountain, *the* ridge. It's returned. I mean *I* have; *I've* returned. What's gonner happen up here.

# COWLEY

FUCK ME MUN look at all iss an for what? Jes-a rising sun, that's all it was. Fuss about fuck all. Jes-a fuckin blob-a light in-a sky, rising sun or whatever that twat on-a telly said it was, ghost or summun. *Ghost*. Ghost be fucked it was jes-a rising sun. I know cos I saw it.

But Jesus Christ, tho … look at it. Yur's all fires an people on-a beach an a feller on-a decks an I can hear a jenny thumping an yur must be thousands-a fuckin people, an eyr all runnin about an laughing eyr heads off an dancing. Some are on-a lake in a boat an I can hear em singing. *Life is jes a dream*, that's what eyr saying. Loads-a dogs running and jumping about, kids, oldies, some of em using crutches, in fucking wheelchairs, even, one-a two. One feller comes past me on his sticks an A see that he've only got one leg, the poor cunt, and he's not old; youngish feller. Someone else, a woman iss time, comes by with a stick n all, but it's a different kind-a stick, a white one that she's tappin on-a ground like cos she's blind. Got some sunnies on and it's night-time but it's not dead dark cos of all-a fires an lights n stuff. It's all jes fuckin mad. A know that fuckin *lodger* showed me bits on his screen like but being up yur is not the same. As jes seeing it on-a screen A mean.

A go down onto a bit of-a beach, where-a biggest fire is. Some black shape against-a flames says *Shwmae Cow* and A say *Ello* back at him even tho A don't know who he is. Didn't recognise-a voice, like. It's not cold up yur but A sit down next to-a fire. Don't know why. Some feller, shaven head cos A can see-a light reflectin off it, says:

—Need a drink, son? Go a can could yew?

A nod me head an he passes me one.

—Yur yew go, brar. Welcome.

Brar. Cunt called me brar. But A jes tell him *diolch* an he holds his own can out at me an A knock mine against it.

305

—Just arrived, is it?

A nod me head again.

—Well. *Croeso*, man. Welcome up here.

A wanner speak to him, ask him something, A don't know what, jes something about what-a fuck is going on, but he moves away so A turn me back to-a fire an drink me beer an look out at-a lake. People are in it, splashin. Jeez, some people are being fuckin baptised; eyr being tipped backwards under-a water an then lifted out again splutterin by some other buggers dressed in white. A see things on rocks; babies' shoes an hats, scarves, gloves, little crosses made out-a sticks. Some people walk past me, into-a lake, an A see that eyr not wearing shoes or socks an some of eyr feet are bleedin. One feller with a big mad white beard comes out of-a darkness carrying a cross over his shoulder; a big one, like, not a little one, looks like he've made it himself out of fence posts or somethin. A woman who's walkin with him stops, takes off her shoes, puts pebbles in the shoes an then puts em back on again an carries on walkin. What the fuck? What's she do that for? Daft bint. Must be fuckin agony, mun.

All iss stuff is going on. An yer's-a music n all, an-a hundreds-a people, running around mad or sitting around-a fires or doing little dances to-a music. It's, it's, it's jes fuckin mad. An what the fuck for? All it was was-a rising sun. An all this stuff going on, iss, iss craziness … it's fuckin amazing, it is. Never thought it'd be like iss up yur. Iss is am-*ay*-zin, aye.

# EMMA

CHRIST ALMIGHTY. DID I do this? Am I responsible for all this? I turn to Bas and ask him the question but he doesn't hear me cos he's just gazing, like, just looking around in a kind of wonder. So I ask him again, and give him a nudge with me elbow:

—Bas.

—What?

—Did I do this?

—Do what?

—All of this. All these people. Did I kick all this off?

—I suppose you did, kind of. Yeh. It was you that got the ball rolling. With that blog.

God. God. I see it all – the people and the fires and the lights, and I hear the noise, and I smell all the smells, and I feel like, I dunno, the conductor of an orchestra or something – all this huge, amazing movement and I'm responsible for it happening. I kicked it all off. Well, me an that glowing shape ... I suppose, really, that I should be feeling some kind of powerful way or somethng but I don't; I just feel in a kind of trance, that's all. And thank fuck that my digital footprint is a small one and I never put any images of meself up on me blog pages or Facebook or anything cos if I did then maybe I'd be getting mobbed or something now like a film star or a singer. Maybe they'd all go into some kind of mass hysteria and rip me to shreds or crucify me. I dunno. I don't know anything, it seems. This is all too much to take in.

—Em. I'm gunner have a look around, alright? Just have a wander. You'll be alright on your own?

Bas also looks kind of stunned; the pupils of his eyes are huge but sort of empty as well, and I can see tiny fires reflected in each one. And I know exactly how he feels; for some reason I need, at the moment, to be on me own up here. I need to wander through it all, take it all in, at my own pace and in my own company.

—I'll be fine.

—It's safe up here. You'll be alright up here. If you need me then comen find me, okay? Or give me a bell. Think you can get a signal up on the ridge.

Which is a daft thing to say because if the only place we can get a signal is up on the ridge then we won't be able to call each other unless we're both on the ridge and then what would be the point of calling each other? But that seems unimportant.

—Alright. Thanks, Bas.

—What for, *cariad*?

—For bringing me up here, like. And for looking out for me back down there.

—Ach. He flaps his hands. —No bother. I should be thanking *you* for making all this happen. I'll see you later.

We go off in opposite directions, him towards the ridge. I look up at it and see people on it, beneath a big moon. Some of them are dancing. That was where I stood. Where *we* stood, me and those two blokes – the nutter and the other feller. Seems a fuckin age ago now. Some of the people on the ridge are women – that shape. Bits of them shine blue in the moonlight, and then a big puff of smoke from one of the beach fires rises up and hides them and I feel something warm and wet nudging my hand and I look down. It's a dog. Smiley scruffy sheepdog with a waggy tail.

—Hello, boy.

I ruffle his ear and his tongue comes out. Makes me think of Waldo which makes me think of my mam and dad which makes me think of Tomos so I crouch down and start talking to the dog which he seems to like. His entire body shakes in something a bit like happy delirium.

—He's not bothering you, is he?

I look up. An older woman is smiling down at me. She's got loads of hair.

—Oh no, not at all. The opposite. I like dogs, me.

—He's not usually this friendly. Taken a bit of a shine to you for some reason he has.

She takes hold of his collar with, I notice, a hand that's missing a couple of fingers. Farming accident or something, must be. But when I stand up she rubs sweat off her forehead with the back of her wrist and pushes her hair up and I see that she's got a big scar there, big dent in the bone. I'm guessing car crash. But there's a thing that comes off her, a feeling sort of; I don't know what it is but it makes me think that she'd be a good person to spend some time with. I just know that I'd enjoy being with her, like. Her and her happy dog. Whose head I pat again.

—He likes you, he does.

A tall young man comes up behind the woman. Must be her son, I suppose, although he looks nothing like her, but she gives him a grin as if she's dead pleased to see him. Tomos again – with another little twinge in the breast, an ache like, between the boobs.

—What's his name?

The young man says something that sounds like 'R2'.

—Like in *Star Wars*?

—No no. And then he says it again.

—Say again, slower?

—Arrn. Two.

—Strange name for a dog.

—There's a reason behind it, says the woman, and then, to the dog: —Say bye to the nice girl.

—You're off?

—Have to be. Been up here since yesterday.

—We have to find my uncle, says the lad with this kind of intense stare and I see him, properly, for the first time; there's something, er, what, un-normal about him. Can't quite put me finger on it but there's something a bit out of the ordinary going on with him, the way he talks, in his eyes. But he's like his mum, and his dog, too – for some reason I want to spend some time with them. Want to tell them about the woman that glowed and about how I'm responsible for this gathering on top of this hill and I'd like to drink with the woman and ask her about her injuries and ask her why, why, *why* this fuckin craziness recently, why am I sore and tender between the legs and why do I have hand-print bruises across my body and why do I have the feeling that I've just narrowly escaped something very, very bad. There's absolutely no reason to think that she'd be in any way able to answer that question but the urge to ask it is a strong one.

—I've only just got here, I say, too quickly.

—Have you? Well. Enjoy it. We might be back tomorrow.

—With my uncle, says the young man. —We have to find him now.

—Look out for me if you come back up, I say. I blurt. Why am I doing this?

—Will do, says the woman. —It's wonderful up here.

—Tara then. Hope you find your uncle, I say and then turn away so I don't have to watch them go. Why? Why the fuck would I do that? What's going on up here?

I go down, onto the little pebbly beach at the end of the lake. There were some people sleeping on this, last time I was up here. I remember looking down at them all from on top of the ridge; there were some tents and smoking firepits and people in sleeping bags like giant slugs. I remember the mist rising off the lake in weird shapes. How quiet it was. Not like that now, tho – there's so much stuff going on that me eyes don't know where to look, there's people gathered around the fires and in the water and standing around in groups or dancing and running. All ages – from babies held to their parents' chests to people so old they need sticks to move. Even some in wheelchairs, although not all of them are old, just, like, not able-bodied. A woman walks past me, tottering on high heels, and she sees me looking at her and smiles and says *hello to you, pretty woman* in a deep man's voice and then behind her/ him, a man comes up, lumberjack shirt, tush, the works, and asks me how I'm doing in the high voice of a woman. This is crazy. A lot of people are wearing masks, all sorts of masks; bank-robber's masks, bandannas worn bandito-style across the face, even the heads of animals or famous people. And the music; a song starts, I don't know what it is, but it's gorgeous, the huge opening chords kind of spread out across the lake, guitar and saxophone and some feller crooning about how he was born to be with me; well, he says 'you', but I know he means *me*. I smell the gorse all kind of coconut-y and the pissy tang of skunk smoke. I see some faces that I recognise, and not in a pleasant way – Marc and Llŷr and their mates, older guys like who've never grown out of their wildness and have reached the age now where that's stopped being cool and has become sinister and a bit pathetic, but even they are laughing, enjoying themselves, lying back all relaxed on the pebbles and passing round a spliff the size of a pool cue. This is – this is – up here is a glimpse into how life could, *should*, be. I sense no anger. There is no violence simmering underneath the surface. It's kind of – fuck, how can I say this – kind of like, up here, everybody is living how they're supposed to live. A little boy comes up to me and he holds out a shoelace or something. Maybe he wants me to put it back in his shoe. But when he holds it up in front of my face it wriggles and writhes.

—Look at this, the little boy says. —Isn't he lovely?

The snake wraps itself around the boy's wrist. Never been scared of snakes in that girly way, me, and I touch the small head; I've held snakes before, lots of times, when I was a kid at Trefenter, and it always surprises me how dry they are to the touch. Not slimy at all.

—He's brilliant. Where'd you find him?

—Over there on a rock. Gonner put him in the long grass where he'll be safe.

—Good boy. That's a good idea.

About Tom's age, this boy is. And acting in the way that Tomos would; making sure the snake is safe, that's exactly the kind of thing my son would do. The little lad goes off with the snake, showing it to everyone and they all react to it with fascination and even a kind of wonder; they're not just indulging the boy, they really seem to be interested. I'd expect at least one or two to scream and run away, but no; even the snakes are liked up here. This is a good place. A huge EU flag flaps against the sky and I get the stars confused.

The voice wails out, yearning, all the way over the mountaintops. Behind me I know that those mountaintops just go on and on; look at this place on a map and it's just featureless squares. I start to feel a bit dizzy, spinny in the head. I did this. I did this. A feller with a topknot comes up to me, shows me a stack of postcards, rifles through them. They all have the same image of the lake on them – the lake that's right in front of me.

—For sale, he says. —Two quid each. Souvenir. Wanner buy one?

I laugh. —Why would I wanner buy one? I can see the bloody lake, man. It's right there.

—To remember it by, tho. Have a look. Quality, these.

I see them gleam. —You've *laminated* them?

—Aye, told you; quality. Last for ever, these will.

I laugh again; not nastily, like. This feller's funny. —Mate, why would I wanner buy a picture of something that I'm looking at right now with my own eyes?

He nods his head all, like, crestfallen. —That's what everyone keeps telling me, he says, and shuffles off. Daft bugger.

I watch a woman in a wheelchair get wheeled into the lake until the water is up to her chest and only the top curves of the wheels can be seen. The people with her lay their hands on her head and close their eyes. I start to feel a bit dizzier so I move away, further down the beach towards the pine woods where it's not so crowded. Find a rock to sit on. I can smell meself – me feet, me 'pits. My fanny, which starts to sting against the rock. It feels raw – rubbed ragged and raw. Parts of me hurt where they've been grabbed and yanked; my neck, my shoulders, and, especially, those meaty bits where the arse becomes the back; I imagine those bits almost black with bruising. A great big sudden cheer goes up from a section of the crowd for some reason. I see a vicar – dog collar, cassock, full kaboodle – kneel at the lake's edge, dip his fingers in the water and then cross himself and kiss the knuckle of his thumb. He walks past me and I look up at him but he doesn't even realise I'm here – he's lost in thought. He moves behind me towards the ridge and I stay staring ahead, out at the lake. The waters of it are dead still like oil but the reflections of the fires and lights on it make me think of the Northern Lights. Or pictures of them that I've seen. I've never seen the Northern Lights in real life and probably never will.

This world is truly mad. I'll never understand it. And I don't understand meself, either; I mean, what the fuck have I been doing ... what the fuck have I been doing with myself. It's not just the body. That's not important. But I mean why have I been acting like I have, ripping away another protective shell I had, which wasn't much to start with, and putting meself out all fuckin, all fuckin raw and exposed. I have a son. I haven't even spoken to him on the phone. Haven't even texted him. I have folks who must be worried sick. My boy, Tomos, my lovely boy. Scared of the lows he is. And instead of being with him and watching him grow and develop and instead of holding him to me and feeling him all warm, instead of baking biscuits for him and protecting him, being there for him, what have I been doing? Say it, woman, say it straight; you've been fucking everything with a dick. And some things without. You've been letting men put bits of themselves in your cunt, your face, your arsehole. Letting them grab you, hurt you. Use you. Because. Because – I don't know any fuckin because. I don't know any why. Because it seemed like the only thing to do. Because it made the blood go fast. Because it made everything else go away. Because what is wanted, no, demanded for my life is the worst fucking thing I can imagine because I want to feel like I've been born. Because when I saw that glowing shape in the sky it was like, like the light in the hospital room must've shone when I was pushed and pulled out of my mam. I went down on my knees on a pissy floor and tasted the insides of a woman called Meg and she tasted fuckin brilliant and I made her pant and gasp and crush my head in her thighs and I made her gush into my face and that was all there was. God. God. Because hands on me, grabbing me, yanking me, that skin on my skin leaving red marks that turn darker, the slack faces above, like light, like flames, like I was glowing too.

I put me head in me hands. I don't want to see anything for the moment. Is this shame? No it's not shame. Is it *fuck* shame. I don't know what it is but it's not *that* because I refuse to feel that. I will not feel how they want me to feel. Guilt, aye – how can there not be that when a lovely little boy is wondering where his mam is? Of course there's guilt. But never shame.

—You alright?

I just nod. Don't look out from behind my hands, I just nod.

—Yeh sure? Cos yeh don't look alright if yeh don't mind me saying. Anything I can help with?

It's a man. It's another fucking man. I feel a touch on me shoulder, gentle like. Better be nice, just tell him you want to be left alone for a bit. I drop me hands.

Aye, I'm fine. Just—

—It's you. I *thought* it was. What's the matter? You look pure heartbroken.

Instantly I recognise him.

—Why are you sad? he goes on. Look at all this. Isn't it ace? And it's got something to do with us.

Adam, I think that's his name. Adlad, I've heard people call him. Of course I recognise him. He walked up the ridge behind me so he could get a good look at my arse. I heard him panting, and I'll bet it wasn't entirely due to the exertion of walking up the ridge. He squats down in front of me. A whiff comes off him, sweaty like, unwashed, but I can't exactly complain because I'm minging like a farmyard as well.

He points to the sky, and the music in it. —Dion, he says. —Can't beat a bit of Dion. Knows his stuff, this DJ, whoever the fuck he is.

I look at his face, the bits of it I can see lit up by the lights of the fires. He looks a bit wrecked, if the truth be told; his skin is all burst-veiny and there are big bags under his eyes. Bags? More like fuckin suitcases. The skin on his lips is so dry it's flaking off. His hair's all ratted. He tries to run his fingers through it but they get snagged in a knotted clump and he looks at his fingers and smiles at them.

—You recognise me, yeh?

I nod. —Course I do.

He nods back. He seems to be finding it difficult to look at my face, to meet my eyes. —Why are you sad?

—I'm not sad. Just, y'know, just …

—Overwhelmed?

—Yeh. Overwhelmed. It's a bit much, this, innit?

He nods again. It's strange, this; I'm feeling like I felt sometimes when I would wake up in bed next to someone I didn't in any way like. Kind of awkward, embarrassed. Nothing bad, particularly – no dislike or anything like that, just this faint sensation that I'd feel better if I wasn't in his company.

—What have you, erm ... what's been ...

He trails off. He seems to be feeling the same way. He picks up a pebble and studies it then drops it. Rubs his palm on his knee.

—There's nothing to be sad about.

—I know that, I'm not sad. Told you.

And now his eyes meet mine. Tiny fires in his. His jaw goes a bit juddery, like he's scared of what he wants to say, and he licks his dry lips. I look back at him. He says:

—Christ. That was close, wasn't it? That was really fuckin close. Closest I've ever been.

I swallow back, in an instant, a nanosecond, the words *what was* because I know exactly what he's asking me. There is no need for him to explain himself. So now it's my turn to just do a little nod for an answer.

—Alright, he says and stands up. I hear his knees crack. His hands are level with my face and I see them, big, the knuckles, the nails all bitten.

—How long you staying up here for?

I shrug. —Dunno. See how it goes.

—Aye, yeh. Me n all. Fuckin loving it tho.

—Me too.

—Sure I'll see yeh soon, then.

I watch him walk off, down the pebbles, towards the fires. His jeans all baggy on his bony arse, his hair up in a cowlick on the back of his head. He turns into just another black silhouette in front of the flames.

Don't think, just yet. Look at the colours reflected in the water of the lake. The song changes and I recognise this one – it's 'No Surprises'. Except there sometimes are, if you go up, aren't there? A rowing boat comes out of the lit-up lake and a feller jumps out and drags it up onto the shore and other people jump out of it there. The bank of trees at the far end of the lake is a black barrier. Stars above it but the moon is behind me, up above the ridge. The ripples caused by the boat shine orange from the firelight. I stand up. Don't know what I'm gunner do, just head down towards one of the fires I suppose, where the people are, but the bloke who dragged the boat out of the water sees me and comes over. Don't think.

—You alright, out here on your own? Feeling okay? Wanner come on a boat ride?

Christ; another man. There's always another fuckin man.

—It's lovely out on the water. Geese and ducks and stuff. Saw a big fish leap out, long as me arm he was. Incredible.

That voice. That accent. The slightest of lisps. They come out of the light behind bar counters or out of a group of others like them or out of cars or out of doorways and they say things that I've heard so many times before. But, God, what is this place, because here is one saying something about birds and fish and coming at me out of a lake mad with lights and I know him, fuck, I know who he is, what is happening up here, what have I caused.

The dreads have been shaved off. The clothes – just a shirt, now, tight to the shoulders, none of the ragged tie-dyed smocks. And I can't see the eyes or their colour because the light's behind him and his face is in shadow but I just know those eyes are the exact same blue as those of my little boy.

He stands there like a statue. Water drips from his fingertips.

—Fuck me, he says. —It's you.

—Weasel, I say. —Fuckin hell it's you.

# UP HERE

AND THESE COLOURS, pink and milky, making of the lake's waters the liquids on which infants are brought into the world. At the edge, where the water laps at the land, the damp earth nibbles and sucks at the feet of the people as if hungry for them to return. When feet exit the water or are pulled from the scrim of mud the sounds made are sighs and groans. This goes on. A barn owl takes the pale scorch of itself from drumlin-hump to top of rock. The words *such a pretty house* and the ones that follow it prompt a simultaneous soar of voices in which even a few dogs join. So long since this high place up here has given out such sounds.

# ADAM

THERE ARE SHAPES and faces in the flames. A couple of cans turning black, some roundish shiny things which, I guess, are spuds wrapped in foil. Primitive man's telly, this. Kind of stops yeh thinking, like some brainless shite yeh put on the telly because yeh can't think of anything else to do. Stare at it with nothing going on behind yer eyes like the faces on the screen, like a dog watching clothes go round in a washing machine. Except here, tho, in the fire, the shapes and faces constantly change; you recognise something, blink, and then it's something else. That's the difference.

I wanted to crush her to me. It was all I could do not to reach out and grab her and crush her to my chest. Not cos of this — not cos of what's going on up here. And not cos she's fit, either, altho she is. More like the way I want to crush an animal to me, squeeze it too hard. No, not like that; not like she's cute, in the way that a puppy is cute. Protection, then; like I'd want to hold a small child to me in the middle of a war zone — to guard it, like; to keep it safe from harm. No, not like that either, really; there's nothing about her that says vulnerability. But the way she was sitting there, on that rock, with her head in her hands, the toes of her feet turned inwards, and you could see them toes, like, in them shoes she was wearing. Big cork wedges. All the night sky above her. The ridge behind her, and it was on top of that that I saw her last. I'd been blimping at her arse. And now, now ... I don't fuckin know. I noticed a couple of little bruises on her neck, just below her jawline. A curl of hair was in her ear. I had to get away before I reached out for her, before I could stop meself.

Like a leaping are, now, some flames. Spring out into nothingness. And now a cobra rearing back to strike. And now the planet Saturn.

—Yew look like yew need a drink, feller.

Some shaven-skulled boy is holding a can out towards me. I take it from him. —Ta mate.

—Just arrived?

—Not long, aye.

—Well. *Croeso*, butt. Welcome up here.

He walks away, into the darkness just beyond the light of the fire. Nice of him, that, to give out the bevvy like that. It's all chilled, as well, and wet; he must've been using the lake as a fridge. I look down at the ring pull. Beads of water on it. Christ I'm dry. That crack and hiss that will be made when I open it.

Not yet. Not yet.

—Yew gonner drink that or jes fuckin look at it? Cos if yewer not, I'll have it.

I look up and I see the big rampant dragon on the wide neck, and I feel like a fuckin pinball – I'm being bounced all over the place. Bet if I just stood here for long enough I'd see everybody I've ever met who's still alive, like what they say about Euston Station.

—Alright mate.

He looks down at me, intensely like. The reputation this boy's got – I mean, I've known people like him – my own friggin father, for one – and they have these fuckin eyes, these eyes like coal but with bits in them that glint, bits that you know, in certain circumstances like, would kind of break apart and meet again and become bright and empty. And this bloke should have eyes that do that, given his rep, and maybe he usually does but now, here … well, Christ, there are even crinkles in the skin around them eyes, smile-lines like. If he's as keen on violence as I've heard he is, from many people, then he's left that behind, back on the lower ground. He's fucking grinning at me.

—Look oo it is. *Shwmae* butt. How-a fuck are yew?

Bit of an orange glow from the flames on the skin of his neck. You could imagine that the dragon's breathing fire, like dragons are supposed to do.

—This is fuckin mad, man, innit?

He nods. —It's am-*ay*-zin it is. Yurd it was all going on up yur like but A didn't fuckin expect this, did yew?

I shake me head.

—Jes seen some people getting fuckin baptised, I yav. In-a fuckin wheelchairs, some of um. An a feller carrying a great big fuckin cross up-a hill. Yew seen it? It's mad. Iss got something to do with us?

—With us? What, me and you?

—An that girl. Y'know her. That time we climbed-a hill.

—Why would it? I say, but that's not at all what I meant to say. I'm feeling the way I felt when I met *her*, just now; a little bit, what, fuckin awkward. Not like I'm getting the same urges or anything, I mean there's no way I'd ever feel the need to reach out and grab this feller to me chest, but still. Feel me eyes getting shifty. I'm looking over his shoulder, at the lake and the people in it. I reach down to scratch me knee. A new song starts up: 'This Magic Moment', the original Drifters version. And it makes me think of that *Sopranos* episode, towards the end like, when Tony and Bobby fight each other and it's like these two mountains of meat crashing into each other. There was a lake there, as well.

I make my eyes meet his. He's just said something, responded to my question like, but I didn't catch it. So I just tell him that I've just been speaking to *her*.

—Speaking to who, butt?

—The woman. The one who was with us when we went up the ridge. She was sitting just over there.

I point, but I see that the rock's empty now. —Well she *was*. Must've gone somewhere else.

—I'll have a look out for her, then. Wouldn't mind a word. An yew, how've yew been keeping? Look a bit fucked, like, yew do. To be honest.

Which is what I said to *her*, isn't it? And now I see marks on the feller's face, some small cuts around his eyebrows, and what I took to be shadows beneath one of his eyes is actually a shiner starting to fade. He rubs at the stubble on his chin and I see some cuts, deeper than the ones on his face, on his knuckles and for some reason I get a very faint whiff of curry or maybe that's just my imagination because when was the last time I ate anything? Fucked if I can remember. Suppose I must be hungry.

—Nah. I'm alright. Well. Getting better, y'know.

He nods. —Aye, I know. I know that, I do. So what yew gonner do with that can, then?

I'm still holding it, unopened. Dangling by me side. Me hand comes up and holds it out to him. —You can have it.

He takes it and goes immediately to open it but then he looks at me and something, what, some funny thing passes between us. I don't know what it is, it's something invisible; his eyes seem to connect with something, no, *understand* something that's coming out of mine and he gives a little, firm nod and holds the can at his side.

He pats the breast pocket of his shirt. There's a bulge of something in there, maybe baccy box or something, and he pats it and sniffs and gives me a nod and then goes off with his can, just like that, just wanders off down the pebbles, towards the ridge. I hear the hiss as he cracks the can and see his head tilt back as he drinks from it. Looks like he's gazing up at the stars but he's not, he's just drinking. It seems like I can hear a helicopter away up in the sky and then the DJ, whoever it is, puts on 'P is the Funk' and that'll do. My knees start to move. Grooveless land. Think I'll head down the beach towards the main fire, join the people there and have a bit of a boogie. Back down in the town I may not have anywhere to live anymore but for the time being I'm not in the town, am I, I'm up here.

Pinball again, getting bounced around, because who's this coming towards me, almost running towards me with her arms outstretched and shouting:

—There you are! Jess told me you were here! Come here!

Ah, Sally. Lovely Sally. My arms get stretched out too.

# COWLEY

An A see her by-a fire. With some feller who A don't know. A go up behind her an tap her on-a shoulder an she turns round an looks at me, at me face an en at me neck, me dragon, like. Fit as fuck iss woman is, still is, even if she does look fuckin knackered.

She says somethin but A don't hear it proper. Me arm's coming up and me hand's going into me pocket. Am taking out that song-machine an Am giving it to her an why-a fuck am A doing this?

—What's this? she says.

—Prezzie, A say. —Sfa yew, it is. Want yew to have it.

—Why?

—Jes do. No reason. Cos of all iss stuff.

Now me arm is pointing at things, like, at fires an people an-a, a lakes n stuff. Don't really know what Am doing, to tell-a truth. Jes feels like somethin Am needing to do. A don't proper know what's going on yur.

—Is this the iPod that you ...

—It is aye, A say an then pull me hand down cos, fuck me, it's reaching up again, like, going up to touch her, touch her on-a face or-a shoulder or something an it's all A can do to stop meself from doing it. Nowt fuckin pervy in it like but it jes wouldn't be fuckin right mun. Not up yur, it wouldn't. So A jes give her a nod an A look at-a bloke she's with an give him a nod n all an then A walk away. Don't look back.

Coulda sold that thing, flogged it for a few quid inna town. Why did A give it to her? Aye well. Found-a fucking thing anyway, didn't I? Cost me not one penny an A couldn't even work-a fuckin thing. Sure she'll get more use out of it than me an she deserves a prezzie, that one. Looked knackered she did. Buggered. An Av got me beer an it's fuckin lush, it is, going down tidy an me belly feels like it's laughing its arse off. Different world up yur, it is.

A look around. See Marc n Griff n them boys, mates-a Ikey, climbing into a rowing boat an pushin emselves off into-a lake. A see loads-a people, people who A know have been an maybe still are junkies an alkies, women who A know have turned tricks from-a caravan parks. Every fucker's up yur. A see some women which avter be men dressed as women – A mean, a big hairy hands on um, some-a um've even got fuckin beards, fuckin gobs an teeth all red with lippy. Jeez-us. Iss is one mad fuckin place. An am jes standing yur avin a good look like with me can, watchin it all going on, no weight in me pocket now, an A feel, like, A feel – slooooooww release. That pill A took, last time I was up yur – maybe iss is it, kicking in *now*, all mellow. *Dead* slow release, innit. A mellow man again, I yam.

Think A could live up yur, me. Rest-a me life. Build a log cabin. Grow veg n ganj. Set up a still. Do fuck all sept tend me crops an drink me moonshine on me porch n smoke me weed and look up at-a stars. Get fish from-a lake. Keep some fuckin chickens, even. Some chookchooks. An some fuckin hiker'd come up yur – no, some stew-dent from-a uni would come up yur looking to dig up some old coins or tools or somethin an she'd see me in me cabin and she'd be all like *ooo, man-a the mountains, ooo what's it like to be so free* and she'd move in with me to get away from it all, from all-a shite that happens to yew when yewer not on-a mountain like an we'd set up a life together with our vegetables an chooks. And we'd do nowt but shag an get drunk an smoke ar weed. And we'd get a dog. No, fuck that, we'd train a fox, jes me and her an ar pet fox. We'd train him to hunt rabbits and we'd eat stew by-a fire and foxy would go-a sleep all curled up on-a rug.

Christ almighty. What *is* iss fuckin place.

A stand and drink. A watch a girl walk past, see the arse on her in them leggings all tight she's got on. She walks into-a trees. A can hear a feller's voice in them trees, shouty like, but he doesn't sound pissed off or anything, jes, like, excited. Like he's telling an interestin story or somethin. A music's loud an yur's a sound of all-a people an A think A can hear a helicopter, up in-a sky like cos where else would it fuckin be, but when A look up A can't see it; jest-a moon above-a ridge, *that* ridge, an A can see some people on it looking at eyr phones ey must be cos ey've got, like, light in eyr hands – like ey've caught light. Like ey've caught stars. Oh fuck off.

Now I can hear a woman singing about a monkey.

A take me can around-a ridge, where it's darker cos it's away from-a fires. Couple-a candles on-a rocks an some torch-things outside some tents but that's it – no firelight yur. A wanner see what-a ridge looks like from this side of it, I do. Wanner see-a place where I stood, with them other two, an see if A can maybe stand under a place where that thing floated, like; aye it was only-a rising fuckin sun or something-a do with that but A wanner see if A can bring-a memory back or somethin like that. Go through it again. A know that's not gunner happen cos, well, it's night-time now an it was day-time then but maybe if A jes stand yur an wait for a bit ... jes see what happens ...

On-a other side of-a ridge is a giant fuckin bat. Not really, it's jes some cunt in a cape, but ee looks like a giant bat. He must-a been sitting down cos he stands up when he sees me come round-a corner. A moon's shining right down on him, on his head. A see that white band around his neck. A see the way his top lip comes out over his bottom one. A see his fuckin eyes, them fuckin eyes on him, A see em go all fuckin big an wide when he looks at me face. An a feel all-a fuckin fires up yur come inside me an A feel meself fuckin burning and A know what-a word for this is an a beer in me gob goes all horrible and sticky.

—Is that ... oh Lord, is that ...

And that's all ee says, all ee *can* say cos Av stuck the nut on him and he's down. Cunt's down. A boot him and fuckin boot him, yur's a fuckin screaming noise in me head an ee curls up underneath his cape an ee's shouting an then some twat sticks his head out of-a tent:

—Oi! It's not about that, up here! This is not the place for that stuff!

A chuck me can at him, half full n all, an tell him to fuck off an A grab ahold-a Father Williams's legs an A drag-a cunt across-a ground, across-a stones, an A see his hands scrabbling at-a ground tryna hold on an A drag him an boot him in-a bollax an A can hear him fuckin crying. Crying like a kiddie. Yur's a boggy bit on-a other side of-a track an A feel it squishing under me feet an some stinky water splashes up an A grab-a bastard's head an A push it down hard. A grab ahold of his manky grey hair and pull his head up. Mud all over his face, his tongue wrigglin about in it like a horrible fuckin worm. Feel the shame yew cunt.

—Oh God I'm so sorry! So sorry! Forgive me please I—

Feel the fuckin hate. Feel my fuckin shame. A dunk his head again. Press down on-a back of his perverted fuckin head. Bubbles burst up around it. All fizzy, as if his head's an Alka fuckin Seltzer. Is arms n legs are kickin an waving and going mad. A pull his head out again an bend down and scream into his face.

—Sick cunt! Sick cunt! A kid! A little fuckin kid!

In-a mud he goes again. Am gunner *stand* on-a back of his head. Am gunner *stamp* him down into-a fuckin mountain. Drown him in-a mud. Take iss sick twat out of-a world so he can't hurt any more kiddies. Make him know what it feels like to drown. Have no fuckin control. Iss is what yew did to me and Rhys my brother yew twisted sick fuckin pervert scumbag fuckin evil fuckin sicko cunt. Feel my fuckin shame.

—No! Stop it! Let him up! He's drowning!

Someone else shouting from a tent. A go to reach for a stone to fling an as A do that iss fuckin Williams squirms over onto his back and his arms reach up. A remember them reaching too fuckin right A do an Av wished for years that A fuckin didn't. Grab that hand. Bend-a fuckin fingers back til ey go snap.

He's proper crying like a little fuckin babby. Not so nice is it, yew fuckin—

—Please. Please. Forgive me. I am so sorry. Believe me when I say that you do not hate me as much as I hate myself. I was wrong. I am wrong. Please. Please.

Ee takes my hand in both of his. Yer's mud and spew and stuff all over his face and God how easy it would be now just-a stamp on that fuckin ugly face. Stamp it with me boot. Not stop fuckin stamping til it's jes another patch-a mud, a puddle-a red fuckin mud up yur on iss mountaintop at-a bottom of iss ridge. Where I stood that time not long ago an saw that rising sun.

Ee's breathing like he've jes ran a mile. Is eyes all big n white in is muddy, pukey face. Is hands are dead tight around mine. Fuckin old man, now. Fuckin old cunt. Manky old twat. What must he be seeing, what must I look like now hanging over him. He's like that sheep. My face. A moon behind me head, that's what he'll be seeing. A moon behind me. My teeth. I could bite his fuckin nose off now I could. Jes rip it off with me fuckin teeth.

—I *know* what I did. Believe me my boy I *know* what I did. Please. Please. Put it on me, now. This is your chance to take all of the pain I gave you and give it back to me. Put it all on me. I am so sorry.

Haven't got-a first fuckin clew what-a sick twat's going on about. All I know is that he looks like that sheep. And like Rhys did all them years ago when we were fishin for sticklebacks in Plas Crug ditch an ee fell face-first in an I had to pull him out. Covered in shite. Crying n all, like iss twat is now. Iss, iss man – iss old man – he's not a man anymore. Not a giant coming towards me in a small room in a church. All he is, all he is at the moment, now, is *this*.

God. I can't be arsed. I jes really cannot be arsed. A move away from him an sit on a rock.

—Oh bless you, he's saying. —Oh I am so sorry. So very very sorry for what I did to you all.

A moon's shining down on him like a spotlight. A sit on a rock an watch him kind of flop out of-a mud, drag himself out of-a mud. Iss old man. It's like he's coming out of it – like he's coming out of-a mountain. Being born by it. God almighty what is this fuckin place, what's going on up yur. Iss *cunt*.

# UP HERE

THE BEAT IS brought down; some people on the beach recognise the song as 'Monkey 23' by The Kills and they yell in unison and if it could be danced to they would but it is instead part of some settling, some stint; small things with wings relax in leaves and pass the torch of insectile purpose to moth and May bug. These rise moonwards, fuzz the wobbling air behind those that top the ridge with light held in their hands, soften their silhouettes as if therianthropes they are, in the initial throes of shifting shape that they too might rise, dissolve and drift, take themselves upwards into owl-light, shredded now by metal blades, a din and frenzy dampened by height and other more grounded sounds. Still there are eyes up here, in the emptinesses that join the stars, eyes that see everything they need to see but not the ghosts, never the ghosts: not the Gwrach y Rhibyn, her of the swaying drool and the tongue kissy-kissy for blood, not the rag-clad armies that yet harass and hack. Nor the blood that drips invisible from the leaves or the tunnels that capillary the peaks – the mines and dungeons and guerilla redoubts. What is seen and transmitted by these high eyes could never be such things; only the shifting shapes of citizens, made luminous on a distant screen, and their traffic in a place where such traffic has been deemed unwanted. Yet how they move, these shapes, even in this lull; how they move, and meet. A woman's voice wails *it makes me act like that* and how could it not, even as a tremor begins in the mountain's guts, a rumble in and on the roads that lattice its shape when seen from above, a thrum as of mass movement of, say, armoured men and their machines. A leap in the epoch about to happen. The mountain will not be split, no, but so stuffed with history is it that its matter is leaking out and has ruptured seams.

# THIN AND GREY

AND THE MADE-GREY ones are still at it in their remote bunker, fixated by the screens. Ever-alert here in this bunker where all light is artificial and every colour is bleached. There is much whiteness on the screens, much that glows, thermal imaging magicking breath and blood into phosphenes, bioluminescence, and termites on a mound these screens could be capturing but termites do not move like this, flitting from one to one in a magnetism divorced from utility and dictated only by will. The fingers tap at the keyboards and the image on the screens lurches queasy away from the black splat of the lake and now there is a road below, and many vehicles. Some of them look like horseboxes and others have numbers on their rooves. The headlights dipped or even entirely off for stealth and surprise and if they convey people the glow of them cannot be seen through the glass and steel that holds them and moves them up towards the lake and its grounded galaxy, its earthed stars that drift apart and re-form and drift again and always incessantly form new shapes. Eyes stare, afar. Fingers tap at keyboards and that is the only sound in this distant strengthened room. Orders and instructions are transmitted out of here and into those vehicles that move in one vertical rank up towards the peak where people have been turned into beacons.

# ADAM

I WISH I had Sally for a ma. I wish Sally was my ma. She's only a few years older than me but, I mean, she's holding my hand in both of hers and she's looking into my face and she's going:

—Are you *sure*? You're absolutely certain sure? Is this you telling me lies?

She cares, like. She worries herself sick about me. Wish I was younger, smaller, so I could just curl meself up against her and let her put her arms around me and tell me nice things.

—Positive, I say. —Abso-lutely positive, Sal. Hundred per cent.

—Cos yew even still stink of it.

—I know I do. Told yeh, it's been bad. But it's not anymore.

—How many times, tho, Adam love? How many times? And the next time—

—Might be me last, aye. I know that. But each day as it comes, isn't that right?

She lets go of me hand, stands back. Her daughter's face in hers. Or hers in her daughter's, I suppose I should say. Cos Sally came first, like, into the world.

—Christ, *sons*. She shakes her head all sad. —Nothing but trouble. So glad I had my Jessica. What substances?

—Ey?

—What did you use? How bad did it get?

She grabs hold of my left hand in both of hers and she turns it so that the inside of my arm is exposed to her. This touch I don't like and I pull me arm, yank it back to meself.

—Aw c'mon, Sally, don't do that. And do yeh really need to know?

—Yes I do. I need to know how much I should worry about you.

—Why?

—*Why*, she says. Cos it's what I do, *cariad*. And plus it's me job, look.

She tugs one side of her fleece out towards me to show me the crest sewn into it. It reads 'Cysllt'.

—Know what that means? Contact. It means *contact*. So here I am, contacting. Outreach is the word and I'm reaching out.

—I know all about it, Sal. What it is. When did yeh get the job?

—Don't change the subject.

—This *is* the subject. This *is* the subject. I'm changing nothing.

—Which is precisely the bloody problem.

—Oh Christ.

I can't help it; I start to laugh. It's her — she's just got a way about her that makes me laugh, even now, even in these circles we're going around. I just can't stay pissed off at her. Bit irritated I was at that arm-tugging stuff. But now we're just looking at each other and laughing.

—What's so bloody funny, then?

—Just you. You make me laugh.

Out of the crowd of people on this beach, all the different people and all the different things they're doing, comes a smiley feller with a bristly head. He's beaming at us both.

—Well don't youse two look happy.

Irish accent.

—*Are* yis?

—Are we what, mate?

—Happy, so?

—*Course* we are, feller. Why wouldn't we be?

—No reason at all, sure. Keep up the laughing.

He hands me a spliff, unlit. He points it at me but it's Sally who takes it and puts it behind her ear.

—Free sample for ye. Give it a blast and if it does the job for ye then come find me so. I'll be around. Or just ask for Liam. Ask anyone.

—Alright, man, ta.

Another freebie. What'll be next?

—Incredible, this, is it no? says this Liam feller, and sweeps his arm around him, over the lake. —As it fuckin should be, am I right?

—You're not wrong, I say, and he laughs loud, altho it wasn't funny. Then he grabs me shoulder and gives it a bit of a friendly shake and kisses Sally on the cheek and he's off, he's away. I turn to Sal.

—See?

—See what?

—That spliff. I didn't touch it, did I? Left it for you.

—That's cos it's not Class A. Had it been a crack-pipe, tho.

—Had it been a crack-pipe I would've done exactly the same thing. Don't believe me if yeh don't want to but I wish yeh would. Only thing I need now is a hot dog or somethin cos I'm fuckin ravenous.

And soon as I say that I realise how empty my belly is. Can't remember the last time I ate anything and I imagine me stomach, the organ like, all shrivelled up like a walnut. Sally tells me to go with her and she leads me further down the beach in the direction of the trees at the bottom of the ridge, *the* ridge like, where there's another fire, a smaller one, with a big blackened pot in it. Close to it and I can smell it now. People are sitting or standing around eating a mush off paper plates.

Sally says something to this Gandalf bloke and he ladles stuff out of the cauldron onto paper plates and Sal passes one back to me.

—What is it, Sal?

—Beans. I think. Does it matter? It's food, innit? Get it et, boy.

She finds a space on the pebbles and sits down and I sit next to her. She gives me a plastic spoon. I dig in. At the first swallow me throat kind of constricts but as soon as the food hits the belly I can feel the burst of energy from it, the goodness in it like, and then I'm shovelling it in. I think I even make an *mmmm* noise. Me body gives out a sort of physical sigh. I look up at the stars and I see a big white bird move across. Maybe the same owl. I see bats. I see a bigger thing move across the sky and think that I can hear it, faintly, behind the music – whuppa whuppa.

—Think there's a chopper up there, Sal.

She gives a shrug. —Wouldn't surprise me if there was. They're not liking this, y'know.

—Who isn't?

—The, y'know ... authorities, like. See the EU flags? This is treasonous, now. We're traitors. Have you not been watching the news? Or the podcasts?

—Can't say I have.

—Saw a couple yesterday on someone's smartphone. Some twat going on about this being private property or something. They seem to think this is some kind of Occupy thing. Haven't got a fucking clue. They just don't like it. But, like, they're okay with Rhos being closed down, aren't they? She shakes her head. —Wankers. This fucking country's gone insane.

I see a skinny guy – *really* skinny like, I mean emaciated-looking – at the fire, holding his plate out for food. He's wearing shorts and red socks. They're *very* red, his socks, like those bits of pimento you squeeze out of an olive before you put it in your martini. Olives? Martini? Where the fuck have these thoughts come from? I've never had a martini in me life.

—Did you ever think this would happen?

—What, Sal?

—All of this? After you saw that, what did you call it, that shape in the sky?

I swallow more food. —Is that what kicked all this off?

—No doubt about it. It was the blog.

—What blog?

—The woman you were with, when you had that, that apparition, she put it up on her blog. Went viral. We spoke about this, remember at the polytunnels?

The polytunnels at Rhoserchan. Another life. Back behind me. Not for the first time I wonder what the *fuck* I've been doing.

—It took on a life of its own, Sally's saying. —For some people it's just a party but for others. I mean look at him.

She points with her spoon at some feller wading through the shallows of the lake. He's got a long beard and is wearing a soaked white robe and, God, he's carrying a full-size wooden cross over one shoulder. No one else is paying him any attention.

—Been doing that for days, he has, Sal says. —Just wandering around with his cross. An all the people in wheelchairs and stuff. And, *Duw*, it seems like everyone that's been through Cysllt has come up here, all the junkies and alkies, all the prozzies. Self-harmers, all of them. So many familiar faces up here. I don't know why this has happened but it all started off with that blog. What was it you saw, Adam love? You and that blogger woman?

I feel a rumbling in my belly. The food; it's started something off. Some faecal thing.

—I really don't know, Sal. Can't say. A shape, that's all it was. Like a person. It was shaped a bit like a person.

—They're saying it was a Brocken spectre. Know what that is? Like a shadow on the air. Just a, an atmospheric phenomenon. Easily explained. But this, tho, all this, this isn't easily explained, is it? What's going on up here, like.

I look around. —Maybe people just want to have a party, Sal. Get together. An excuse.

—Yeah, but. She points again at the feller with the cross. —People like that. He's not just partying, is he?

—Maybe he is, in his own way. Who's to say?

I know that sounds very fuckin dim but I don't really want this conversation. I don't really want to think about what's going on up here. Maybe later, like, at some point in the future when all of this has wound down and burnt itself out, maybe then will be the time to think about what it all might mean. If anything, and if at all. But to discuss it now, in the middle of it, when it's all going on – that doesn't feel right, somehow. Feels not just futile but pure wrong, as well, kind of, what ... well; fuckin rude. Kind of impolite. No, that's not right. All I know is that I don't want to do it. And there's a rumbling in me belly, faint at the mo but getting louder.

—Not now, Sal, anyway. Yeh don't erm, decompress when you're still under water, do yeh?

—What the fuck does that mean?

—Like, how can yeh debrief when it's still going on? After something's finished, *then's* the time to talk about what it might mean. Or might've meant. Cos you don't know how it's gonna end, do yeh? While it's going on, it's just going on. It's just happening, knowmean? It's like, how it ends is what gives it the meaning. Like a full stop.

Sally laughs. —That's the addict talking, Adam love. That's an insight into the thought processes of the addict, that is. The ride-the-tiger thing. The all-there-is-is-the-moment thing. The, the eternal present.

I laugh as well. —And that, that's the social worker talking, innit? That's the I've-read-some-books-and-been-to-a-few-lectures thing. You gobshite.

—You arrogant twat.

And we have a little laugh together. And hug each other with one arm cos we're still holding our plates. Which are now scraped clean so we chuck em in the fire and sit down on a rock to have a smoke an then Sally makes a lot of things okay; she asks me if I've got money, I tell her I'm skint, she says I can go and work in the outreach thing, there's a few openings and they favour ex-users, like, people who know what they're talking about, she tells me that she'll put in a word for me and I'll have no problem getting a job. She asks me if I've still got me flat and I tell her probably not, no, and she says I can move in with her; tells me that her Jess has just moved out so she's now got a spare room. Then I tell her that I'll need to fetch me cat from Rhos and she says that's fine as well, cos her own tomcat not long ago died and she's missing the feline company. So then I tell her that she's a pure fuckin angel and that in the space of a few minutes she's just sorted out my entire friggin life. She tells me to stop giving her the big head. Tells me again that it's her job. Cysllt. So then I tell her that the food has given me some crampings and that I need a toilet and she points towards the trees.

—What, there's a bog in there, is there?

—Kind of. A long trench, like. A latrine. D'you know what to do?

—I imagine so, yeh; hang me arse over the edge and drop me kex. Course I know what to do, girl.

—Aye, but then you kick soil over it and put some leaves on it. There's all wild mint and stuff in there, y'see. Keeps the pong down.

—Alright.

I go across the beach, weaving through the people like and into the trees. Under the music I can hear the sound of a man's voice, loud, and then I see him, standing by a sign with '*Toiledau*' painted on it, kind of druidy, mad beard on him, white smock kind of thing, and he's right off on one, ranting away to some cool-looking girl chewing gum with her arms folded and her hair pushed back under a bandanna. She's just standing there, hip cocked, looking at this bloke giving it laldy:

—Because this is the age of the snoop and the snitch and the curtain twitcher! Of the bigot! This is one of those moments in history when the people of Britain have let themselves become enamoured of their own viciousness, d'you hear me, to hate the poor, not poverty itself, and to disdain the vulnerable! To be swift to condemn and slow to forgive! Such is the temper of our scapegoating age and such will tempt the fires that cleanse! The waters! See how they rise! And so we strip ourselves of the necessary qualities of life and have nothing to be taken at death! So we—

I like this feller. He should be on *Question Time* rather than at the entrance to a communal bog on a mountaintop. And I like the girl too cos she just looks at this feller, blows a great big pink bubble, waits for him to take a breath and then pops the bubble and says:

—Aye, there's lovely, but do you mind letting me get past, now? Cos I've got the turtle's head, I yav.

A laugh jumps out of me and gets everything moving fast inside and I think I'm gunner shit meself so I leg it past the girl and the ranter and into the trees. Follow me nose down the path to the trench which is a bit *off* the path, in the thick trees like where it's more private, turn me back, drop me kex and let it all out. Jeez the relief. The stink isn't too bad, surprisingly, from the trench; you can smell it, of course – I mean it's a long ditch full of shit and piss, how could you not smell it – but it's not overpowering cos it's masked by smells of earth and herbs. And it seems like it's been dug, designed, in such a way so that every few yards there's a big low branch that hangs over and makes a kind of blind to separate each person. Clever, that. A whiteness catches me eye and I look and see some toilet rolls slotted onto twigs. God – everything's been thought of, it seems. Wouldn't be surprised if there's some handwash somewhere and a canister of Febreze.

I lean forwards to pluck one of the toilet rolls and at this angle I can see between the trees, to the ridge, see the big moon above it, the people on it, the dancing shape of a woman, some others around a pinprick of light which I know must just be the screen of a phone but which looks somehow magical. Christ it all looks fuckin magical. Wiping me arse as I am and it all looks, *is*, fuckin amazing. And I wonder why you don't come *now*. Why you don't do something *now*, here, with all these people to see you. All these people up here, with their camera phones, eyes and memories. I mean, any shape in the sky that wasn't a bird or a bat and everyone would become a baby. Every single one. Because they – because we—

The bushes around me start to shake. I see small animal shapes leap and dart through them to the left, away from the lake, further into the mountains. The branches above me snap and clatter and I look up and see bird shapes doing the same thing. Everything is in a hurry to get away. I look to my right to see what might be scaring them and I see the far end of the lake, by the road, and the trees all lit up; headlights, beams, torches, like the forest is on fire with white flames. My heart leaps. I feel almost sick. Something huge is happening. I see a helicopter rise like a giant insect over the treetops and I see its searchlight move across the lake water towards the gathered people. Like it's hunting for them. I hear its rotors. I hear the music, not fully drowned out yet, change to 'Jump In The Line'. Something is happening. Some *things* are happening – a lot of things are happening. I finish wiping me arse and chuck the bog roll in the trench and rip up a few handfuls of leaves and chuck them in after it. Air freshener, kind of. But then, very quickly, the smell from the trench becomes very fucking bad, horrible, and I go through the trees towards the beach where everyone is looking up at the helicopter hanging above, caught in its blinding light they are, the racket of it, and everyone in its too-bright light looking all exactly the same and I can't make out which one is Sally, or Sion, or Benji; I can't make out any individual face at all.

# EMMA

—Who was that feller?

—Just some feller I know.

—Looked rough as fuck. Why'd he give you that iPod?

—Dunno. Present. Just wanted to do something nice I suppose.

—Did you …

—Ey now. Don't go there. Don't spoil it before it starts.

He looks all sad, his lip sticking out all sulky. I touch him on the knee, just a tap. Daft sod.

He's pitched his tent next to one of the walls of the old ruined houses and he's made it all cosy inside – there's a sleeping bag and a washing line with socks on it and a little table with a lantern on it and, Jeez, he's even made a bookshelf. It's a proper little temporary home. The lantern is lit and it's giving off this warm glow and through the open tent flap I can see the lake a bit below and all the people moving around it and I can hear the music and see it all in the light of the fires. Not far from the tent, as we were walking up to it, it was a bloody orgy – most of the other tents had people shagging in them, judging by the noises like, and one feller was on his back in the grass getting a blowjob from someone with a hairy back, not necessarily another man – I mean, there *are* women from Tregaron up here. And just outside the tent I'm in, Weasel's gaff like, I noticed a sculpture, a thing that looked like the skeleton of a fantastic animal, made out of sticks and rocks with a sheep's skull for a head with colourful flowers in its eye sockets and I asked him about it and that's what he is now, he said, a sculptor – he makes things from discarded stuff, rubbish like, driftwood, stuff like that. Got a website. Had a couple of exhibitions down in Bristol, where he's been living for the past few years. Makes a living from it.

—Keeps me out of their clutches, he's saying now. —Know what I mean? Below their radar. Don't need anything from them, no benefits, nothing. The less I have to do with those fuckers the better. Sooner have them think I don't even exist.

I'm gonner wind him up again; I can't help meself.

—Yeh, well, you're safe, aren't you, in yeh little burrow, under the ground? Only danger is when you go out to nick one of the farmer's chickens.

—Ey! Told you, less of the fuckin weasel!

—It's what you called yehself.

—Aye but not anymore, I was an arse! I've grown up now!

—Oof. Touched a nerve there.

He's smiling – I mean he's not really pissed off. But I'm enjoying meself.

—What's it like in the winter when yeh fur turns all white? Is it hard to recognise yehself? Do other weasels and stoats—

—Will you shut the shite up? It's fuckin embarrassing me. I was such a dick.

He puts his head in his hands and rubs his short hair vigorously and looks up again, still with a bit of a smile. Shakes his head. —Me name's Dylan. That's me real name.

—Dylan?

—Aye, yeh. Me mum was a big Dylan Thomas fan. And me dad was a big Bob Dylan fan, so what else could they call me? Inevitable really.

—It's a nice name.

—Common tho, in this part of the world.

—Doesn't matter. Still a nice name.

And then, and then ... I was going to save the news; maybe get a bit drunk before I told him. If I told him at all. Dutch courage like. But this talk of names – it seemed to be the right time. And, again, I just can't help meself:

—Do you want to know what yeh son's called?

The smile goes. Even in the low light I can see his eyes and the colour of them; the almost black ring around the blue.

—My son? I don't have a son.

—You do. He's called Tomos.

—You mean—

—When we shagged in Ynyslas dunes that time. Remember? Seven years ago. You came in me and I got preggers and I had the baby and he's a lovely little boy and he's called Tomos. You'd fucked off, remember? Done a runner.

He looks down at his hands. —Are you certain he's …

—Oh man.

—I know. I'm sorry for asking. But you've gorrer admit that at the time you were—

—Fucking everything with a dick, I know. But yes he's yours. I knew the moment you came. I could tell. I heard a kind of click. And anyway all you've got to do is look at him. He's the spit.

He swallows, and if he was a cartoon drawing there'd be a word balloon coming out of him containing the word 'GULP'.

—Is he …

—What?

—Is he cool?

And that's the best thing he could possibly ask. That's the best response I could ever have hoped for from the man who is the father of my boy. *Is he cool* … what a brilliant thing to ask. —He's the best, the coolest little boy you're ever going to meet. Do you *want* to meet him? *Yma*, here he is, look.

I take me phone out and open the photo album and there he is, my boy, in a Spiderman outfit from two Christmases ago. I give the phone to Weasel. No – to Dylan.

—That's him. That's your son. Must be like looking in a mirror, aye? Well. A mirror into the past like.

He looks at it for a long time. I look at him looking at it. The music outside is now a deep drumbeat and there's the sounds of the people too but in this tent it seems as quiet as a church. He touches the screen of the phone dead gently with a fingertip. Hands it back to me.

—I'm gonner go outside for a minute.

—Okay, I say, and he crawls out of the tent. I put the phone back and spin sideways on my arse so I'm looking straight out of the tent flap. Legs crossed under me. I see the shapes of the people down there against the flames and I see the firelight reflected in the surface of the lake. I could, what, *bask* in this I suppose, in what I've made happen up here, even if I didn't mean it to happen; I mean I could just enjoy all of this, what's going on. They don't know that I'm in some way responsible for it, all they're doing is having a good time. They don't know what I saw. Christ, *I* don't know what I saw. And Weasel, no, Dylan, he hasn't got the first clue either; just, like the rest of them, he saw all the images and read all the stuff online and he came up here to see what was going on. The origins of it don't matter to the people up here. They've come for many reasons, not just one. Most of them - nearly all of them - don't know who I am. Or what I've seen. Or even that I'm here, with them.

Tomos not being near to me is like a weight. The absence of him is heavy. I can feel it, like, feel the hole; I could put it on one side of a scales and a, a fuckin *truck* on the other side and they'd be in balance. Wonder if it'd weigh as much as Dylan. Wonder if they'd balance each other out.

There's a movement in the grass outside the tent, around the base of that sculpture. Strands move, part, and then there's a little face looking at me; beady eyes, whiskers. A rat. One of them mountain rats with the humps on their backs and the snaky tails that Waldo used to catch hundreds of; he'd bring them to me with his tail all waggy and drop them at my feet and sometimes they'd still be alive and he'd pick them up again in his jaws and crunch them some more and drop them again and still they'd try to crawl away, all broken. Horrible, like, but Waldo was just doing what he thought he should do. And so I'd pat his head and call him a good boy but I'd feel bad for the rats and I hated having to finish them off - slamming the spade down on them, *ych y fi*. But this feller here - he's in no danger. Well, as long as he stays away from the dogs on the beach he's not. And he's not scared of me, either, sitting back on his hind legs, his tiny paws at his chest as if he's praying. There's a carrier bag of stuff in the corner of the tent and through it I can see a Ginster's wrapper so I reach towards it, slowly like so as not to frighten Ratty, and delve inside and take out a half-eaten sausage roll. I hold it out towards him. He's interested, and his nose goes mad with the twitching, but there's no way he's gunner take it out of me hand so I throw it towards him and as soon as it hits the grass he's snatched it up and vamoosed. There y'go, Ratty-boy. Take that back into yeh burrow for yeh babies and yeh wife.

Rats getting married. Him, in his tiny top hat and tails, his whiskers waxed like a hipster's 'tush. And her, with her whiskers sticking through the holes in her veil and her tail held up by the bridesmaids, which would've been mice, wouldn't they? And a badger for a vicar.

I take out the iPod. Why did he ...? God knows. Just passing on a reminder of *that* morning, I suppose. Don't know what was going through his head. Normal rules don't apply up here. I turn the machine on. Battery nearly dead. Screen glows in me hand and all the music goes on outside and something that sounds like a helicopter but that could just be in the music. I scroll down through the playlist. Whoever owned it originally had awful taste cos it's all dire chart stuff, Ed Sheeran and Little Mix, but then there's three songs together in a row that stand out: Nick Cave's 'Dig Lazarus Dig!!!', 'Misty Morning, Albert Bridge' by The Pogues and Iggy Pop's 'Real Wild Child'. After them it's back to the crap again: Meghan friggin Trainor. But them three songs ... scrolling down, in the quiet of a morning, and with a fuller battery and the internal speaker on ... tired and fuzzy ... and with a crap pill ...

Oh Christ. I start to laugh. All of *this* for *that*? You've got to be fucking joking. Is that it? Oh my God. This is fucking ridiculous. The whole thing from what – chance. An accident. And the morning sun rising. Oh God this is hilarious. What a fucking laugh.

The music outside changes to 'P is the Funk'. Me knees start to jiggle. I chuck the iPod away somewhere in the tent. The blog. The madness. The storm I was in. This, here, on this mountain. And all because ... all because ...

I hear Dylan's voice from outside: – What are you laughing at? and I can't really answer him and then he appears out of the warm night and gets on his knees and leans his top half into the tent and what's this, now, he's putting his face in my neck. His breath is hot on my skin. I cup the nape of his neck in my left hand.

—What's so funny?

—Nothing. Doesn't matter. What's this? You okay? Overwhelmed is it?

He shakes his head. —No. Not really. Don't know what I am. I've got a son. I'm a fuckin dad. What were you laughing at? I heard you laughing.

I shuffle back on me arse to make room for him to enter the tent and we sit cross-legged facing each other. There's sweat on his face but the moisture in the corners of his eyes – well, that just starts to turn me on.

—I always liked you, he says. —I mean I thought about you a lot after that night in the dunes. There was something different about you.

—So you did a runner.

—I had dealers after me. Bailiffs as well. It was me own safety I was thinking about, at the time. There was a feller called Jerry who I heard was gunner stab me up. Give me a shanking. I had to leg it. But I never stopped thinking about you.

—Shite, I say, and laugh again. He carries on:

—No, it's true. I always wondered what might've happened had we, y'know. If we had've tried to make a go of it like.

—What would've happened? A junkie who liked to think he was, was a fucking weasel in human form and a promiscuous depressive. What d'you *think* would've happened? One of them great big houses down the Llanbadarn Road? A luxury flat with a nice view of the sea? Or, or …

I trail off. Dylan nods his head. The heat comes off him in a breeze. I can feel it on my skin.

I ask him: – Don't you have a woman? Has there been anyone else?

—A few, but nothing serious. I mean dates, like, they're always … I mean, you go for a pee and you come back to the table and there she is, swiping fucking right. Looking for someone better. Can't be doing with it. Sooner, y'know, casual pick-ups and that. More honest. Nothing else.

I won't tell him. Not even if he asks. I will not tell him about the rips in me skin and the bruises and the stink of piss in the knees of me jeans. Might tell him about the shape, the glowing thing, and what this gathering on this mountaintop is about but I will not mention the iPod. Not yet, anyway. But the bruises at the back of my throat that make it painful to swallow, no, he'll never need to know about that.

—It's all just so shit, he says. —I mean he's six years old. I've missed seeing him as a baby. Never changed his nappy, never heard him say his first word. Everything goes by so fucking fast. I'm gonner be forty years old soon for fuck's sakes.

My gob is dry. I lean back and reach for the bottle of water in the corner by the bag of food and in doing so my top rides up and he looks down at my belly.

—That tattoo. Is that the day he was born?

—It is, aye. I sit back up and take a big swig of the water. So many of them recently, a high percentage like, they aimed at that tattoo when they came. Why? What's going on there? I drink more water.

—You always had the best belly, Em. Still do. Looks even better now with them numbers on it.

He grabs my waist and leans his head forwards, down and forwards.

—Oi. What are you doing?

—I was gunner kiss that date. Can I kiss it?

—You'll see me stretch marks.

—I could not ever care about that. D'you think I'm bothered by stretch marks?

And I can't quite believe I'm doing this but I take his hands off me waist and gently push him back. And I say: – Not yet. Even tho there is a burning where his skin touched mine, just at that slight touch I could hear my heart and feel my stomach go into a lovely boil I still tell him *not yet*.

—Alright. Can I hug you, then?

—You can do that, aye.

I open me arms and he kind of flops into them. I feel his back rise and fall as he breathes. Control, control, here is a plan: in a minute I'll call my mam and dad. I'll walk up onto the ridge where there's a signal and I'll call them and let them know I'm okay and then I'll tell them to put Tomos on and I'll tell him that I love him and that I've got a great big surprise for him and then he can speak to his dad. For the first time in his life he can speak to his father. And then, tomorrow, me and Dylan will go down off the mountain and we'll go to Trefenter. And then. And then.

The one time I took heroin – this is like that (well, after the initial vomming). Cotton wool around my heart, around all the exposed parts. The one time I chased heroin and the one time I looked up into the sky and heard those words and saw that glowing shape. Dig and bridge and wild. How mad and strange. Just a man dicking about with an iPod.

Over Dylan's shoulder I can see through the tent flap. See the lake, and just for a moment it looks like a void, a spread of black nothingness, held where it is and kept where it is by all the stuff going on in front of it, on the beach, the fires and the music and the dancing, moving shapes of people. And there is no fear, for the moment. The void is there and I can see it and smell it but there is a barrier between me and it and if at times it breaks down, well, that barrier can always be rebuilt again. Here I am.

The music changes to 'Jump In The Line'. As it does, I see the far end of the lake, away near the mountain road, start to flash with bright lights and something rises up over the trees there, something big. I can hear it, as well, behind the music. It's very loud. It's a helicopter. And its searchlight is very bright.

—Dylan, I say into his warm ear. Whisper it, like. —Something's happening. Something's going on.

# COWLEY

- Aw STOP begging, mun, fuck's sakes. Making me feel sick yew are. Listen to yewerself. Stop it.

Sfuckin pathetic, iss is. He've got all mud an puke all over him he has an he's on his fuckin knees with his hands at his chest like he's fuckin having a pray. Making me feel horrible, he is, an fuck knows iss sick cunt has made me feel horrible before an Am not having him doing it again.

—Oh thank you thank you I know I do not deserve this kindness from you I—

—What av I just said? Fuckin stop it, now. Stop fuckin begging. Shut-a fuck up.

Ee sits back on his arse an wipes his face. Like a little fuckin kid he is. Like Rhys was with them sticklebacks. Well, with*out* them sticklebacks it should be cos ee never fuckin caught any, did ee, ee fell flat on is face in-a mud.

He coughs. —Is. Is there anything I can say?

—Anything yew can say? What does *that* mean?

—To make it better. To make amends.

*Make amends.* Fuck's sake this man has no idea what he's done.

—How did you know it was me?

—Pardon?

—Last time yew saw me was when A was a kiddie an Am not a kiddie anymore. Look at me.

—You're not a kiddie, no. But there's the boy in you.

—Oh fuck off. Better than you being in the boy.

Ee pulls a face at what he's jes said as well he fuckin might.

—I mean. What I mean is. You don't look much different. Bigger and stronger that's all.

—Too fuckin right bigger and stronger, cunt. Don't yew fuckin forget it.

A face comes out of a tent and I flick it a V and it goes back in.

346

—Healthy. That's how you look now.

—Stop looking at me then.

He looks away. God, he looks stupid.

—But all *that* is is flesh.

—Ey?

—Fallen flesh. Fallen so far.

—Fuck yew going on about now? If yewer not on yewer knees fuckin begging yewer talkin fuckin bollax. Am yur, now. So are yew. Yew know what yew did to me an Rhys n probably loads-a others n all.

—I'm sorry. So, so sorry.

—Aye, yew've said. A thousand fuckin times.

—And grateful.

—Grateful? For what?

He looks at me again. —I would deserve what you could do to me now. There would be no judgment.

I laugh. Can't help but laugh. —I know *that*. Any judge'd give me a fuckin medal.

—That's not what I mean.

—Well what *do* yew mean, then? No, don't tell me. I don't fuckin care.

How could I ever have been scared of iss man? Ee's nothing; ee's sitting yur in-a mud covered in is own sick and shite and ee's jes been crying and begging and now ee's talking bollax. Ee's fuck all, mun. Ee's jes a little boy.

—Did you see her?

—What?

—Were you permitted to see her face?

—Who, her with-a stars? I touch a place behind me ear. —How'd you know about her?

—Her with the stars? Yes, and everything else. Everything. And you ask me how I know about her. I'm a man of the cloth, how could I *not* know about her? And yet I have been denied her.

—Which serves you fuckin well right, A say, altho A haven't got-a first clue what he's arsing on about.

—Her with the stars, he says again. —That puts it better than I ever could.

And, *Duw*, now-a cunt *smiles* at me. I can see his teeth through-a caked shite on is face.

—What's to fuckin grin about, mun?

Ee doesn't answer, jes wipes his face again with his sleeve. An then, *then* ee puts his fingers in his gob and rootles around in yur an pulls something out, looks at it, an en holds it out towards me in his hand.

—Take this part of me.

—A tooth? Fuck off, manky cunt. What would I want *that* for? Put it back in yewer gob, mun, fuck's sake. Keep it to yewerself.

Ee looks at it again an sniffs and then puts it in his pocket. Fuckin *mochyn*. I must-a booted im harder than I thought. How could I ever have been scared-a him?

—So what happens now? ee says, an A can see-a gap in his teeth. —Where do we go from here?

—'We'? What's iss fuckin 'we'? A don't know about yew but I'm gunner go back to-a beach an get drunk and have a bit of a boogie. That's me. Haven't got a clue what *you're* gunner do, like.

—And I'm forgiven?

Ah, mun, so *that's* what he's after. *That's* what he's tryna get out of me. And he has to fuckin ask it? Sitting yur like he is, he has to fuckin ask it?

—Put it iss way, mun. Yewer talking-a me, aren't yew? I mean yewer *able* to talk, like, yewer fuckin alive and breathin. What does that tell yew?

Ee says something but A don't hear it, it's jes sounds, cos Am rememberin, for some reason, iss time ages ago when A met another dog-collar cunt in a pub. Pissed as arseholes, ee was. A knew who ee was, like, from-a Sunday school, but iss was ages after that, like. An A was getting pissed with Bernie and iss bugger staggered over to us at-a table with three whiskies and told us ee remembered us an we clinked glasses an drank an ee told us a story an it went:

Adam an Eve in-a garden of Eden. Adam says to Eve: isn't iss fuckin great? We live forever, we shag all-a time, everything is jes fuckin lovely an anything we want we jes ask for it and it gets brought to us. Isn't this jes fuckin brilliant? An Eve said: Aye, I know. It's jes not enough, is it?

An en ee buggered off laughing, iss dog-collar cunt. A saw im after, in-a alley next door to-a pub like, in-a pool of is own piss. Lifted is wallet n all, if A remember rightly.

Ee's looking at me, Williams is. A hear that song start up, a one about jumpin in-a line or whatever it is. A see that one-a Williams's eyes is starting-a close up an then, fuck, there's noise, all noise, and ee gawps up into-a sky an A look and see a fuckin helicopter, coming over low, an yur's lights everywhere. Everything's lit up. —See that? a say, to wind him up. —Yewtree, mun! Come for yew, ey have! but he's not listening, an in fact he's up n running around-a ridge, into-a lights. Everything's bright, dead bright, and dead fuckin loud. Something's going on.

# THE FORCE

UNSEEN, THE DARKER swells of hills against the night. Unseen the bats that dart, the owl that glides, a secret squeezed from the black. Unseen too the hedgehog that is burst beneath the wheels of the lead vehicle and squirts guts for the corvids to pick at later, also unseen. And the cleg-flies that curl around grassblades, their bodies glittering with mould spores that eat into their tiny brains. And the postures of these dying flies, their heads down as if in abjection: all unseen, in the passing darkness beyond the headlights' blurts.

Inside the lead van a phone is passed back from the front seat.

—Have a look. Textbook. This is the Beanfield. See what are taken out first? The vans and that? Get rid of any shelter, see. Shock and awe is what it is. Confuses the fuck out of them. Here ya go, bang, now you've got nowhere to hide. While they're busy digesting *that* data, you wade in. Textbook.

Faces lean in, around the screen. Under the noise of the engine the screen gives out its soundtrack: shouting, thuds.

—Before your time, that. Remember it well, me, tho. A hand reaches and takes the phone back. Fingers tap. —Orgreave you've seen, right? Fingers swipe. —Ah, here. This is the kettling of the student protests. Watch the movement. See how it's all done in concert? All together? That's what went wrong in 2011 but we learnt the lessons for the anti-austerity stuff. Didn't we?

—Certainly did, Boss, a voice in the van replies.

Again the phone is passed back and again the faces lean in, lit up by the screen's light. Outside the van the high places go by. The screen freezes.

—Signal's gone, Boss.

—3G shite. Middle of fucking nowhere. We're nearly there anyway.

The phone is handed forwards. The satnav's female voice tells the driver to turn next left.

—The fuck are we?

—Middle of nowhere. That's all you need to know.

Glitter of a lake on the right-hand side.

—Is this it?

—Does it look like it to you? There's no one there.

—But that's a lake.

—It's not the one we want. Listen to what the satnav's telling you.

The van swerves around the lake and the vehicles behind it follow, in a chain; another riot van, a few Range Rovers, a horsebox, another riot van. The lights of them up here, in this thin air, will-o'-the-wisps that burn too bright and which move with rare purpose. Through the beams the white moths tumble. Some splat into the windscreens and leave buttery smears on the glass behind the grilles. What a place for ancient gods. And the closer the convoy gets to the lake the more there is to un-see; trackside analoys topped with relics – a pair of spectacles, a football shirt; bullawns on the boulder-tops, most baked dry in this humming summer, those few shaded ones still retaining a scrim of slimy moisture in which entire cosmogonies of strenuous careers continue and which release tiny flies, gnats and midges upwards into the sticky night. And then the snapping bats. And glow-bugs like the eyes of ghosts cowed by the brighter phantoms and seeking bracken anonymity.

The convoy climbs. Around it the ridges serrate the holes between the stars.

—Who's this cunt?

There's a shape in the road, a man, legs apart and his hand held out, palm flat in that gesture that says STOP. The lead van slows and the vehicles behind it do the same, crawling forwards slowly until the blunt bonnet abuts the man's knees. Standing there in the cone of light.

Passenger-seat leans his head out the window. —Police business, sir. Get out of the way.

—No.

—No? I said get out of the fucking way.

—And I said I won't.

A sigh. Passenger-seat gets out of the van and approaches the man. The two of them face to face in the slice of light on the mountaintop. The idling engines.

—What are you doing up here? asks the man.

—I don't need to tell you anything. Except to get out of our fucking way.

—I know where you're going. It's not an Occupy thing. It needn't concern you.

—It's private land and it's being occupied. In my book that makes it an *occupy* thing. He does the air-quotes with his fingers.

—It's public land.

—Oh, d'you think? Nowhere is public land, matey. It's all privately owned. And the owners want you all off it and it's our job to get them what they want.

The exhaust in hanging phantoms. There could be a nothingness all around.

—Where's your number?

—Must've forgotten it. Silly me.

—I want your number.

—Do you? Well you aren't getting it son. And I've got *your* number, by the way; idle parasitic trespassing scumbag who'd sooner live in your own shit than do a decent day's work. Sound about right? Now are you gonna move aside and let us pass?

The man stands firm. Looks about himself calmly, almost pleasantly detached.

—Answer me. I'm a policeman. You *will* be arrested and taken in.

No answer. The policeman takes his cuffs from his belt then he too looks around, at the lack of habitation, at the night unpricked by house lights. And he hooks the cuffs back on his belt. And then the truncheon comes up and comes down against skull and a cheer goes up from the lead van and a horn is honked three times in triumph and the unconscious body is dragged to the side of the track and dumped there and some blood blooms on the bilberries.

The policeman gets back in the van. Has his back thumped and hair mussed. —Drive on. And that's the only thing you need to know, lads, up here: No. Fucking. Nonsense. Nip it in the bud. Let's get this done. Prepare.

The convoy shunts into motion again and inside the vehicles visors are lowered, stab vests secured, black tape pressed across numbers. Shoulders are rolled, neck bones and muscles popped. Outside the helicopter comes out of the moon to a loud cheer from inside the vehicles and now between the trees can the lights of fires be seen. *Turn left* says the satnav. *You have reached your destination.* A line of cars blocks further approach so the convoy is halted in the trees and they get out of the wagons, the bulked-up figures, hefty, faceless behind masks. Bludgeons are slapped against gauntlets. Balls of booted feet are bounced on. Amongst the trees and beneath the swooping moon and the clattering bank of the chopper all is psyched up. Horses are released to stamp and snort and be mounted and strut side to side, turn around and then around again in dark dressage. Once this place saw horses. Such animals. And once this place saw armour. Never this neon and never this need, *that* need, at the far end of the line of parked cars, on the fiery beach, the little people ranked there now to stare upwards at the hovering machine and its hanging light. All the little white faces looking up. Rang, once, to steel on bone this place, all of a roil it was. And now the lake a shimmer of bioluminescent stew.

They advance as one, tutored in this. The riders above the ranked helmets. The roll of clubs on shields, that drumbeat now. Batons expanded and tonfas twirled. Canisters of pepper spray capture light and gleam like a beetle's wing-case.

# UP HERE

She was nice, that lady who touched the snake's head. Nice pretty lady. And the snake was nice too with his tiny tongue that came out and flickered.

The little boy in the tent looks down at the surface of his cup of juice, balanced on a rock. It ripples because there is a movement on the mountain that makes it do so. He remembers the scene in the first *Jurassic Park* film and tells his mum that dinosaurs are coming.

—What? His mother looks up from her sketchbook. —What did you say sweetheart?

The little boy points at his cup. —Dinosaurs coming. Look.

And too there is retreat of small things, across the hilltops, amongst the undergrowth, between the trees: low quadrupeds with tails down leaping over fallen logs and from high branch to high branch, away from the lake and deeper into the massif where there is no human need played out. Some burrow wriggling into the earth; some slip into cracks. Others rise upwards on hauling wings and become specks shrinking against the yellow moon. On kukri wings the sand martins return to their warrens. Hares re-find their forms. Onward comes something else. *Dinosaurs* says the little boy in the tent once more to his mother.

# THE FORCE

The bellies of the clouds above would be lit with this as if with stored lightning but there are no clouds above. This scald of a summer. Only the beam of the chopper and the drone follows it like a remora, the gnatty hum of its rotors submerged in the blare and blatter of the blades. Everything seen, witnessed:

Troglodytic they come from their tents and bashes and burrows to be broken on the shore in the charge. The decks dragged from their podium and shattered beneath hooves, ending jaunty Belafonte and now is all screams, in these high lands, the screaming out of throats and the thud of baton and boot on bone, gloved knuckle, and it seems a release of some sonic storehouse in the stones roundabout, some sound memory of steel on steel. Roars of outrage find their partners separated by centuries. Everything seen:

The stimulants in the fast-working faces. Shatter the champing jaws. In the red of the fire light. Caught in the 'copter-beam. Trampled tents. A gauntleted hand grabs a hank of blonde hair, drags a woman across the pebbles, between the sprawled bodies. The scalp rips up behind the ear and exposes tattooed stars which blacken with blood and the neck and face around them bruises, breaks under the blows of a truncheon. Teeth tinkle out. A man dressed in a robe has his cross smashed and is pushed beneath the water and told to walk on it instead. Belly-crawling and broken on the beach. The drone sees it all; the helicopter lights it all up. The people are kettled into the lake, now a slick of blood that hands reach through. Arms wrap around children but some children run alone shrieking. The horses circle, stamp and snort and so do the armoured men. Batons are brought down. Batons are brought down. Again again again. Bone is splintered and skin is split. A big man with a dragon on his neck roars like that dragon and rises out of the water holding a boulder above his head but before he can bring it down on the nearest helmeted head he is bludgeoned back beneath the churn. Batons hack at the black water. Fingers crunch beneath heels. A half-naked man, shirt torn away from his chest pounds across the beach, stumbling over bodies, screaming for someone called Emma; a tonfa is whipped from horseback, shatters his skull to eggshell. Belly-crawling and broken on the beach. Visored eyes consider the rasher of skin caught on the gauntlet, inked with stars, discarded with a flick. The slack torn face is still pleasing in its forms and a boot ensures it will never be so again. A dog-collared man is helped to his feet by one of the black shapes; *Sorry you had to see this, Father. Get yourself away from here. Go safely, now.* Wrists are clamped in cuffs. A mouth is shouting so that mouth is punched, its accent stoppered; the following collapse tears the shirt completely away and reveals a date tattooed below the collarbone: *And that's your first day sober, I bet? God, you people are so predictable.* That collarbone is snapped. The ribs beneath it too. The batons fall and fall and skin swells and splits and teeth lie amongst the pebbles like pebbles themselves and sprayed gas turns eyes to bleeding slits and mouths to whooping holes. Lungs rattle and expel, as do stomachs. Skin become bubblewrap. The dark figures pick across the twitching retching beach and still the batons rise and fall and it's finished, now, whatever it was; what was happening up here is done, now. All over. Ended. Behind the rocky ridge a sun burns brightly and waits to rise again.

# ACKNOWLEDGEMENTS

Much of this novel was written whilst under employment at Wolverhampton University. My thanks there to these fine people (with apologies to anyone I've forgotten): Ade Byrne, Sam Roden, Roz Bruce, Rob Francis, Bas Groes, Paul McDonald, Glyn Hambrook, Jacqui Pieteryck, Dew Harrison, Frank Wilson, Ben Colbert, and Candi Miller.

In Mostar: Mirko Bozic. How I love your fierce and undefeatable city.

In America: Bill Parry and Frances, Jim Gregory and Rachel, Willy Vlautin and Lee. Zoe Fowler, too, both there and here.

Thanks to Nicoletta Laude.

Thanks to Chris Taylor and Beth.

Thanks to Rupert Crisswell.

Thanks to Gary Budden.

Thanks to Angie McAuliffe for sharing the invaluable wisdom of her boy Ollie.

Oh, and as far as I know, Cardiff City Council does not, never has, and never will utilise anti-homeless spikes.

And I actually like Tregaron, very much; honestly I do. It's a joke. To prove it, I'll buy all of you a pint in the Talbot tomorrow.

Thanks to some of the *Stinging Fly* fellers in Dublin: Declan Meade, Sean O'Reilly, Thomas Morris.

penguin.co.uk/vintage